Collected Writings

A bust of Olive Moore by sculptor Sava Botzaris (ca. 1933)

OLIVE MOORE

Collected Writings

Dalkey Archive Press

© 1929, 1930, 1932, 1934 Olive Moore
Corrected texts and appendix © 1992 Dalkey Archive Press
All rights reserved
First Edition

Library of Congress Cataloging in Publication Data
Moore, Olive.
  [Selections. 1992]
  Collected writings / Olive Moore.
  I. Title.
PR6025.O575A6   1992   823'.912—dc20   91-29755
ISBN: 1-56478-000-7

Partially funded by grants from The National Endowment for the Arts and The
Illinois Arts Council.

Dalkey Archive Press
1817 North 79th Avenue
Elmwood Park, IL 60635 USA

Printed on permanent/durable acid-free paper and bound in the United States.

CONTENTS

Celestial Seraglio   1

Spleen   109

Fugue   233

The Apple Is Bitten Again   335

Appendix

    About the Author   421
    A Note on the Texts   425

CELESTIAL SERAGLIO
(A Tale of Convent Life)

Le laisser consommer cette union que je désire, mais qu'Il désire si fort Lui aussi!

Quand sera-ce cette rencontre première et dernière? Première, parce que je Le verrai pour la première fois après L'avoir tant appelé! Dernière, parce qu'elle consommera tout et qu'elle ne finira jamais! Il sera là, devant moi, pour moi toute seule. . . . Oh! son regard, ses bras tendus, son dernier appel: "Viens maintenant, viens vite."

Oh! vite, Jésus! . . .

Je me mets là, toute vide et altérée, et je colle mes lèvres à la blessure de son Cœur. Et son Esprit, qui est l'Amour, entre en moi avec son Sang béni, et il me remplit. Oh! qu'Il remplisse le pauvre petit vase, qu'Il l'inonde, qu'Il déborde. . . .

"Jésus, que veux-Tu que je fasse?"

Méditations de Sœur Marie Saint-Anselme

N ow, there were two ladies, a mother and her daughter, and they lived in Brussels," began Sœur Damiana, a last look over the class to see that all hands were folded on the desks before she began the Sunday story. "They were very rich ladies, and though they once had been devout and had done gladly their work for the poor, they gave themselves up to the vanities of the world and now listened more to the voice of the Devil than to the voice of Jesus. Wherever the Devil beckoned they followed. They went to the theatres in silk dresses cut immodestly at the neck; they gave themselves up to their appetites and ate whatsoever they desired; and forgot to tell their Father Confessor of their greed. They led a life of vanity and pride, and the Blessed Virgin would see Her Son gaze sadly on the pleasures which were leading them away from Him, and say: 'Do not punish them yet, dear Son, they will repent.' "

Sœur Damiana paused and changed her voice. "You must remember, children, that le bon Dieu, Who watches over you always, and sees each unkind thought as it comes in your mind, and hears each angry word as you shout it at your friend, and writes it down in His big book to which you must answer at the Day of Judgment, does not punish you until He sees the Devil has almost won you for his own. Only then does He punish you to save you from torment everlasting."

"But to resume. The rich lady and her daughter did not repent; they continued to buy jewels and fine clothes to deck themselves with on their visits to balls and to theatres, following always where Satan led them. And one day they forgot to go to Confession. On that day the Blessed Virgin wept. . . ."

A pause; a quiet survey of the grave faces in the hushed room; a moistening of the lips as the climax approached.

"That night, returning very late from a big ball given in their honour, the mother said to her daughter as she was getting into bed: 'Daughter, we are so happy that I feel sure God has forgotten us.' " A pause.

"The next morning, the next morning when the mother awoke, she called to her daughter: 'Daughter, open the shutters and let the sunshine into the room.' The daughter looked at her mother in surprise. 'But, mother,' she said, 'the shutters are open, and the sunshine *is* all over the room.'

"You see, children, she was blind. God does not forget."

"But . . . but . . . I don't call that fair . . . I call that a horrible story . . . I think it was *mean* of God . . . I don't think she meant to be bad at all . . . I call it cruel to make her blind for going to a party. . . ." Joyce Carr, normally so short and chubby, seemed to tower unfamiliarly above the frightened class, her freckled face red with indignation and confusion, stammering her protest in a tear-thick voice. Stammering it, moreover, in English, which was forbidden.

In a heavy silence the class waited for her to resume her seat, and eyes bulged at her as though the Devil who had just spoken through her lips was now about to rush out from them. Some, despite their curiosity, turned away, feeling it almost a sin to look on her.

But Joyce, red and angry, kept her eyes on Sœur Damiana, and stood her ground. The nun's mouth was deliberately narrowed and stern, and her face, not unpleasing when relaxed, was shrunken and cold in an effort to keep her displeasure under control before the class. She must ignore the triumphant half-smiles the English girls were signalling among themselves. She must remember the girl was English and a Protestant, and she must be lenient, as it really mattered so very little. . . .

"You will now stay in during the hour of recreation," her words came clear and hard like the Father Confessor's voice when he was grieved, "and copy the story as you remember it, as many times as it is possible, and bring it to me personally before breakfast to-morrow. I also place you under the ban of silence until that time. Children, you may go."

There was a sigh of disappointment. All over and so soon. And Joyce let off so lightly.

E mily Jennings is being sent away! Have you heard?"
"No!"

"Yes, she is. Marion told me. She saw Emily go into Sœur François' room and come out all red and crying. Marion doesn't know properly what it's all about, but it's pretty bad, she says. She says it's something about things one shouldn't tell. You know. She says Emily told Margaret something *awful,* and Margaret, like a silly ass, went and asked Sœur Mannes if it was true, and Sœur Mannes said No, but who told her? Margaret wouldn't say at first, but Sœur Mannes told her she wouldn't tell anyone, so Margaret said Emily. Then Sœur Mannes went straight to Sœur François and told her everything, and had Emily fetched from history class. Wasn't that mean? Just like a beastly Belgian. I'm sorry for Emily, though."

Leisurely, arm-entwined, they wandered by the trees. After a pause. "Do you know what it was Emily told?"

"No, *honest.*"

"Yes you do. You just won't tell me. I told you what Marion told me about. You know."

"Well, I don't. I wish I did. Besides, Joyce, you know I tell you everything. But I can't tell what I don't know, can I? I did hear a little bit, but it didn't sound sense. I heard Dorothy and Mona whispering about it in Chapel this morning. Something about a baby being born without a head. But that couldn't be all, could it? You don't get expelled for *that.*"

"I bet you know something more, Mavis. I bet you do. You just won't tell me, that's all. I won't be friends any more. I'll go back to Margaret."

"O, Joyce. O, Joyce. I don't know what Emily told. I really don't, Joyce. I'd tell you everything. You know I would. I don't know what Emily told, but I know something else. You know what I told you about girls getting all big up there when they grow up? Well, Marion told me . . ."

"No! *Really?*"

"Um."

"But how?"

"Well, Marion said . . ."

"Good lor'!"

"You see, Joyce, I do tell you everything. You won't go back to Margaret, will you?"

"Darling!" Joyce beamed into her friend's serious eyes, "of course I won't. Look, Mavis, I'll tell you something I heard Violet Gray say to Mona last night. She said: 'Read Genesis XXXIX, 7–15.' I turned it up immediately but I can't make anything of it. See if you can."

Joyce pulled a small Bible from among the lesson books under her arm.

They read it very carefully, a finger pointing under each line, and at the end lifted puzzled faces to each other.

"Lie with her?" echoed Mavis. "Lie with her? But, Joyce, what could he lie to her *about?*"

A violent rap on the shoulder caused them to snap the book to. It was Sœur Etienne, who took the afternoon recreation. "Pas à deux," frowned Sœur Etienne, "pas à deux!"

Frustrated and indignant the two friends spied round the playground for some small child whose ears they need not fear. For a chocolate or a holy picture any lonely infant would allow herself to be dragged round by the hand, while oblivious to her presence the confidences could continue.

"Joyce, have you read that bit in the Solomon's Songs?"

S he, too, had been a wayward child; and often vain of the silky hair that on week-days was drawn back in two smooth plaits. Like yours. But darker, and so obstinately curled that her father had had to lick it smooth with a brush dipped in syrupy beer. Especially when she was caught at the mirror.

Sœur la Bienheureuse Imelda drew out her coarse white handkerchief and gently dabbed at the tears on Mona's cheek, smiling the slow, thin smile for which she was loved.

It was Sunday afternoon and they sat together on a bench beside the lake in the Quartier des Dames. A mist of April green covered the fronds of willow leaning to the water's edge suggesting the cool glaze of a waterfall and the branches above them shone with moist buds.

From the Grand Boulevard came an even drone pierced by sudden shouts and the rhythmic clack of the hockey players.

Tears gathered again and trickled down the cheeks already puffed with crying. "But I am sixteen," protested Mona, "I'm not a child. I know my own mind. I do: and I'm not going." She paused expecting a protest. None came, so she continued hotly. "I don't want to go. I want to stay here for ever and ever." Sœur Imelda continued to smile, and Mona gulped "with you."

She, too, had said she did not want to go and finally that she would not go, and then that she would never be wicked again if they would only let her stay. She had cried and prayed for weeks, so that she was all numb and quiescent when finally they came to fetch her away. "God has brought her to contrition," he misinterpreted. But she had hated him too much to hear one word he said that morning. Afterwards, even long afterwards when through the Divine Mercy and the constant intercession of the Blessed Virgin she could accept the memory calmly, if not yet with love (O dear Mother forgive me!) for her battle had been a stern one for such poor strength, she could not remember her father's last words. She remembered only how Jeanne had rushed at her and clung to her neck as they cried together, and how Jeanne had screamed and kicked them as they were torn apart and she was hurried from the door into the carriage.

"I've said so in every letter for the past month." Mona wiped her own eyes this time for Sœur Imelda was staring into the lake. "They only say it's nonsense at my age to want to become a nun. And in his last letter daddy said I am obviously being led astray—what did he mean by that?—by people who ought to know better."

"It means that your parents love you very much, and perhaps they need you in the home," said the nun, turning from the water and taking the girl's hot hand.

"O, I don't know about that," said Mona half-aggressively. (Strange people, these English! Who, then, do they love?) "I've got two brothers and three sisters. They'll not miss me much, I'll bet. They won't let me have my own way, that's all."

"So you have brothers and sisters at home, too?"

"Mm. Five. Dick comes first, he's the eldest. Then me, and then John, he's fourteen. And then Mildred and Doris and Joan. Joan's only eight." She stopped: racially she felt uncomfortable speaking about her home.

"I had a little sister, too," said Sœur Imelda, stroking her hand. "She was twelve years old, with big dark eyes in her little face, often sad. She was not like me always noisy and laughing, but quiet like a mouse and shy."

Something in her voice made Mona hesitate. "And did she die?"

"No," said the nun. "Only for me. Everything outside dies, my child, when you take the veil."

She seemed to have been ill a long time, and when she woke it was to a lethargy of prayer and duty. Her habit of keeping her eyes fixed in a distant sightlessness gave an impression of divine abstraction, and many of the nuns began to hope that in this handsome girl a saint was to be given to the Convent. A year passed.

One morning, a week before she was to be ordained, she failed to rise from the communion rail. She made three lunges like a sick horse pulling at a heavy load, and remained half-lying on the floor, deep sighs coming from her throat. Her mouth fell open, and the host which she had just received slipped from her tongue on to the rise of her black dress, and there lay for an awful moment until Père Joseph stepped from behind the altar rail, and with gentle fingering replaced it in the chalice. Panting and still unable to close her mouth she dragged herself to her elbow, and some nuns rushing to her, half-led, half-dragged her down the aisle.

After that it was known that God had spoken, and His message was clear to all who had witnessed the distressing scene at the altar rail. She returned to bed. The Chapel bell tolled morning and evening, and each day prayers for her recovery were added to the Mass, and sometimes even to the grace before meals.

Exultation was in the air. Even the smaller children seemed aware that something unreal was happening, and hushed their usual exuberance. The tension was like the silence in which one listens to a heart beat, restraining the breath.

"But I shall have you," said the girl earnestly, "I shall not need the outside world."

Sœur Imelda gave no sign of having noticed the warmth in her voice. She shook her head. "You are so young," she said, and searched Mona's face with her fine eyes. "And you are emotional and rebellious. O, yes, you are. I have watched you. If to-morrow you had no home to rebel against you would soon find something else. I know. How will you hide all that, dear child, under your new habit? Or do you think that under a coif your thoughts will be so different. For how long?"

Tears started again down Mona's smudged cheeks. "But I can try. I can learn. If I could be like you some time, I shouldn't care. . . ."

Sœur Imelda said sadly: "But a life is such a long time. . . . You are young: you do not know. Afterwards it will be too late."

Mona made no reply. Could this be the afternoon of which she had dreamed for the past month? To culminate in a rebuff. Furtively she turned her head aside and blew her nose, which suddenly re-echoed in her astonished ears like the bursting of a hundred paper bags amid wild applause.

Only the Mother Superior remained unmoved by the excitement following on her illness. Sœur Marie-Joseph saw no trace of the miraculous in the altar scene. Despite the thirty years of unquestioning love and devotion which she had brought to her task, the natural shrewdness of her peasant stock told her that the girl was not sick through ecstasy but through fear. Wide as she was long, wrinkled, robust, beloved by all, she would insinuate herself into the sick-room many times a day on such child-like pretexts as bringing a rosy apple or a new holy picture to the patient.

One day the Mother Superior's little meddler-coloured face had peered down into hers, and finding her awake, she had said: "I am writing to your father, child. He must come and take you away. You must not be forced into doing what you do not wish to. He will take you home again."

The white face with its fine, wide eyes had looked back at her without surprise or hope. "It is no use. He will not take me back. If he did, it would only be to send me to a different order. He means me to be a nun."

"Nonsense," said Sœur Marie-Joseph, placing her donation on the bed-table. "We shall see what he has to say when I tell him that you are ill."

It was no use. "I have no son to give to God," the letter ran, "but I have a daughter. My vow then is fulfilled. Am I to sin against Him and His Holy Church because she is vain and stubborn and fond of the pleasures of the world? Tell her . . ."

When she had read the letter she handed it back to Sœur Marie-Joseph without comment. She smiled. Her acceptance of its finality surprised even herself. She felt neither anger nor disappointment. It was as though for the first time she heard and understood her father's point of view.

Sœur Imelda remarked as though finishing her thoughts aloud: "But then if you desire it so much, and it is of your own free will that you take the veil, you may not find it difficult. But do nothing in a hurry. Promise me you will do nothing in a hurry, my dear child, until you can answer every doubt in your heart." She was suddenly so serious that she seemed to Mona almost on the verge of tears. "And then if your decision is irrevocable, if you must go your own way, always remember afterwards, should you grow restless," she hesitated as though uncertain whether to continue, "always remember that youth is a very short period of time; it will wear away quite quietly. It will be gone before you know how."

The tea-bell clanged in the distance. The nun dipped the corner of her handkerchief in the lake and wiped Mona's hot cheek. Perhaps understanding that from the girl's point of view she had not been altogether sympathetic, she bent down and kissed her lightly on the forehead. Mona crimsoned with pleasure, and shyly happy she took Sœur Imelda's arm as they hurried together through the avenue of trees into the Grand Boulevard.

Mavis sauntering leisurely in to tea paused at the gates to let them pass, without raising her eyes from the book she was reading.

"That is a clever girl," said Sœur Imelda when they were out of earshot, "and one day when she grows up she will be very beautiful."

A pain stabbed at Mona's heart. She felt wicked and very angry with herself, but she could not help it. She heard herself saying: "And doesn't she know it! If she looks in the glass much longer she'll get a squint!"

"There, you see!" cried Sœur Imelda, shaking a finger at her, her eyes bright with laughter. "My dear, dear child!" She laughed aloud at Mona's discomfiture. "You see!"

The revelation came abruptly. A picture postcard passed from hand to hand among the few, the very few.

Mavis, now fourteen, was included because of her age and popularity. At fourteen one was assumed definitely sophisticated. It was the age at which one was admitted to the whisperings, the guessings, the titters, the gropings; the results of which were ludicrous in the extreme; conclusions so irregular that only abortive guesswork bred of an aggravated curiosity for forbidden things could have reached them. Added to the thrill of 'knowing' was the pride at being among the favoured few who permitted themselves these confidences.

One must not betray that one understood nothing; or understood so imperfectly as to be puzzled at the nonsense. Strange jokes must always be greeted with laughter: loud laughter, often before the point was reached. As when that odious Ellen O'Brien, leaving at Christmas and good riddance, had flounced up to a whispering group and said maliciously: "You infants don't know anything. I've got a terribly wicked rhyme; see if you can understand what this means." She looked slyly around and lowered her voice mysteriously: "How does a mouse when it spins? Answer: 'the higher the fewer.' Get it?"

Without hesitation the whispering group replied scornfully: "Of course we understand it. Every word. Perhaps you're not as clever as you thought you were, Ellen O'Brien! We know exactly what *that* means." At which the odious Ellen O'Brien went into shrieks of wild laughter and ran away shouting that it was too good to miss and that she must tell the others.

It came as a shock to Mavis when, after furtive looks to see that no nun was around, the postcard was placed in her hand. She had not known. She still was not quite certain; but she had no intention of exposing herself to any malice, or risking the indignity of being considered 'innocent.' So she gazed at the picture with an emphasised indifference and wisely kept her counsel.

It was a statue. A white marble statue, that struck her for all her morbid preoccupation as being somehow something supremely beautiful. A naked man with a lovely girlish face, and curls twisted on his shoulders. His feet were bound with sandal-laces and a small wing grew on either heel.

She handed it back with a studied smile. That then was the difference. Men did not just wear trousers and talk in deep voices and have short hair. They were not simply girls one fell in love with.

Then a thought came to her. A thought so terrible it gave her a sensation of giddiness. Was she sinning? Was it a sacrilege? Was God watching her now? Would He write it down?

But the thought persisted and would not be denied. Wretchedly she sought her friend.

"Joyce, you saw the picture with the little wings on the feet? . . . Joyce, I've thought of something awful . . . I daren't hardly tell you . . . Joyce, *Jesus* couldn't have been like that, could He?"

Even Joyce, who was the same age as Mavis but considered herself considerably older and more erudite on 'things,' was shocked at so appalling a suggestion. But that was not all. Guiltily Mavis followed up her query with something even more unforeseen.

"And Joyce, you know all that about . . . you know. Well, Jesus couldn't have been born that way, could He? *He* was brought down from Heaven, wasn't He?"

The two friends considered each other with scared, unhappy eyes. The trial of faith was ghastly. Would God, Who must be listening, strike them both dead?

Joyce hastened to mend matters. "O, *no,*" she breathed, "O, *no,* Mavis. How could you think anything so wicked! Everybody else, of course. But not, *not* Jesus."

The matter was settled, the tension relaxed. But fear still dogged Mavis for her terrible doubt.

That day and the next she was very careful how she moved, especially on the stairs. On the stairs she must walk cautiously and very slowly. God might throw her down.

The second day having not merely vanquished the stairs but sustained no injury during play-time, she understood that God was not angry and had by now condoned the incident.

T he greater part of Mavis's energy and attention were focussed on Joyce. Their days were passed in passionate misery when quar-relling; or in ecstatic admiration of each other when at peace. The hardy friendship flowering after many years, jealousies, and threats, was sealed with a pin blood-dipped from each wrist. Their signed and sealed agreement lay rotting under a chosen tree in the Boulevard.

Yet for three days they had not spoken; nor strolled, linked, about the playgrounds; nor waited for each other at the classroom doors. Those who believed Mavis to be the slave were surprised to see that it was Joyce whose eyes were red; Joyce who gazed in the direction of her friend's averted head: Joyce who passed the forlorn notes which went unanswered.

Truth to tell, Mavis, while assuring herself that a disillusioned heart must renounce friendship for ever, was enjoying herself considerably. Joyce's treachery had wounded her, but decidedly it was gratifying to find Joyce mourning the loss so openly, so abjectly continuing rejected advances. Mavis had expected to bear alone both the hurt and the loneliness; her friend's unforeseen self-effacement made her reckless and a little hard. She should be forgiven; but not yet.

Pleasantly from her first humiliation Mavis knew the first sweets of power. A fine, head-rearing sensation with a tingle of pins and needles down the spine as on that day someone had said to her: "Ida James says you're the prettiest girl in the school." Ida James! A big girl of seventeen!

It came again now, as they ran to her: "Joyce is crying her *eyes* out, Mavis. *Do* come and make up." Calm narrowed grey eyes looked beyond them in a peculiarly offensive way. No. "O, Mavis, you *are* cruel!" That pleased her more, far more, than being thought pretty. O, Mavis, you *are* cruel!

All the more so, thought Mavis angrily, because they owed her that at least. She had been the injured party long enough, guarding her secret in the face of insults and inaccuracies. Now for a brief space she was lifted above her persecutors—whom her friend had lately joined —and if, in tasting power, they gave her without knowing it something hitherto undreamed of: let them!

O, Mavis, you are cruel!

Something Mavis did not fully grasp made life at moments unbearable. She realised she faced alone a hostile fate from which all other girls in the school seemed immune. For this she must pay the penalty of sneers and whisperings, without hope, no matter what qualities she possessed in herself, of mercy or forgetfulness. It was as though a snake, devised especially for her injury, lay concealed in the grass, wary for her tread. And all because someone had started the rumour (The Angel, I'll bet!) that there was something . . . shsh . . . about her parents.

Mavis was aware, though at first she had not noticed it, having been at the Convent since she was small and usually spending her holidays travelling in Belgium or with an aunt in England, that her parents differed from those of the other girls in that they arrived to see her separately. If at Christmas her father arrived for a few days, she could be sure that for the summer holidays she must expect her mother. Her father, a great red-bearded man with fine grey eyes and large milky hands covered with tufts of red hair, would supply the deficiency gruffly: "Your mother, my dear, sends her love: she was unable to come with me this time." Her mother, of a young elegance so unusual in Convent mothers as to become an object of romantic passion among the girls, would say: "Mavis, your father sends you this picture book; he will try and be here in the spring."

Followed days by the sea, Mavis never doubting but that one parent at a time was sufficient for a daughter to cope with.

Until the day Milly Martin had taken her aside and sniggered: "Mavis, is it really true your people are separated?"

"Separated?" echoed Mavis, bewildered but on her guard.

"Well . . . you know . . . not together. . . ."

The blow had fallen. But Mavis, momentarily inspired, smiled at Milly, who was two whole years her senior, as one smiles at a fractious child. "Silly!" she laughed. "Who told you such absurd lies about me? Why mother and daddy are devoted to each other!"

She carried it off this time because Milly was a guileless, kind-hearted girl incapable of real malice.

But victory was not always so easy. She was suddenly aware that she was regarded as something apart; a curiosity to be questioned; a mystery to be solved. Quick to spy veiled allusions to her parents her sensitiveness made her abnormally cunning in her evasions. Bravely to herself she faced their lonely visits; their hurried, infrequent letters written invariably from separate addresses and bearing punctilious reference to each other's health. Pondering these injustices her heart was heavy with a dull resentment against those who had put this indignity upon her. A sullen dislike of her strange parents took root, and grew in times of provocation to a resentful hatred. At such times she would plan elaborate escapes so that *they* should never find her—or at least not until they could be made to promise never to be seen singly near the Convent again. For this she traversed an immense amount of snow and endured the pangs of slow starvation; and after the reconciliation she flaunted her united parents in the playground arm-in-arm, and bowing right and left to the assembled, tearful enemies who once had taunted her.

Since her childhood Mavis had seen her parents all too rarely to have known the delights and warmth of family life, as lived, it seemed, by others. An only child, her attitude of censorious detachment seemed to her in no way unnatural. Had she been told that children do not censure their parents, she would have replied, bitterly enough, that other children perhaps had no reason to. She had always admired her mother's elegant beauty, but was subdued by her light impersonality which gave

Mavis the impression that her mother had come to visit any neat and good-looking little girl who might care to be taken to the sea for a short holiday.

Of her father she thought with pleasure. She loved him in a shy, thwarted way, and sometimes longed to love him more warmly if only he had not always been snatched from her after the brief weeks they spent together exploring solitary villages along the Belgian sea-coast. He had a hearty masculine generosity which pleased Mavis more than her mother's elegance and she felt he was fond of her, though of course he couldn't be, to make her the laughing-stock of the school as he did.

They would sit together under the striped awning of a small restaurant looking over the bright sleepy square, and he would talk to her in his serious abstract way of many things of which she understood nothing at all, they made so little sense, but was content to loll back and let her father's fine deep voice lap her about like the water lap-lapping from the deserted street-fountain through the hot summer afternoon. "There is always time to undo the damage they are doing to you now, child," would rumble from the tangle of rusty beard. "Heaven's nearer earth than Olympus and it's as well to mount by easy stages of kissing an authentic piece of the real Cross. You may attempt the other ascent later." What it meant never mattered, as father disliked being interrupted.

How pleasant the holidays were with father! One need not be on one's guard for fear of being considered unlady-like or wicked. Lady-like was a word he never used. He never said: "Little girls must eat what they are told. Do stop frowning in that sulky way. It makes you look *so* plain." Or questioned one off-guard on abstruse dates and the capitals of the Empire. Father was of opinion that a healthy girl is reared on the sweetest sugar cakes, and ice-cream, and big glasses of sticky lemonades. He would take a large white card from the waiter and say: "What do you say to a raw juicy steak covered with questionable vegetation—possibly mushrooms?" Unlike mother who never consulted her at all, and was always harassing her to replace her knife and fork between mouthfuls.

But he came too seldom and for too short a time. She was not sure she really loved him, now that she had found out. He was in league with her mother to do her harm, making her 'different' from girls whose parents arrived always by twos, irreproachable, superior.

"Who are you spending your holidays with?" would come the honeyed, mock-innocent taunt. To be answered with grave dignity: "I am going to my aunt's."

And now Joyce, her own Joyce, had come so low in losing an argument as to strike: "Anyway I'd be less conceited if *my* father had to leave my mother at home every time he came to see me!" "No use her crying *now*," thought Mavis angrily as she watched the intermediaries running back to say, no, she would not come. "She said it, and she can't take it back ever again."

O, why were parents so hateful! She did not altogether understand in what particular hers differed from ordinary parents. She only knew they were the cause of her distress and humiliation, and that they must know this, and that quite obviously they did not care.

Until Jeanne van Kampe, the daughter of prosperous local peasants, arrived and diverted the curiosity to herself. Stumpy, fat, a square of Flemish face and two thin fair plaits reaching to the ground, Jeanne went unnoticed until the day she made her astounding revelation in history class, when Sœur Mannes had been called from the room.

She was talking animatedly to the girl beside her, and both were laughing. Then Jeanne's voice was heard above the entire class in angry imitation: " 'Non, jamais!' screamed my mother at him, 'I will not have him killed to-morrow. I will not. He is not fat enough. Another fortnight at least!' 'I say he dies to-morrow,' shouted back my father. And then my mother lifted up the frying-pan and banged my father on the head till he cried for mercy." The fat Flemish girl gurgled at the recollection. "O, they fight like cocks those two!"

Everyone knew before the recreation was over.

It was shocking, but what could one expect from a common Belgian peasant girl? It was shocking that she showed no delicacy in concealing the matter. No one *need* have known. And now obviously there was nothing to be gained by discussing it, seeing that not only would she not care what was said, but would have been surprised to hear that anything could be said.

Meeting Jeanne in the corridor soon afterwards Mavis stopped her. "Jeanne," she said gently, eagerly, "your parents really quarrel?" "All day!" answered Jeanne, without surprise or interest. "They have been married such a very long time."

To her astonishment the English girl with a small laugh that was more a rumble of pleasure, took three large chocolates from a paper bag, and pressed them into her fat dimpling palm.

At the summer vacation Mavis was even more fully and unexpectedly vindicated. To the amazement of the entire school both her parents arrived to take her away for the holidays.

Mavis remembered every moment, every word, every gesture of that wonderful day with a vividness that was to remain with her for life. They must have wondered at the sharp cry of rapture that came from her as she rushed at them through the doorway of the *petit salon*. At the haste with which, overruling all excuses, she insisted they must visit the classrooms ("Other girls' parents *always* do!" she pleaded. Which, after all, was true.) and she between, a hand to each, pink with happiness in the doorways, the focus of all eyes as each class rose respectfully to the nun's signal "Levez-vous, mes enfants."

True they had no sooner arrived in Antwerp than her father complained he could not stand the damned bells, and that if he was to do any work on the proofs he'd brought with him to finish in peace, he must get away from this unearthly din. The blur of their lifted voices had droned through the wall of their room until she fell asleep. The following afternoon he caught a boat home. He pressed half a sovereign into her hand with affectionate instructions about making herself ill, and she clung round his neck and kissed him with such fervour that, highly gratified, he promised to return at Christmas.

Mavis would have preferred her mother to have gone home instead. But even that meant little to her now. She had won. She was free. She was now quite ordinary.

"John the Beloved is here!"

Mavis knocked the lesson book from her friend's hand, and stood before her breathless.

"Oooo. Where? How d'you know?"

"Saw 'im. Saw 'im with my own eyes. Saw 'im getting out of a cab as I came round the Chapel door carrying the altar cloth for Sœur Benôit. Old Damien was muttering something feebly in his beard, and Sœur Marie-Joseph was making no end of a fuss over him. I heard him laugh! I wanted to catch what he was saying and went very slow as though the cloth was too heavy all of a sudden . . . only Benny twigged and hurried me round the corner. Anyway, he's here. Think he'll preach on Sunday?"

"Oooooo. 'Spec' so. He always does. Going to tell the others?"

"Not much! Let 'em find out for themselves. Come on, let's hang round the Chapel. He might come out of the *p'tit salon*." Joyce hesitated. "Come *on*, bell won't ring for another quarter."

"But Mavis, can't you go alone? I don't know a line of to-night's lesson, and there's two pages on Charlemagne, and you know how ratty the Angel gets with me at history class. . . ."

"Rot." She dragged her reluctant friend on to her feet and tugged her away. "Learn it in Chapel. I'll prompt you."

"Où allez vous, mes enfants?"

"To the Chapel, Sœur Vincent. I lost my handkerchief there this morning."

"This morning? Ah, then you can surely wait for it another quarter of an hour. The bell will ring very soon."

"Beast," muttered Mavis through her teeth, as they wandered back to the Grande Cour to endure the tail-end of the recreation hour, "mean beast, jumping out on one like that. Never mind . . . p'raps he wasn't there. . . . Shall I hear you your dates?"

But such news, however jealously guarded, was not to remain one's own for long. By supper time everyone had heard that Père Jerome had arrived to visit his brother, and that, before leaving, he would take the High Mass on Sunday and preach at the Benediction in the evening.

Will he take Confession too? Haven't heard. Probably. Anyway we get a sermon. And if he does take Confession only the R.C.'s benefit. Lucky things! Think of asking him to forgive you your sins. 'Nuff to make you sin on purpose! O, Milly, how could you! Anyway they can't read the Old Testament like us Protestants, and lose no end of fun.

In Nomine Patris, et Filii, et Spiritus Sancti. Amen.

Mes enfants, je desire vous parler ce soir de l'immense bonté de Jésus, qui dans sa tendresse infinie vous veille du mêmequ'un berger ses brebis adorées. . . .

All was subdued after the incense and the singing, and, in a moment not unlike that in which, reflecting idly, one watches long the fire's heart-beat as twilight fills the room, Père Jerome's voice came warm and masculine through the quiet Chapel. To his listeners, nervously eager, his speech seemed as clear as though engraved, or as boldly gilt and carved as the letters over the great crucifix hanging high above the altar behind him. As he preached he smiled, and made play with his hands, and once when he laughed outright at his imitation of the Devil replying to Our Lord, even Sœur Mannes, that martinet at devotion, forgot to rebuke her girls for joining in.

It was Milly Martin who thought of John the Beloved, that Easter day they met in council in the old fir tree near the orphanage grounds. Mavis and Joyce, and Marion Moore, and Milly, and Violet Gray.

That had been the first of his infrequent visits, and they had discussed him excitedly as someone gay and impersonal sent from the outer world. Of course there was Monsieur le Curé, lazy, amiable, and obese, with his black three-cornered hat and its pom-pom looking absurdly small over the pink hanging face; or there was old Père Damien so bent and frail as to be taken no more seriously than a pious ghost; or there was Père Antoine, squat and gross, who made an ugly white foam round his lips during his Lenten sermons. Yet they never seemed to call for discussion, even apart from being fixtures.

"Did you notice," asked Violet Gray eagerly, "what a jolly voice he's got? I dunno, but he didn't seem to be jawing at us like the others do. Why, even Mavis behaved herself and forgot to fidget for once." She dodged a kick from her aggrieved example. "And did you see how Sœur François laughed when he gave the illustration of the man and the pig in the pond? First time she's ever unbent as far as that, I'll bet!"

"And did you see," volunteered Joyce, "how his eyes twinkle all the time, even in the serious bits? He keeps looking as though he's going to whistle and say suddenly: 'You poor things, take a holiday now and enjoy yourselves!'"

"He has such *lovely* eyes!"

"When he looked at me with that jolly smile he's got, quite a long while . . . after that do good to your neighbour bit . . . I couldn't help it, I grinned all over my face."

"How like your conceit, Mavis Clare! So he looked at *you*, did he? That's news to me!"

"Meow . . . puss-puss . . . p'raps he was searching for you, Marion darling, far back in the fifth row, and caught sight of me instead in the first. Did he look at me, Joyce, and didn't I grin back, or didn't he?"

Of course Joyce said yes.

It was after the din had subsided that Milly Martin voiced her inspiration. She said: "I think Saint John, whom Jesus loved best, must have looked as he looks." So he became Saint John and John the Beloved, which had also the merit of putting a nun off the scent if a 'thought' was found scribbled in the margin of a lesson book. For thoughts became quite frequent in Bibles and text-books.

His teeth are very white when he smiles.

I do admire black eyes.
My beloved feedeth among the lilies, heavily underlined in the Song of
Songs.

One day Marion was helping Sœur Etienne to arrange some fresh linen
in the reception quarters of the building, when in a small parlour they
found Père Jerome reading. Sœur Etienne, who was about to lay the
linen on the table, turned quickly and shyly away so as not to disturb
him, when Père Jerome, closing his book and looking up with a slow
smile, had laid a restraining hand on Sœur Etienne's white sleeve, and
had said gaily: "Restez, ma sœur, restez, je vous en prie. Je m'ennui tant
tout seul. Il n'y a que les mouches qui me tiennent compagnie . . ."
   Marion said that Sœur Etienne laid the linen down on the table as
though the appeal had been a command.

A meeting was called in the old fir tree near the orphanage grounds
to discuss what should be done about Tony Grüdel.
   Was it a genuine conversion or was it simply swank? And if swank, as
was only too generally suspected, was she to be allowed to continue
currying favour with Sœur Mannes by this disgusting display of holi-
ness in Chapel? And should one continue the present persecution, or
was she in future to be left in peace?
   It was put forward that perhaps Marion Moore had gone a little too
far in emptying an entire pepper bag between the leaves of Tony's
prayer book, causing the spluttering German girl to be led from Mass
in hysterics.
   But Marion in a tirade both eloquent and shrill had vindicated
herself completely by charging Tony with a breach of faith.
   "You girls know," proclaimed Marion, striding a higher branch
more easily to dominate the assembly, "that Tony was pledged to us for
history class. After all, she *is* one of us though she's taken to carrying on
like a holy martyr to show Manny how she loves her. I said to her:
'Tony, this is an attack on us English and on our religion—yours as
well, sausage—and will you stand by us?' I said: 'We're on strike in
history class to-night because they've got some beastly things about our
King in it.' I said: 'That's because it's written by foreigners: he wasn't
like that at all, really.' Well, she knows English all right, girls, and I
took her right down the page and told her where it came to Henry VIII.

'All these bits,' I said, 'where it calls him sinful and arrogant, and blasphemous and godless, and headstrong and wicked—I under*lined* them forrer—were written by the enemies of England, and you're not to say them. You say hm-hm, like a loud cough, but don't say the words. You listen how we read it. *This hm-hm monarch whose hm-hm ambitions lead to the hm-hm break, etc.*' Well, Tony swore, and Mariechen Lunt and Ellie Walter came on our side as well. And what did she do, the fat German coward? What did she do?" They knew only too well. "Let us down 'cos she funked it when her turn came! Insulted our history and our King (Marion flung up her arm as if it held a banner) in front of a lot of sneering Belgian girls. What did you expect me to do, girls—kiss 'er? Wish I'd thought of something worse than pepper! I've got a better one next time!"

Three rousing cheers were given. The punishment, though severe, had been just.

"But does she mean it?" considered Mavis seriously, "or is she fooling us? There's Mona, she's nuts on being a nun, but she doesn't go about like a dying duck in a thunderstorm and throw a fit if she whiffs some incense."

"It's swank," said Violet Gray scornfully, "she's got two new holy pictures Sœur Mannes gave her pinned above her bed. And I've heard her on her knees saying her prayers hours after the light's out, hoping that Manny will find her when she makes a last tour of the dormitory."

"What I don't like," said Joyce, "is the way she gets let off her lessons now that she's so pi. I'll swear Sœur Mannes passed her over on purpose in sums yesterday, because I'd learnt the one after hers and hadn't bothered about the others, but she passed right over Tony and I got the wrong one, and a row. And you know what The Angel's like about leaving the class—well, Tony put up her hand three times in Histoire Sainte and The Angel only nodded and let her go. I put up my hand, and I really wanted to go, too, and she took no notice. I thought I was going to burst. If that's not favouritism I'd like to know what is!"

"But she's awfully funny to watch," gurgled Marion.

She was awfully funny to watch. "Let's watch Tony go to heaven!" But only her immediate neighbours got the full fun out of the apeing and tittering that went on around the florid German girl at her prayers.

How intently Tony prayed! The colour of her plain pink face would deepen to a mauvey red, and her eyes would rest on the blue vault of the Chapel, where the Holy Virgin spread her star-stained cloak about the saints, with the golden dove at her head and Jesus, thorn-crowned but smiling now, beside her, in a wide appealing stare which seemed to lift her to the heavenly feet and carry her beyond the worldly sniggers and fun-pokings which somehow, far far below, beat about her impotently as angry rain-drops on a window-pane.

Sometimes when the Holy Mother seemed to have taken elsewhere her attention and protection, and Satan was so very near, Tony would seem to drag herself clear by tightly shutting her eyes as though warding off a dreaded blow, and pressing the crucifix to her moist lips. She would sway and shiver and rock her head with the fear-closed eyes, and those on either side of her, impressed for all their grinning, would hear her muttered: "Jésus, Jésus, pardonnez-moi . . . mon Sauveur. . . ."

Especially during High Mass Tony's antics were not to be missed. Then it was no use tittering; there was no approach. She was beyond all reach. From the first organ note, and the Kyrie Eleison heralding the Litany with its repetitive fluted Ora Pro Nobis, she was visibly set throbbing. As the first fresh incense drifted in low smoky clouds, chaining the senses, Tony would seem about to swoon away, only to be held erect by a Hand stretched down to succour her.

Her singing was full-throated and heavy, and tears would well from her gentle blue eyes at the sweeter and intenser passages:

> Sur cet autel où mon âme l'adore,
> Jésus y est, et la nuit et le jour. . . .

She would begin quite softly, hardly louder than a moan, unconsciously reserving herself like an artist for the supreme moment, and her voice gradually rising would send out its final startling cry in the triumphant culmination:

> Voilà ce cœur qui vous a tant aimé!

O, Tony was well worth watching. Watching for the tiny beads of perspiration forming on her round blonde forehead presently to swell and trickle down her face unnoticed. Watching her plump fingers shaking as the chaplet slipped past them until at last they found the cross and pressed it to her lips with an inarticulate murmur. Watching how her face would swell, particularly her lips, and her eyelids become puffed and red-rimmed.

Yet the last dip of hot fingers in the benetier on filing out would end the ecstasy, and tired and quiet she would become an easy target for pent-up wit and vindictiveness.

But Tony was a good girl, empty of resentment or anger. She suffered much from home-sickness, and loved to talk of the mischievous exploits of 'Bubchen,' who, with his three small sisters, she had left behind her in Germany. She would run to a group of girls with a photograph, post-card size, in which appeared a large, prosperous-looking greengrocery. In the doorway stood a fat woman in a clean apron holding a small fair boy, and three little girls sat stiffly on three little chairs in front of her.

Really! had no one a family but Tony Grüdel? When the group was English a faint sneer would follow Tony's stout back as she departed with her postcard. "Fancy showing her grocer's shop like that!" Marion Moore would say. "And fancy her mother in a common apron. . . ." For Marion had a photograph of herself radiant in a frilly white lace frock, an immense pale blue satin sash around her waist and two blue satin bows on her hair, holding a fine new bicycle erect while behind her curved a vast canvas road edged with misty trees.

When told by Violet Gray that in future she was to be allowed to monkey about as she liked in Chapel, the grateful Tony put both her fat hands over her face and burst out crying, and would have liked to hug Violet, only Violet said she didn't care about kissing, thanks, especially a girl who blubbed like a baby over nothing.

There were some thirty German girls all told. They were most orderly and unassuming, and mixed little with the English girls to whom they were 'The Sausages.' Among them was Ellie, with her two dark plaits wound about her ears and her nightingale voice. The Germans would be seen during recreation piloting Ellie into a quiet corner of the play-ground where her lovely voice, lifted like a jet of diamond-white water, called them home again in lush May songs and sentimental *lieder.*

Sometimes a knot of English girls would stand apart and watch the happy incongruous group with grins of contempt and impatience.

They had locked Hazel in the grenier again, and her screams could be heard faintly down the loop of the banisters to where, in the remaining moments of the after-tea recreation, the girls were assembling for evening chapel.

Joyce walked back from the orphanage grounds thinking of Josephine crying silently against the wall of that low stone building which looked always cold, the tears running down her face on to her pinafore.

"Je suis une mechante fille . . . je suis une mechante fille," she had sobbed, and that was all she could be made to say. The white veil of a lay sister could be seen against a window, and Joyce had thought it wise to leave. "Tiens, prends mon mouchoir," she had said, for obviously Josephine possessed no such convenience, and with the handkerchief had pressed two sous, all that remained of the week's pocket-money, into her hand.

Now she remembered that she had forgotten to ask Josephine whether she was wearing drawers or not, and that she and Marion had a bet on it of two pencils and a new nib.

Josephine was reputed to be not a good girl. Once, having refused to carry the orphanage banner in the Christmas procession because, she explained, it was too heavy for her and she might fall, she was punished by having to go without her drawers for a week; a punishment especially severe during recreation for frost was on the stones and benches. Angele Latier had found it out, and it was so funny, that ever afterwards any-one accompanying a nun on an errand to the orphanage, always asked Josephine whether she wore drawers or not, and there was always a bet on the reply.

She was late and had to walk up the aisle alone.

Under cover of passing her a hymn-book Violet Gray whispered: "They've locked Hazel in the grenier again. She's making a ghastly row!" and Joyce went quite white and felt almost sick. ("O, you should have seen J.'s face! She went *green*. . . .")

Not that she even liked Hazel. Indeed she rarely spoke to her, a clumsy undersized girl whom everyone agreed was 'not all there.' But she could not bear it when they locked her in that awful place: the thought alone seemed to drain all her blood away in fear, as in those terrible dreams she had and from which she woke in a cold sweat. And there was Hazel now, screaming away with everyone shut in the Chapel far out of hearing. It was like torturing a dog; or throwing stones at a sick cat as she had once seen the children in the village do. And thinking of it her heart went hot and beat loudly and at a great pace. "They'd not lock me up there!" thought Joyce fiercely, "I'd break their rotten door in, and they know it, too!"

A touch on her arm, and Sœur Mannes frowned into her turned face. She opened her prayer-book and picked up the thread mechanically.

Mon Dieu, je vous aime par dessus toutes choses, de tout mon cœur, de toute mon âme et de toutes mes forces . . . parce que vous êtes infiniment bon en vous-même et infiniment. . . .

I wonder if He loves us all the same way, or does He love some of us more than others? Sœur Imelda, for instance, more than Sœur Benôit, or Lucy more than Marion, and I wonder who He likes best in the whole school. He can't love Hazel much or surely He would open the door, as He did for Peter, and show them what He thought of their beastly tricks. She must be frightened now: it was getting dark. All the rats, all the noises in that horrid cistern, all the dark shapes of the trunks and the nearness of the ceiling that your head hits when you stand up, and always seems to want to smother you.

Of course it was The Angel. Only Sœur Angelique did things like that. But what can Hazel have done this time? No one else was put in the grenier and left to howl themselves sick. Hazel was eleven now and though she was still sometimes 'dirty,' it couldn't be that. The punishment for that was to stand in the middle of the dormitory with one's drawers on one's head for fifteen minutes before getting into bed, and let all the other girls see and laugh at you. And, anyway, that only happened to the little ones in Sœur Osana's dormitory, and they went to bed a full two hours before the other girls.

But even for telling a lie, it's too much. Why doesn't she tell her mother? Why doesn't she get her people to take her away?

Another touch on the elbow. Really Manny is maddening to-night. Does she come to church or pray or to watch *me?*

Mon Dieu, je me repens de tout mon cœur, d'avoir offensé votre souveraine Majesté et votre bonté infinie. Je déteste tout mes péchés pour l'amour de vous, et j'aimerais mieux mourir que de vous offenser encore. Je me propose. . . .

Joyce remembered the first time she ever heard Hazel crying, crying in that weak awful way of a new baby, through the classroom window in the recreation grounds. She had climbed up one of the columns supporting the arch of the terrace and seen Hazel over Sœur Angelique's knees, her drawers off, and The Angel, horribly hot in the face, beating away with a steady rhythm. And climbing down she had picked up three large stones and sent them flying through the window squares. The punishment, somehow, hadn't mattered. . . .

At last they were filing past the Chapel entrance. On the pretext of tying her shoelace she managed to remain at the end of the line and escape detection as she fled up the stairs to the topmost floor where at the top of a small ladder stood the grenier door.

She knocked softly. Hazel? Hazel? It's me . . . don't be afraid. There was no reply, and, although she waited some time, no sound. She must have cried herself to sleep, thought Joyce, as she made her way slowly downstairs again.

But this time Hazel had not cried herself to sleep. She had screamed till her voice gave out and she was tired of screaming. And when it had grown so dark that even the sound of her own sobs had terrified her beyond endurance, she had thrown herself in a panic from the narrow port-hole window. She had landed on a roof some twenty feet below, where bruised and unconscious she had been found by frightened lay sisters, and rubbed with oil and taken to bed.

The next few days Sœur Angelique's narrow face was defiant and self-conscious, and her eyes knew how to avoid the deliberate questioning stares directed at her. It was sweet to kick the fallen lion while one could.

Hazel became the heroine of the hour. The smaller children brought to her bedside offerings of holy pictures and chocolate cream: the older ones promised her their protection.

She was not locked in the grenier again.

W ell? What is it?"
"You needn't keep on saying that and making it all the more difficult to tell. I wanted to confess something. I haven't got to: but I want to."

"You've said that three times already. What is it?"

"All right, you needn't be so sharp, Mavis. I don't have to tell it. I wrote that note 'cos I felt it wicked not to tell you: but you can't bully me into telling, and you needn't think you can."

"O! *Idiot!*" Mavis jumped up from the grass in a temper and stood over Mona as though she would have liked to beat her. "Idiot! Getting me to waste all my rec when I wanted to be with Joyce hanging about here over a silly confession I never even asked for. What is it? Quick! or I'm off."

"I tell you I don't have to tell. I'm doing it of my own free will and I call it beastly the way you're treating me," and Mona broke into loud sobs.

"O Lord deliver us!" cried the exasperated Mavis, "you know, you'll make a fine nun. You'll begin to blub if they put their hands up to leave the room. And if they answer back I 'spect you'll faint. Well, keep your silly secret. I'm off," and away she started towards the hockey field.

But Mona was up and after her in a flash. Confession was good for the soul, and she hadn't been meditating on this one an entire week for nothing. "Mavis, come back. O do come back. I'll tell it now. I really will." She caught her up and hung on to her pinafore. "I've meant to tell you for ever so long. It's about something I said to Sœur Imelda about you. . . ."

Mavis sat down suddenly and took a long breath. "It's not . . . you didn't tell her . . . you couldn't have told her what I told you about. . . ."

"Thank you," sniffed Mona, "I'm not a sneak, whatever you like to say about me, Mavis Clare. No, it's something I said about you, though. And it's true, too," she added fiercely, "but still I shouldn't have said it. But it's no good going and confessing it, if I don't tell it you as well, it's still a sin."

"Don't you go putting me into your confessions," said Mavis aggressively, "or I'll have a few things to tell your beloved Sœur Imelda about you myself. I s'pose you told her I was conceited or something. Is that it?"

Mona turned a deep pink. "It wasn't quite like that . . . and . . . and, anyway you are, you know, Mavis. Everybody says so. Only I got so awfully jealous when she said you were nice-looking or something that I said you didn't half know it, too."

Mavis considered this a moment, and felt surprisingly elated. "Did Immy really say I was nice-looking?"

"Mm." Mona saw her elation and suddenly found her confession more painful than she had expected. "And I said: 'Doesn't she know it too!' and that if you looked in the glass much longer you'd get a squint. That was a sin," she added primly, "and I've wanted to confess it ever since."

"Funny," said Mavis, who hadn't troubled about the tail-end of Mona's confession, "I never even knew Immy had noticed me, or rather I always thought she disapproved of me and Joyce."

"Saying you're nice-looking doesn't mean she doesn't disapprove of you," intercepted Mona quickly. "She never said anything about your conduct being nice. And I'd rather she praised my conduct than my face, anyway."

"Would you, Mona? Would you really?" considered Mavis with a subtlety of which she was quite unaware. "I dunno. Everybody's good. . . . I s'pose I can't feel your way about it 'cos I'm not an R.C. Somehow, I wouldn't care a hang if I'd only been called a good girl . . ." and without warning, at the back of her mind an echo suddenly said: And nor would she. . . . She wouldn't have bothered to confess you that . . . and something seemed to show her Mona very far below gazing up at her, and lots and lots of girls, ugly girls, very far below, all gazing up at her, and not because she was good at all; and she tossed back her curls with the air of a pretty circus pony, and felt proud.

"What was it Immy said, actually?" she inquired with an affected innocence, "anything particular, or just that I was nice-looking? . . ."

But Mona could be cunning, too. She had little cause for liking Mavis Clare and more cause than she cared to dwell on for avoiding her. She's mine, and *she* shan't take her from me, thought Mona, and said: "I don't remember properly now. It was the afternoon I spent with her in the Quartier des Dames, and when we came in to tea she noticed you at the gate and said: That's a nice-looking girl, and I said you knew it, too, and if you looked in the glass much longer, I said, you'll get a squint."

Still Mavis was loth to believe it. She wanted more than this cold appraisement of her charms, and she was disappointed. Besides, Mona's voice lacked conviction.

"Are you sure that's *all* she said, Mona?" she wheedled. And Mona answered in disgust: "Yes, *all.* Aren't you ashamed of yourself, Mavis Clare, fishing for compliments that weren't ever given?"

Mavis changed her tactics. "If you tell a lie at Confession you've done a double sin," she brought out menacingly, "and it's as good as if you'd never confessed. I heard The Angel telling Angèle that last week over stealing that jam."

"I've not told a lie," said Mona fiercely, "I've confessed all I've said about you and I haven't told a lie. It's you who's sinning with your conceit and your fishing. I haven't told a lie, so there!"

"Then what're you so red in the face for if you aren't telling a lie?" pursued the inexorable Mavis; "you're jealous, that's what you are, and that's another sin on the top of your lie, and your confession's only half a confession, and that's another sin. And that's three in one afternoon." She stood up and with an odious air of conscious virtue made great play at patting her skirts straight. "All right, goody-goody," she looked down meaningly into Mona's indignant face, "don't tell me if you don't want to. . . . But look out for yourself. . . . Perhaps I'll take her away if I like. . . ."

All colour left Mona's face. She swayed slightly and caught her hands together as though to steady herself. She felt as though she had been half-strangled. Even tears failed her. "You couldn't!" she screamed after the disappearing Mavis, "you *couldn't* . . . you, aren't good enough . . . you *couldn't* . . . she wouldn't look at you. . . ."

"Can't I?" Mavis shouted back. "Can't I? We'll see. . . ." And just as she was turning the corner she looked round again, and making sure that Mona was looking, she made a long face and put her thumb to her nose.

I t was said that Sœur Damiana's eyes had filled with tears when her beautiful black hair was cut off, and this so endeared her to Dora Jennings that she took her as her *flamme,* and made herself ridiculous. No one else considered Sœur Damiana worthy of serious attention. For Sœur Damiana had been too recently Eileen O'Connor, and Eileen O'Connor had been merely a large, red-cheeked girl from Dublin who took the veil under the influence of Sœur.

And Sœur, head of all the English nuns, was cold and disdainful like a great lady moving among suppliants; and tall and very pale with unsmiling hazel eyes of gimlet intensity; and with hands memorably white and fine. And everything about her had the unreality of a milk-white unicorn.

But Dora thrived on ridicule; and she had a secret which she treasured even more than her fine new mother-of-pearl rosary with the pretty ivory and silver cross, and the small silver links between the beads.

One afternoon she had crept quietly to the Dormitory to make an apple-pie bed to repay Mavis Clare for her latest behaviour towards her beloved, when suddenly she became aware of someone crying in a cubicle at the end of the room.

Dora held her breath and waited a moment, fearful of being discovered. The sobs not only continued: they grew louder, and all at once they became so heartrending that she put down the wet sponge and the hair-brush, and forgetting that she was liable to heavy punishment for being in a dormitory at five o'clock in the afternoon, she ran towards the sound.

There sat Sœur Damiana on her narrow bed, her face hidden in her pillow, so abandoned to her weeping that she never even felt Dora's arms go round her waist.

Dora found herself trembling so much that she sank on her knees and laid her head in Sœur Damiana's lap and soon was crying almost as loudly herself. It was awful to see her beloved gulping and blowing her nose and then finally making an effort to tidy up her face as though nothing unusual had happened. It was so awful that she kept her face hidden in the heavy cream skirts and averted her head until it was all over.

When she did look up she found Sœur Damiana looking down at her, her face so red and shiny that it might have been polished. Dora wondered how one comforted. She stammered shyly: "Was it . . . was it the sewing class?"

Sœur Damiana nodded. She did not seem to find it strange that Dora should be sitting at her feet consoling her.

What a pandemonium it had been! And what a headache she had had! The entire class had been against her, egged on by the older girls in the back benches. It had been worse than ever to-day, with that new trick of each row standing to attention at a signal, and shouting: "*Sœur Eileen O'Connor, puis j'aller à la cour?*" and following the "No" with a loud groaning in which the entire class joined. *Sœur Eileen, Sœur Eileen, Sœur Eileen O'Connor,* they sang in chorus. Six times this had happened. She did not care to call another nun or to complain to Sœur, or show in any way that she was incapable of controlling her new classes.

Dora watched her face anxiously. "It wasn't me, was it?" she inquired, and was surprised to see Sœur Damiana smile. No.

"Was it Mavis Clare?" asked Dora threateningly. Again No.

"Because she's a beast. I hate her," said Dora. "She thinks she can do whatever she likes, and she gets all the other girls to do as she tells them. She even cheeks Sœur Macky; and she took Josephine away from me, too. I'll pay her out one day!"

"You're my *flamme*," said Dora gazing up at Sœur Damiana, her cheeks scarlet. She had never had her to herself before. "You've been my *flamme* for three weeks now."

Sœur Eileen—Sœur Eileen O'Connor took both Dora's hands in her own. She seemed to have forgotten that only a moment since she had been crying wildly as any schoolgirl. "That is very nice of you, Dora," she said a little breathlessly, "thank you very much indeed. I wonder why you chose me?"

" 'Cos I love you best," said Dora, "I love you better than anyone in the whole school. What's your favourite colour?" she added shyly.

"Blue, I think," said Sœur Damiana after a moment's thought.

"Then I'll put blue ribbons in my underclothes instead of pink," confided Dora, "and I'll work you something blue for Christmas. And I'll fight everyone who's rude to you in sewing class."

To her surprise this was greeted with a burst of laughter. "I shouldn't do that," Sœur Damiana advised, "perhaps it's best to leave them alone. When they get used to me they'll be better. But there is something I'd like you to do for me, Dora. Can you give me your promise?"

"I'll do anything, anything," gasped Dora as though about to be commanded to deliver both eyes on a dish in emulation of Saint Lucy.

"Then promise me you'll never tell anyone that you found me crying. We'll make that our secret."

A beautiful intimacy seemed to Dora to have sprung up between them. She looked round Sœur Damiana's cubicle, aware that no girl had ever before seen it but herself. Like all cubicles of nuns who superintended dormitories, it was curtained apart and was spacious enough to admit a small *prie-Dieu* beside the bed. In a corner stood a brown oak *lavabo,* a large linen-bag, and a cane chair. A small crucifix hung on the white wall, and a picture of the Holy Family and another of the Virgin alone, were pinned beside it.

Dora saw the edges of Sœur Damiana's pink flannel nightgown sticking out from under the pillow, and then, looking up towards the head of the bed, she saw something which seemed to her so dreadful that it haunted her in dreams for weeks.

It was a large picture glued to the wooden partition above the bed, and on it was an enormous grinning skull, which, by a trick of shadow, projected itself far out of the picture, and gave her a cold tingle down her spine. Around the skull were flames, the flames of Hell, filled with hideous devils threatening with their pitchforks the tortured bodies of the damned, whose arms were raised in agony. Under Death's grinning face lay a scythe and an hour glass. And a long bony finger pointed in triumph to the large black lettering beneath it all:

CETTE NUIT PEUT-ETRE!

M avis read the note passed to her under cover of the noisy scraping of the chairs moving towards the VIe Station de la Croix, *Une femme pieuse essuie la face de Jésus.*

Dear Mavis, please be friends again it was all my fault yesterday what she really said was There's a pretty girl and she's awfully clever Will you walk round with me after supper I'll wait for you by the pump you can have that chalk pencil if you like   M.

At the next movement *Jésus tombe pour la Seconde Fois,* she turned and nodded to Mona, and they smiled together affectionately.

From her new position Mavis could see to the back of the Chapel, where, under the vase of lilies beneath Saint Anthony, Sœur Imelda knelt with her head bowed so low that only the white band across her forehead was discernible.

The sight did not give her the thrill she had expected.

Du 22 avril au 1er mai. Retraite.
Soir.

> *"Moi, je t'aimerai."*
> Et moi?
> *"Toi, tu me laisseras faire."*
>
> *JESUS!*
>
> *Méditations de Sœur Marie-Saint-Anselme*

It seemed incredible to Mavis that, with the exception of the respite allowed between twelve and one o'clock, she had again not spoken a word throughout the day.

Hunched up, both elbows on the desk, and her chin resting on her hand, she wondered how she could have given way to the mock-heroic impulse which had landed her in this interminable Evening Meditation when she might have been in the recreation room walking round with Joyce. She wished irritably that the hum of voices and the sudden trills of laughter were less persistent in their re-echoing. By the intervals at which the laughter occurred she guessed that they were Où allez vous comme-çá, Marianneke, Marianneke? She was good at Marianneke.

Otherwise the silence was broken only by the crackle of turned pages and the leafy rustle of knitting needles.

Sœur Marie Imelda, who took the Meditation Class, was bent over her desk, apparently copying from a large book. Her fine white hand moved slowly and evenly across the page. Now and again she raised her head and passed a grave look over the class. Most of the girls were reading; a few were knitting or embroidering; here and there a prayer-book or a cantique lay open on a desk.

Tony Grüdel, the only other Protestant girl beside Mavis taking the Retreat, was saying her rosary, her head against the wall, her eyes tightly closed and her lips moving continuously, happy in her orgy of undisturbed prayer. Her plain pink face oozed a pious stickiness. Mavis longed to rush across the room and in front of everybody deal a few resounding slaps on its shiny roundness and throw the rosary out of the window. Without knowing why, Tony at her prayers always seemed to her a particularly stupid and unpleasant sight.

At intervals Mona turned her head and looked at her very deliberately, and when she met her eyes looked away again quickly. Mavis knew what she meant. Ass! She thinks I'm taking the Retreat to charm Sœur Imelda! Once when Mona looked round, Mavis shook her head vigorously and smiled. She meant "It's all right. Don't worry. I'm not. I don't want her!"

All at once Sœur Imelda raised her head and caught their by-play. Mona turned quickly round, crimson with unhappiness; she would have liked to flatten herself abjectly against the floor; but Mavis took a malicious pleasure in staring insolently into Sœur Imelda's eyes, conveying: "I'm not afraid of you. *I'm* not Mona!"

To help the time pass she turned again to her book. It was a fat illustrated volume on the Lives of the Saints, A to L, and had been dealt to her by Sœur Osana, who had charge of the religious books from the library to be handed, during Retreat, to those who had no needlework.

The pictures were very horrible, Mavis thought, as, with an effort, she compelled herself to look again at the more gruesome ones. She had never seen anything like them before; had never imagined such people could exist, and she longed to be sharing them with Joyce. Particularly the one of the screaming man in a hair shirt being pushed from a high rock, an enormous stone hanging from his neck, and black water spread very far below him.

And the picture of Sainte Bolonia, with, in the background, the hillside on which she had tended her sheep and where her pious ways had first attracted attention. There was the wide strip of river dividing the fields, and on it moved Sainte Bolonia, headless. But in her outstretched hands lay her smiling head casting a shining circle of light on the waters from its halo. Sainte Bolonia was carrying her head across to its burial-place.

Then there was the hideous full-page picture of the two women; one on the rack, blood streaming from her sides in which hung great iron hooks; the other on her knees, tied to an iron ring in a stone, her back ravaged by the scourges of her torturers. This was a peculiarly realistic picture, and there seemed to be, Mavis noticed, a great many people looking on at the martyrdom. Probably took place in a public park, she thought, noticing in the background a tree, near which a large fire was being kindled. Beneath it was written: "The Holy Virgin Thea, to whom her virtue was most dear, reproached the Judge for his injustices. Enraged by her remarks he caused her to be inhumanly scourged, then stretched on the rack and her sides torn with iron hooks until the bare ribs appeared. Valentina, a pious Christian Virgin of Caesarea, who had also consecrated her chastity to God, cried out to the Judge from the midst of the crowd: 'How long will you thus torment my sister?' She was immediately dragged by force to the altar, stretched on the rack, and the Judge commanded that her sides be more cruelly torn than any others. Being at last wearied of tormenting them, he ordered the two virgins to be burnt together."

Ugh! How shall I sleep after all this! What horrible nightmare things everyone was doing with such joy. There was the Blessed Catherine of Fingo's picture, which made one feel even more sick, because it was uncanny as well as frightful.

A hideous grinning man in a funny Eastern dress was standing over the Blessed Catherine, wiping an enormous curved sword. The victim's headless body lay over a block, and a pool of blood flowed from it. But the horrible part was that three heads were bounding over the ground, and yet each head bore an unmistakable likeness to that preceding it, and they all somehow belonged to the Blessed Catherine. Reading the text Mavis learned that the Blessed Catherine had been executed at Nagasaki in Japan; and that it is said that when her head was cut off it rebounded three times, each time calling loudly the names of Jesus and Mary.

What would mother say to a book like this? wondered Mavis. Mother who once said to her as they were making a tour of the classrooms: "How can you bear all these statues covered in blood, my poor child? It is all so barbaric," without realising (Mavis was sure of this) what a sacrilege she had uttered. What *would* mother say to the picture of Saint Arcadius who was chopped clean in halves, with his feet and legs and arms and even his fingers separately cut off and lying near him in a dark mess?

Saint Arcadius had a lot of writing under his picture and Mavis read it raptly, her curiosity getting the better of her horror.

"Then said Arcadius: 'Jesus Christ is my life and death is my gain. Invent what torments you please; but know that nothing shall make me a traitor to my God.' The Governor, in a rage, paused to devise some unheard-of torment for him; hooks seemed too easy; neither plummets of lead nor cudgels could satisfy his fury; the very rack he thought too gentle. At last he said to the ministers of his cruelty: 'Take him and let him see and desire death without being able to obtain it. Cut off his limbs joint by joint, and execute this so slowly that the wretch may know what it is to abandon the gods of his ancestors for an unknown deity.' The executioners led Arcadius to the place of execution: a place dear and sweet to all who sigh after eternal life. Here the martyr lifted up his eyes to Heaven, and implored strength from above. He then stretched out his neck expecting to have his head cut off; but the executioner bade him stretch out his hand, and joint after joint cut off his fingers, hand, arms, and shoulders. Laying the saint on his back he cut off his toes, feet, legs, and thighs. The holy martyr held out his limbs and joints one after another, repeating with invincible patience and courage: 'Lord teach me thy wishes,' for the tyrants had forgotten to cut out his tongue. After so many martyrdoms, his body lay a mere trunk weltering in its own blood. Even the executioners were moved to tears. But Arcadius with a joyful countenance, surveying his scattered limbs all around him and offering them to God, said: 'Happy members, now dear to me, as you at last truly belong to God, being all made a sacrifice to him!' And turning to the spectators he said: 'Your gods are not gods: renounce their worship. He alone for whom I suffer and die is. . . .' " But Mavis could read no further.

She felt shaken. Her breath came in short gasps, which sounded to her noticeably loud in the surrounding silence. She leant her head against the wall to steady herself. She wished she had never opened the book. Never, never would she cease to be haunted by the terrible things she had seen. Devoutly she wished she had brought her Bible from Chapel instead and searched out some 'bits' so as to be one up on the others later.

How she longed to be in the recreation room, shouting as they tried to pull her away, over the white handkerchief. Où allez vous comme-çá, Marianneke, Marianneke? Où allez vous comme-çá, Mariann-E-K-E. Cherchez des pommes-de-terre, Marianneke, Marianneke. Cherchez des pommes-de-terre, Mariann-E-K-E. She was almost humming it aloud. And then a good tug, and a jerk, and over they came, and again she won and everyone was surprised at her strength and swore it was a trick. And secretly she was just as surprised herself.

She found Sœur Imelda staring her straight in the face. A something hostile and questioning was in her eyes. Mavis, red in the face, thought: "I'll look you up now. I hope you're being drawn and quartered, or hung by the heels with the blood trickling from your nose."

Half-way down the I's. *Imelda, La Bienheureuse, Vierge. Page 321.*

La Bienheureuse Imelda was being neither drawn nor quartered, nor was her head anywhere but on her own neck. She had a full-page picture; and it was a restful and a happy one. In a beautiful dark chapel with the nuns and the girls kneeling just where they knelt in everyday life, a lovely girl with her face lifted to the altar, her arms outstretched imploringly, knelt in the centre of the communion rail. Above her head rested a Host rayed like a star.

She read: "Although scarcely eleven years old, the little Imelda, who had just entered the Dominican Convent outside Bologna, was already known for her piety and zeal. Owing to her extreme youth she was refused Communion, though she so ardently desired it. One day, when all those who were old enough to receive it had left the Communion rail, the Host, in answer to her prayers, came out of the Tabernacle and stood in the air over her head. The priests were greatly surprised, but discerning in this miracle the Divine Will, they brought the paten and gave her the Host. So great was her joy that she died immediately."

Mavis stared in astonishment at Sœur Imelda, almost believing she had discovered a secret from her past life. Unaccountably she felt relieved that the miracle had been so mild. How she would have hated to have thought of her ever afterwards with her head in her hands, or stretched on a rack, or slashed with swords and having salt rubbed in her wounds! Some puritanical strain caused her to desire her martyrs goreless and restrained in death. She now knew that the Blessed Imelda who had died so young, and Saint Elizabeth of Hungary, whose skirts once filled with roses, were the nicest saints of all.

The bell rang at last and she walked straight into the group, of which she herself had so often been leader, eager by horseplay and sarcasms to trip the unwary into breaking their silences. They were ready for her. She had meant to show by a grimace that it was all a mistake, and that she wished she had never been let in for it, when someone gave her arm a vicious pinch hoping she would cry out, and she immediately assumed a mournful dignity, meeting their attack with such pained surprise that she even deceived herself into believing she was enjoying it all. Perhaps she was. Even Joyce received such a look of what was presumably an admixture of pride and sorrow as Mavis passed on her way to the dormitory queue, that she howled in astonishment: "Good Lord! She's gone pi!"

She little guessed the effect of the Blessed Catherine of Fingo on her friend's sleep that night.

N ow a change came over Mavis. She could feel it circulating as something physical within her, such as seasickness or giddiness in the head. Sitting tense on her hard rush seat while Père Damien spoke to them all of humility, she was intensely aware of being different from what she had been on entering the Chapel twenty minutes ago.

She sank herself deeper into this sensation of difference. On the walls of the Natural History class was that picture of the glossy golden snake lying beside its empty skin. She leaned her head against the high back of her chair and closed her eyes, shedding, she felt, a skin. An ugly skin; a layer of sin; dark and pursuing like a shadow, which was what Père Damien was calling sin: *une ombre, nos ombres à nous tous.*

Still with closed eyes and head thrown back she thought of Sœur Vincent de Paul, because of whom she had undertaken the Retreat. Sœur Vincent, the wide, kindly Flemish nun, who had said in front of everyone, simply everyone, that it was a pity *la petite bavarde* was a Protestant and so was not taking the Retreat—only that could stop her tongue. She had said: "Can't I hold my tongue? Can't I! I'll show a foreigner what an English girl can do when she wants to!" It had become a patriotic issue, backed and counter-backed; yet Mavis knew in her heart that patriotism had not been the reason for her coming forward at all.

Mona thinks I'm doing it to get Immy away from her. But I'm not. I don't want her; although I threatened to take her away; although I *could* get her if I tried. O, easily. Ever so easily. I'd only have to turn pi a bit and run and fetch her books and learn my Histoire Sainte a bit better.

The shedding of the skin called for humility; called for charity; for sacrifice. If only Mona could know how innocent Mavis was of bad intent. Not only that, if only Mona knew how she had renounced her desire; had deliberately turned away from Sœur Imelda (whose conquest was unquestioned from the start) to save her pain.

Mavis was on the point of believing this when she opened her eyes to look towards Mona's chair and her eyes met those of Josephine Mars, who must have been staring at her for some time. On seeing Mavis's eyes open and staring straight at her Josephine went crimson and looked away, and Mavis reddened, too, in surprise. Quickly it had flashed through her mind: she was thinking how pretty I looked like that . . . with my eyes shut . . . like, like . . . what did Sœur Marie-Joseph once say? . . . like an angel in a Holy Picture . . . un ange d'un tableau saint. . . .

But now she was different; she remembered how different she was to be in the future. Oh, what she must overcome! How big her shadow was! Probably bigger than any other shadow in the school, if the truth were known. Vanity, sloth, greed, temper . . . but above them all, above them all towered Vanity.

Why had anyone ever told her she was pretty? Why had Ida James, a big girl of seventeen, ever said that she was the prettiest girl in the school? And having said it, why, O why, did they come and tell her about it? Before that she had not known, not cared, not understood how nice it was to be prettier than other girls.

Why was someone always saying: I wish I had hair like yours, Mavis? Wish I'd your teeth. Oh, *you* needn't worry with eyes like that. And why was that itchy feeling down the spine so pleasant as one replied politely: I like your hair so much better, Doris? Or one simply said nothing at all. Why should one long to grow up, to grow up quickly, to put up one's hair (Mavis knew exactly how her hair was to look, in fat bronzed ringlets and little plaits interwoven with a velvet ribbon and a few pads, like that illustration in the *Sphere* that Violet Gray received last month from home) and wear long skirts, and have a waist no more than eighteen inches, and have a fine full figure like Zilla Ray on the picture postcards? And . . . and charm . . . tall men with deep dark eyes like John the Beloved; only real men one could dance with, and who would fall on their knees at one's feet like in the picture called 'Bliss' which Milly Martin kept under her mattress.

Mavis knew exactly how everything would be; she was rehearsing it more and more frequently these days. The first meeting; the proposal; the first kiss; the wedding dress of stiff cream satin; the engagement ring that was causing her so much thought in the choosing. But she would renounce it all. Vanity. She would begin by giving herself a penance. She would write

I must not be vain.
I must not be vain.
I must not be vain.

five hundred times, and not with that double-edged nib she usually used for penance writing.

Neither must she look in the glass; or only once in the morning to see if her collar lay straight. But no more in windows or the glass doors of the refectory. She must not put that little crimp in her hair with the two bent hair-pins—always pretending it grew like that. She must not wear the big black bow at the back, considered so becoming; but must do her hair flat in two straight plaits without the crimp or the pretty bow. Instead, two plain slides at the bottom of each plait, even on

Sundays. She must perform acts of mortification, because vanity, she remembered Sœur Damiana once saying, was the ugliest and most severely punished of all sins. Sœur Damiana also said that if Jesus told the rich man that he could not enter Heaven unless he gave up his wealth, He also told Mary Magdalen that no girl who was pretty and was fond of her prettiness could ever be admitted into the presence of His Father, but would be unconditionally passed over by Saint Peter in favour of the plain ones.

To illustrate this Sœur Damiana had told the story of the vain woman who was very rich and given up to sin and pleasure. Mavis had wondered and wondered about her so often since hearing her story, and had dressed her up and coloured her in a hundred different ways. One day a gentleman, one of her many worldly friends, came to see her (*un beau monsieur, un monsieur du beau monde* had been Sœur Damiana's words) and he brought her a necklace of precious stones; a wonderful necklace which outshone all the jewels of the Madonna in the Cathedral of Louvain. The woman was so dazzled by the earthly splendour of the gift that she ran with him to her mirror and he clasped it round her neck. But when they looked, they saw in the mirror, not the necklace, but a big green snake lying coiled three times round the woman's neck.

But after that? What happened then? Qu'est ce qu'elle a fait alors, ma sœur? But Mavis never heard the end, though it caused her fevers of ungratified curiosity and speculation. Sœur Damiana knew no ending; could never see that the story needed an ending. It was a message from God to all guilty of the sin of vanity.

For a fortnight afterwards Mavis had kept her necklace of blue Venetian beads snug in her handkerchief case. For a long time now she had ceased to speculate on the woman and the serpent-coil; but Père Damien was bringing it all back with his angry words on sins like shadows closing in on all who were not warned in time. Afterwards it might be too late, he emphasised. Mavis gave a little shudder as she realised her escape. Never to have known. To have grown up, to have grown old, to have reached perhaps to twenty-five, and never to have known that there was no hope of ever getting into Heaven if one were pretty and vain. In the future it would be as though she had no face. Or rather as though she was someone she had known a long time ago and almost forgotten. The pretty, sinful self she knew so well would be dead; and if she still happened to be pretty and they told her so, she would not believe it; she would not listen.

There was something new and exhilarating about sacrifice. Sœur

Marie-Joseph had once told her that Saint Catherine of Siena, in after years, confessed that her greatest difficulty in mortifying the flesh had always been to overcome sleep, of which she was very fond. Ever afterwards she had liked Saint Catherine immensely; but just now she thought of her with a faint contempt. It seemed altogether too childish compared with overcoming vanity. Almost it made her laugh aloud to think of the absurdity of bothering to overcome sleep!

So great was the change within her now, that she felt herself assuming an entirely different expression. She looked at the angel, the one with stars in her auburn hair and the tall lily in her hand on the Virgin's right, and secretly hoped she was growing like that. She felt intoxicated with a pure and solemn happiness, and joined in the Benedictus in a clear, fluted voice which, she could not help noticing, although for the moment divested of earthly thoughts, made a warm and charming sound.

Walking down the aisle on leaving the Chapel, Mavis did not stare around at her friends and smile, as was her customary exit. Instead she kept her eyes fixed steadily in front of her, and about her expression there was something gentle and aloof. It was not altogether her fault that in a far corner of her mind a small voice goaded her with the reminder that this was perhaps the most becoming expression she had ever used.

Mavis came out of the Retreat with flying colours. Three whole days and not one word spoken. Her enemies were confounded and had to content themselves with a few sneers at girls who will go to any lengths to show off. But it was none the less a triumph, and the English-Protestant section was overjoyed.

Joyce won a bar of cream-chocolate from Josephine Mars; a ready-reckoner from Edith Malcolm; an india-rubber and a coloured lead-pencil from Milly Martin.

Mona lost an embroidered collar to Marion Moore.

Violet Gray lost two double-nibs for penance writing and her new pencil case. Serve you right, said Mavis, for not believing I could do it!

Janet Cairns lost a lace holy-picture and a stick of licorice.

Molly Tindall won a piece of velvet hair-ribbon, against which she had wagered a pair of quite new kid gloves with the third finger of the right-hand glove split.

Mavis won admiration and envy, and two of the smaller children, overcome by the glare of her sudden popularity, chose her as their *flamme*.

She was again friends with Mona, who had at last reluctantly accepted her word that she had no dishonourable designs on Sœur Imelda. Mavis secretly wondered if it was any use having designs honourable or otherwise on Sœur Imelda. There was still that something hostile and questioning in her eyes which she had surprised there during the Evening Meditation, the second night of the Retreat. As though she knew something about her; as though she could see straight through her, and was not impressed.

When it was all over she had gone up to her, very modestly, and not at all expecting praise for what she had done, and had said with a shy smile: "I *did* keep the silence, ma sœur. Every minute of it."

Sœur Imelda had looked at her quite kindly, and even smiled. But what she had said had been altogether unexpected: "Mon enfant, souvenez vous que'on n'employe jamais la sainte réligion pour plaire à sa vanité."

Her voice had been gentle; but Mavis had felt her cheeks burn as though they had been slapped.

N ow then, you two. Stop that at once. If The Angel catches you there'll be a row."

Marguerite von Dadels, who was using her feet as both her hands were being held behind her back, explained angrily, administering a good kick on the ankle. "She's taken my confession. Si, she has and she can't deny it. C'est moi qui vole les pommes cette fois-ci."

Jeanne Martelle, who had a grip on her arms and was twisting them with relish, denied it equally angrily. "First she said she'd steal the apples, then she said she'd steal the handkerchief, so I said I'd steal the apples, and now she's in a temper 'cos she says it isn't anything very bad stealing a handkerchief and that I've got the best sin."

"You let go her hands," commanded Joyce, who delighted in putting things right as she called her zeal for interfering in the quarrels of others. "Or I'll report you to Nicky, and we'll see who steals apples or not."

Released, Marguerite rushed at Jeanne and gave her a last violent kick on the shins and then darted quickly behind Joyce's skirts for protection.

"Now then," said Joyce with considerable dignity to the furious Jeanne, who was making vain efforts to reach Marguerite, "you shan't touch her. I won't let you. How can you be such a coward as to hit a little one two years younger than yourself?"

"As she's two years younger than me, I steal the apples," said Jeanne with ten-year-old logic. "An' anyway, as my turn for Confession comes before hers I can have what sins I like!"

"O but you can't," cried Joyce, who cared nothing for logic and a great deal for her reputation as champion of the weak. "You can't steal the apples this time 'cos you stole the idea from Marguerite and then twisted her arms for it. . . . There's a double sin already. And *you* can't either," seeing Marguerite's triumphant face, which immediately soured, "and unless you both make it up at once and promise me not to use the apples I'll speak to Père Damien about you and he'll tell Sœur Veronique."

The response was immediate. Père Damien's complaints to Sœur Veronique were uncomfortably effective. Sullenly two hands were extended and clasped. Two small sullen faces tried to look as though they did not long to fall on this importunate *Anglaise,* give her a sound beating, and then return to their fight in peace.

Joyce saw only the triumph of virtue, and virtue must be rewarded. "Tell you what I'll do," she said graciously to the crestfallen pair, "I'll think you out some new sins; nice sins which you have never used before."

This time there was no mistaking the effects of her arbitration. Here indeed was practical interference! Were not the godless English girls the best and most suave liars in the Convent? Smiles and exclamations broke out, and the three of them sat down on the last stair but one, more comfortably to resolve the problem.

"Now what have you done really naughty this week, Marguerite?" began Joyce.

"Nothing," said Marguerite, seriously considering the question. "Nothing at all. I've been a good girl this week. I offered it up to Saint Catherine for my sister who's got the fever, comme j'ai promis à maman. . . ."

"But you must have done something wrong sometime," exposulated Joyce.

"But no. How could I?" asked Marguerite. "I offered the whole week to Saint Catherine. I made 15 hours of silence, 22 acts of charity, 20 acts of mortification, and 5 hours of prayer. Can't remember any more, but I've got it in my desk."

"But surely you made a slip somewhere? How about your sums, did you copy from Madeleine again?"

Marguerite shook her head. She remembered nothing.

"But I know something she did!" put in Jeanne triumphantly.

"You don't."

"I do. You told me yourself on Wednesday night."

Marguerite hung her head; even her ears crimsoned. She whispered something in Joyce's ear, and gabbled: "It wasn't my fault, really and truly it wasn't my fault. I couldn't help it. I put up my hand four times and Sœur Mannes took no notice, even when I went up and asked her she wouldn't let me go. So I couldn't help it. . . ."

"Even if you could, you couldn't confess it," said Joyce decidedly. Belgian girls never seemed to realise what was proper and what was not. "Anyway it's not a sin. One can't help things like that when one's little, but you might remember you're getting a big girl now, Marguerite; you're nearly eight. What about you, Jeanne, this week?"

For Jeanne, too, it had been a flawless week.

"Can't think of anything," she sighed, "don't think I could've done anything this week. Haven't quarrelled even, 'cept this morning with Marguerite, haven't told any lies even . . . haven't done anything . . ." she ended lamely, aware that she was not being believed.

Joyce sat silent a while considering her verdict. She assumed a dictatorial and grown-up manner as she turned to Jeanne to deliver it. "You shall say," she declared, "that you hit a little girl two years younger than yourself. That's a new sin, and it's quite a bad one too. And it's true. You can add that you're far too proud and that you need more humility. That do?"

Jeanne paused to consider whether this did not sound too sinful. Stealing apples, even imaginary apples, was so much milder than hitting a companion. Yet it was nobler to shoulder the heavier and truer sin, even if it meant a longer penance. She nodded, but showed no enthusiasm.

"And you, Marguerite, you can say that you can't overcome your greed, and that you asked for three helpings of potatoes at supper, pretending you hadn't had any yet. How d'you like that?"

Marguerite agreed eagerly; she liked her new sin. Any sin was better than having to steal a silly pocket handkerchief just because you happened to be two years short. Also it was almost true. She had tried to obtain a second helping of jam on Sunday by pretending that her saucerful had been stolen; she had failed, and now she remembered the incident. (But Saint Catherine could not reproach her with that as the week began at Mass on Monday morning, and Sunday was well outside her province.) Gratefully she threw her arms round Joyce's neck and hugged her.

Just then the tea-bell clanged, and the two little girls jumped up and raced each other down the corridor, Marguerite's long, fair plaits leaping behind her.

Joyce hurried towards the refectory through the *grande salle,* hoping to find someone who knew more about the wives of Henry VIII than she did. After Chapel it would be too late.

A nd I wore a white frock all embroidered, and a pink satin sash, and a white embroidered hat to match with a big pink bow on it, and white boots and stockings, and long white gloves, and so did the others, and we all carried mother-of-pearl prayer-books," declared Marie Lutt, describing to a small audience, which included Sœur Mannes, the joys of her sister's wedding in Brussels, at which she had been bridesmaid.

"And then we all went in the carriages home, me on mother's knee as we were a place short, and there was the great white cake like a church with angels all over it and silver flowers, and much, much too grand to cut, as grandmother said. And we could all eat anything we liked, pain d'épis, des glacés aux caramelles, un enorme gâteau de noces, et une grande pièce faite au nougat brun, *et un enorme gâteau au moka,* and when they were all busy singing and playing games, I went round with Etienne and we counted the dishes, and *there were thirty-two different things to eat on the table.*"

Unable to contain her envy Hazel hazarded: "And did you try them *all,* Marie?"

Marie made round eyes; the memory was painfully sweet. "I ate some of them *twice,*" she breathed.

Hazel writhed, tormented like a wretch in Purgatory who may imagine Heaven but never glimpse it. "O, Marie," she cried, "O, Marie, I wish I'd been there, too! O, I wish I could be a bridesmaid! O, I wish I could be married now, and eat whatever I liked for ever and ever! O, wouldn't that be loverly!"

Marie from her unique experience of the gay world was about to reprove such raptures with disdain, when Sœur Mannes ran forward scattering the little group, her face grey with fury. With a shrill high shriek such as a dog gives out when trodden on, she seized Hazel violently by the shoulders and struck her twice across the face.

"How *dare* you? How *dare* you?" she fumed, bringing out her words with difficulty, while Hazel covered her crimson cheeks with her arms, and the other girls stood dumb with surprise. "How *dare* you corrupt these girls, your own companions, with your vile thoughts? Wishing to be a bridesmaid, wishing to be married, wishing to be led to the altar, wishing for all the greed and worldliness which Jesus died to save you from. Talking about marriage in God's very house: bringing sin to His very doorstep. Placing lascivious thoughts into the minds of His lambs. Go into that corner and stay there for the rest of the hour, and ask the good God to forgive you and cleanse your mind of evil. Meditate on Saint Agnes who went to the place of execution, Saint Ambrose tells us, more cheerfully than others go to their wedding. Whoever speaks to that girl during this recreation," said Sœur Mannes loudly, as Hazel walked towards a pillar, sniffing audibly, "will conjugate the verb *obey* five times, and bring it to me before going to bed to-night."

H ard tears of rage shone in Joyce's eyes as she glared helplessly round the little group surrounding her in sympathy.

"Just you watch me. I'll pay her out, I'll pay her out!" she gasped, "how *dare* she treat me like that, and in front of the whole class too! And what for?" She made a gesture of appeal, amply answered by the perplexed shrugs of her supporters. "Because I said something that occurred to me about her story! Why, I thought she'd be glad I took any interest in it, she's always saying I don't listen. But I'll pay her out—you wait!"

Exactly how Joyce was going to pay Sœur Angelique out the group tactfully refrained from inquiring. The fact that she had expressed her intention to do so was enough. It was a popular and common intention.

"It's no use writing home about it 'cos all letters are read, and you'd get it back. But you can tell Sœur Veronique about her," suggested Milly Martin, studying Joyce's freckled and ugly face with interest.

"A lot of good that'd do!" snapped Mavis, who had one arm round her friend's shoulders, and wore a possessive air of mourner-in-chief. "If you go and complain to Nicky about anything she always thinks it's really you who's in the wrong. But if you go and complain about The Angel then she *knows* you're in the wrong." She pushed back a red curl from Joyce's damp forehead.

"That's true," said Violet Gray, "there's nothing much to be got out of Nicky unless you complain about Immy, or someone else she doesn't like. Remember when The Angel smacked my face once during Histoire Sainte? Well, all Nicky said when I complained to her was," here Violet pursed her lips and assumed a thin drawl which was meant to give the impression of being high up and far away, " 'Sœur Angelique may have been a little hasty on this occasion, which may also have been one of extreme provocation for her, but you must remember that discipline must be imposed or the classes would immediately get out of control.' " Violet stopped mincing. "Think of calling The Angel's temper hasty! And discipline! My hat!"

"Just you wait. I'll pay her out," repeated Joyce, blowing her nose with a loud finality suggesting the prophetic trumpeting of her revenge. "I'll teach her to make a fool of me in front of the whole class. I'll teach her to pull my ears in front of the others, and all for nothing too. I'll show her whose ears she can pull. You wait. I'll think of something that'll make her look pretty small, if I have to get sent home for it."

They saw Sœur Damiana, who took the tea-time recreation, approaching to warn them about being a group; so the six girls linked arms and marched brisky towards her. Whereupon Sœur Damiana, seeing the charge though pretending not to notice it, turned aside and rapped two small children on the shoulder, asking them brusquely what they meant by walking round in twos, and scattering them in search of another sharer of their secrets.

Joyce had been perfectly sincere in her interruption during Histoire Sainte. She had merely voiced an idea which had come to her mind quite suddenly and which she felt would be welcomed as a solution to the mystery. However often she recalled the scene that had followed she could not in her heart discover where she had offended, or how she had deserved The Angel's humiliation of her.

The examples of First Miracles had been extraordinarily interesting, and Joyce had listened enthralled, for she loved a good story. But the evidence in Saint Ignatius de Loyola's case *had* seemed stretched a trifle thin, and always would seem a trifle thin no matter how many times her ears were pulled.

"Saint Ignatius de Loyola's first miracle," Sœur Angelique had said, "was as follows: One day on hearing that a poor man called Lasano had hanged himself on the beam in his chamber, he ran to him and cut him down and remained praying by his body for a long time until the man came to himself, though he had before seemed perfectly dead to the bystanders. Lasano made his confession and received the sacraments, and soon after expired. And all the people went away marvelling at a man who had seemed perfectly dead returning to receive the sacraments and repent through the prayers of the saint."

"But," Joyce had hazarded, feeling that an explanation of the phenomenon was desired, and contracting her eyebrows in her seriousness, "but perhaps the spectators were wrong, and perhaps he wasn't perfectly dead after all. . . . You know," she explained gravely, "people who hang themselves don't *always* die."

There was a moment's surprised silence, broken by a few titters, before Sœur Angelique reached Joyce's desk, took her savagely by the ear, jerked her off her seat, and led her, crimson with surprise and shame, into the middle of the room.

Here, following a tirade from which she salvaged only the stray "We'll see who can joke on sacred subjects to amuse her friends," Joyce stood with her hands above her head for the remainder of the lesson meditating revenge, from methods of pushing Sœur Angelique down the stairs, to hiding her spectacles at the bottom of the box in which the chalks were kept.

Throughout the following week Joyce was unusually polite to Sœur Angelique. Her conduct was irreproachable. During the following Histoire Sainte her concentration was exemplary and she twice answered questions, once on Saint Catherine of Siena's age on taking the veil and again on why Saint Peter desired to be crucified head downwards, which apparently had evaded the rest of the class.

It was, therefore, especially noticeable that from the following Histoire Sainte she was missing. The more so as M. le Curé was present, as was his custom, it being the first Sunday of the month.

A more receptive mind would perhaps have noticed the subdued excitement apparent among certain of her friends, noticeably in the movements of Milly Martin, who had already chewed a large slice from her india-rubber although the lesson was but fifteen minutes old. Certainly Sœur Angelique noticed her absence, for she turned to Mavis and asked: "Where is Joyce Carr?" Mavis, surprisingly red in the face, replied: "I don't know, Sœur Angelique. She must be coming. I saw her on the stairs." Half an hour later The Angel repeated her question, and Mavis, more red in the face than ever, replied: "I don't know, Sœur Angelique. She must be coming. I saw her on the stairs."

And exactly ten minutes before the lesson ended Joyce entered the classroom with a gentle, wide-eyed look of innocence that checked Sœur Angelique's frown as she said: "Who has given you permission to absent yourself during an entire hour, we would like to know?"

Joyce, with a little curtsey to Monsieur le Curé, gazed appealingly into The Angel's face and said sweetly and clearly: "I couldn't get here sooner. I was saying my prayers."

"Saying your prayers?" echoed Monsieur le Curé, amused at this novel explanation of unpunctuality.

"Mais, oui, Monsieur le Curé," replied Joyce demurely, "I was saying my prayers on the stairs . . . like Saint Frances. Sœur Angelique was telling us about her last week. She was so good that as a novice she said a Hail Mary on every step whenever she went upstairs. I . . . I remembered that . . . and I . . . I, too, said a Hail Mary on every step as a punishment for being naughty in Histoire Sainte two weeks ago. . . ."

The child's face was so serious, and it was so obviously a case of well-meant but misplaced zeal, that Monsieur le Curé forebore to smile. Instead he patted Joyce on the head and said in his kind voice: "Sit down, sit down, my child. But remember in future that what is becoming in a Saint is not always becoming in a little girl. Please overlook her lateness, ma Sœur," his jolly face beamed on Sœur Angelique and her class, "the little one meant well, and, enfin, she will not do it again."

The nun smiled back at Monsieur le Curé without opening her lips. Indeed, her face was a study of baffled rage. When Joyce took her seat at Monsieur le Curé's request, and continued staring up at her in mock-innocence, her face flushed a hot scarlet; it was obvious that she was fully aware of the fact and that the knowledge only heightened her discomfiture and her colour. Her face seemed to exude a poison of fury, like a snake surprised. Her hands were clenched on the desk, and for a moment the look in her eyes was so malignant, that Joyce had a moment's doubt as to the wisdom of her prank, and thanked her stars that Monsieur le Curé had been there to condone it.

Beneath these misgivings ran an undercurrent of contemptuous amazement that Monsieur le Curé actually believed in her escapade and could not see what was obvious to the entire class: its effect on Sœur Angelique. But she did wish that Violet and Mavis would stop joking and whispering together in the back row, prolonging the agony by their silly sniggers.

That she should apologise occurred to her, but was dismissed at once. "She'd think I funked it," thought Joyce wisely. "She'd think I was frightened of her, and then in future she'd always pick on me. No fear!"

The sun was at its spinning, and its web hung heavily over the leaves of the chestnut trees and the vast green sheet of meadow near the orchard which marked the southern boundary of the Grand Boulevard.

The feel and the smell of heat were everywhere. Even the lake looked hot in its metallic radiance, and could be seen like a polished pebble glittering through the far end of the long avenue skirting the Quartier des Dames. Only the clump of old fir trees near the hockey field remained darkly untouched by this all-golden activity, as though an enmity existed between the two which no temporary compromise of a summer's day, however lovely, could adjust.

It was a Sunday afternoon in early July; and it was three o'clock, as the bell in the brown Chapel-belfry was remembering with a strident tongue. Remained two full hours to be lazed away before the tea-bell sounded. Lazed away indeed; for who could find energy for games in such heat? The alternative lay in the reading-room, where one must sit silently over one's book under the unrelenting vigilance of Sœur Mannes. No; better to lie out on the grass and loosen the neck of one's high black frock and knot a handkerchief into a cap to protect one's head from the sun; and whoever chose might take the floor with a story, while one improvised daisy chains (which drooped before they were finished) or lay with closed eyes and forgot to listen.

The avenue of chestnuts which strode straight through the Grand Boulevard, making of one side the enormous meadow primly cut into gravel paths, tree-groups, and many bushes, and of the other the hockey field and tennis courts, ended on an eminence, as though to enable it to take a long proud look at itself. Anyone standing on this eminence at this hour could have judged the listlessness of the afternoon's mood by the small black groups of girls stretched full-length about the grass, or moving slowly over the gravel walks like enormous and lethargic black beetles; and by the absence of all the shrill discordant clatter escaping from an army of girls freed for the three glorious hours of the Sunday afternoon recreation.

Only Armande Delacroix welcomed this unusual inactivity which the heat produced. It meant that while everyone was too indifferent to undertake the exhausting task of minding other people's business, her actions could pass unnoticed, and her scheme, who knows? be carried out.

Certainly on any other day her movements would have caused considerable comment and interference. For Armande was hanging about the row of outdoor lavatories in the *grande cour,* opening each door wide and standing at the entrance of each for a few seconds at a time. She was doing this all alone, and as soon as anyone approached she took refuge in one of the lavatories and shut the door until they left. This had been going on now for an hour and ten minutes.

Armande welcomed the thick heavy heat of the drowsy afternoon. Heat was bad for drains, how often had she heard that! It made them smell, nastily. And bad drains were bad for health. Were not diphtheria and typhus and many other dangerous diseases due primarily to bad drains? And any disease would do so long as it got her sent away; and this was about the only way she knew of getting ill other than falling down and breaking a leg, which was not infectious and was therefore useless for her purpose. Concentrating on her misery and praying to be smitten with any illness which bad drains bring in their wake, and smitten as quickly as possible, please, Armande went conscientiously sniffing up and down the unsavoury row of doors.

She had been crying a great deal all the morning, but was not crying now, though her eye-rims were red and swollen. Walking up and down outside the line of cubicles she was taking deep breaths of bad drains with a malicious and desperate zest which left no concentration over for tears. She wanted to be ill; dangerously ill. She wanted something frightful to happen to her, something which would compel them to send her away; something which would make it impossible for her to remain any longer. But above all she wanted to die.

She wanted to die because she had never known such misery, and saw no relief unless they brought back Angeline. For if Angeline and she were not to meet again, what was there left in life?

They had been parted almost without warning, and so there had been no long farewells. Only a hurried vow never to forget each other and to meet again very soon, though how they forgot to say.

The day before yesterday at ten o'clock in the morning Sœur Marie-Joseph had come into the geography class and beckoned to Angeline, and taken her away. Her mother had come to fetch her. She was in deep mourning. Apparently Angeline was needed at home now, and besides she was nearly sixteen and quite a big girl and hardly needed more schooling, her mother said. And yesterday morning at five o'clock, while Armande lay staring at the ceiling trying not to make a noise with her sobbing, Angeline had been packed into the Convent omnibus with her mother, and driven to the station, never again to return.

Everyone pitied her now, that she knew, and knew that though she hated it, it was well-meant. Had they not been known for their rare and cloudless friendship? For three years now there had been in life only each other; the familiar inevitable pair, Angeline with her brush of small fair curls and Armande with her warm, dark hair in two plaits caught up with ribbons in the nape of the neck. Always happy, always together.

With a look of desperate and heavy passion in her large blue eyes, Armande traced and retraced her steps, thinking of her friend. They had spent their last evening together in tears in a corner of the *grande cour,* as far away from the noisy rest as they could be. Angeline would begin to speak and Armande would burst out crying, and then, consoling her, Angeline would start crying herself and in her turn was comforted, and so it went on as the hour shrank with a vicious haste.

Armande had kept on insisting that she, who after all was left behind, was the more miserable of the two. "Tu m'oublieras! Oui, oui, je sais bien, tu m'oublieras!" she kept crying. And Angeline had repeated passionately in her gentle broken voice: "Je ne t'oublierai jamais, jamais. Je n'aimerai jamais personne que toi. . . ." She could still feel the soft warmth of Angeline's full lips as their mouths clung together in a last kiss, and the pressure of Angeline's fingers over her own. She would always feel the soft warmth of Angeline's lips, and the pressure of Angeline's hand on hers.

Armande stopped for a second time that afternoon, lifted up her skirt, and pulled a letter from her little pocket tied round her waist with tapes. When she had opened her desk yesterday morning it lay on top of her books. Angeline must have run to the classroom at the last minute and placed it there to comfort her when she was gone.

It was a long letter of six full copy-book pages written with a violet pencil, with many watery smudges as the ending approached. Each time Armande read it she added new smudges to those of Angeline and through her tears the writing precipitated itself lengthwise across the page, crumpled into a heap, dissolved into starry and indecipherable points.

It was doing so now; but she had her letter well by heart and fought her way through the tearful fantastic obstacles, feeling pleasure at the unhappiness the familiar words caused her. Especially towards the end.

"It is not possible, dear, dear Armande, that we who love each other so deeply should not meet again, of that I am certain. When you are crying I shall be crying too. Do not forget me, for I shall love you always."

"And now I'm all alone," cried Armande in an agony of sudden tears, leaning her head against one of the doors, and groping blindly for a pocket handkerchief.

It was here that Sœur Imelda found her ten minutes later, still leaning against the door and talking aloud between her sobs.

The nun guessed the reason for the outburst and put her arm round Armande's shoulders to lead her away.

"Come, come, Armande," she urged. "A big girl like you must not give way like this; you set a bad example to the smaller children, besides aggravating your own unhappiness in this silly fashion."

But Armande had no use for the cold comfort of reason. She moved her shoulders angrily to try and shake off Sœur Imelda's hand. "A lot I care what example I make!" she cried passionately, "I shan't be an example much longer, I'm going to be ill, terribly ill, and then I shan't be here to *be* an example. O, I hope I die!" she sobbed, her face distorted with misery.

This time she found herself sobbing against Sœur Imelda's stiff guimpe while the nun stroked her hair, dispensing a half-pitying, half-impatient comfort. After the first fury had abated she noticed that Sœur Imelda's guimpe was no longer stiff-starched like a plate, but more like a sheet of sodden and sticky paper; yet rather than remove her face and confess to the damage she had done, she continued a monotonous half-sob and kept her cheek glued to the wet paper, until a voice said gaily: "Must I risk my death of cold by getting wet through, Armande, or would a handkerchief do as well?"

No, it was too bad. Sœur Imelda must always have her little joke, the whole school knew that, but to laugh at such a moment, Armande thought, was too callous, too cruel. She jerked her head away as though a needle had been stuck in her cheek. She would have liked to refuse the handkerchief, only it was such a vast and inviting one. She took it sullenly and began a furious drying up which almost rubbed the skin from her face.

When she had partially regained her self-control she looked up at

Sœur Imelda, and by way of justification gulped angrily, "I know I look silly to you. You don't know what it's like to lose Angeline. I don't suppose you ever loved anyone as we loved each other. . . ."

"Not an earthly love, certainly," agreed Sœur Imelda, not without sympathy.

Armande stifled her desire to cry "Then you don't *know*." She said instead: "I'll never love anyone but Angeline, never, never. You don't know how that feels . . . I'll never have another friend again as long as I live. If I live to be a hundred I'll never want anyone but Angeline . . . and I don't want to stay here now that she's gone. . . . You don't know how I feel . . . nobody knows . . . I'm going to be ill. . . . Terribly ill. . . ." Alas, Sœur Imelda could not guard against a faint curling of the lips. "I am. I *am*." Armande reddened angrily: "I'm going to get typhus or something horrible . . . from smelling bad drains . . . O, I hope I die . . . I hope I die! . . ." She was crying again into the vast and inviting handkerchief.

Sœur Imelda put her hand on Armande's shoulder and led her gently but firmly to a bench near the swings. "Listen, Armande," she said, "have you thought how very wicked it is to talk of getting ill? Have you thought what *le bon Dieu* will say when he hears you? Have you thought about your parents who love you so dearly?" She waited a moment to let that take its full effect. "I know it is hard to be separated from Angeline, but surely you cannot love your friend better than you love your mother and father?"

Armande had never thought of that. Besides, it seemed hardly a fair comparison. Of course, she loved her parents better than anyone in the world, she supposed. Yet for the first time it occurred to her, not without a shock, that she had always been so glad the holidays were over so that she could come back to school and Angeline. She was almost appalled at her own wickedness as she remembered that she had never felt anything like this on saying good-bye to her parents. Must be because she knew she'd see them again, she decided half-heartedly. Sœur Imelda was obviously waiting for an answer, so she shook her head obediently.

"Then, my dear child, do not you see how transitory all this sorrow is?" (No, no! cried Armande in her heart, she doesn't know. . . . She never loved anyone like this. . . .) "Love like this you owe your parents, your sisters, and your brothers. But even before them, Armande, you owe this love to God. He alone can comfort you. You need not tell Him why you cry, because He knows. But you can pray for your sorrow to pass. And it will pass. Yes, yes, it will pass." Sœur Imelda took Armande's hand in hers and stroked it. The girl was quieter now, but she made no comment. "Armande, why not give this week to Our Lady of Sorrows?" Sœur Imelda pleaded. "Have you thought how small your sorrow may be compared with Hers? Every morning when you rise dedicate the day to Her, and you will see how soon your sorrow will grow less."

Armande said slowly: "I'll try . . . I will try . . . I'll give the week to Our Lady of Sorrows . . . but I shan't ever love anyone else. I *couldn't*, not if I lived for ever and ever. . . ."

Sœur Imelda stood up. She was pleased that she had made head-way with this obstinate girl, who now showed signs of being more reasonable.

"Come to the refectory and help me count the tablecloths," she said (scattering to the winds all Mona's secret hopes during the past week). She saw Armande's reluctance; she must be patient with her. "Come," she said gently, "I'm going to keep my eye on you, Armande, for the rest of the afternoon."

Silently Armande followed Sœur Imelda through the maze of stairs and corridors.

She would give the week to Our Lady of Sorrows, and She would help her. But deep in her heart Armande listened to the voice which was telling her, so clearly it came that it might have been a warning from God Himself, that this had been love, and that never again in quite this splendour and strength would it be repeated.

O ne day Sœur Marie-Joseph appeared in the sewing class leading by the hand a little girl in a blue check pinafore buttoned down the back. There followed a whispered consultation between Sœur Marie-Joseph and Sœur Damiana, after which the little girl was placed on a chair near Sœur Damiana's desk and given a large picture-book to inspect at leisure.

Before leaving the room Sœur Marie-Joseph patted her on the head and placed some sugared almonds in the little pocket of her blue check pinafore. The little girl was apparently too shy to look up and say 'Thank you'; instead she began furiously turning the pages of her book to show, possibly, that she was paying it the grateful attention it deserved.

"C'est elle!" hissed Jeanne Martelle dramatically to all near enough to hear. The news spread rapidly, and there was much covert inspection of the newcomer.

She was about eight years old. Two very small plaits of brown hair reached almost to her shoulders. Now and again she raised her eyes from her book without raising her head and peeped at the class out of enormous brown eyes which seemed to usurp all the available space in her face, and gave her the appearance of a very timid and melancholy dormouse.

Soon she appeared at all the lessons of the smaller children, at first on a chair near the nun's desk, turning the pages of picture books, until finally she was promoted to a desk of her own where she sat with her hands folded on the lid, focussing her soft dark eyes on the blackboard or on the nun in charge of the class.

She arrived at ten o'clock every morning and left at five in the evening; and already the entire school was aware that this was the Jeannette Dubois, daughter of Madame Rose Dubois who kept the little sweet and pencil shop at the turn of the road towards La Monnelle. They said she was attending the lessons through the charity of Sœur Marie-Joseph who had seen Jeannette in the street one day and had learnt her story from Monsieur le Curé.

Even the smallest child had heard that Jeannette had no father. The children noticed that while no mother and no father made you an orphan and an object of pity, no father made you nothing and yet an object of shame; and they wondered why. They had strict instructions to be kind to Jeannette and to play with her, but never to mention her home or ask her curious questions.

It was difficult to follow the first part of the instructions however conscientiously one strove to be kind to Jeannette and to play with her, because Jeannette never seemed to know how to play, except by herself. In all the games she hung back and spoilt them by her shyness, so that it became kinder to let her sit by herself on a bench as she preferred, gazing at all that went on in the playground as though it were a scene from another world.

But one day Jeanne Martelle having struggled with her curiosity long and ineffectively, sat down beside her and said: "Is it true you haven't got a father like other girls?"

Jeannette fixed her with her enormous brown eyes and answered immediately, as though repeating a phrase she had learnt for such occasions: "Je suis comme le p'tit Jésus, je n'ai pas de père. Maman dit que le bon Dieu est mon papa, et que le p'tit Jésus et le p'tit Saint Jean sont mes deux frères. Et que quand je vais au ciel je les verrai."

Jeanne Martelle had been deeply shocked by this blasphemy and had felt it her duty to relate the entire conversation to Sœur Imelda. Much to Jeanne's surprise and disappointment Sœur Imelda said nothing at the time.

But the following day during the needlework hour Sœur Imelda entered the class and went across to where Jeannette sat resolving the problem of her first knitting needles. She whispered something in Jeannette's ear and placed on her desk a large packet of cream-chocolate.

Jeannette put out a small finger and traced the gold lettering on the shining packet. She seemed dazed by the munificence and unexpectedness of the gift. She dared not look up while she knew that Sœur Imelda still stood over her. But as soon as Sœur Imelda moved away she turned her small flushed face, and her large eyes followed her every movement till she left the room. Only then did she enter into possession of her gift, and taking the packet reverently in both hands, placed it in her desk, hiding it well away under all her lesson books.

J oyce came out of Sœur Veronique's room closely followed by Sœur Angelique. She held her head too high, and looked as though she was impersonating Marie Antoinette on her way to execution; but Sœur Angelique looked satisfied with herself and her prisoner. Mavis, who had flattened herself against a column for the last half-hour waiting for her friend to reappear, realised her effort had been in vain, and that she would have to wait until the *promenade* to hear the result of the momentous interview with Sœur Veronique.

As she stood in the street struggling with her glove-buttons while the crocodile was performing the neat convolutions essential to its formation, Monica Watson tapped her on the shoulder.

"I've got to walk with you, Mavis," she announced.

Mavis shot up like a piece of released elastic. She stared at Monica as though she had never beheld so loathly an object. "Who says so?" she demanded, in her haughtiest I'm-the-prettiest-girl-in-the-school manner.

"Sœur Osana," shrugged Monica. "She says Joyce is going to walk with her at the back to-day."

"Blast!" said the furious Mavis. "That's The Angel. . . ."

"You needn't think it's any fun for me, you know," sighed Monica plaintively. "I don't want to walk with you. I've got friends of my own, thanks."

"Which way are we going?" said Mavis, who ignored all unfriendly remarks.

"To Le Calvaire, Sœur Mannes said."

Mavis found comfort in this. It would take a quicker eye than Sœur Osana possessed to keep an eye on them at Le Calvaire.

The afternoon was hot, and the crocodile shuffled along the road at a leisurely pace. It filed up the narrow village street, where covetous eyes were cast at the caramels and sticks of licorice in the post-office window; and past M. le Curé's square red house with its carefully arranged flower-beds and tall iron gateway. Here it took the first turning on the left and, leaving the narrow lane, came out on the wide dusty high-road, which the eye could follow far into the distance. On either side the corn and turnip fields swept flatly on, their monotony enhanced by the clumps of trees at regular intervals. Now and again a farm was passed with its heavy odour of pigs and manure, and its inviting pump to which the more audacious ran and held up their mouths to catch the drips until a nun caught sight of them and shooed them off, while luckier ones dipped their handkerchiefs in the rain-barrels and cooled their faces.

What an interminable walk for a summer's day! There was Sœur Osana sending a girl on ahead to suggest to Sœur Mannes that perhaps they ought to stop at the *chapelle* for a prayer, as they passed it. Only because she felt that such mortification of the flesh could be overdone when one was approaching the late fifties. But Sœur Mannes, too thin and too wiry, was afraid there was not sufficient time, and suggested that Sœur Osana might more carefully superintend her girls at the back of the crocodile as their pace was unpardonably slow.

At last the familiar hillock with its frilly rows of pines was seen, and then attained, and then entered. Slowly the crocodile advanced, up, up, up, the long pine-bordered avenue which cut straight through the centre of the mount; and behold at its summit, silhouetted against the deep blue sky, the three enormous crosses bearing their gaunt and dramatic burdens.

That moment always held its thrill, even though in some strange way the sight was an unfriendly one. From far the figures at the foot of the centre Cross might have been those of neighbouring peasants resting after their pious pilgrimage, but as one drew near they assumed enormous proportions, and could be recognised as the two mourners: the Magdalen with her arms embracing the foot of the Cross, and the Virgin Mary, her painted brown eyes staring in abject misery at the ground.

Once both the women's dresses had been a violent blue and white, but the blue had faded and the white had grown grey through the five-year vigil which they had always to endure before another coat of paint was forthcoming. The right hand Thief, who, like his fellow ruffian, had his great plaster arms tied with ropes, had had the colour of his face so worn away through his constant gazing at the sky that it was impossible to guess what colour it once had been, as even his beard was washed white by the rain and bleached a dirty yellow by the sun.

Here Mavis received always the impression, which never diminished with familiarity, that had she possessed a ladder sufficiently long she could have leant it against the sky and climbed straight into Heaven, which seemed always to rest on the tops of the trees in which the space had been cut for this strange and awesome shrine.

A hundred yards from the top of Le Calvaire a signal was always given, after which the neat reptilian formation dissolved into a disorderly straggling troupe which reached the summit as best it could.

As Mavis had calculated, Sœur Osana, who was fat for such a climb even in the winter's cold, was now more concerned with her own exertions than with the guardianship of the nimble Joyce who sprang always maliciously ahead of her. At the summit she was joined by Sœur Mannes, who listened patiently to her sing-song irritation. After all, said Sœur Mannes, preparing to say her rosary, orders were orders, and neither of them had any say in the matter of where the children were taken, winter or summer. True Obedience was the child of true Humility.

Joyce joined Mavis deep in the thicket of leggy pines, well screened from the sight of the rest. This was forbidden, but they felt reckless and angry.

"What did she say?" burst from Mavis.

"No Tourelles."

"For whom?"

"For me, of course."

"The *beast* . . . O, the beast! . . ." breathed Mavis.

Joyce's lips were trembling. She was trying to be brave, and it was difficult. Tourelles, the culmination of the year, to which one counted the days even before June was out! And this was her last year.

"I knew I was in for it as soon as I got into the room. . . . Sœur Veronique said: 'I understand it was you who led the girls out of Chapel on Sunday night when M. le Curé held up the reliquary? What have you to say for yourself?' You know how small Nicky can make you feel!" Joyce almost gulped her words down. "But I didn't say a word. Wouldn't have been any use anyway, I knew The Angel had said it all first. Sœur Veronique asked her: 'She was the first to leave?' And Angel went into a long rigmarole. She said I'd corrupted the other girls . . . though she couldn't be sure you hadn't had a finger in it as well. . . . 'How many left the Chapel?' put in Nicky. . . . 'Eight in all,' said The Angel, but that I left first and that it was obviously at my signal that the others rose and followed me. . . . Then Sœur Veronique asked me if it was true that I had told Tony Grüdel that in a book I saw during the holidays I'd read that there were hundreds of bits of the real Cross in all the convents and churches and I'd added 'enough to make a forest,' and had I also said, Nicky went on, that wild horses wouldn't drag me to kiss the bit of glass containing one of these hundred pieces of the real Cross, which M. le Curé held up on First Sundays. . . . I said, 'Yes, but not quite like that, Sœur Veronique . . .' and The Angel chuckled, 'O, I'll bet she said worse than that. . . .' "

"The *beast*," put in Mavis.

"Then Nicky took on that angel voice, when you know you're going to get it thick. She said: 'But you know you have never been told to assist at any of the ceremonies you don't wish to attend, except, of course, to attend Chapel, which is compulsory, have you?' . . . I said no. . . . 'And that you are not expected unless you particularly wish to do so to follow the example of the Catholic girls at their prayers?' . . . I said no. . . . 'You know that if you had come to me or to Sœur Angelique, or to any nun in charge and said you intended to leave before the end of Benediction on certain Sundays when M. le Curé holds the reliquary to be kissed, you would have been granted permission gladly to do as you pleased?' . . . I said yes. . . . 'And knowing that you have entire freedom in these matters you amused yourself stirring up rebellion among your Protestant friends and walking out of Chapel ostentatiously in front of the whole school?' . . . so I said yes again. . . . And then The Angel began. . . . Jove, you should have seen the rage she worked up! . . . She told Nicky that I came to Histoire Sainte to mock at her and make the class laugh . . . she told her about Saint Ignatius and the prayers on the stairs . . . and she put it on so thick I didn't recognise myself. . . . Of course Nicky knew it all before, but she pretended to be shocked and upset and . . . oh well . . . no Tourelles . . . that's all."

"Can't you go to Nicky and say you're sorry or something?" suggested Mavis desperately.

"What's the use?" said the dejected Joyce, "she'd forgive me, O so nicely! . . . but no Tourelles for me . . . I've tried it before. But I didn't cry," she remembered, "I never said anything at all . . . I didn't let them see . . . I'd rather've died. . . ."

In the distance they heard the clapping of hands. Sœur Mannes was marshalling her crocodile. They ran quickly through the trees and fortunately arrived on the outside of the mass of girls before any order was apparent.

Mavis kept her arm round Joyce's neck. They both felt utterly miserable.

"Listen, Joyce, I'll stay with you," said Mavis. "I've been to Tourelles four times now . . . I don't care a hang . . . it's the last time anyway. . . . We'll spend the day in the orchard and get out into the village through the hedge . . . you know how. . . ."

But Joyce shook her head. Such self-sacrifice would make her even more unhappy. For the first time she showed signs of tears. "O, Mavis, you mustn't *think* of such a terrible thing," she cried, "I couldn't bear that . . . I couldn't. . . . After all, it is my punishment. . . . I'd never forgive myself if you stayed with me . . . and besides, The Angel'd be so pleased . . . she doesn't like you much either, you know. . . ."

"Tell you what I'll do then," said Mavis, "I'll lend you *The Three Musketeers*. . . . Mm . . . I've got it . . . it's under my mattress . . . Dolly Jennings lent it to me. . . . Only don't let it get pinched. . . . You'll like it. . . . I haven't got very far. . . . Immy nearly caught me with it in geography last week. . . ."

Here Monica Watson walked up and said plaintively: "Here I am, Mavis. And you, you're wanted. . . . Sœur Osana is looking for you all over the place. . . . She's wild. . . . She's already sent off three girls to look for you and they all say they can't find you anywhere. . . ."

In the distance Mavis heard her friend's voice protesting shrilly: "But I was standing near the second Cross all the time . . . yes, all the time, ask any one you like. . . . Mais je vous le jure, Sœur Osana . . . tout le temps. . . ."

Je viendrai à Lui comme une épouse, parce que dans sa tendresse incompréhensible Il m'a choisie et m'a offert son Amour.

"Viens, dit-Il, ma colombe, ma sœur, mon épouse" . . . J'étais esclave, Il m'a libérée; j'étais infirme, Il m'a prise dans ses bras; j'étais pauvre, Il m'a ouvert son infini; j'étais aveugle, Il m'a parlé à l'oreille, si doucement, que j'ai cru mourir de bonheur. . . .

Et après cela, Il m'a dit: "Je serai ton Epoux pour l'Eternité!" L'éternité! . . . c'est-à-dire toujours, toujours, toujours, sans déclin et sans lassitude. . . . Alors je me suis levée de ma misère et j'ai tendu mes bras vers Lui.

Oh! Le voir maintenant! . . . O Jesus, ne retarde plus trop cette heure de notre Rencontre. Ne tarde plus, j'ai tant hâte. Mais en attendant:

"Jésus, que veux-Tu que je fasse?"

Méditations de Sœur Marie Saint-Anselme

L e plus beau destin," Sœur Vincent had said, "c'est le martyre." Melanie repeated the words to herself as she stood in her chemise and stockings behind the curtain of her cubicle, and, her underlip caught tightly between her teeth, pulled in by a fraction of an inch the piece of thin hairy rope which she wore round her waist on her bare skin. This done she put on her knickers and her petticoat, ran to her *lavabo* and began conscientiously applying her soapy sponge to her neck and ears.

Melanie always paid particular attention to these since finding glued firmly to her desk-lid the sheet of paper bearing in large and insolent capitals:

Melanie van den Bluk.

We don't want a girl that comes from Hulbeke,
Comes from Hulbeke, comes from Hulbeke,
She might wash her face, but she won't wash her neck,
So we don't want a girl that comes from Hulbeke.

Yes, those beastly English girls had been responsible for that; they could wash their necks but they couldn't say their prayers! And though

Melanie was not inwardly converted to the belief that a neck desires daily washing, she took the hint. One never knew what those nasty godless foreigners would think of next.

Yet when she came to do her hair it could be seen that she had unusual and important uses for soap and water. Carefully, a frown between her eyes, she wet her palms in the basin and rubbed the soap into them till a profuse watery glue was produced; then with both palms stiffened she drew them tightly over her hair on either side of her face. Soon it became stiff and sticky, and her beautiful curly hair, of a rich chestnut colour, hung in an unbecoming lankness, which ugly effect seemed to afford her complete satisfaction. Now she tugged her hair tightly back from her face and wove it into two thick plaits, so tightly that her eyebrows and forehead were stretched painfully back.

Nothing now remained of the froth of chestnut curls which gave her usual face its pleasing cherub-look. Yet there was a suggestion of a smile round her mouth as she surveyed this parody of herself before jamming her black straw hat on the top of the drowned-rat effect, viciously releasing the elastic so that it gave her chin a sharp sting.

And she was still smiling as she marched up the aisle to the brave Sunday morning sound of the organ which always made High Mass seem like the prelude to a holiday. Melanie was anxious to start her prayers, but she could not resist looking towards her friend Berthe Jadot. Berthe, waiting for the look, had her eyes fixed on Melanie.

They smiled. Not at each other, as the cynical Violet Gray, amazed at their ridiculous appearance and assuming it to be some practical joke, thought. Violet saw a grin. Actually it was a slow feline smile which seemed to hint at some deep and secret pleasure shared and remembered. After which both Melanie and Berthe gave themselves up to their devotions; so completely in Melanie's case that she would have continued kneeling after the others had left had not Sœur Mannes rapped her on the shoulder.

Outside the Chapel they had to put up with a great deal of fun-poking; and they received it with the same feline smile of secret joy, so that it was taken to mean some form of practical joke which doubtless they would divulge later.

"Help! What've you done to yourself, Melanie?" cried Mavis, passing her in the *grand cour.* "You look like a drowned rat!"

Melanie was on the point of retorting "Not everyone in the school is as vain as a peacock!" when she checked herself and passed on with her secret smile. "All her hair scratched back and a grin like a Cheshire Cat" said Mavis to Joyce on the way to breakfast.

At breakfast both Melanie and Berthe refused sugar in their coffee, and Berthe, who was watching her friend from where she sat and had just taken a second *tartine,* seeing that Melanie took only one, returned the second to the dish that was being handed to her.

At *goûter* they both refused their dish of apricot jam, Berthe giving hers to Dora Jennings, who sat beside her, and whom she rather liked. But Melanie got up and walked across the refectory and gave her jam to Marion Moore, whom it was known she disliked almost to the point of hatred, since the day Marion had emptied a bag of pepper over Tony Grüdel's prayer-book. And although it was understood that there was to be no suggestion of rivalry between the two, Berthe's face was flushed as she watched Melanie resume her seat.

During the Evening Recreation they sat together on a bench at the far end of the Boulevard pondering Berthe's suggestion that they should revert to their normal appearance. Melanie held out against it obstinately. "Why *should* we?" she wailed plaintively.

"Because we're too conspicuous," Berthe explained. "Everybody laughs at us; they think it's a joke, and that only makes us look silly. . . ."

"That would not have troubled Sainte Claire . . ." murmured Melanie, as though to herself.

"It doesn't worry *me,*" said Berthe, stung by Melanie's smile. Come to think of it, virtue was making her unbearably arrogant. "I'll put up with all the sneers . . . no one was more sneered at than Jesus . . . don't I know that? . . . but it's silly to attract attention when there are so many things we can do that'll feel worse, and that they won't even guess at. . . ."

"I can stand their sneers," smiled Melanie. "Didn't Sœur Vincent last Sunday make a special point of the fact that a saint is always mocked at? *Always.* She said that when that *Anglaise* . . . cette Joyce . . . giggled when she had to read out in the life of Sainte Claire de la Croix that every morning she stood barefoot in ice-cold water while reciting the Lord's Prayer a hundred times. . . . But that couldn't hurt Sainte Claire, as Sœur Vincent said to her. . . . Berthe," said Melanie softly, dropping her voice almost to a whisper, "Sainte Claire twice received Holy Communion from Jesus Himself. . . . O, it must be glorious to be a saint . . . and deserve so much. . . ."

"That girl's friend Mavis said to me yesterday when I was telling Tony Grüdel how the replica of the Crucifix with a piece of the Crown of Thorns and even the sponge was found in Sainte Claire's heart after she was dead, 'O, but that was hundreds of years ago! There aren't any saints to-day! . . .' I thought, yes, you know a lot, you English! . . . Melanie, will it be long before we *know?* . . ."

"It may be years and years, Berthe. . . . Sometimes it's not till you're dead and someone comes to your tomb and you make a miracle that it's even known *at all.* . . ."

"Are you sure of that?" asked Berthe, who, when her friend nodded mournfully, felt a hollow space under her heart. "O, Melanie," she cried, ashamed of her fear but unable to conceal it, "can we go on for all that time . . . and then *never even know?* . . ."

"I don't know . . . I hadn't thought of that . . ." confessed Melanie, "they say that Sainte Julienne never knew, Berthe. . . . You remember? . . . and that no one knew until after her death when they found the sign of the Cross cut into her heart by Jesus Himself, and saw how her hair shirt had all grown into her flesh. . . ."

"But most of the saints *do* know they're saints," remembered Berthe with relief. "Yes they do . . . they know at once and everyone round them recognises it too. . . . What is a hair shirt, Melanie?"

"A hair shirt's a sort of shirt made of . . . of . . . made of hair," explained Melanie. "It's awf'ly rough and scratches you every time you move."

"I wish we could get one!" groaned Berthe.

"Ooo, so do I!"

"D'you remember what Sœur Vincent said of Sainte Claire, that a hair shirt wasn't enough so she wore a shirt with hog's bristles inside cut short . . . and she always slept on the ground . . . and though she was afflicted with continual pain for thirty years she was always happy, and only had a little straw to lie on now and then. . . . Melanie, could you sleep on the floor?"

"I *could,*" said Melanie stoutly, "but how can one get the chance? They'd find me out and then it would all be over. . . . I tried not sleeping all the other night and I kept awake for ever such a long time . . . I heard it strike twelve . . . but I must have fallen asleep after all. . . ."

"O, it's so difficult!" cried Berthe, "no one seemed ever to interfere with Them, or tell Them not to do things, did they?"

"Don't be silly. Of course they did!" said Melanie. "Why, even their own parents tried to stop them from being saints as soon as they knew of it . . . and look at Sainte Geneviève. . . ."

Berthe, who had recently lost her father and who adored her mother, could never work up much enthusiasm for Sainte Geneviève.

Could it have been possible for her to do anything so sinful or imaginative as actually to dislike a saint she would have realised that Sainte Geneviève, left to her judgment, would be spending her time in Purgatory to this day for allowing her mother to be struck blind that morning she refused her her permission to attend Mass.

"Have you ever noticed, Melanie, that Sainte Geneviève is the only one who ever retaliated on her parents?" she ventured.

"O, *she* didn't retaliate. . . . It was God Who struck her blind, not Sainte Geneviève . . . and besides her mother recovered her sight afterwards when she prayed over her. . . . He couldn't lose a saint just because her mother wouldn't let her go to Mass, could He? . . ."

Unconvinced, Berthe made a noise in her throat and they sat in silence for a little while.

The many sounds which reached them from where the girls were playing, which sounds seemed to rise like a thin steam from off the various groups all contributing to its volume, heightened their sense of isolation from earthly happenings. Though their bench was on the very edge of the Boulevard boundaries they could see in the distance the outline of an enormous black ring which spun round and then stopped and then started off again. Everybody seemed to have joined in the Tiens, tiens, tiens, des bonnes amies. . . . Even their self-willed remoteness could not keep them from noticing that to-night there was somehow more laughter in the game than ever before. But before anything more earthly could intrude Melanie whispered:

"Berthe, does your rope hurt you?"

They were alone, yet both felt that such things could only be becomingly discussed in whispers.

"Yes, it *does* . . . I found a blister yesterday morning when I got up, and this morning there was a little yellow patch . . . but I tightened it just the same. . . . How's yours?"

"I haven't even got a blister yet," sighed Melanie, who could not help wondering grudgingly why Berthe should have been singled out for this especial mark of favour, " and yet I've tightened it as much as I can bear every time. . . . P'raps I'll find one to-night. . . ."

"Have you tried anything else yet, Melanie?" whispered Berthe.

"Nothing 'cept keeping my face in the basin while I said a Hail Mary twice . . . and those two pebbles to kneel on in Chapel in my stockings. . . . Have you?"

"I've done that too . . ." said Berthe, "but I didn't keep the pebbles in all the time," she confessed, "they did hurt so. . . . I did try with the nail, though . . . like the Bienheureuse Christina . . . last night when the lights were out I put it on my foot and took my shoe and gave it a good bang . . . it was a good bang, Melanie . . . but somehow it didn't go right through as it should have . . . it just made a little mark on the instep and wouldn't even stand up straight. . . . And all the time I thought how Jesus must have suffered with those great big nails and the great hammers in His hands and feet . . . and I thought what an awful lot we've still got to do. . . . O, and I put a pin in my forehead too . . . but that didn't hurt as much as I thought it would. . . ."

"Sainte Catherine de Siene wore a crown of thorns at night," murmured Melanie dreamily.

Melanie the infallible! Berthe smirked.

"Only it wasn't Sainte Catherine!"

Melanie raised eyebrows.

"It *was.*"

"Wasn't. It was Sainte Marie Madeleine."

"That is not true, Berthe," said Melanie coldly, for she loved Sainte Catherine de Siene more than all the other occupants of Heaven put together.

" 'Tis true," said Berthe, and quite viciously for a would-be saint. "It was Sainte Madeleine who wore the crown of thorns . . . Sœur Vincent told us so last Sunday. Besides," added Berthe, "Sainte Catherine never did anything like that. . . ."

"O!" brought out Melanie indignantly. "O, how *can* you speak like that of One who . . . of One who . . . Why, she could do things that no one else ever dared do. . . . Didn't she drink the bowls of matter from the wounds of the sick? . . . and once . . . once she sucked an infectious cancer in a poor woman she was nursing. . . . I'd rather walk on any nails or things than do *that,* anyway. . . ."

Berthe ignored the challenge, but smiled and edged nearer to her friend. She wished to offend no one, least of all Sainte Catherine de Siene, whose power Up There . . . who knew? Besides, except for the grudge she bore Sainte Geneviève, she never admitted to a preference in the Saints, who were all, of this she was convinced, blessed equally by God. So she murmured a Yes, that is true, and allowed Melanie the victory.

But there had been something on her mind since Friday last when Melanie and she had first decided to dedicate themselves to saintdom. Perhaps Melanie would be shocked and even angry with her, but it was better to face it, thought Berthe. Jesus did not always reply to prayers at once, and one could be left a long time perplexed wondering what would please Him.

"Still," she hesitated, "Melanie, what's going to happen when we leave?"

"How happen?" Melanie broke unwillingly from thoughts of Sainte Catherine.

"Well, we shan't ever go to dances or parties, or anything, shall we? . . . and we shan't ever wear pretty frocks, or put on coloured hair ribbons or stockings . . . or . . . or ever allow anyone to . . . to like us . . . shall we? . . ."

"I suppose we shan't . . ." said Melanie slowly. "Do you know, I have thought of that, too, Berthe . . . that would be a big sin . . . a terribly big sin. . . ."

But that was not what worried Berthe.

"But if anyone did ever . . . er . . . like us, Melanie . . . we couldn't help it . . . could we? We wouldn't have to do anything . . . anything terrible . . . would we?"

"*Terrible?*"

"Well, like Sainte Lucie . . . (anyway, thought Berthe suddenly, my eyes aren't pretty enough to make anyone like me, so I needn't cut *them* out . . . but poor Melanie's are . . .) who sent her two beautiful eyes to the young man who admired them . . . or like Sainte Alexandre, who walled herself up in a grave for ever rather than have that young nobleman in love with her. . . . Jesus doesn't want us to do anything like that these days, *does* He? . . . He'll see it isn't our fault, won't He?"

Melanie faltered: "I couldn't ever cut out my eyes, Berthe . . . I don't think I ever could. . . ." She opened wide her eyes, large yellow autumn-leaf eyes, appalled at the thought. "But I could cut off my hair . . . I wouldn't mind that at all . . . that's easy, isn't it? . . . And, of course, one has to pray against looking pretty to people. We ought to begin now and say a prayer each day. La Bienheureuse Collette was one of the most beautiful of all saints and was admired by all who saw her . . . and . . . and all the rich young men from the great families in the surrounding country came to woo her, Sœur Vincent said, but she prayed and prayed to God to change her complexion and her face became so pale and thin that nobody recognised her again. . . ."

Which brought Berthe, much comforted, back to her first argument concerning their new hair-dressing.

"We oughtn't to be so conspicuous, Melanie," she urged again. "It's not being sneered at that matters . . . only it is so silly somehow to let them try and guess our secret . . . and it doesn't really hurt much, does it? . . . 'cept at first just a little bit on the forehead. . . ."

"But why should we?" repeated Melanie plaintively, "*I* don't mind their sneers. . . . Look how they sneered at Sainte Catherine. . . ."

And then Berthe held out her arm and whispered: "Twist my wrist, Melanie."

Melanie, serious-eyed, clutched the outstretched hand and began slowly to twist it towards the right.

"Harder," urged Berthe, her lower lip between her teeth.

"Harder still," she gasped ecstatically through quivering lips; and then, "Enough . . . O *enough*, Melanie. . . ."

Ah, it was sweet to bear this for Him! So small a thing in return for His long agony, and yet even so small a thing brought one a step nearer His throne. And it did hurt most terribly, reflected Berthe, easing her released hand this way and that and wondering would she be heard, and would her wrist bear to-morrow the Blessed bruises, and be, ah joy! a little swollen?

Punctually at seven o'clock the girls were marshalled in the Chapel corridor and marched in crocodile formation to the convent door which with its forbidding iron clamps and narrow *grille* must in some previous existence have stood guard at a castle drawbridge.

Here they stood at ease a few moments waiting for Sœur Veronique, Sœur Angelique, Sœur Marie-Imelda, and Sœur Etienne to join those nuns already present. The quarter signal chimed from the belfry, and the crocodile, defrauded by fifteen minutes of its start, grew restive, despite Sœur Damiana's *chuchotement*, and the eagle eye of Sœur Mannes, who saw that already the day had begun to be a trial to her.

The outing to Tourelles was her yearly Day of Martyrdom, and this year it seemed to have begun even before the children were out of the door. "But why let them worry you?" Sœur Imelda had said at supper the previous night when she had protested weakly against having to accompany them again: "Do not be so fussy with them; it is their holiday and they are young. And besides, they are such good children. You might as well be angry because a little cat scratches you as be hard on the girls *au jour de Tourelles*." Which was neither sympathetic nor understanding of Sœur Imelda, who had always an eye to her own popularity; whilst she, Sœur Mannes, knew only her duty to God.

However, she noticed with some satisfaction that a remarkable amount of soap and brush work had been done. Indeed, only on prize-giving day could such an array of smoothly plaited heads and neatly gloved hands have been seen.

Pretty white lace collars relieved the best black Sunday frocks and peeped above the pelerines; best black velvet and satin hair ribbons were at the ends of pigtails; best black shoes and stockings; best black gloves clasping small purses; and here and there a piece of jewellery, a best bracelet; a new mother-of-pearl chaplet in the hands of the devout; or a small gold brooch placed to advantage; and the best black Sunday straw hats, stiff and shining with an extra inch on the brim and a small velvet ribbon round the crown. Even Sœur Mannes had to admit that the trim uniformed crocodile did not disgrace the Order. Every second or third girl clasped a flat black shopping-bag in which was to be brought back the painted *pain d'épis* figurines, the chocolate angels, and all the happy tinsel gifts of the Fair.

At last the head nuns arrived and the heavy door swung open to reveal the ten large coaches, each with its row of seats on either side, and its two brown horses tossing their festive manes bound with coloured silks so that each time they shook their heads they seemed to be tossing a handful of confetti over their polished necks.

That was the one touch of gaiety allowed; and at the sight of it good behaviour was thrown to the winds and a shouting and a scrambling broke out which showed that the holiday (and Sœur Mannes' secret agony) had begun in earnest.

There were cries of friends separated by the crush into different coaches, and last-moment exchanges at the risk of losing one's place altogether; there were hats and bags dropped over the sides of the coaches which had to be rescued by gymnastic feats over the edge of wheels; there was a gay jangling of harnesses and a great deal of whip-cracking and shouting from the coachmen who entered into the spirit of the day; and opening and shutting of the front door as latecomers appeared shamefacedly, to be hurried by agitated nuns into the remaining empty seats of the last coaches; and in the excitement the quiet ones sat more quietly than usual clinging mutely to their happiness, and the noisy ones were noisier than ever it seemed possible for anyone to be, scattering theirs abroad in a happy farmyard din.

Sœur Osana was adjusting the bolts she hoped for the last time that morning, when Mavis rushed towards the door, her hat in her hand, her pelerine unbuttoned.

"Quickly, quickly! O, open it quickly," she cried, dancing from one foot to the other in an agony of apprehension. Sœur Osana fumbled at the bolts. "Mavees," she said, "put a pin in the Holy Robe for me, petite, yes? The pains in my legs are so bad, yes?"

"All right," shouted Mavis, darting into the street, "I'll put a pin in for you. . . ."

"Don't forget, little one! I'll have something for you when you return," cried Sœur Osana, watching her running up and down shouting for a seat.

There was no seat, but Germaine Lafitte, on the third, sat up in front beside the coachman; and as the first coachman was still arranging himself on his little bench Mavis ran up to him and, before she could be stopped, put her foot on the wheel-spoke and vaulted up beside him.

Her heart beat very fast wondering who would be sent to fetch her down again, and feeling giddy at the thought of being sent back before the whole school. (O, I shall kill myself, I shall kill myself if they do!) But Heaven or the coachman or the horses themselves decreed otherwise, for before she had properly regained her breath, eight golden chimes rang out on the air and the houses were moving past on either side to the castagnetting of hoofs and wheels over the cobbled village street.

For once the caramels and sticks of licorice in the post-office window met with no response; they might have been so many slate pencils and india-rubbers. Monsieur le Curé, a smile on his round pink moon of a face which, with his perilously perched beret, would have made the fortune of a music-hall comedian, was standing at his handsome iron gateway ready to wave as the cortège passed.

"Come with us, Monsieur le Curé! Come with us!" yelled the holiday-makers. Monsieur le Curé made a trumpet of his hands. "I fear the horses would not like me!" he shouted in comic despair. "But we would, Monsieur le Curé!" came the answer. "Ah, well, next time for certain, *mes petites!*" he trumpeted, going through the yearly ritual with becoming solemnity.

They went straight on towards the ugly red inn at the cross-roads where the toy tram-train to Brussels stopped, to keep up the villagers' pretence of communication with the outer world.

Outside the inn door Jeannette Dubois in a clean white pinafore, too long, and ill-fitting with that look of rebellious exile peculiar to charity clothes, was standing with a handkerchief in her little hand to be waved as the coaches passed. Graciously inclined on this happy occasion the occupants of the coaches fluttered their handkerchiefs in reply, and a few of the smaller children called shrill greetings to her.

In her own surroundings Jeannette seemed to have lost a good deal of her shy mouse air, for she pushed open the door and piped eagerly: "Maman, maman, viens, viens vite!" A clean stout woman in black came out and on seeing the cortège began curtseying to the nuns as they passed, her face a picture of humility and gratitude. The two could be seen waving from the door until the last coach turned the corner into the long avenue of trees from which began the long country drive to Tourelles.

Le bon Dieu seemed always to take this day into His especial care. It was a dull heart that did not believe this to be so. And it would have been a poor mind that could have been persuaded into believing that the great stretch of shining blue above them was not the Virgin's cloak lent for this day to protect Her Own, but was due to the judicious choice of a day in the last week of the hottest month of the year, in which skies might be relied upon to behave themselves.

Mavis watched the dusty yellow road disappear beneath the horses' hoofs, and hoped that the journey would never end. She sat very stiff, her head thrown back, and looked high out over the long, dusty, tree-bordered road, possessing it wholly. Isolated and high, her head almost touching the first low branches of the passing trees, she sat enclosed in her possessive happiness, not desiring it to be shared or intruded upon by anyone. She removed her thoughts from Joyce; from Sœur Veronique and Sœur Angelique, who were actually in the last coach of all, and yet had seemed to be sitting menacingly on either side of her until now; from wondering why Jeannette had waved so eagerly knowing all the time that she would never be allowed to share such a day with them; from the chatter and snatches of hymn tunes rising from the coaches like their heavy breath. (Beneath her in the coach Sœur Etienne's voice said: "Suppose those who have brought their rosaries began a little prayer. Come, Angele, you begin, and the others will take it up where you leave off. . . .")

A warm breeze lifted the heavy fringe of chestnut hair on her forehead and played soothingly round her head. She had forgotten to put on her hat, and she was unaware of this even though it lay on her lap and her fingers were twisting themselves about the elastic.

The ceaseless clop-clop-clop gobbling up the long country roads, the wide shady branches holding out their leaves in a gesture of grave and spontaneous homage; the height at which she sat, all these played up to that urge, that cold near-tyranny which was breaking out now at odd moments through her childish exuberances and enthusiasms. When, as now, in an uncomprehending exaltation she longed to be a queen, or an emperor, or a devil, or a peacock. When she wanted to be still for long periods of time and never be touched or spoken to; when she wanted to stare in front of her, as she did in Chapel when this mood came on her, until the candle-flames dissolved into a single spluttering and blinding radiance through which she went on staring in a trance until her eyes ached, or a chair grated noisily and woke her. Strange thoughts came to her then. Once she had said to Joyce: "I want to see what Sœur Mannes looks like without her coif." And sure enough she had stayed awake until long after Sœur Mannes had been heard getting into bed; and had crept to the end of the dormitory and slightly moved the curtain, and seen Sœur Mannes' head on its pillow. The sight of the black, cropped mop had given her an indescribable nausea, as though something horrible and hitherto unguessed at had been revealed to her, but which she still failed completely to grasp. She had crept back to her bed wondering how the desire to pry had come to her, and feeling that she had been well punished for her wickedness.

The large man beside her with his square red face under its frizz of black hair, his warm black eyes, and his thick, friendly moustache, cracked his whip through the air to make things gay for the pretty little girl sitting so quietly beside him. Ah, poor little one, she dared not even smile at him for fear of the dragons watching her! The good man wanted them all to laugh and sing together, and was sorry to see so many young creatures bleating their prayers out loud, instead of shrieking and fighting together as his youngsters did when out with father for the day.

At ten o'clock they came to a halt outside the *herberge* on the outskirts of Lemur. The coachmen after a display of inter-shouting seemed to agree on the main point, and getting down from their perches entered the *herberge* just as a large-bosomed smiling woman in a spotted cotton dress came out to greet her visitors. Following the polite comedy (for had she not seen to the filling of the jugs of milk and the assembling of cups and mugs an hour since?) of a consultation with Sœur François, during which were enumerated all the attractions of the house from lager to grenadine, she bustled back into the inn calling loudly: "Allons, Jeanne! Allons donc, Henri! Du lait pour les demoiselles. Dépêchez vous donc!"

"Always milk!" wailed Milly Martin, ignoring Sœur Mannes' Tck

Tck. "We might as well be babies!" Milly Martin's idea of a holiday drink was *chocolat,* thick, odorous, and very sweet, such as one drank when taken to Brussels to have one's tooth drawn.

A girl of fourteen in a neat blue dress appeared with her arms full of brown enamel mugs and glasses, and began placing them in rows on the long wooden table outside the *herberge.* A young man in a workman's blue blouse followed her with two large enamel jugs of milk. She said something to him as they arranged the table together. He coloured and then grinned, showing his square peasant teeth. He went again into the inn and returned with his arms full of mugs, followed by Madame carrying a third enamel jug and a platter of small *tartines.*

Then began a general filling up and handing round, starting with the head nuns and their coaches, and spreading to the rest amid a great deal of unruly shouting and impatience. For as long as he could the young man remained at the table near his mother, handing her the mugs and performing various inconspicuous tasks while his sister took round the filled mugs on a tray. He took obvious care to keep his eyes fixed on what he was doing. But the young girl must have complained to him about his laziness, for an argument broke out among the three, after which, looking sheepish, he took up the next tray and approached the coaches awkwardly. He was a commonplace, handsome youth, and the interest was immediate. All those who had not been served began reaching for a mug, and on achieving one, instead of handing it on as was proper, they kept it as though it contained an especial charm. And those who already had mugs of their own suddenly made a generous gift of them to their neighbours.

Angele, who had a blue mug on her lap, suddenly pinched Mavis on the behind. "Want some milk?" she cooed invitingly. "You're too high up to reach for any." Incensed at this public affront to the back of her and understanding the wherefore of Angele's solicitude, Mavis shouted: "Try and get rid of it on someone else; and you dare touch me again, you little beast, and I'll give you something you'll not forget!"

"Mes enfants, mes enfants!" protested Sœur Etienne wanly.

"Have you had any milk yet, Mademoiselle?" asked the young peasant, suddenly appearing below her and glancing up for one bashful second. Mavis shook her head, too embarrassed to speak, and with an awkward movement of his thin hand he held a mug high, blushing like a girl. Mavis blushed as she took it from him; but already he was down the line handing a mug with exactly the same question, blush, and movement to someone else.

The girls sipped their milk slowly, making it last a long time; but it was no use. Madame bustled round with a great clatter of efficiency collecting her mugs herself, and making sure that none was missing. Henri had gone into the house and did not appear again, although it was quite five minutes before the coachmen were in their seats and the horses moved off; handkerchiefs fluttering towards Madame and her daughter.

Now that the horses were refreshed the dull flat countryside, which not even the lavish sunshine could inspire, was shed at a sharp pace. It was to repeat itself for two more hours. A few stone houses ending in an *herberge* and a village was passed; long stretches of field, a few trees along the road, and another farmhouse was left behind.

But now Mavis had other thoughts. At intervals she looked down at the receding road beside her into two bashful dark eyes, and the thirsty far-travelled Princess deigned to accept the cup of goat's milk from the handsome shepherd boy who sought death for her sake.

Suddenly a shout was heard; other shouts followed, and behold a great deal of pointing and clapping of hands. Sure enough, far away to the right could be seen the vast cross-crowned dome of La Miséricorde. "I saw it first! I saw it first!" clamoured a hundred voices.

The coachmen grinned and whipped their horses up. It was an essential part of the holiday ritual to enter Tourelles with a fine clatter over the cobbles, as though invisible fireworks were being let off under the horses' hoofs. Soon Tourelles could be seen round the bend of the avenue; and the dome of La Miséricorde, its great breast lifted to the sun, could be seen to be of a heavenly blue mosaic surmounted by a golden cross, and covered with enormous golden stars that leapt and sang together in the strong sunlight.

"Come with us, Mavis, do!" urged Violet Gray, as the girls got up from the *déjeuner* of cold meat, pudding, and fruit, which had always to be eaten at the Hôtel de la Reine d'Espagne before they could be turned loose until five o'clock.

"I've got to go first and stick in a pin for Sœur Osana. I promised her," said Mavis, who not having Joyce was willing to join any group that would have her. "But that won't take long and I can find you soon."

"We'll be on the flying-boats," Violet shouted after her.

Mavis trotted across the diminutive Grande Place, with its fringe of chestnut trees and its square of old and crooked houses, which seemed to support one another like a troupe of sick mediæval beggars pausing at the church door in the expectation of a miracle. Quickly she passed through the giant doorway of the courtyard and into the cool dark heart of La Miséricorde.

Again that impression of old old women with many black petticoats and frilled white lawn caps tied under their old chins. Always kneeling about on floors, legless, half-human, although hundreds and hundreds of chairs stood unoccupied.

As always the miraculous statue of Jesus was besieged and surrounded. Twice now Mavis had promised to stick pins in Jesus' robe, and on each occasion had regretted her promise as soon as she found herself in front of Him.

Because, when she stood in front of Him, there was no doubt, so well had the sculptor done his work. The figure seemed real; too real. It was little more than natural size, and showed Jesus with a crown of thorns on His head, from which the blood dripped over His wan and sorrowful face. His arms hung down in front of Him and His hands were tied together with real rope. They, too, had blood on them. The figure was covered with a dull purple robe, a seamless robe, which fell in heavy pleats from neck to hem, and was tied with a thick black cord. And in this robe thousands of small steel pins shone like star dust.

Although Mavis's middle-class patriotism and Protestantism were already (in common with those of the other English girls) flowering aggressively in an alien country, she would not have dared to doubt that this was really the robe Jesus wore during His agony, as they said it was. Jesus stood weary-eyed and ill-used for the world to gaze at, and the seamless robe must be His own, or He would not have allowed them to place it on Him, and to come strangely with their little pins to do Him homage.

Mavis took a pin from a square wooden box and dropped a sou in the slot. Awkwardly, nervously, she approached the figure and, placing the pin neatly in the purple sleeve, murmured: "Please, Jesus, this is for the pain in Sœur Osana's legs. Please take it away from her. Amen."

That's over. What a relief. She tiptoed through the forbidding dark space of the great church, pausing to watch a young woman in a heavy black veil kneel at one of the confessionals and pull to the curtain, and then out through one of the side doors into the sunshine. This was a way she could not have used before as the small green lawn on which she found herself was unfamiliar. A path lost in a wide curve led apparently to the front of the church and into the Grande Place. In front of her stretched a long low wall, whitewashed a delicate green, and cut into the centre of it a severe wrought-iron gate stood unlatched.

An impulse for which she could not account, for her mind was with the roundabouts and delay was foolish, made Mavis walk to the iron gate, push it open and pass through.

She found herself in the deep grass of an orchard, staring at the most beautiful sight in the world: warm ripe fruit hanging heavily in their leaves from the arms of a tree. She stood a moment uncertain what to do next, but feeling no desire to pick the fruit. Then a little way away from her she saw a brown figure bending over a large flat basket, like the ones the lay sisters brought into the kitchens every Friday from the bakery. The figure straightened itself and she saw it was a monk, a Franciscan from his brown habit and white rope, with a fluff of white hair on his temples.

He saw her, studied her a moment and beckoned. Mavis, though the back of her mind was taken up with roundabouts and gingernuts and the desirability of not wasting time, walked quickly towards him over the deep grass.

"You want some fruit, little one?" asked the monk as she came near. "Then fill your pockets with what you like best. But don't despoil our little orchard," he gave a high thin laugh, "because it is really extraordinary how you young ones can hide it all away!" He was an old man, a very old man Mavis thought, thin and tall, with a long and gentle face from which two grey eyes gazed peacefully. Although his mouth was so shrunken he still had all his teeth; and his voice was friendly and reassuring.

She put out her hand and picked a beautiful red apple, but she felt it right to say, as a sort of grace before eating: "I didn't come to pick the apples. I really didn't. I wanted to see what was on the other side of the gate, just because I didn't remember seeing it before. But thank you very much for this one." After which display of good manners she felt entitled to bite.

The old man asked her all about herself and even listened to her replies, and then went into a long description of the apple-wine and the preserves which were to be made from the fruit, for which this had been a blessed year.

Mavis began to pick the apples with him and roll them into the basket, while he cooed away like a wise and elderly pigeon, making speech seem natural in the quiet, sun-speckled orchard given up to the green silence of the summer heat. As they worked he pointed out to her the butterflies and followed their flights with his finger, but told her never to steal them from the air they loved, because *le bon Dieu* had placed them as a crown on the earth.

He made her pause several times to catch the humming of the bees; he said she must never be frightened of them. "But they sting you!" cried Mavis, "even if you don't move they still sting you!" He explained that the bees sang their little hymns and that if you liked their singing they could never hurt you. They knew at once those who liked their hymns from those who did not. Mavis had never thought of that. She had thought their hymns were a warning that they were coming to sting you.

Once when he moved to another side of the tree she saw his wrinkled feet through his sandals, and remembered something she had often puzzled over. "Don't your feet get awfully cold in the winter without stockings on?" she ventured.

The old monk laughed. "Not after forty years of no stockings!" He bustled among the clusters of ripe apples, taking their energy into himself. "At first it is very cold, a true punishment. But then you are young, and you welcome the cold and the punishment. Soon there is no more punishment. The feet are happy whether it is cold or warm, and they even laugh at the rain. And then when you are old . . . well, then you are only glad that your feet still like you and carry you about with them, though just a wee bit too slowly sometimes."

"I wore socks," said Mavis, "till I was ten. But now I'm too big for socks, of course. I never found it cold, either. But I wouldn't like to have to go without stockings all my life. A girl couldn't very well, could she?"

The fruit in the large basket began piling up rapidly. An eager childish rivalry broke out and they both darted hither and thither and came back with their arms full of apples, calling to each other to come and see who was working the hardest. The old man's pipings and the young girl's shrill answerings scattered through the sun-heavy boughs, and hung in the air as a music to which they moved and gesticulated.

Suddenly a third was in the picture, a monk with a young face and fine eyes and a ring of black hair round his head.

Mavis stopped laughing and prancing about. She heard the old monk saying: "Ah, you are marvelling at my industry, brother. I'll whisper to you: *le bon Dieu* took pity on my old bones and sent me down from Heaven His prettiest angel to help me. Do not talk too loud for she will fly away. . . ." The old man made a comic gesture of apprehension.

Mavis understood that she was not wanted any more and must go away. She was sorry it was all over. She was aware again of herself and her surroundings and she remembered the Fair, and wished the old monk could come with her and see all the exciting things that were happening on the other side of the wall. She no longer saw him as old, but as wise and happy and eminently desirable as a companion.

She approached, making a little curtsey, and he took her hands in both his, saying gently: "Dear child, thank you for your sweet company. . . . Surely I have seen one of God's own angels, so good and so beautiful. . . ." He made the sign of the Cross on her forehead with his thumb, and murmuring something about not wanting to go, Mavis curtseyed again and ran away towards the iron gate.

As she stood under the roundabouts trying to catch sight of Violet Gray, the old monk's last words sounded in her ears above the crash of the hurdy-gurdy. *Si sage et si belle.* Unconsciously she turned it all back on herself, spoiling it with the cheap romanticism of adolescence . . . si sage *et si belle. . . .*

Violet was nowhere to be seen. The roundabout rocked and thundered past, emitting harsh tormented shrieks as though about to give birth to another painted monstrosity.

On the bosom of its gaudiest offspring, a scarlet swan ostrich-crossed, Milly Martin came to rest a few feet from where Mavis stood.

"Seen Violet anywhere?"

"Mm. She went off with Marion and Doris some time ago. Dunno where they went, though. Why don't you come up and have a ride? 'S my fourth."

"I was thinking that I ought to do my shopping first," said Mavis doubtfully. "Y'see I've got Joyce's seven francs to spend too. I must get the things she asked for. . . ."

"I get my things last," said Milly, " 'cos otherwise the chocolate melts and everything gets sticky and the sugar breaks off. . . . Wait for me, then; it's my last."

But Mavis was already being tempted by an emotional parody of a peacock in its mother's earliest and happiest manner. Early because it showed every symptom of decay and approaching senility, and happy because only a person of a young and courageous fancy could have conceived such a robust and indelicate travesty.

She lowered herself into its hollowed back and leaned against the garish and dilapidated tail thinking how jolly it would be to have all chairs made like this. And desks too, so that one could really share one's desk with one's lesson books. Put a little board where the neck is, and have the inkpot in the eye.

A groan, a splutter of song, and the peacock moved unwillingly up an incline, Mavis holding her breath; but Milly Martin swaying in her swan's sixth embrace, curled her spidery woollen legs insolently round its hooped and gracious neck.

Now arm-in-arm they pushed their way through the crowded confetti-movement of the Fair.

The air was dizzy with coloured sound and coloured movement, bearing its quivering restless burden through and over the crowd and up into the thick sunshine. Colour hung on the air; flying-boats waved through it; banners wrestled with it, flopped, waited, came up again for more; grinding shrieks tormented it; tunes and laughter shot up to join it. Everything was loud, hot, prismatic. Everything swam, fidgeted, flashed, and rebounded. And everywhere the thick brush strokes of the afternoon sun pricked out, enhanced, and selected.

The two girls were eager, but hard to please. With youth's parsimoniousness they stubbornly exacted full value for their money. More often only to gaze was almost enough, thus accumulating another bar of chocolate cream, or an extra Saint Antoine in *pain d'épis,* or a coloured picture of La Miséricorde, on frilled paper, blessed.

"Let's go on the Cake-Walk!"

"But he only lets you walk over once, and it's twenty centimes."

"Let's go on the flying-boats!"

"You only get five rounds, I've been counting, and it's twenty-five centimes."

"Well, we must do *something. . . .*"

Mavis spied Armande by a stall of *figurines* in pink sugar, holding a little statuette of the Virgin and Child, sticky and tinselled, and arguing over the threepence asked for it. As usual now she was alone.

"There's Armande again," said Mavis, "she's by herself. Let's ask her to join us."

"O, don't!" said Milly swiftly and breathlessly, pulling at her arm. "I want us to go somewhere . . . and a third's no good. Besides Armande's so sulky these days . . . and she'll blab anyway. . . ."

Mavis sensed something forbidden, and momentarily her heart failed her. She ought to have known better than to ally herself to Milly Martin for the whole afternoon. Milly was always very daring and very boyish and forever boasting of how her brothers took her with them on all their holiday escapades. It was always Milly Martin who cried: "Who'll dare me to hide The Angel's specs?" "Who'll dare me to upset my coffee over the refectory table?" "Who'll dare me to say my sums backwards to Manny to-night?"

And Mavis at bottom, just as eager to break rules, must break them in her own way and at her own time, and not when someone else insisted on her breaking them, and in their way.

So she listened and withdrew her arm petulantly.

"O, but we can't do that. You know we can't. You know we mustn't. We're supposed not to know about it even."

"Well, we *do* know about it," Milly grinned, "and I even know where it is. And we've never really been *told* not to go, 'cos they don't even know it themselves . . . so we're not really doing anything very wrong . . . besides nobody will see us!"

"Yes they will," said Mavis doggedly, "they're sure to. O, you needn't think I'm afraid," seeing Milly's lip lift in a sneer, "I've dared worse things than you've ever dared, anyway. . . . Yes I have. . . . Anyway I don't want to go much. . . ."

"O yes you do!" said Milly wickedly, "you're dying to go. You know you are. Only you just don't dare. You daren't do anything without your precious Joyce . . . that's what it is. If you weren't afraid you'd come."

Mavis flushed with sudden dislike and anger. It was so nearly true and she knew it, and she hated Milly Martin for knowing it too.

"It's your last year, isn't it?" said Milly.

Mavis nodded.

"Well, it's mine too. So what can they do to us?"

That was true. Only a week to the holidays and then a couple of months to Christmas. What could they do?

Still she stood angry and irresolute. "All right, then," said Milly, "I'll go alone. I ought to have known you wouldn't dare do anything if Joyce Carr wasn't here for you to show off in front of!"

Yet strangely enough she stood her ground and questioned Mavis with her eyes. It was obvious that she wanted her to come, that she didn't seem able to go without her. Despite her threat she hung back. She was even afraid lest she had already gone too far. In her heart Milly had always wanted Mavis Clare for her friend, had chosen her at sight, and had wondered ever since how she had been taken from her by the fat and speckled Joyce.

They stood a moment eyeing each other uneasily, and then Mavis said: "All right. I'll come."

The thing to do was not to be seen together, and to look as though they were wandering quite aimlessly.

"I'll go ahead," said Milly, "and you keep me in sight but keep a long way away and don't look as though you're looking. Stop at some of the stalls and things. It's at the other end of those trees; and you'll see me go in. . . ."

Off wandered Milly, Mavis lounging casually in the same direction. At a stall she bought a long bar of cream-chocolate for one franc, and at another a large bag of coffee caramels for seventy-five centimes. She felt this easy, light-hearted bartering to be a masterstroke of subtlety.

Then Milly disappeared, and shortly afterwards she was joined in the dirty striped tent. Furtively they sidled round the sanded ring, gripping hands, and keeping close together.

Neither of them had expected it to be quite so appalling. Every time she looked at something new Mavis gave a little squeak of dismay, and now and then they turned their heads aside. It seemed so very unreal, so untrue, so ugly, and so unlike anything they had seen before.

When the Bearded Lady suddenly smiled at Milly and held out a picture postcard of herself saying in a gruff voice: Deux sous, mes petites, they both leapt back, their mouths open stiff with horror, and then ran to another corner of the ring. She followed them with her eyes for a nightmare moment and said something to the fat dwarf sitting on a chair beside her. It was obvious that she was extremely angry. It was more obvious that the two children were very frightened.

The long thin man with the elastic skin slipped off his dressing-gown and wearily prepared for work. He looked round to make sure that all attention was focussed on himself, made a few mournfully jocular remarks, and taking hold of the flesh in his chest pulled it out about seven inches in front of him, looked at it, seemed to recognise it, released it, and bowed. Oo! came Mavis's metallic hiccough of disgust, like the sudden dropping of a coin in church. Milly stood rigid in morbid concentration. Now he was pulling out the flesh of his upper arm. Oo! hiccoughed Mavis. Now his neck flesh came right out in his hand. Oo! Now his right cheek stretched far and thin between his fingers. Oo! (O, do stop that, hissed Milly through clenched teeth, digging Mavis with her elbow.) Now his yellow hairy leg flesh stretched far out and jumped slackly back again. Finished now, ladies and gentlemen. The Elastic Man reached languidly for his dressing-gown and resumed his seat. The tension relaxed, the two made swallowing noises in their throats and averted their eyes from each other.

An enormous balloon-like creature of a peculiar white flesh tint and with heavy black hair clipped short in her neck and a black clipped shadow on her upper lip, waddled uneasily round the enclosure holding out a heavy inflated arm to be pinched.

The two drew sharply together as she passed, staring at her vast tower of a body and the long thick crease that rose from the top of her pink cotton bodice exposing a large piece of swollen and divided flesh.

A dark beautiful doll with a high curved bust and baby hands studded with diamonds and gold, stuck out a red tongue at them and wrinkled up a piece of putty nose while they stared at her. "And to think that I could push her over with my little finger," whispered Milly indignantly, as they glared and moved on.

Then they saw the half-thing without legs, though one foot dangled somewhere in the middle of it as though it grew from the base of the stomach, and with two half-arms, thin stumps of grey flesh, bound with gold bracelets. And Mavis after one look at the squashed, pushed-in face, said: "Let's get out or I shall be sick or something," and even Milly looked away.

They hurried to the door and so far forgot themselves in their eagerness to escape as to leave together. Once again the confetti-movement of the Fair enveloped them; this time with the caress of bright wings of guardian angels waiting for their return to the light.

"Lord, you look green," said Milly shakily, "pull yourself together for heaven's sake or they'll guess. Here, eat some chocolate."

"O, isn't it lovely to be outside again!" breathed Mavis, trying to laugh away her haunted face. "O, Milly, I'll never go near anything like that again. Never! You wouldn't think they could live, would you? I thought I'd die when that fat woman came at us. . . ."

They dragged along sucking their chocolate sticks, trying to rid themselves of their dark secret on the streaming sunshine that was as reassuring as day breaking in on a nightmare.

"Come on! Here are the swings. Quickly!" cried Milly, suddenly running towards an empty painted boat with a soiled rope hanging down the middle. Quickly Mavis scrambled in. She understood what Milly meant. Here was safety and everydayness. They swung backwards and forwards over the crowd, half-seeing familiar faces and black hats and flying pelerines dotted about all over the ground and tossed into the air like themselves; and the full horror of the thing they had just witnessed began slowly to leave them, to submerge itself in the clamour and colour in which they made only two black specks, fly-dirt, in a worn-out swing.

The strong sunlight would have none of it, and was teasing them into being children again.

"Swear you won't breathe a word to anybody about what we've seen?" said Milly, pulling their little boat up and down with the piece of soiled rope.

"Swear," breathed Mavis.

"Not to *anyone*," emphasised Milly.

"O well, I must tell Joyce," remonstrated Mavis, "but I swear not anybody else, and I'll make her swear too."

"I don't see why you should tell her," said Milly crossly, "she's sure to tell."

"Joyce'd never tell if you *killed* her," said Mavis fiercely. "I'll swear to anything, but I won't swear not to tell Joyce." So Milly gave it up.

They spent a long time on the swings, and then crossed to the flying-boats, where they met Violet Gray, climbing down from the platform.

"Hi, Mavis," shouted Violet, "I've been looking for you everywhere. Where've you been all this time?" She ignored Milly Martin.

"On the swings an' all over," lied Mavis cheerfully. "I looked everywhere for you and couldn't find you, so I went off with Milly."

Violet came very close and lowered her voice to a whisper.

"Have you been in the little blue tent at the back of the switch-back?" she asked.

"Haven't been in any tent. It's forbidden," said Mavis. "What's there?"

"A woman on a tight-rope," whispered Violet, "and a funny man making jokes. She balances all alone with an umbrella over her head. O, it looks *lovely*. You can't think how lovely it looks. Why don't you go? It's the small blue tent at the back of the switchback; you'll see a picture of her outside. Outside the tent I mean."

"Want to come, Milly?" ventured Mavis, hoping she would say no.

But Milly, whose curiosity was insatiable, said yes.

They found the tent and its picture where Violet had predicted, and after furtive looks to reassure themselves that they were unobserved, they raised the tent flap and darted through.

Nothing to terrify them here. They sat close together on a bench toward the back of the tent and stared at the small sanded ring in which a square fat man with a purply-red face was talking loud and fast. A wire was stretched between two poles from end to end of the tent. All of a sudden a small woman with very yellow hair hanging sweetly down her back, and bound on the forehead with a piece of satin ribbon, was walking slowly toward him. A pink tarlatan skirt with many frills reached her knees and below that were cotton stockings of a deep muddy pink, creased round the ankles and at the back of the knees. On her feet were flat satin slippers with rounded toes; one a dirty grey white, the other a faded pink. Her fingers were weighted with enormous hoops of coloured stones, that flashed at the little gestures she made as she minced toward the fat man. He stopped his patter and his smiles abruptly, as though a tap had been turned off behind his face, and bowing absurdly low to the audience and to the lady, he said in mock obsequience: Look well, Ladies and Gentlemen, for you see before you the One and Only Lolà, Queen Beauty of Tight-Rope Walkers.

There was a small splutter of applause, at which the lady also bowed low and smiled, showing two bright gold teeth and two or three spaces where teeth should have been. Then she placed her foot on the fat man's hand and helped herself on to the wire with her hands.

There was a good deal of preliminary swaying, during which the two girls sat in agony, as though she was about to fall and be killed to atone for their wickedness in sneaking in to watch her. But the lady righted herself. After all she had only been playing with them, as a juggler plays with the balls which he knows cannot escape his fingers.

She shivered the wire a little with her feet, swayed her arms and shoulders to and fro, and with another smile all round, started down the wire with a curiously restrained and yet elastic step. She stood on one foot and smiled; and then on the other foot and smiled; and then she ran up and down the wire with an ugly wading movement, taking deep steps across space as though she was running up the stairs three steps at a time. Then she raised her thin arms high above her head and became very still, conveying that she was now about to do something so difficult that the audience must hold its breath, like a prayer, to sustain her during its performance. And as all eyes popped at her, scared and tremulous, she slowly raised herself on to the point of the grey-white toe, and then after a slight pause and another effort, raised herself on to the pink toe, and thus went drifting down the wire grinning, triumphant, except for the two or three teeth which were missing.

Just then, as though his own silence had become unbearable and oppressive to him, and must be shattered at all costs, the large man's throaty voice shouted:

"Messieurs et mesdames, savez vous la différence entre une vache et un homme?" His grin stretched across his face into a purplish-red mask of comedy. He was so obviously and infectiously pleased with himself and his remark. People began grinning, realising he was up to some mischief.

"Evidemment vous ne le savez pas," beamed the large man. "Eh bien, je vous le direz: Une vache boit de l'eau et donne du lait: mais un homme boit du lait et donne de l'eau."

There was one loud guffaw and then everyone joined in. The rickety wooden benches rocked with the laughter of the people balanced on them; even the wire-walker did risky things with the wire to show how she enjoyed the fat man's joke, and he, of course, laughed louder than all of them.

The two girls sat dumb and shocked, and stared at all the mirth and at the purply-red gestures of the fat man. Now the golden-haired lady bounced up and down the wire like a much-used but still active ball. She kept her mouth with its spaces of missing teeth open all the time in a grimace of welcome. Her whole face seemed to be petrified into this perpetually grinning acknowledgment of the homage and admiration forever wafted to her from the changing squatters on the wooden benches.

After that it was all over, and the large man and the pink lady were bowing this way and that, and then again, and then returning for more, and finally disappearing behind a curtain flap, the audience seeing itself out at the canvas doorway.

This time the sunshine and the noise did not strike them so dramatically or so gratefully. It was merely like coming out into the Fair again. Perhaps it was only natural that after the unbearable excitement of the first tent, they should feel cheated and unimpressed.

"I can't see what Vi thought was so lovely," began Milly, kicking a stone out of the path.

"Nor me," said Mavis sulkily. "Did you see her gold teeth all shiny? And black holes all round her mouth. She wasn't a bit like the pictures you see of tight-rope walkers, was she? Why, I call her downright ugly!"

"I wouldn't like to have to monkey about on a wire," said Milly, "would you?"

"O, I dunno, I would rather. Only a nice one of course, and all in pink satin, not a silly cotton thing like hers." Mavis thought of all the people looking up, always looking up, looking up at her, breathless and admiring. But she kept that bit to herself.

"Did you hear his joke?" ventured Milly.

What a silly question. Of course she had heard the joke as well as Milly Martin had.

"Awful, wasn't it!"

"Mm. Wasn't it!"

"How he could say it all out loud like that and not even blush or anything!"

"I felt *awful* when I heard it," admitted Mavis, "I felt all hot, like losing your drawers in the street or something."

The bond of the wicked joke became a magnet drawing them close, for suddenly Milly thrust her arm round Mavis's waist and said quickly and hotly: "I wish you'd be my friend, Mavis."

"But I can't," said Mavis confused, "I'm Joyce's."

"Yes, I know," stammered Milly. "But I wish you had been my friend instead of hers. I've always wanted you for my friend, Mavis, ever since I saw you standing on the refectory table smashing all the handles off the cups at prize-giving. . . . D'you think Joyce'd mind if you were my friend instead?"

Really! Would Joyce *mind;* when she'd break her heart. "Of course she'd mind," said Mavis angrily, forgetting that a moment ago she had felt flattered and powerful. "Joyce and I have been best friends for two years. I can't leave Joyce just because I'm asked to."

"No, I s'pose not," said Milly, whom love seemed to have made unusually humble and self-effacing. "No, I s'pose not. But you might have chosen me, Mavis, instead, in the first place 'cos I'm much more like you than Joyce is. . . . And I know something nice that I could show you . . . er tell you . . . if you were my friend. . . ."

Mavis looked sympathetic but helpless. Curiously enough she had not grasped the significance of Milly's last sentence.

Yet even though she felt flattered and powerful, she remembered that she did not really like Milly Martin. No, she was too domineering, too similar without being pretty; too possessive and too quick. She could never have chosen her as a friend, never. Yet she felt intensely proud that Milly wanted her for a friend; indeed, had wanted her so long a time now.

"Let's do our shopping now," she said primly, taking Milly's arm and squeezing it. O, she must be so kind to Milly, so considerate. She must stoop and be so good to her. And for once the vivid and independent Milly seemed unaware of any patronage. She saw Mavis smile and thought how lovely she looked, and ached in her heart to have her for a friend.

The shopping proved a long and tiring business of choosing, and arguing, and dragging about from one stall to another in search of non-existent bargains.

All at once, her bag full of cakes and chocolates and sugared *figurines,* Mavis felt tired. The day seemed suddenly and unaccountably ended for her. She seemed to have been put down at the end of her finished day without explanation or excuse. She was aware of a heavy throbbing in her forehead and a beating behind her eyeballs and she wanted to be sitting in the coach driving back over the long yellow road, between the trees and past the peaceful farmhouses.

More than happened through the whole year had been crammed into one day, and she was hot, tired, and dusty, and she wanted to cry a little with irritation at everything happening at once, when each little bit could have had its own day and been spread over a long period of time.

Now she was upset because her feet ached in her heavy black walking shoes, and the elastic under her chin had suddenly become tight and vicious. She wanted to put her face in cold water. She wanted to cry. She wanted to relieve herself. She wanted to make no more effort, but just to shut her eyes and find herself in bed in the dormitory.

She wished the signal would sound for the reassemblage. She didn't care that Milly Martin loved her and secretly ached for her to be her friend. She even didn't care that an old man had thought her good and beautiful.

For a moment she almost wished she had spent the day with Joyce, fat, speckled, obedient Joyce, lying on the grass in the Quartier des Dames reading *The Three Musketeers.* I wonder how far she's got, thought Mavis. Further than me, anyway; but she mustn't tell what happens.

"I wish it was all over, and that we could start back again," she said sulkily to Milly, as she squeezed some last apples into her full-gorged bag, risking its seams.

"Jove, I don't!" said Milly, with her sharp bark of a laugh, "I wish it'd begin all over again. I wish it'd go on for a week and then a month."

And then Mavis knew why, wrinkling up her nose and looking sideways down her cheeks, why despite the flattery and the power and the frustrated desire welling up in secret prayer to her, the hearty and sufficient Milly Martin was never to be her friend.

Mercredi 7.

Je me tiendrai devant Lui comme une toile devant son
Peintre. Je me livre a Lui et je Le laisse faire. . . . Je n'ai à me
soucier de rien qu'a ne pas me dérober ou changer par mon
impatience le plan qu'a conçu pour moi son Amour.

Je reste là devant Lui. Je Lui dis que je L'aime et que je Le
supplie de me travailler malgré mes cris et mes résistances. Et
puis, tachant de faire taire tout en moi, je Le laisse imprimer
son image adorée sur sa petite toile blanche.

Pour reproduire ton image.

"*Jésus, que veux-Tu que je fasse?*"

Méditations de Sœur Marie Saint-Anselme

W hy, you're crying, Solange! Yes you are! You needn't duck
your head like that, Solange, because you're *always* crying."

Solange first rinsed the floor rag in its mess of dark water and its
layer of brown soap scum and then slowly, unwillingly, half-raised her
head. Round her large blue-flecked eyes were dark dabs of tears and
dirty fingers; her nose shone hotly, and her expression was stubbornly
unfriendly at the unwelcome intrusion.

"I am not crying, Mademoiselle."

The white veil of the lay sister and the white bands on her chin and
forehead made her look forlornly young, hardly more than fourteen,
although she would be nineteen in the spring.

"But you *have* been crying; you can't deny it. Your face is all dirty
and you'd better clean it before The Angel comes along and sees you."

Mavis was on her way to the library to replace *Forty-two Stories of the
Brave and True for Girls*. And here scrubbing away at the classroom floor
was Solange, with her white veil not too clean and not too straight, and
with that lost look, that mute hang-dog humility, that left one undecided whether to comfort or kick her. Solange, who would one day
cease to be a cry-baby, and would take the black veil and even teach
in class, though she had been at the Convent herself since the age of
eight.

"You do cry an awful lot, don't you?" insisted Mavis, at her pin-
pricking again, and scrutinising her rudely and deliberately.

"Not very much, Mademoiselle," replied Solange, tremulous under this deliberate and arrogant scrutiny.

"Well, anyway, every time I see you anywhere you're *always* crying. Everyone calls you The Cry-Baby, you know." Mavis lowered her voice to an insinuating whisper. "Are they very mean to you? The Angel gives it you a bit, doesn't she?" The last whispered too eagerly.

But Solange had no confidences to impart. She shook her head wearily.

"And tell me," pursued Mavis, "is it true that you have to do all sorts of penances and for quite small offences? Is it true you had to stand with your tongue out for an hour yesterday while everyone else was eating, because you answered Manny back? And did Sœur Marie Augustine really say that you ought to be *thrashed* for your laziness. Jove, she's a mean beast. . . ."

Tears gathered in Solange's large blue-flecked eyes, such beautiful eyes, more beautiful than Mavis's own, had the comparison occurred to her. Obviously she intended to make no confidences, and to be party to no exchange of secrets. It was not that which she resented. But her heart was torn in her fierce peasant pride at this raking up, this discovery and bandying of her shame.

Did they know, then, of the thrashings even before she received them? If that were so how much more the blows could hurt! And the silly insolent Miss was looking down her nose at her with a mocking, dirty, suspicious knowledge behind her eyes, was looking down at her as she knelt (no not at her feet because the Miss had stationed herself at her knees), and at the bucket of brown water and its dark soap-scum.

"Poor you!" chirped Mavis, taking Solange's silence for acquiescence. "I wouldn't put my tongue out, I'd *stick* it out right under their ugly noses!" And then remembering, "Is it true that Sœur Marie-Joseph is very ill?"

Solange fought the trembling of her lips. "Yes, very ill, very ill indeed, Mademoiselle."

"Is it true she's going to die?"

"They say she won't live long now," said Solange in a low voice, turning her head towards the open classroom door to make sure that they were alone. "Sœur Veronique told Sœur Etienne at breakfast this morning that now her stomach has swollen right up and goes on swelling, and that she suddenly gives loud cries of agony; and she moans a lot and prays all the time, saying the end is near. She has never been ill in her life, and now she cannot move for pain. And she is so old and so good . . ." added Solange gravely.

Mavis stood like a bright bird, unable to take in the significance of Solange's sad voice. The holiday frock of blue alpaca, with its prettily embroidered cuffs and collar and its little silk bow at the neck, made her feel very fine and self-assured. The young lay sister looking up at her felt her pride and self-assurance and marvelled at her foolish pleasure in her own prettiness. It had never occurred to Solange, who used the piece of cracked glass above her *lavabo* only to see that her coif was tied correctly, why even though one practised meekness and docility, true emblems of a gentle heart, one could still be as a thorn in the flesh of those whom one served. Meanwhile Mavis, smiling down at her, used all her wiles, as was her wont when assuming herself admired.

"Will she last out the holidays?" she asked anxiously, though Sœur Marie-Joseph was hardly a reality to her.

"Perhaps. The doctor says this disease often lingers a long time, and it hurts a great deal. He says it would be better if she could die now, as she prays to. . . ." Solange bent her young face to her floor washing and put her capable hands back into the dirty water.

Mavis, watching the long shooting movement of her arms and her heaving back over which the white veil crackled like tissue paper at each lunge, said primly: "I may be going in to Brussels this afternoon with Sœur Damiana, she's going in to order the new lesson books. . . . Isn't it a pity the holidays come to an end so soon, though you don't seem to get much holiday, do you?"

But Solange, knowing that she was trying to point out her blue alpaca holiday frock with its embroidered cuffs and collar and the little bow at the neck, went on with her work as though she had not heard; as if to emphasize that she did not like her very much and considered the intrusion at an end.

U seless to pretend that Joyce lied. Was she not truthful to the point of priggishness?

Then, why, seeing that on Joyce's own admission the matter was unimportant, why this sudden distaste for her company? Mavis knew only that it was not jealousy. She would not admit to jealousy. She could not be jealous of a fat plain girl with freckles, who happened also to be her best friend. Then why this angry throb in her blood every time she thought of it?

Anger? "But what right have I to be angry?" asked Mavis of the

Chapel ceiling. "Joyce *is* my best friend, and we're awfully fond of each other. And perhaps I'm only angry because it happened to her first. . . ."

For Joyce had returned from the holidays kissed. True, Mavis had to keep reminding herself that it had been only a peck on the cheek from a cousin two months older than Joyce herself; yet it was a kiss, an experience which not only raised her in the esteem and envy of all the older girls, but which actually placed her in value considerably above Mavis in her especial game of confidences.

And it was foolish to pretend that Joyce had confided only in Mavis's jealous ear. Now that she remembered, Joyce had not even taken the usual precaution of beginning: *Swear* you won't tell *anyone*. . . . And was she not friendly with everyone now? Were they not all hanging round her neck, and wasn't Joyce just lapping it all up and becoming daily more condescending in manner?

Last night walking round during the Evening Recreation Sally Davies had come running up to them and, ignoring Mavis, had burst out: "O, Joyce, I've been looking for you everywhere to tell you . . ." and then she had placed her arm round Joyce's neck and shshsh'd in her ear, whilst Joyce giggled away knowingly, and then said "O, nothing!" when asked later, much later, for Mavis was too proud to show curiosity or impatience at this comedy, what Sally Davies had said.

It was not that Joyce made much of it; which irritated Mavis almost beyond endurance. She could tell her story ten times without altering one word of it, and each time on coming to the point could shrug her shoulders and emit a clipped giggle as though nothing more unusual than a mosquito bite had taken place. And Mavis, revolted, was going about with a sour face which was being delightedly misinterpreted as jealousy.

It seemed that Joyce had been standing at a window staring into the garden and wishing it would stop raining, when her cousin Bertie, who was two months older than herself, had crept up quietly behind her, tapped her on the shoulder so that she turned her head in surprise, and then had leaned forward and kissed her on her left cheek. After which he ran straight from the room.

The running from the room seemed particularly comic to Mavis, who, after hearing the incident related for the twelfth time, found herself wondering maliciously whether Cousin Bertie was also red and speckled, with puffed cheeks and fat hands dimpled like those of his cousin.

No, it was not jealousy that made her blood throb when she thought of it; and she thought of it continually. It was certainly not jealousy that had made her run away into the end lavatory to be alone and cry so bitterly that she surprised herself. It may have been suspicion. It may have been fear that knocked warningly at her heart, and all unconsciously made her pause, as imaginative youth must always pause, before entering a world which the mind has peopled too lovingly.

"But what was it *like?*" she had appealed.

"Wasn't like anything," Joyce had replied. "Just like a sort of dab. Just as if you'd poked your face with your finger. Heavens, I *was* surprised!" And, unmoved, she went on to tell how sheepish Cousin Bertie had looked when next she saw him in the schoolroom at teatime.

Then it had not been like the picture 'Bliss' which Milly Martin kept under her mattress. Nor even like 'Young Love,' which Marion Moore had once passed to her in history class. Not that Mavis cared very much for 'Young Love,' although the girl with her pretty curls and tennis racket was rather like herself, they said.

She preferred 'Bliss,' with the low tight black velvet gown from which a small slipper glanced from between the heavy folds of the velvet train, and then the gleaming black hair of the man's bent head on which the moonlight fell through the open windows of the ballroom.

It could not be as Joyce pretended it had been; and it was not as Joyce pretended it had been. If it was merely a dab on the cheek from a fat cousin, pictures like 'Bliss' would not be painted.

Besides which Mavis remembered that Mona MacDowell had once confessed to her that she would gladly suffer ten years in Purgatory if only Sœur Imelda would give her one small kiss, or would allow her to place her arms round her neck and tell her that she would love her always.

A nd I don't think I *like* boys," said Joyce, much later. "They're rough and ugly. And my cousin Winifred said that men are all covered in long curly hair from their necks down; nothing but hair, all over. I don't think I like that."

"I'm quite sure father isn't!" inserted Mavis quickly.

"Well, my cousin Winnie said they all are; and she says they look horrid. She's watched them bathing, and she says she got an awful shock the first time she saw that her father had his arms all covered with thick curly hairs. She said it made her quite sick as she hadn't expected him to be like that. . . ."

"But Milly Martin's got hair all over her legs and she loves showing them too," said Mavis, defending her picture postcards, "and she's not a man. And just look at Sœur Osana's hands. . . ."

"That's only two out of all us hundreds," retorted Joyce, "and *all* men are like that only much worse . . . and you needn't look as if you didn't believe I'm telling the truth, Mavis, because Winifred knows about everything . . . and she says men look just like monkeys, except for their faces of course. . . ."

S œur Marie Thérèse had a skin so white that it was said that milk flowed in her veins instead of blood. And when she spoke, snow.

Least popular of all the nuns, the excitement of mystery hung about her, partly because she was haughty and cold with the children; partly for her smile, evoked rarely and not forgotten; partly for the sinister effect her presence seemed to produce on the other nuns. Even Sœur Imelda, so gentle in her speech and manner, would address her curtly and sharply on entering the sewing class to bring altar cloths to be darned or the lace-work of the Communion cloths to be repaired by those most skilful with the needle.

And Sœur Marie Thérèse would raise black burning eyes and, in front of all the children, fail to notice Sœur Imelda, or Sœur Damiana, or Sœur Augustine, whilst staring them full in the face. A child would giggle nervously. A group of friends would titter maliciously. Ah! to be able to stare out of such fiery black eyes in unseeing insolence! But it was not insolence. Sœur Marie Thérèse did not see them; did not seem to see anyone, and therein lay her power.

She had, as it were, burst upon the children. As a rule they knew their nuns well before they became their nuns. Glimpses could be caught of white-veiled novices on their way to Chapel, or seated during High Mass far back in the alcove where the nuns sat to the left of the altar, or during recreation, or on Feast Days, or at their menial duties in the kitchen or on the farm. There was preliminary gossip; it was known who they were; whence they came, whether they were destined for the Convent or the Convent orphanage. So that when one of these emerged black-veiled and in control of such and such a class, all one need do was go and be rude for a few weeks by way of initiation, and afterwards adore or leave her alone should she prove unworthy of attention.

Sœur Marie Thérèse carried mystery to the point of never having been seen or heard of as a novice at all. One Sunday afternoon she had arrived in the refectory as the children were having tea; said grace; wandered slowly in and out of the refectory tables; said grace; and saw them out into the playground for the fifteen minutes preceding Benediction. And the mask she wore caught into her coif—for it could not be a human face at all this piece of stretched white flesh, so thin, thin-nosed, thin-lipped, eyebrow- and eyelashless, with two black holes burnt in—made an immediate and hostile impression.

After that it became great fun to watch Sœur Marie Thérèse make the same impression on the nuns. That she was not liked among them the least-interested spectator could not fail to see. Not that to all outward appearances she was anything but silent and modest and willing to do the work of three when asked, and forbearing with the children to a degree which even Sœur Eileen O'Connor must find quixotic. And suddenly, from whatever she was occupied at on the desk, raising her eyelids, dead-white, transparent, lashless as an eagle's and resting on the class her burning eyes, the noise would cease, and the children catching their breath would stare back, acutely aware of their heart-beats. For she saw the children very well and it was not insolence in the look she gave them.

Mavis, turning the heel of a grey woollen stocking with an ill grace and an unkind thought for the virtuous orphan who must needs wear the finished article, caught at its meaning and whispered to Joyce: Quick. Watch her now. How she hates us! Poor thing.

"Why poor thing?" said Joyce, watching Sœur Marie Thérèse as told, and hating her in return.

" 'Cos she doesn't like it," said Mavis, dropped a stitch, dropped several more trying to pick it up, put the knitting in her mouth and was silent, thinking of things more urgent than Sœur Marie Thérèse's smouldering and dissatisfied eyes.

It was Violet Gray who said: "Cæsar had black eyes like that; and now we know he made his soldiers' knees knock every time he looked at them!"

"I like her," said Mavis, raising a chorus of derision and disbelief. "I do," said Mavis fiercely. "I *do*. She isn't soft like all the rest. She doesn't care. I think I like her most awfully!"

And Mona, thinking of her own gentle and soft-eyed *flamme,* laughed loudest of all.

Then came Dora Jennings and said that Margaret had told her, who had been told by Gwen, who had it from Ellen, who had it from Jeanne Martelle, who slept in the next cubicle and swore to the truth of it, making the sign of the Cross three times and turning round and bobbing to the new moon, that when Sœur Marie Thérèse took off her shoes she hadn't any *feet*. Instead she had (whisper-whisper). No! Yes. No! Yes. Truth. Jeanne said so. She was the *Devil*. Or anyway she wasn't human.

And then Sœur Marie Thérèse was not seen ever again, and was said to be very ill. But there was no hushing of bells, or telling the children not to play so noisily during recreation, nor were prayers added to Mass as was customary when someone was gravely ill. And then the rumour. Not that Sœur Marie Thérèse was no longer in the Convent but that she had gone. That she had run away.

Joyce with a week's pocket-money and two lace holy-pictures wormed the whole story, or as much of the story as she could, out of Jeanne, the orphan, who was now promoted to helping in the third refectory. Jeanne had heard it said that Sœur Marie Thérèse had lowered herself out of the window of her room which gave on to the edge of the Place des Dames, well in the middle of the night, about two o'clock, said Jeanne, and had walked the five miles to the station and probably caught the six o'clock train to Brussels. The window of her room had been found closed, a chair placed near it, the rope attached to it falling straight from the window to the ground.

And when she had vouchsafed all this information Jeanne suddenly went off into a high and sinister falsetto laugh, and putting her lips close to Joyce's ear had hissed: "I'd give this fifty centimes piece and a *dozen* lace pictures to know who held the chair!"

To which Joyce, trembling, and feeling as though her curiosity had led her into the presence of Satan himself, said with dry lips: "*Held the chair?*"

"But yes," hissed Jeanne, fixing her with narrow and malicious eyes, "someone must hold a chair, you know, or it falls out of the window after you."

"Tell me," stammered Joyce, her knees feeling weak. "O, do tell me . . . I'll get you another fifty centimes piece. . . ."

"I don't want your fifty centimes piece," said Jeanne, letting out another harsh, high-pitched laugh. "But I said I'd like to know. . . ."

And Joyce, reaching the door, and with her foot on the top step, ready to rush at top speed down the stairs, her mind a jumble of devils and the smell of sulphur, gasped: "How do you know, Jeanne, that it was *two o'clock*. . . ."

Suddenly Jeanne's face went angry and distorted, a look of fear crossed her eyes and then a look of hatred which remained. She made a step, stopped, then shook her fist menacingly at the retreating Joyce: "I don't *know* that it was two o'clock, Miss Pig-face," she hissed. "I said that perhaps. . . ." She made a further step, her voice rising in anger and her teeth showing. "And all I've told you is lies . . . *lies* . . . everything . . . I just made it up as I went along."

But Joyce, white with horror before the anger in Jeanne's face, was rushing down the stairs two at a time, and racing over the formal lawn of the Visitors' Garden, which was forbidden, and out among the reassuring sounds of the Grand Boulevard, where safety lay.

M arion's active eyes sought Sœur Mannes, now fourth from the end. Again she experienced that sharp, odd, and novel sensation which she did not altogether understand, and which she liked. She knew that she ought not to be watching and that she was intruding on something entirely personal and sacred, but she could no longer help it, it gave her too intense a pleasure. It was no longer a question of intrusion; she was compelled against her will.

From her position in the front row, the Communion rail was so placed that she was kneeling almost at the end of it, and she could follow undisturbed and to her heart's desire the uplifted heads and thrust tongues and shades of devoutness in the lip contortions, and the exact moment that M. le Curé began slurring his words and swallowing the tail-end of his Benediction. Indeed Marion's concentration was so remarkable that one morning she counted thirty-three different ways of sticking out a tongue. (It became almost an obsession with her that she would never know M. le Curé's secret opinion of some of the breath breathed into his face.)

Yet on that particular morning she had noticed nothing unusual in Marguerite van Dadel's behaviour as she bumped down, thrust back her head, opened her mouth, stuck out her tongue, withdrew it, bowed, and trotted back to her seat; though as usual she eagerly felt rather than saw Sœur Mannes' slimy tongue shoot out and return, and knew that the nun's eyelids were quivering as she dragged herself out of her lizard-like absorption.

So that when questioned Marion could truthfully say that she knew nothing and had noticed nothing. The whole school, when questioned, had noticed nothing peculiar in Marguerite's behaviour; not that this was believed.

Suddenly Marguerite's name was spoken in a whisper, and Marguerite, half-frightened, half-resentful, moved slyly and silently among them, not unflattered by the interest she was creating. That no one was allowed to speak to her was no hardship. She had never been a very communicative or popular girl.

Sœur Gonzaga, the tall bronzed English nun, at once the pride and delight of the English section for her heavy laugh that struck one like a crash on the shoulder and her unusual masculine habit of striding through the corridors, both hands deep in her pockets, whistling the comic tune of the moment, was seen to take Mavis aside before supper, and Mavis was very red in the face on her return to the queue.

"Much better own up to it and get it over, my dear child," was Sœur Gonzaga's advice. "It won't be half as bad now as it will be when they find out for themselves, or when Marguerite confesses, which she is bound to do. Take my advice and do it now."

"But I don't know anything about it!" groaned Mavis on the verge of tears. "I wish I *had* done it, as they suspect me anyway. . . ." Which made Sœur Gonzaga think her stubborn as well as dishonourable, and wish she hadn't wasted her breath. Almost all suspected Mavis; a few decided for Joyce, though Milly Martin and Violet Gray were also mentioned as possible accomplices.

And nothing would have been known had it not been for Père Damien's interference. For Marguerite told him everything at Confession, after two bad dreams and one rather blurred vision of *le p'tit Jésus* resting on her cubicle partition, weeping.

Père Damien decided that the severest punishment he could give her, that is to say, the punishment which would be the most difficult to perform and therefore the most acceptable to Heaven, was to tell everything to Sœur Imelda and abide by her verdict. And Marguerite had told Sœur Imelda everything; everything except the name of her accomplice.

After Holy Communion on that particular morning Marguerite had returned to her seat with the Host in her mouth, and she had kept the Host in her mouth. She pushed it a little to one side so as not to swallow it, or inadvertently bite on it, and she had kept it there until after Chapel, when she was to meet someone secretly.

They adjourned to the end of the Boulevard, and there Marguerite had opened her mouth and shown the Host intact. No, she had not touched it with her fingers or taken it out. This point had been discussed before, and it had been decided that that would be going too far.

But Marguerite had, and she was thoroughly frightened and ashamed of herself now, broken off a little piece with her teeth. It had been a grave and terrible moment for both of them; and also a little disappointing. There had been no Blood, the Host not even turning a Pale Pink; and so after that Marguerite had swallowed it. . . .

"We didn't mean anything wrong," Marguerite kept explaining between sobs, "we only wanted to see the miracle. We wanted to see if it would turn into Blood, like it did in the man's handkerchief when he took it out because he didn't believe. . . . We only wanted a *sign*," wailed Marguerite, convinced that even a lifetime of prayer would not wash her clean again.

"You may be glad you weren't both struck dead. That would have been the sign you deserved," said Sœur Mannes nastily, angered by the tolerance Sœur Imelda was showing the girl.

Four days passed and Marguerite, too sorry for herself still to appreciate the novelty of her position, became hourly more pathetic and more frightened as she waited for her accomplice to reveal herself and confess her share in the deed; by far the larger share, for Marguerite knew she would never have thought of it all alone. She had capitulated only after a long and cunning temptation during which she had been assured, if it succeeded, of a double vision of the Blessed Virgin and Saint Catherine.

And then on the evening of the fifth day, in the middle of the ninth Station of the Cross, Tony Grüdel's nose suddenly poured blood all over her prayer book and the front of her dress. Down went Tony's head on her arms. She trembled from head to foot. She moaned, she wept, she clasped and unclasped her hands and shook them towards the altar; and after a sickening display of hysteria she was led half-fainting from Chapel, the blood all smeared over her face and hands. She remained in bed for a week, and it was rumoured that her beloved Sœur Mannes had interceded on her behalf and that the affair was now at an end, though no one knew how that end had been accomplished. When Tony reappeared, more fervent and more subdued than ever, no one dared approach her or ask her any questions.

Not that they wanted to, now. There was too strong a sense of having been cheated; of having been fooled out of what should have been the most memorable dramatic event of the year. And one in which beyond a doubt Heaven would eventually have vouchsafed a Sign.

Τhe Mother Superior lay in state.

Infinitely small and wasted, her hands clasped the wooden crucifix of her brown rosary; her round medlar-coloured face twisted in a last grimace of pain, unreal and unfamiliar. (Only Angeline, noticing this, found it not kind of God to allow a face that had held a smile for all to finish in such disharmony.)

The mouth was sunken in and had drawn the cheeks after it, so that the cheekbones shone like old ivory. The eyes were not shut, and through the narrowed eyelids they seemed, in their glazed fixity, to count the children shuffling past. The thing from which she had died made a sudden lump in the stillness of the bed; the large curve where the stomach lay pushed the bedclothes before it, spoiling the symmetry of the laying out.

Beneath the long ebony Crucifix at the head of the bed two tall candles burned; at the foot a lay sister swung a censer at intervals, casting through the hot cell and the acrid-tasting candle grease sudden jets of scented smoke.

On the narrow bed Sœur Marie-Joseph lay helpless in a gnarled and discoloured parody of her daily self. She might have lain for years under a hot disfiguring sun and been slowly charred to this painful rigidity. A coarse grey counterpane stretched tightly across the bed, like the open untroubled smile of someone kind and elderly; and through the black hole in the middle of her small sunken mouth she might have been calling out to them to pull it up over her head and hide her from sight.

Sœur Marie-Joseph bore uneasily her lying-in-state; and only the bells from the Chapel belfry wearing away the afternoon with their incessant and monotonous clanging, touched to solemnity the otherwise unpleasant.

The younger children headed the procession, taut and excited in their Sunday clothes. The nervous rustle of their little rosaries was like the scrunch of a boot through brittle leaves. *Je vous salue . . . salue . . . soit-il . . . soit-il. . . .* They might have been frying their words for all the hissing and bubbling that went to produce them. But they shed no tears. Sœur Marie-Joseph had gone straight to Heaven, and was even now kneeling under the Virgin's blue cloak, telling Her, so Sœur Damiana had assured them, of the good children she had so unwillingly left behind her on earth.

That had been found the best means of softening the news of her death. The children had burst into quick and angry tears, appalled and thwarted. For Sœur Marie-Joseph was loved. She had been the Mother Superior now for over fifty years, and it was whispered that some of the more educated nuns resented the protracted reign of this simple and devout peasant woman from a neighbouring village.

Not so the smaller children. Perhaps they understood that the little withered old woman was the only nun who really loved them as though they had been her own. There was no awe or fierce shyness as at an intrusion when her brown and pleated face would peer round the class-room doorway, or be suddenly recognised among them in the Boulevard at recreation time. Even if one stood disgraced in the middle of the room, or sullenly with one's face to a tree while the others tore madly past, one was not afraid. Her vast pockets were inexhaustible and they held for all. Down went her two crinkled hands into their depths, to emerge with caramels and coloured biscuits . . . from the Virgin Mary, dear children, to give to you all . . . *le p'tit Jésus* begs you to divide them charitably. . . . He said He will not watch because He trusts you. . . .

"Only think, children, she will tell them all about you!" Sœur Damiana had said. Will she tell of me? And me? And me? And ME? "Of *all* of you—but not of those who continue crying," Sœur Damiana had answered, inwardly amazed at the immediate response she met with.

Well, she had arrived some time ago and had had plenty of time to talk. She was watching them now as they shuffled past in their Sunday clothes, not daring to look too closely or too long at the bed and keeping tight hold of their beads.

For all Heaven was watching them now. Sœur Damiana had said that when Sœur Marie-Joseph looked through the clouds she could see straight into their hearts, as clearly as though the top part was water and the heart was floating clear with writing on it. But she did not say who would bring them sweets again, and give them cakes and pictures when they fell ill. They no longer cried; but they were not comforted.

The older girls, more curious and more cold, passed deliberately through the cell, taking in as much of the details of decay as possible. She meant so much less to them. A smiling symbol; not to be feared and therefore not to be respected; someone who might one day, it was said, become a saint.

It was the outer aspect of death that was exciting. . . .

The new head nun, Sœur La Bienheureuse Imelda, stood in the corridor watching the procession's slow progress. Her dark, handsome face was taut and unsmiling, and appeared by a trick of shadow down the nose more forbidding than usual. Mona MacDowell, so soon to see it for the last time, stared in an ecstasy and told herself: "When I'm twenty-one I can do as I like, and then . . . then I'll come back and then she'll know. . . ."

Nearby Sœur Veronique and Sœur Angelique stood together smiling behind their hands. They seemed to have forgotten that Sœur Marie-Joseph lay dead a few yards from where they stood, in full view of the children, enjoying their joke. Now and again, as though recollecting themselves, their faces would reassume set, authoritative expressions, whereupon one of them would speak softly out of the corner of her mouth, and up would go their hands again, ineffectively concealing their merriment.

Straight as an arrow and as purposeful, Sœur Imelda kept her eyes on the procession, and gave no sign of having noticed their presence.

O utside it was ink black, and precisely flung pebbles of rain struck the window-panes in long, flinty darts. At intervals, flattening one's nose against the glass, one could see on the dark, flat, escaping earth, shadowy trees, low houses, and squares of yellow light; and one breathed *Home!* and *England!* because one had landed at Harwich two hours since, and because fourteen is the age at which one still breathes *Home!* and *England!* on returning home for the holidays. . . .

Heavy-hearted, the two friends sat arm-in-arm. They seemed to have said all that there was to say and still to have left so much unsaid.

"Won't it seem funny not to wear our black hats any more?"

"Won't it seem funny not to have to go to Chapel at seven every morning? And think of never walking in another procession and picking the rose leaves and mint off the ground before The Angel pounces on us!"

"O, The Angel wasn't so bad . . . considering . . . and under Sœur Veronique's thumb all the time, poor old thing. . . ."

" 'Spose she wasn't. I wouldn't like to be in her shoes for life."

"Nor me . . ." said Mavis, "didn't old Mona carry on when she left her Immy . . . and yet Immy wasn't so very nice to her, seeing how Mona had been keen on her for years and years . . . I told her so many a time, only she only wanted to claw my eyes out . . . she thought her Immy was a saint!"

"Mm . . . and I've seen Immy send her to bed without saying good-night to her night after night, for some silly thing like not being in time at the supper queue . . . and she knew that Mona would cry herself to sleep all right. . . ."

Black-hatted girls were rushing wildly about the corridor shouting their farewells. There was a medley of cries and shrieks, and handclasps and kisses, with everyone trying to appear just so much gayer than they felt.

"She'll have to look out for herself now . . . and serve her right . . ." mused Mavis.

"Who?"

"Immy, of course. Mona won't be there to adore . . . and she'll have The Angel and Nicky to reckon with, poor dear."

"D'you think it's true they didn't want her as head nun, and that Nicky wanted Sœur Mannes instead?"

" 'Spec'so. She hates Immy."

"So does The Angel."

"Yes, but she didn't before Nicky began it . . ." Mavis reminded her. "I wonder why Nicky suddenly turned nasty and got The Angel over on her side. . . ."

" 'Cos she couldn't get Immy there, I 'spect," said Joyce, nearer the truth than she suspected. That last, glacial, Tourelles interview pricked her into saying viciously, "I always hated Sœur Veronique . . . she's like an iceberg coming and nosing up to you. . . . She'd freeze a summer's day. . . ."

"Well, serve Immy right," repeated Mavis, as there rose up in her mind the memory of how two fine dark eyes could bring the blood into her cheeks as though they had been slapped. "She isn't God Almighty, though she may think she is. . . ."

The lights outside grew perceptibly stronger and brighter. The end was very near; and there were vows of eternal friendship between the handing down of bags and the adjustment of coat-buttons.

"D'you think your people'll let you come down and stay?" queried Joyce for the third time.

"You bet they will!" said Mavis with a conviction she was far from feeling. "Is Newcastle nice?"

"Ooo . . . it's the loveliest place in England . . . far nicer than your London, 'cept that you've got the Zoo, of course."

Which reminded Mavis. "Lord! I hope they won't start asking me the capitals of Europe before to-morrow, anyway."

She used 'they.' Not for worlds would she have betrayed that even now, within ten minutes of her arrival, she was ignorant as to who would meet her; or whether she would be met at all.

What would Joyce, kind, affectionate Joyce, think, Mavis asked herself bitterly, if she knew that she had even no idea with whom she was to spend her holidays? Her heart contracted at the thought that perhaps her whole life would be spent in the one long secret battle of guarding her 'difference' from the world.

Now was the moment for something memorable and earnest in the way of parting speeches; yet neither could think of anything adequate to the occasion. And time pressed hard.

Probably they would never meet again, though they refused to admit such a possibility. New sights, new friends, might separate them for ever. Now was the moment for tears; yet Mavis, so adept in the use of the right moment, found no tears, and few of the correct emotions.

" 'Spect I'll miss old Mavis," thought Joyce sullenly. But she also was surprised at finding no use for the nice clean handkerchief she had prepared for the occasion.

Suddenly, like a quick and irrevocable decision leaping to the mind, a diffused yellow light poured through the window, and the train slowed gently into Liverpool Street Station.

Feeling vaguely bruised, vaguely unhappy, they saw that the Great Moment was almost past, yet neither could muster the appropriate tear. "Get them to send you to Paris too," urged Mavis, "promise to study ever so hard if only they'll send you. . . . Here's your bag, darling. . . ."

And Joyce between kisses vowed: "You bet I will! Don't forget to write . . . and tell them Mother will *love* having you for Christmas. . . ." They moved through the carriage door on to the platform, clasping suitcases and coats.

"Why! there she is! . . ." shrieked Joyce, "look, *there's* mother . . ." and with a final "Don't forget you've *got* to come!" she tore down the platform towards a little bundle of a woman who held out two plump arms.

Joyce gone, Mavis said a few last good-byes.

Now, indeed, she felt alone; alone and unutterably miserable. She looked round but she saw no one; no one belonging to her. So they had not come. Of course, they must have forgotten the date. . . . Everyone seemed to be rushing madly at everyone else. Everywhere arms seemed to be outstretched and embracing. Good-bye, good-bye, good-bye; good-bye everything and everyone. What should she do? Who took charge of children left on platforms? She saw herself sitting all the night through in the dark, beside her trunk and suitcase.

But she must not cry. She must not show how frightened and humiliated she felt, and how bitter the tears tasted, caught up in a knot in her throat. Did they, the others, notice that she was alone? Of course they did. To gain time she bent down over her suitcase and became busy with a strap.

The pretence was becoming useless; she must have been playing with the strap for quite an hour. She heard no sound, she saw no light. The last taxi must have clattered away; the last train had left the station. And still no one came and asked her what she might be doing alone on a railway station platform after midnight.

She would brave it out. She must go to the station-master and tell him her story. Tell him that she was a schoolgirl home for the holidays and whom no one wanted.

She raised her head, and beside a luggage rack stood a tall, bearded man in an unusual felt hat and stubborn clothes, loose and aloof, staring down at the children; and as she caught sight of him her heart beat so quickly that it seemed to her to tremble.

Dear father! Dear, dear father! I shall love you all my life, now! For ever and for ever.

And suddenly she noticed, with no small surprise, that the platform was crowded with parents and children and piled luggage; and that people were still kissing and calling to each other and finding each other unexpectedly, and hailing cars and taxi-cabs. And the clock above the refreshment room said exactly ten minutes to eleven. Seven minutes only, then, had she been standing there!

He had not seen her; and feeling suddenly self-conscious and grown-up, she walked up to him and said: "Here I am, father!" and held up her face.

SPLEEN

and the elephant said to the flea: don't push.

G oats with long purple udders and sly drooping faces passed, trailing a strong smell of goat. She watched the woman take from her skirt a piece of bread, break a corner and give it to the child, a calm socratic child with stony eyes, and return to her business of bringing her stick down sharply across the undulating hindquarters of her goats, undulating slowly over the long Saracen road, their heavy purple udders swinging pendulously to the bleating of their neck-bells. Soon they would be far away, small dark pellets of their own dropping, the woman dwarfed to the size of the child, the child scarcely discernible, passing out under the archway to the town. As at a signal the bells of San Soccorso would give out a wild and shrill salute, rushing out on the air as a flight of famished gulls, scattering the evening mood in noise and restlessness. Six o'clock.

How well she knew it all. Morning and evening she had seen them pass, the same woman with angry pointed cries, the same stick, the same blows, possibly the same petticoats, the same children grown to grandchildren, the same goats perpetually renewing themselves, replaced, undulating, docile, the same purple udders, the same golden satyr-eye half-closed, the same acrid smell of goats passing; and twenty-two years had made it hardly more real to her than on the morning on which, leaning out on the ship's rail, her eyes set to the horizon, she had seen the island lying in glittering staccato relief on its sea-bed of plumed green, the crisp blue-green of early maize. She had looked down at the fishermen's boats come to fetch the passengers and their goods and had seen a vast tangle of heaving reeds under their covering of light sea, the marbled floor of the sea from which Foria rose, and it had seemed to her like the surprised dark suspicious stares at herself, at her wedding ring, at her sole companion the round young peasant woman from Piacenza carrying her baby, which she had endured these three weary days. And then back again and up at Foria, crowned by Mont' Epomana its tip still lost in the morning clouds, its colour-streaked waterfront heaped like the bright scrapings from an artist's palette. Journey's end and the angry cries of the Piacentina refusing in the name of the Blessed Virgin, protectress of all things helpless, to jump in a boat overstacked with wine barrels and melons, and not until the child had been taken from her, leaping full strength on to the feet of the water-seller who had been prying up her petticoats.

What would dear Stephen and Stephen's father and pouter-pigeon mamma and Dora with her pale protecting eyes, lovesick, and that sullen snub-nosed girl lost among the underhousemaids who had been rescued, and Barrett who so despised hesitating inefficient orders, and the interminable procession of other hired people at Sharvells which people such as Stephen and his pouter-pigeon mamma considered necessary to the well-being and upkeep of dear Stephen and pouter-pigeons, what would they say could they see her now sitting between the Piacentina and the garlic-thick melon merchant, shirt open to the waist and black energetic hair bristling thickly down his chest; her small patent leather feet, so correct, so refinedly helpless, looking out from under the heavy folds of the blue serge skirt of her travelling costume, ample, braided, the cape coming to her elbows covered with the very latest ornamentation in shining silk, heavy, solid, expensive; the hat a masterpiece of discretion, four brims of fine straw, laced and interlaced, escaping, recaptured, poised well forward on the brow and held there by coils of hair, an elegant misshapen mass of curls and puffs leaping forward and outward from behind the ears.

What would they say to her sitting among the wine barrels and the melons and the garlic-reeking unclean foreigners, her patent leather foot nudged at intervals by the melon-merchant with the naked bristling chest?

She has gone back, back to where she belongs. For the best. As I said at the beginning of this painful. I know. I know I should not say so, but I did say. And it is always a mistake to raise people from. The crimson satin walls of the dining-room and the vast curved window admitting one to the finest view in the county.

Ruth. Dearest Ruth. Dora's pale protecting eyes, lovesick. Do not let them make you unhappy.

Madam, Barrett says. Her heart dropped down into the tangle of weeds, but it was only the Piacentia assuring her charge that he was the most beautiful, beautiful.

Soft and caressing the blue air as she raised her head. She had felt all at once sick and so tired. In a few minutes the journey would be at an end, for ever. Never again to move from the niche which she had found for herself; nor answer questions.

She laid her fingers on the water as in a vaschetta d'acqua santa. It was warm. Of course, warm. Warm water, blue-shining water, radiant water, Italian water. Of course Italian water, for she was in Italy. At last and for ever, and only three days since she had sat in the waiting-room at Victoria and the boat train had seemed to be delayed for many hours only to crawl away for many hours more and no nearer France; and suddenly some-one was thrusting a brown face down into hers and shouting at her, menacing her with teeth strong, sharp and white as sea-foam.

—Sbarcate, sbarcate Signori! shrieked the face.

—Quant' è simpatica! nodded the admiring melon-merchant, staring at her delicate frightened face drooping beneath the weight of her four-brimmed hat and elegant mountain of hair. But the water-seller staring through the heavy expensive travelling costume, said he did not think she would be of much use, that meagre foreign type never was, and spat out something that put the men in an uproar and set the Piacentina's face on fire.

—Sbarcate, sbarcate Signori! shrieked the face again, and now thrust out a long gnarled branch of an arm and jerked her roughly to her feet. And Ruth who did not want this arm had found herself clinging to it despairingly. She was tired sick and giddy with sudden fear. How they had frightened her that first morning! The sudden rough jerking to her feet had come as a blow across the face. All that had been warm and blue had turned heavy and menacing. What would become of her she had wondered foolishly if she disobeyed? Beneath her the small boat swayed and beat the water, the hot intense sand blazed up in to her eyes as she stood swaying idiotically with the boat and clutching heavily at the neapolitan's arm, like some-one blind caught in a panicking crowd.

She had been aware of rows of brown faces and foaming teeth gathering on the jetty and hemming her in, leagued against her with this savage to whose arm she was hanging. If she moved she would step into the very midst of their shouts; then she must stay where she was for fear of treading on a grinning mouth with a voice shrieking out of it like an evil flame. The shouts grew louder. The neapolitan's face came down close to hers and out of the mouth came the shrill snapping of a thousand twigs about her ears. Quickly she pulled her head away, but held on, held on with her feet pressed tightly together and swaying to the nightmare rhythm of the boat. All at once a black spot dissolved and blotted out the other detached black spots and was standing by itself on the swaying sands calling to the face itself, and the face was calling back, beating the twigs about her head and eyes. The sky fell beneath her feet, a thick glittering canopy of sand swung above her head and with it mouths, dark heads, sounds, shook, dissolved, flashed by and swung back again and up and back again and up. Her eyes closed, drowning in heat and terror. She was swung up suddenly and the sands passed away beneath her and she was carried nearer to the detached blot. The sounds it made were quite different from the sounds she had been afraid to step on. They were soft, reassuring sounds; gentle, caressing sounds; restful as hands trailing in cold water. Cool, cool, cool, and kingcups, and cool beads of water on grass, lush, tangled grass, odorous earth-hair to lay a forehead on. Such had been her first and vague impression of Donna Lisetta, and in all the twenty-two years of her life on this strange dark-hearted island, it had remained and strengthened. The sound of the voice calmed the panic that possessed her, and she saw that the sands were passing away under her because the neapolitan was running across them with her in his arms, and out on to the stones of the little port where he placed her in a carriage with an awning and a tasselled horse. Placed her gently and with a smile, nodding; his teeth in his lean dark face showing strong, sharp and white as sea-foam.

Beside her on the empty seat they wanted to put the Piacentina and the baby. No. O no. She waved them away with a feeble hand. No. She looked around her helplessly as though making her way through a fog. She wanted the blot, the voice, the cool woman with the cool green voice that had calmed her panic.

This made no favourable impression on the italians. A young mother and waving away her own child? It could not be. The Piacentina and the baby were pressed forward again; actually her foot was on the carriage step. But again Ruth waved them feebly away; even going so far as to put out a weak hand and give a feathery brush which was meant to be a strong push to the Piacentina's shoulder, pushing her away, far away and out of sight and into the sea if necessary.

The Piacentina got down and looked with round astonished into round astonished eyes. They were saying something. They were going to start shouting again and beating her over the face and eyes with shrill crackling twigs. Her head rolled feebly on her neck; it was growing heavy again and out of control. She began to cry drearily, unable to control the hiccoughing of her sobs. She wanted to dissolve completely away in the tears pouring over her cheeks.

Here was a singular treat for the Forians. Not since Giachino's woman had run into the piazza with her head cracked from eye to jaw and the blood making a pool sufficient to bathe an infant in, had there been so much to gape at. Indeed there had never been so much. What more common, after all, than to see one of their womenfolk with slit jaws, or more rare than an elegant foreign lady, a lady of evident distinction and richly dressed, blubbering like a sick child under their hundred eyes? And the elegant foreign lady would have sat there all day and blubbered while they stood around and watched her, had not Lisetta rescued her again, climbing to the empty seat and taking charge of her head by resting it on her shoulder.

—E stanca, la poverina, said Donna Lisetta to the staring eyes. Stanca, that meant tired. The first word she had understood for so long. Yes, yes, yes. Si. I am tired. I am stanca, si. Stanca. I am tired. But she was safe. She wanted to tell them to put the Piacentina in a carriage too. But she couldn't. She hadn't the strength. And besides she no longer cared. Let her find one for herself. Or let her walk.

They swung round and up a narrow side street, out on the miniature tree-bordered piazza, through more narrow streets and more turnings, under a crumbling fern-covered archway and out on the long straight road leading away from the town. She had seen nothing but the hot powdery road rolling away beneath her, and that imperfectly and through a mist. The unaccustomed heat, the yellow glare, the dust, were as a blanket held gently but persistently over her face and head. She submitted to it and fell soundly asleep on Donna Lisetta's strong black-silk bosom.

They carried her to her room and left her sleeping. They hesitated to leave her, the three women who had seen to her undressing. Looking down at the pale soft face on its pillow of coarse hand-woven linen they felt her to be altogether too fragile, too docile, and entirely helpless. But they were quite wrong. For all her endearing gentle appearance she was not a little mad, quite capable, and very determined.

A thin howl, drawn out and ending abruptly in a shriek, startled the air. The evening steamer from Naples came round the bend of the porto, conveying its awareness of its importance in the evening life of the island; all the very blue water to itself. It was always the first to break up the evening peace getting in its noise before San Soccorso which had to wait the hour but scored in a ten-minute vengeful display of farmyard cackling.

There was a sudden kindling of movement on the goat road; road which, legacy of Saracen conquerors twelve hundred years since, the Forian traitors to this early blood ridiculously called Via dei Angeli. Absurd as the crosses and campanili attached to the humped and tiled mosques and remnant walls of pagan temples scattered in profusion over the island.

The road was busy at this hour. Human caryatids moved over it, crested, placing their feet swiftly and surely in a nereid-swing of the hips, their long dark petticoats beating about their ankles. Monumental, eternal, these women as they swung past with rhythmic tread, the red clay jars motionless on their firm heads. In single file whole families moved along, graded from the tallest in front to the one not more than five years old, her miniature jar tilted perilously on her little head but more often hugged safely in her arms. The women's hour.

When the boat has passed on to Castoli its next stop on the island, the road would be broken-up in a clattering of hoofs, in the ai ah ahs of raucous donkey boys, blows, angry sounds, the thudding of bare feet, cart wheels grinding, the crack of swirling whips. Men and boys returning from the port with barrels of wine and oil, the huge piled baskets of scarlet tomatoes, the ice in the long plaited sacks which they plaited themselves and sold in Naples. Dark and wiry, they ran shouting about the road beside their beasts, beating them, cursing them, urging them, leaping ahead and leaping back again, as though they were the last of a victorious army homing in triumph with their loot of conqueror's gold. And they did this morning and evening with the same unquenchable vitality and noise, the arrival of the Naples boat transforming them from dark silent effaced creatures into this torrential outpouring of masculine energy, ravaging them, driving them angrily unsparingly as they drove their beasts.

But the crested women with nereid-swinging hips moved in their slow-measured step, monumental, eternal. They were going to the wells and fountains of the town to fetch water. In the morning before the sun was at its height and in the evening when it was spent, they moved over the Saracen road to fetch the water, evenly, calmly. Unlike the men it evoked in them no sense of triumph so that they brought no battle-fever, no heroics, no mock-splendour to the doing of an everyday task. So much the worse for them, she had always thought. For their reward their half-hour of shrill clatter at the well, water-jars swung to their head cushions, and back again, nereid-swinging, calm, eternal, empty and joyless.

She too could carry a water jar on her head, the fine english signora; though having found that it was not as difficult as she had supposed she had long ceased doing it. Secretly she had lowered herself in their esteem; though not secretly for she knew it well enough and who, after all?, can keep respect for twenty-two years because of an arrival in an elegant travelling costume with braided cape and exquisite pointed shoes. Too much mystery for respect, thought the islanders. No letters. No visits. No family, then. Ah-ah these cold foreign women who look one steadily in the face and make no distinction in their talk. Men in petticoats, poor godless creatures. But Ruth had found her niche and was never again to explain herself away to anyone but herself, and had even ceased to do that for a very long time now.

Strange that in twenty-two years her environment and existence should have become scarcely more real to her. But she had never belonged, although at first young, eager, she had tried. She waited. She seemed to be resting there; a stage on a journey she was not conscious of desiring to complete. Ruth herself was unable to understand how, entering as she did into the heart of the place and its people, she was yet unable to make them hers. Her days had passed in caryatid calm, empty, joyless, undeviating, as she had willed. For always she was fair. She never forgot it was of her own choosing. That she had thrust herself on them, had insisted on their having her, years before foreigners were heard of on the island.

Now of course they were fairly common. The Naples passenger boat that once had called weekly, now called twice a day, and on Sundays there were crowded excursion boats bringing the neapolitans to bathe and picnic. White stark hotels were being conjured up, and the townspeople let rooms all through the summer and autumn months and were growing rich and impudent on it. In Naples one day she had been startled by the sight of a large garish poster in a Tourist Agency window. Foria had been promoted to Agency patronage. Entering she was supplied with an illustrated booklet and dates and times and guide services. True, Foria had no Blue Grotto as had its prosperous neighbour, but it had been no less the pleasure ground of Rome's wealthy and notorious; and Horace himself gazing out from the Bay of Baia (at the island said the booklet) had proclaimed it the loveliest sight in the world. The Agency now having cast a belated eye in the same direction seemed grateful to Horace for this remark; it received an entire page to itself.

On her way home, waiting at Baia for the steamer, she had searched the horizon for Foria, yet although the evening was of that limpid vibrating kind in which one reaches out a hand to touch objects many miles distant, and although she could see plainly the menacing twin humps of Capri and the rounded Procida, she could not see the particular island which, in the Agency booklet, Horace had had in mind when praising the loveliness of the Bay. Unless his eyesight was finer than mine, she reflected, which I doubt. All of which meant that the island was attracting the attention of the mainland, and that the attention of the mainland as the stark white hotels showed, was worth attracting.

But Ruth knew a time when children ran behind their mothers' skirts at the sight of her, and could not be coaxed away until she had passed. And she had liked it enormously the fierce shyness of the children and the morose savage shyness of their elders. Silent indifferent dark-hearted people. At first (she could now laugh at that early fear) they had seemed altogether sinister and hostile to her. It was so unlike anything she had ever known and herself so very much in their power. But she had liked their self-contained impertinence, their complete absence or understanding of respect or deference. Once beyond her first and physical fear of them she had liked at once these people who rarely talked. At first she had thought they sat about silently because, not being able to understand them, it was useless to address her. But not a bit of it. They spoke rarely because they had rarely a desire to speak. And Ruth coming from a world where talk if not spontaneous must be induced and where the larynx was the most productive part of the human body, loved and marvelled at these people for their silences. Twenty-two years remained an unreality; but she had been grateful for the silence. She was her sole companion. I am, she quoted Donne, the self-consumer of my woes; and was glad that her years had not been spent in the wetting of other people's shoulders in attitudes of varying despair.

Not a little mad and very determined the englishwoman who was never seen to handle her own child, but gave it to others to wash and feed and showed distaste when they caressed it. The Piacentina left a week after their arrival, and besides her wages Ruth gave her more than half her wardrobe; all the pretty elegant clothes her purple-dark italian eyes coveted. I do not need them, she said, indifferent, when the girl hesitated. I shall wear what Donna Lisetta wears. But the silly girl, seizing both her hands and covering them with kisses, persisted in treating it as a sacrifice and behaved much as the beggar must have behaved on getting Saint Martin's shift. And ever since she had worn the accepted peasant dress of the island, the dark sprigged apron, the dark tucked blouse, the long dark petticoat. She wore no stockings even in winter when the Graecale swept cold and clear over the Bay; she disliked zoccoli for their dreadful clap-clapping on the stone floors, and wore instead light low-heeled shoes sent especially from Naples. She cut off her elegant mountain of hair to the neck where without effort from her part, fortunately, for she had no intention of making such effort, the ends curled up and made her look more fragile more docile than ever. A little novice, said Lisetta, watching the rigid rejection of all clothes and elegances associated with her former life; and a little angel she added when Ruth's shorn tails of hair curled like altar candles in June. Not until her early thirties did Ruth let her hair grow again and make a twist of it in the nape of her neck as the other women.

From the start Donna Lisetta accepted her new lodger without question and was immensely proud of her. She accepted also the bundle of white clothes that rarely cried and remained motionless for hours on end.

S ome-one was calling her. She answered through cupped hands winging her voice like a planing bird. Graziella, Lisetta's eldest daughter, carrying a plate of grapes came through the doors leading to the veranda alcove where Ruth lay prolonging the afternoon siesta into the early evening. Was she going to the town? asked Graziella. She was not. Because I am, and la *mamma* says I am to ask if there is anything you want there. Only the day's papers and more of that red wool for Concetta's new jersey.

At the mention of Concetta's new jersey Graziella tightened her lips and stared sideways down at the grapes. What a monkey childishness! Ruth looking at her knew very well what that grimace was intended to convey. Here was Graziella, a new bride and well into the fifth month of her first child, screwing up her face because Concetta, her fourteen-years-old sister, was to have a new jersey knitted for her by the Signora, and not only a new jersey, bitterly, but a red one. Stupid and ridiculous creature! But a splendid thing from the polished obsidian head on the strong neck set well back and emphasised through years of water carrying to the narrow naked feet, dusty and just now none too clean. Pomona sulking, Artemis tamed and fertile in the name of the Father, Son, and Holy Ghost.

—When I go to Naples on Thursday, Graziella, said Ruth slowly as one enunciates to a stubborn child, I shall bring you back a thick coat, long, with a good warm collar, because it will be cold very soon and we must see that you are kept warm and happy now. (Why was she always going out of her way like this to propitiate these childish dark-hearted people to whom she was less than nothing, and must go on for ever being less than nothing no matter what she did, because the only tie they understood, the blood-tie, was not there?)

Immediate smiles, stammers, ecstatic gratitude, and the Blessed Virgin invoked and thanked personally, dear protectress of all things small. But. But. How should she say it? The Signora must not think her ungrateful. The Signora must not think she could refuse so great and desirable a gift. But. But. You do not want a coat? O yes. Indeed yes, Graziella wanted a coat; wanted a coat more than anything in the world except. Except? Except a silver offering Signora? Afterwards? Perhaps Signora? O, the offering! But you will get that in any case. Surely (gently), you knew that, Graziella? (Of course she knew it, confirmed that Madonna-monkey look that creeps slyly into such eyes in un-guarded moments.) That would be seen to in Naples as well, but later much later. More smiles, more stammers, more gratitude to the Blessed Virgin and herself sitting jointly hand in hand; and Ruth was left to her evening solitude again.

Three years after she came to the island she had placed a silver plaque for Graziella, a smiling cherub head addressed and dated, in the Church of Monte Vergine to thank the mountain goddess for Lisetta's safe delivery; and another for Concetta when her turn came. How grateful Lisetta had been! for she was on the point of offering up her best white coral earrings which, returning them hastily to their little box, the Virgin could not have liked nearly as much. For now both Graziella and Concetta were represented in Heaven by images such as old Celestino with the engraved silver heart which he had offered up thirty years ago for the cure of his left arm (hearts being nearly five lire cheaper than arms) and which he had never ceased to boast about, could bite his fingers at.

And already it was Graziella's turn. A sense of pleased wonder came over Ruth as she took in the import of this thing which she had known from the start and but now realised. She anticipated her next trip to Naples; saw herself once again chosing, suggesting, harassing the silversmith with requests for a doric simplicity whilst fingering the most choice examples of his perplexed and tortuous baroque. Dear strange adopted people! After all she had made them hers, and she liked them the better for never completely accepting her.

She leaned forward to watch Graziella below pass swiftly sinuously between the vines. Already the rise under her sprigged cotton apron was well-defined. Balanced against the rigid set of the girl's smooth head it seemed to urge her forward in a victorious sweep, as though she continually pushed aside an invisible obstacle and the conquered path unwound itself before her proud feet.

L eaning forward to watch her from sight Ruth thought: where she treads flowers should spring. And she waited a little breathlessly for the earth to respond, to give a sign, to welcome fecundity as Ceres passed. To break up gladly in a ribbon of buttercups. Set a thousand birds to sing. Leave a primrose in each footprint. Instinctively she still turned to meadow-flowers and grass in this grass-parched birdless land. But Ceres passed with her hot dusty feet unheralded, between the dusty vines, along the hot dusty road, a small grey cloud of dust pursuing her heels to the town.

—Yet there should be flowers! she thought foolishly, almost passionately, as though the earth had nothing more urgent to do than break in coloured flames around the feet of pregnant young females off to gossip at the public fountains. Yet not so foolish seeing that it had done so once. Once when Botticelli's miraculously burdened women had passed the earth had answered and caressed their narrow feet. Once, but not again. Not that one believed; not that for a moment one believed that Sandro's Graces could produce anything more real than doves, or singing birds, or cherub heads for the rapturous upholding of celestial feet. Or that his Spring winging divinely across canvas had done more than break in the load of flowers her long fingers were scattering.

Not that one believed, but that one wanted to believe. The hand turning the pages of her book trembled. She ought not to let her mind pursue the subject; and she knew by her quickened heart-beats that it was now too late to withdraw again into her trained impersonality.

Graziella was not afraid; not in the least afraid. These women knew no fear. At most a faint superstitious dread that after its birth the child might be taken from them to live in Paradise, the little innocent. But who would grudge, as she had once been horrified to hear Padre Antonio explain, who would grudge Our Lady such a gift: She whose mother-heart had been left torn and bleeding?

And scarcely any pain at all. Like the gypsy or nomad women kneel-ing behind a hedge, exerting themselves, picking it up, wrapping it round, and starting after the caravans moving unconcernedly away. Nothing at all. One day she would return from the beach or from the town with the day's papers, and Lisetta would run out to her with a face of beatitude announcing that Graziella had been delivered of whatever she had had to deliver, and Graziella, completed, would be sitting up in bed, the sweat still on her smiling face, accepting the cup of zabaglione and the figs, and the next day she would be up and about, singing to her infant, feeding it, washing it, ravished with delight in it, and binding it in the mummy-bands of a della Robbia holy child until only its face, surprised and formless, was visible. And from first to last no fear, no despair, no mental torture. Nothing that was known to colder northern women, over-civilised, over-sensitised, bearing their children in an agony of pain and bewilderment.

Her lips quivered uncontrollably. To steady herself she leaned against the pillows of her chair and stared over the blue shining water of the Bay to where, on the horizon, the evening sky prepared for an Ascension. Only to find the tears pouring down her cheeks and that she was crying silently. Who hadn't cried for so many years now! All the tumult and frustration hidden for so long in the background of her mind, denied, ignored, refused a hearing, lain suppressed and fermenting, seemed to be pouring out over her face as she stared at the piled clouds coming up over the edge of the Bay. How unprepared, how defenceless she felt before the suddenness of the attack!

Was it possible that because a girl with her apron jutting out in front of her passed through a vineyard, twenty-two years must melt away like a pear-drop on a child's tongue?

Plaintively and helplessly impatient her voice came to her again over the years. *But you see I do not care for men, Dora. I do not care for women. Why can one not have something else, something different, something new, something more worth having if one has to go through all this?*

She said it to Dora because she knew of no one else who would even try to understand, and because Dora loved her and being a woman could not dismiss and pooh-pooh-my-dear everything she said as the natural hysteria and lack of mental balance usual in pregnant women. Not that she was altogether fond of such dog-like devotion. Ruth liked clear decisive people. But talking to Dora was like talking aloud; and she had never talked to Stephen who was so evidently proud of her just now.

One morning on opening her eyes she was awake as though she had not slept; and she knew instantly, as though she had said her thoughts aloud, that there was but one person in the whole house to whom she wanted to speak or listen, and that this was the sullen snub-nosed girl lost among the underhousemaids, who had been rescued and had now had more than a year in which to be grateful to little Mrs Philmore the vicar's earthly comfort, creator and organiser of the local Ladies Needlework Guild with its many divisions, subdivisions, charitable activities and interferences. Sarah. Sarah Minchin. She wanted to talk with Sarah Minchin. But it was obvious that Ruth being who she was and Sarah being what she was, not even the morbid desires of pregnancy could make it possible for them to meet as equals. Apart from the tongue-tied embarrassment Sarah would experience if her lady who was not such a very real lady at all if only poor Sarah knew, plucking with young anxious fingers at the embroideries on her dressing-gown should say: Tell me, Sarah, is it true that you tried to kill yourself? You were frightened? You were angry? Tell me, Sarah. Because I too am frightened. I too am angry. Do other women feel about this as I feel?

To which Sarah had she not been well-versed in the abject and resentful deference of her class, apart from the tongue-tied inexpressiveness that sat upon her in a perpetual sulk, might have said many bitter and salutary things on the ease of protected motherhood. Even so the disgraced and retrieved Sarah could have said nothing which in her heart Ruth did not know, or had not recapitulated many times to self-aggravate her misery and confusion. Why am I not thankful? Why, why should I mind? I have always liked children; and children have always liked me. But she did mind; and the incredible thing was that it sometimes seemed to her that something outside herself minded even more than she did.

At first she could not believe it even though her face had that momentarily pinched grey look which is the first outward sign of pregnancy, and morning nausea was frequent. But when there could be no possible doubt as to what was the matter with her, Ruth was shocked, herself, at the horror that came over her. Why? Why should I mind? There was no answer. She was like a woman possessed. She was a woman possessed; and she was horrified at the possession of herself by this thing she neither understood nor desired. And yet in her despair her rational self could stand aside bewildered and appalled by the horror that possessed her; as though a part of her were trying to remain aloof and sane in the midst of acting a nightmare.

Perhaps it was the indelicacy of noticing such things that kept
Stephen from seeing her as anything but grey-faced and preoccupied,
which would take its course; but for all the cunning of her heightened
sensibilities to protect herself, Ruth could not protect herself from
Dora; and yet Dora who loved her and as a woman should have tried to
understand, was not a little shocked at what she guessed and almost
surprised. For Dora was one of those women who for all their contempt of men and marriage are passionately fond of children and would
make splendid mothers were there any known means of making them
such. Yet more shocked than hurt, so awful was it to her to see her
idolised Ruth's strained and frightened face, and to surprise her with
eyes red from secret crying. Who would have suspected, thought the
anxious Dora, that all this lay buried under Ruth's gentle detachment,
under the dear eagerness which one could not help loving her for, and
instantly. And all for something which should have glorified her and
which Dora had always imagined she would accept calmly and gladly,
and not with revulsion and a face like a tragic mask, except for the
mouth which was contracted and nervous.

The unhappy Dora watching her move restlessly about the room
misunderstood it all completely.

—Dearest you must not believe it as unpleasant as is supposed. The
pain is over very soon. And they say that afterwards women forget their
pain no matter how intense it has been at the time. That is nature's
compensation.

—Pain? echoed Ruth startled, standing quite still and looking at her
with a stupid dazed look on her pale face. Pain? But I have no fear of
pain, Dora. Not pain. Why should you say that?

Which saved her from explaining, for what is there to explain to one
who thought of birth in terms of physical pain?, that were her child
presented to her in her sleep, as it were, painless, immediate, she still
would not want it. And that that was exactly the reason of her fear: that
she did not want her child. Dora she knew would have done her best to
say what was becoming to the occasion. This was a phase which must
pass. Many women must say much the same thing faced with the
coming of their first child. At which she could have cried for infinite
relief. Only to know that the answer to that is: until the child comes,
and then the mother loves it. She must. It is nature.

Then she was wise to keep her thoughts to herself; for in her case it
did not seem to be nature, even though to persuade herself she would
repeat, the water-drop wearing away the stone: when it comes. Lame

comfort. She knew otherwise. She was not of those who can question and answer to their advantage. Nor fearing the answer could she refrain from questioning. At night how plausible they became these inner pleadings by which she explained and condoned herself to herself, to her immediate surroundings. But as each new day which was to herald and accept the decisions of the night became but a restless wait for a return to the sheltering isolation of the night, back to the tortuous self-persuasion which the day would have nothing of, she seemed to herself the evil queen of the tales of her childhood returning at midnight to her witchcraft.

For how can one love a thing one does not desire? Perhaps because it is usual to love one's child. Then I am not usual. (How easy to accept this in the darkness of the night when the unreal becomes the obvious!) Because she knew that not wanting the child now she would not want it later. She knew it was not possible to her to love a thing she did not know or had not seen. How can one? Yet I am expected to. All women do. I am a woman. Therefore I do. And if I do not? (And at a movement real or imaginary within her.) When I breathe, it breathes. When I feed, it feeds also. Against my will. Yet when it had finished using her for its own purpose, she must welcome it and say that it was hers and that therefore she loved it (all women do) at once and without question. When it had had nothing to do with her from start to finish.

— Yet creation, Ruth, is a wonderful thing, had said Dora yesterday, hoping, looking vaguely helpful and helpfully vague.

— Is it? she questioned of the darkness, although at the time she had smiled submissively enough to please, for she knew better than to trust her secret perplexities to friendly but unfollowing minds. Is it? Do you believe that? Or are you repeating what we have all been taught and taught not to question. (After all, considered Ruth not without bitterness, what had been her friends' efforts to comfort her? It is a phase. It is nature. It is a wonderful thing.)

But I want to know what is the use of it all. Can you not try to understand me, Dora? She did not want the stories that calm frightened children. She wanted to know why the child is frightened. To what purpose: to what end? Why do I alone not feel this need? Why do I question where others accept? Why should I shrink from what others welcome? At first in her first terror of herself she had answered: because I am wicked; because I am sinful. But that got one no further than Dora's remarks, and was even more childish.

Perhaps could they see into my heart they would be more afraid even than I am. What to them is such a wonderful thing is to me fuss and ugliness. Ugliness, she thought, refusing to take back the word. And meaningless, too, and dull and hopeless. And knowing that, I am afraid. And they know that I am afraid, and they cannot answer me, but float up to gaze at me, like goldfish in a bowl. (A goldfish, she thought, whose pale evaporating eyes were meant to stare through fishy water and come to the rim of the bowl for a long aching look.) All women do. I am a woman. Therefore I must. To what purpose? If I dared ask them that! It will be like Stephen. And what will be the use of that? Or it will be like me. And what will be the use of that? But I am not to ask the reason because women have ignored the question, smiled, turned aside and talked of love. She tried and could not. Perhaps because she had known too little about love; so that she had no such consolation. (There was no bitterness in the thought. She had known it from the moment they had sent for her after the weeks of separation and she had seen his dear wasted face trying to convey his recognition of her as she had stared down at his bush of snowy beard. Turned all white of a morning, said the bony creature privileged to watch over him, still amazed and incredulous. Why was I not told? cried Ruth, cheated of a part of him.) It must be that she had no maternal sense. None whatsoever. And they regard me as something unnatural and not sane, and they may be right. A woman is expected to have a maternal sense as she is expected to have other womanly attributes. Had I been born blind or deaf they would not expect me to see or hear; that they could understand. A boy is born. Or a girl. A boy. A girl. And you know before hand every possibility of its life, and like a litany the answer is unalterable and as assured. Birth. Adolescence. Marriage. Birth. Old Age. Death.

She paused as though to make sure that it was she who had formed the words: then in the silence she repeated them. Birth. Adolescence. Marriage. Birth. Old Age. Death. That then was their wonderful thing! One had but to wait, one's mind in revolt against one's body, knowing the end and fearing it, and then because it is called nature and because one is told that one must because everyone does, one is to accept blindly what one has resented actively every moment of every day for weeks and months.

She saw it more clearly now, their wonderful thing. Some sudden turning her groping mole-mind had taken and there it was, clear as the daylight that must break upon the room when the great curtains were swung back on their heavy ropes. But the discovery, like the daylight, proved more revealing than comforting. For how does one accept the inevitable?

Because a reason had to be found for the sudden and bewildering revulsion which had taken possession of her like some deadly disease, a form of emotional galloping consumption that ravished her physically and mentally, she remembered the story her father had told her in the heavy brown workroom, untidy, serious, personal, dusty with books and smoke, worked-footstools and large humped chairs with the stuffing falling out of them, and the vast carved oak table heaped with examination papers, textbooks, blue copybooks with names sprawled over them in young difficult boyish handwriting. That had been her first emotional experience of real consequence, but she had shared it with her father whom she loved; and this time she bore it alone and it was nearer and more real to her than anything had ever been or, she felt, could be again.

It was considerable part of the solution. One is not suddenly trans-formed from a negatively peaceful person into a restless fury without cause; and as though to make amends for the pain she was causing her these days, she said it to Dora one afternoon as they sat together gazing out at tulip beds arranged with stiff and formidable precision and colour-graded with monotonous regard for formal landscape harmony, and none whatever for Spring itself.

—My mother, dearest, never wanted me. She found herself saying it without difficulty or shame, talking rather as people talk in their sleep but fully conscious of what they are saying, and prepared to argue it.

Never wanted her! No, and not only had not wanted her but had dreaded the very thought of her and had tried to end it all and could not and with the shock had died and she had been born barely at her seventh month. My father suffered most. It was he who had told her about it, which was brave of him for she need not have known. As the mere thought of him could set her pulse dancing, she smiled as she spoke.

Dora's face was set and unsmiling. What then would she think of me, wondered Ruth keeping her eyes on the formal travesty of Spring, who can find no reason? She had had such good cause to dread the coming of her child. (How one must beg the world's pardon with adequate reasons!) A very sound reason, not a wild intangible reason such as mine, but one real to her and terrible. (Or merely obvious?)

—You see, said Ruth slowly, my mother. My mother was not married to my father. Perhaps that, hazarded Ruth.

(But she said nothing of the handsome girl in the sombre grey fishing village near Portloe, strong-breasted, determined, a large enamel brooch at her throat, and narrow intense eyes that stared from the faded photograph in the carved frame above her father's desk, and made her small daughter's heart beat wildly each time she opened the door and watched them follow her across the room.)

Not that Dora wanted to hear more. She understood that after all these years she had overheard Ruth's secret. The secret of that bearded Jovian headmaster of that novel preparatory school in Hampshire, the widower with an only daughter. Overheard because inexplicably she felt it had not been meant for her, that she should not have been listening. She had been eavesdropping outside a confessional box. She had been listening to a sick person's delirium and some startling thing had been said quite mildly, as though the patient were asking for beef-tea, very weak. You see my mother was not married to my father. Gently: O you did not know that? No, not another cup thank you. Dear, dear beloved Ruth.

—What difference could that make to me? asked Dora loyally.

—But it may make a considerable difference to me, thought Ruth despairingly.

I think, Stephen, said Ruth. I think I carry my womb in my forehead.
—I quite definitely feel it here, pursued Ruth, drawing her brows sharply together and staring across at her husband perplexedly. Whereas I do not feel it here at all (and her hand touched her body). So that if you came and told me that all the time it is growing in my head I should not be in the least surprised. Not in the least. I should say: yes. How strange. I thought so too!

Some there are, she quoted to Dora, whose souls are more pregnant than their bodies. No. Socrates. And no one has ever thought of applying it to women. Why? Because the soul Dora is man's prerogative, and woman is but the eternal oven in which to bake the eternal bun. Nature's oven for nature's bun. Hundreds of thousands of buns daily in a variety of colours and only two shapes. All produced for one relentless purpose. Birth. Adolescence. Marriage. Birth. Old Age. Death.

—I think, said Ruth as she had said earlier in the day to Stephen. I think I carry my womb in my forehead. And I think that that, perhaps, is my curse.

But in her heart she refused to regard it as a curse. Alone, nothing could be more natural than her attitude. She was growing larger now, but that, as she had said about pain, meant nothing to her. She seemed unable to notice it. The pinched early look had left her very soon. For all her despair and resentment she could not prevent the warm peach-bloom of her cheek nor that look of physical radiance peculiar to women who are first loved, which nature insists on in her patients after the first few anxious weeks.

If she was in no way reconciled at least she was no longer afraid. Even at its strongest her fear had been but the temporary expression of her revulsion. Fear, for all that may be claimed for it, is more often cowardice; and in that direction at least she did not err. She had an abundance of courage both mental and physical, and a courage of a sort unusual in woman in that she accepted nothing but that which her mind had tested. She was no longer afraid, nor angry, nor bitter, but she was still in revolt and revolted (for how does one accept the inevitable?) and at times exasperated almost to frenzy by the purposelessness of it all. At first the more she had thought about it the less purpose she could find in it; and now understanding the purpose she could see no reason for it. Then back to the tragi-comedy of the squirrel cage. They won't bake buns? Let them bake cakes. And should they not want to bake even cakes? And not only not want, but refuse? If something outside one refuses: something one cannot control because one cannot fathom? Darkness. But nothing physical. Nor pain nor even death. Futility, perhaps.

One thing she would not, she could not accept: that women went through it all without question; were creatures possessed and content to have no say in the matter. Her mind centred more and more around the thought of what women could have done had they brought conscious thought to bear on what had always been dismissed as a pre-ordained and unalterable task. She found herself believing that had it been left to men centuries of creation would have produced some thing more vital, more exciting. But then men were the active and not the passive instruments of nature. Men questioned. Not from woman that despairing cry: my God what am I in Thy universe? To answer which sails unfurled, wings of birds and angels yielded their secret, the earth rose and parted, was weighed, sifted, spanned from the immensities of its roof to the treacheries of its floor, the moon stuffed in the pocket, the whole held negligently in the hollow of a hand. Man returning the apple to woman who first bade him eat of it; and woman (enclosed in her world within herself) humouring him, placing it carefully out of reach on the mantelpiece above the hearth which was her contribution to the whole, together with the tranquillity, the amorous fidelity, the kind sentimental cruelties necessary to its maintenance and security.

She suggested as much to Dora.

—This, said Dora, still patient, still trying to put some sense into her, this is what woman is made for. After all, said Dora.

—Was made for, corrected Ruth. Was made for.

And in that sentence sprung to defend her as it were from Dora's moral certainties—in that disconcerting way surface sentences have of proving discoveries, releasing their trap-doors at the back of the mind through which the speaker hurtles in the act of murmuring something detached and pleasing (knows that she has lost or won, will leave and nor return, and stay because life is not taken up again after such an interval and there are the children, or will leave that very night and cheat with memories the final loneliness in which all things die, or retreat, or advance, or surrender) she knew that she was no longer alone. Was made for, she had said, more to contradict than to affirm: a sullen child's last word; and had fallen on the discovery that she was not the only woman to feel about her child as she felt. Or rather that it is not only a few unnatural and unbalanced women who feel as I feel. That is not true. They like pretending that all women are born mothers. They like pretending that because women have to be mothers, born or not. That supplies their apology; feeds the conceit that man is an individual and oblivion an illusion; satisfies the weakling's need to have been spawned by divine command and ultimately entitled to equal heritage of a flowering and boundless Paternal estate. And so they pretend that only a few strange and unnatural women have denied this truth to themselves. But that is not true. She knew that now. There had always been and there would always be many such perplexed uneasy creatures, unsure, hesitating, bearing maternity with an ill grace and as something strange and outside themselves. Only their opinion was never asked or heeded. And it all began, thought Ruth idiotically, it all began when we gave up eating grass.

S he was none the less convinced that she was being cheated; was being made use of against her will; was being hourly thwarted. She had the illusion that all these mental questionings, the denials, the whys and wherefores, bitterness and revulsions in which she had been caught since its inception, and with which she had been solely and persistently concerned, had arrested the action of her body; as though this thing was not to be until a satisfactory reason could be found for its being and for her wilfulness in denying it life; as though gestation was suspended until she had prepared herself to accept its consequences.

If mentally she was calmer it was because it is psychically impossible for any emotion, no matter of what intensity, to be maintained at boiling pitch for more than a relatively short period of time. In one torrential outpouring, as it were, the emotional lava overflows and subsides within itself again. Surprised, chagrined, no mountainous upheaval commemorates the event, but a mild stewpot simmer ludicrously out of proportion to the promise of its early wrath! Ruth had, however, the very definite physical sensation of having been badly bruised. So much so that often on turning her head quickly or lifting an arm or moving a foot she felt a pain shoot through her, sharp enough to bring tears to her eyes.

And then one day in her morning bath she noticed for the first time how large she had become. She couldn't believe it. Impossible! Yet it must be true for the water refused to cover her. She lay flat. And still the water refused to cover her. She sat up. Useless. She lay down again. She turned on this side. On that. She lay back flat again, resting her head against the edge of the bath, contemplating; and had to admit. Had to admit. That it was not happening in her forehead at all, but was happening very much where it was meant to happen. That while she had been angry and despairing it was growing. It was becoming. It was happening. The eternal bun was baking in the eternal oven. And all her anger and despair had meant less than nothing to it. All her revulsion had had no effect. For answer a heavy white bubble of a tightly stretched stomach and water below lap-lapping round its sides. She put up a wet hand to her eyes.

But the tears came again, insisted on coming. On an impulse she leaned forward and made them fall in large warm drops on her heavy white bubble of a tightly stretched stomach which the water refused to cover. They fell one by one, quite large and warm, ran down the sides in smooth even rills and were lost in the water lap-lapping below. A baptism. A dirge. A funeral dirge over the unborn. Your burial service, said Ruth, wept fifty years too soon. A white bubble of a coffin and tears dropping on it like earth.

For what seemed a long time she lay back, her head against the rim of the bath, contemplating herself, and seemingly unaware that the water was becoming uncomfortably tepid and that with the cold her skin was showing drawn and mottled. Except for a quick unconscious shiver now and again, she lay without moving and with her eyes half closed, her face taking on the intense abstracted look of a sleepwalker, for she was unaware either of herself or her surroundings. She was aware only of the sudden and appalling change which had come over her and left her numb. Conversion, even a mild and imperfect conversion, is an ordeal; but when it is swift and sudden and complete, when, as it were, there is no mistaking the voice that calls from bells and blossoming apple boughs, or when, again, in the dark forest the hunted stag turns on the hunter and reveals the crucifix upheld between its antlers, it is such a complete and shocking disintegration of the human soul that few, fortunately, are called upon in a lifetime to endure it more than once. Ruth read her message in the lap-lapping of the water that seemed so far away and in the tightly stretched bubble of a stomach that still seemed to her unreal and not her own; and she understood that the search was ended. An answer had been found to her questioning. Something different, said the message. Something worth having. Something beyond and above it all, said the message. Something new.

And now after the dreary perplexity of the past months, the listlessness, the morose staring, there was an unreal and luminous quality about her as though she were possessed of an abundant and inexhaustible fount of serenity of which she alone knew the source. She was transformed; she was radiant. She was excited and very happy.

So it was true that if one asked one received. If one questioned one was answered. Woman was a witch filled with a great and terrible power over mankind. The power of life, of creation, of death. How puny then the thunder of man! Jove's toy squibs. Vulcan's toy swords. Woman's thunderbolt. Miniature gods with life and death in their hands for the dealing. Hebes. Cup-bearers of gods. Chalices in which gods were renewed and born again. And they did not know it. They denied their terrible power because they ignored it. But she was going to use her power. If I am to create, she told the eager creature in her mirror, I will create. Only of course something new. Something different. Something beyond and above it all. Something worth having. She seemed to wing across floors and paths leaving no footprints. Her face wore a smile happy and continuous and if those at whom she smiled doubted at moments that she saw them they were not altogether wrong. She saw them but she seldom noticed them.

Dr Mason may have been a very old man indeed, as she believed, but he had a certain store of wisdom and accumulated facts. True, medically it was one of the most interesting manifestations of induced and sustained hysteria during pregnancy he had ever come across. But being one of those pleasantly tyrannical old gentlemen who claim life-privileges for having assisted one into the world, a service he had performed efficiently enough for her husband, he took upon himself to condone with Stephen exceedingly and give as his private opinion that hysteria in such cases is so nearly allied to madness that it is a great pity, a great pity.

But the change was altogether too harmonious and serene for madness. Secretive, mystic, and the exaltation of power. She was drunk with the terrible knowledge of her terrible power. She took to avoiding the house a good deal and to wandering secretly in the isolated and unsought woods bordering a part of the grounds. Here she would lie for hours on the earth as though embracing it. She had not done such a thing since she was a child and it brought her immense comfort and a spiritual content, in which, as in a trance, the life around her vanished and was forgotten, leaving her alone on her patch of mossy grass among the trees. The first wood anemones lifted fresh white faces from the crisp red undigested leaves of autumn, making starry and melodious patterns which the birds echoed, hung above the downy antlers of the woods like flowers of the air.

Grass had always had an intense and spiritual significance for her. Once as a small child out walking with her father she had pointed with her blackberrying cane to a particularly wild tangle of grass and tufted clover and had said: Look father, earth's beard. All divine and noble beings she had thought had beards: God and her father, and Homer, and Michelangelo, and the lion-hunting frescoed Assyrians, and the earth. Above all, the earth. In the earth's hair you cooled your hands and laid down your face; and its potency was a healing drug that never failed. They cut off Samson's beard and cried: Samson, civilisation is upon thee! And yet she would have disliked Stephen in a beard. Stephen like civilisation was smooth and refined. Dear Stephen.

Stephen who was for ever tidying up his face and composing himself, as an old lady composes her ribbons.

A large yellow leaf running with its fellows before a sudden wind fell in her lap. Ah no, Zeus! she smiled, picking it up, throwing it, watching it leap away, and reflecting how warily one must have walked when to stoop and welcome a friendly cat or lift a half-starved cur on one's lap was to find an amorous god bestriding one or bearing one arrogantly away on perilous and uncalled-for journeys over new and discordant seas! Did anxious parents of handsome daughters, forbidding all kindness to dumb animals, tell fearful tales of the dread seducer who comes in the shape of the wounded bird and gentle treacherous garlanded bull on whose back young innocence is invited to ride? And did young innocence wander forth in the morning blue and search the gracious skies for pursued and palpitating birds, and run secretly to the river's edge in the hope that among the tangled rushes stood the shining and forbidden creature, new-garlanded and eager to be off? Of course they did! by the very frequency with which it happened to these marriageable and disobedient young women borne off in absurd and smiling attitudes to be breeders of gods and heroes.

No, she intended no replica of herself or Stephen. That would indeed be a shocking waste of her new-found and terrible power, laughed Ruth. Something new. Something quite different. Something worth having. Something beyond and above it all. Something free that would defy the dreary inevitable round of years. And she counted on her fingers, pressing them in the grass: Birth. Adolescence. Marriage. Birth. Old Age. Death.

How inadequate, how humiliating, and what a mockery!

Only this could a human being achieve, and then thrust upon him without so much as a by-your-leave or would-you-prefer? Something new, she begged of the grassy beard. Let me be the first. That after all would be but fair. She had thought first. Each day she came secretly to her grassy altar and made her prayer and prostrated herself before the earth as once the greek women had prostrated themselves before the beauty of Apollo, seeking to imprint the divine image on the life within them. Not that she needed to do this for the thought was never absent from her mind, but the ritual pleased her and added to her confidence. She made no actual demands in her prayers, which in the strict sense of the word were not prayers at all but only an aching desire which possessed her utterly and made, as it were, its own demands. There was nothing shaped or definite about her plea. There was no I want this and must have that, with a clear mental image of what it was she desired and expected to receive; and that was the most curious thing about it all. She desired no say in the matter. She would abide by her grassy oracle's decision. All she need do was ask and she would be answered: for had she not been answered swiftly and suddenly when she had given up all hope of having been heard?

She was large now and she moved much less quickly. From the start she had taken sparse interest in the preparations which were going on around her and had left to the ecstatic Dora the many duties connected with nursery furnishings and nursery maids, secretly amused at the thought that the newcomer would require none of these things or persons. But she came very near to anger on finding that the sceptre of all this nursery world was to be borne by a certain Sophia Peadbury, a stout rock-like creature of fifty summers and more, with a square of grey unpolished face; very clean, very correct, conspicuously null.

To Dora she protested.

She had thought it understood that there were to be only young light-footed people in the nurseries.

Young people, countered Dora nonplussed, were very well for the lighter duties, but one must have some one really capable and trustworthy when it comes to dealing with a small child. And her references were excellent. She was with the Downham-Renshaws and the Gawtrys, and was especially and carefully recommended.

So she understood that it was a family decision, and nothing whatever to do with her. It was recognised that such decisions never had, and were unalterable.

Attempting flippancy she wondered: why not Stephen's old nurse?

It had been suggested, when it was remembered that she died two years ago. Would she not have been too old? Eighty-nine; though with all her faculties about her. Did you never see her? She lived in that absurd cottage you always point to just beyond Aldbury Cross. Dora would not have her looking so hurt. It was for the best, the child's best.

She made no further protest. She knew it was useless to let it be seen how deeply she felt about it because to Dora her resentment must seem merely personal and directed against the family. But she was hurt, more hurt than she cared to admit for she must allow no secondary thoughts to divert her mind from its singleness of purpose; and she brooded over it this grey and saddening afternoon in early March as she sat on the stone edge of the lily pond goading with her finger a floating leaf until the water rolled over it, took possession of it and tried heavily to drag it down.

She was on her way back to the house from her grassy solitude and whether because being heavy she grew more easily tired or because the thought of returning immediately to the house was distasteful to her, she sat down to rest. An eighteenth-century nymph on her carved moss-grown pedestal leapt up from the centre of the pool in all her shoddy exaggeration and clumsy effectiveness. Because of a somewhat harassed and weary smile, effaced as it were by a green dipped finger in the days when the conch shells clasped so delicately between her fingers had played water on her face with monotonous insistence, Ruth always thought that she looked more like a young lady who had lost her clothes than like one who should be unaware of what clothes might be.

Then she was not to have (not only as she had expected but had never questioned) she was not to have healthy youthful faces to bend over it, and healthy youthful teeth to smile down on it, and crisp, youthful fingers to handle it, and youthful eyes, and quick youthful voices that had not been trained to servility and righteousness. She was to have the heavy, the conformable, the unwisdom of the too-well-bred. For any child she would have resented this dull and steady routine of guidance; this foreshadowing of the inevitable pleasant-nursery product. For the new and strange being which slowly her mind was bringing to perfection in her womb her resentment was deep and critical.

—You will not like it, said Ruth to the edge of flinty stone which could be seen in the distance half hidden by labyrinths of yew hedge, spacious towering single trees, old walls enclosing separate and tidy gardens, littering the ground which separated her from the house. You will not like it, and it will understand you as little as I do.

That she did not belong she had always known. What until recently she had not known was how very much she did not desire to belong. Which was what Stephen's mother could not forgive in her. There was no gratitude in the girl. Amiable-mannered, quiet and quiet-looking enough, though what Stephen could see in the girl who compared unfavourably, most unfavourably as she had said from the first. People liked and accepted her. Yet impossible, and she could not rid herself of the thought—who had had to stand by, unwilling spectator, and watch the whole unfortunate affair and make the best of it and smile the formal smile she had been taught early, used all her life and found sufficient—that the girl did not realise she had been lifted from genteel poverty to position and plenty. She could not accept (who saw mankind divided by divine and unerring right into two unalterable groups, the group which at Christmas and for sickness dispensed blankets and jars of calves'-foot jelly and the group which at Christmas and during sickness received the blankets and jars of calves'-foot jelly) this total absence of humility, of correct understanding, of grateful acknowledgement. The girl had been rescued from genteel poverty by the foolhardiness of her son without so much as a thank you or a timid smile. It was not easy to forgive her that.

She did not know that Ruth was without gratitude because without knowledge of what genteel poverty might be. Her father's fault, of course. His ideas on education were so far ahead of his times that the book he wrote on his method in 1888 (or was that the year of its publication?) when Ruth was six years old and the only other person in the world presumably aware that such a system existed, was not heard of until about 1909 when Professor August Braunschweig of Stuttgart, discovering the work through a cursory reference in a catalogue of educational text books, descended on the surprised publishers who after considerable delay unearthed a copy (the great moment of my life, the old man was known to say in after years) and was practically handed over the translation and foreign rights as a gift; and having shut himself up for the better part of a year exploded on the german educational world the wonders of the Justin Dalby method. Later Professor Braunschweig following up his success with a Life of his hero, arrived in Havre on a long and enthralling visit to M. Jacques La Thangue, Dalby's life-long friend, with whose assistance, notably in the matter of dates and letters and remembered conversational-scraps, Braunschweig compiled that memorable biography which in its english translation *Dalby of Litherton* sent astonished educational authorities hurrying to their library shelves to see whether by any chance, mislaid, one could never tell.

Arrived in the drear inconspicuous Hampshire townlet Braunschweig found that little if anything was remembered of his hero, except that he died of paralysis in 1904 after having been in a mental home for more than a year following a stroke. That the only person who could have given him such information as he desired was Dalby's housekeeper, Emma Grier, who had died aged seventy-four a month after hearing of her master's death. That he was a widower, no one having seen his wife who died in childbed they said; and had come to Litherton when his little girl was two years old and opened his school on the outskirts near

Barton Common. His daughter? well, she had gone away after his death and had not come back since, nor heard of, married some said, though no one knew rightly to whom; some saying she had gone to live abroad leaving no word at all behind her, things get about and people talk; anyway, she had not been heard of, had not come back, and was not likely to now; and besides you never could tell for the Professor himself was queer at times and kept to himself a great deal and had no friends in the neighbourhood.

They could however point to his grave, of which Professor Braunschweig after placing thereon a large and formal laurel wreath threaded with crimson ribbon and getting the sexton to help him neaten the few square feet of forlorn and neglected earth, took several photographs. They could also point to the rambling creeper-covered two-storey house which had been his school and of which the Professor took several more photographs; as also views of the little town and the cliffs and the sea surrounding and containing it.

Before leaving Litherton which he loathed, partly for its crass and childish ignorance of the daily life of his idol, and partly because the good german was surfeited with the drab and ill-cooked food peculiar to english country inns with their insular insistence on bad beer and whisky, both of which he found undrinkable, he had a stroke of unexpected good fortune. He found in a small dilapidated shop in the High Street two photographs of Justin Dalby. That one in profile, maned and serene as Asclepius, which not unnaturally was the cause of that sustained heroic and fate-defying tone adopted as characteristic of the man by his biographer, and which was later to puzzle and disquiet Ruth who found only the quality of heart-ache in her father's gentle and bewildered face. The other a full-length picture in which he held on his knee a staring child whose long loose curls were brushed gravely from her face, held by a wide black velvet ribbon round her little skull, and ending in a bow on the top of her head. Had Professor Braunschweig studied this photograph more carefully there would have been a great deal less of that thunder-defying splendour in the portrait of his hero which he gave to the world. It never occurred to the excellent biographer lost in opalescent clouds of hero-worship, of theories, notebooks, of the fate-shattering neglect of genius, that Justin Dalby had himself put that ribbon round his daughter's little skull, and following her instructions had tied with infinite humour and patience that precise black velvet bow.

A t school she had been called My-Father-Says. At the end of her first term she arrived home ill, dispirited, and nervous, and a week before the holidays ended there had been a frightful day of hysteria and shuddering and teeth-chattering incoherence. Finally after much persuasion she had showed him the long mark across her palm which she had kept so carefully hidden and where she had been burnt with a poker for misunderstanding some trifling clause in an uncertain code of honour. More unbearable than the burn which didn't hurt now at all, was that they sneered at her unconscious and perpetual references to her father, at her clothes, at her silence which they interpreted as sullenness, at her shyness which they mistook for sulkiness. In short she had been put through all the subtleties of torture inflicted by boisterous normal school children on the retiring and abnormal child. And it was all as nothing compared with her hourly longing to be with her father again.

During her single term at school there was a girl who was very kind to her, came to her rescue on more than one occasion, took her under her protection for she was older than Ruth, came to stay at Litherton, came even now and then to spend her holidays with Ruth and her father and Mrs Grier in the cottage he took year after year beyond Portloe. It was a curious protective friendship this of the older girl for Ruth, the more so because nothing could have been more simple or unexciting than the quiet Dalby household. Whereas after her father's death when Ruth for the first time in her life was seriously ill and lost masses of her shadowy and beautiful hair, Dora taking charge of her again as if she had been a child, carried her off to her lovely home Wrockram, that show-place of the North, where Ruth was never to forget the summer noons through which in her convalescence, drowsing on cushions on the floor of the boat, she seemed to glide over the lake with its hundred turnings, its dragon-fly murmurings, its pale enchanted willows mirrored in the glazed water; and where the following year she met Stephen.

She was not then altogether to blame for her lack of gratitude at being, what were the words?, lifted from genteel poverty to position and plenty. The distinction her father had made as between races, peoples, classes, differed in many ways from the distinctions common to his day (his book being written, or was it published? in 1888) which was a pleasant one of smug imperialism, good queens and good will; and particularly did they differ in their not being calculated on a monetary or patriotic basis. Long before the days of an H. G. Wells popular History of the World on every schoolroom bookshelf together with the mob-educative value of the penny daily newspapers showing that other strips of land can exist and be inhabited by people not necessarily frogs or fools or ignoramuses or bullies, the obscure schoolmaster was insisting in his obscure and modest study that it is as unwise as it is impossible to define where races begin, end, and merge, as it is to define where art and the noises of races such as music and speech begin, end, and merge.

How well she remembered her father telling her that a man is his own reward or his own punishment. Nothing, how well she remembered that dear homily of his!, nothing could alter that. You can no more reward or punish another human being, Ruth, than that being can reward or punish you. And forgiveness. That was the most ludicrous pretence of them all! Never use the word, tear it out, make a little ball of it and throw it in the fire. There was no such thing.

And that afternoon on which, returning from her first Sunday school where Mrs Grier had insisted on taking her (for she had her rights said Emma Grier and one was, after looking after her moonstruck master, to see that his little girl—his little orphan as she called Ruth—was given a good christian grounding in the Word) and over the Sunday crumpets and Emma's Sunday potato-cakes in father's brownly warm and littered study, she had insisted on piping out all that she had heard, and had come to the story of the Tribute unto Cæsar and her father had put down his tea-cup with a great laugh and said: Who but Voltaire could have countered that so neatly? (For he taught her to love France and the french whom he called the modern and socratic beacon of the world.) Ah, that was the way to learn one's lessons! Wrapping up warmly after tea (Emma saw to that) and striding over the cliffs towards Barton shouting after father in one's best french Voltaire's *Discourse on Moderation* in a thin pointed voice, as one struggled against the sea-wind that gathered the words out of one's mouth and rushed them away beyond reach unless one held on and got in first.

There was the day on which for the first time he made her walk barefooted on the grass. The indignant Emma at an upper window shouting that he was killing his own child, a murderer before the Lord, and that if she came to die, poor creature, she Emma was a witness and would tell all that she knew. But Ruth survived to repeat the experiment every morning, putting herself as he explained to her in direct contact with the earth, with the generative power which bore mountains, poured streams, moved sap. He told her to think of this as she began slowly crossing the grass backwards and forwards; and sure enough quite soon the soles of her feet would begin to tingle and impelled she knew not how, with Mercury's wings at her heels, she would begin running, faster, faster, laughing, elated, breathless, glowing. With few exceptions he maintained that most of the ills of the body could be cured by walking barefooted on grass. Moreover this in an age when the human female did not walk for two reasons: tight shoes and propriety. And in this age in which bodily movement in the female was restricted and rendered painful by whalebone and yards of heavy unwieldy cloth, he saw to it that his daughter wore warm lightly woven garments bearing from the shoulders and not the waist. (Alas, how exquisitely droll they found this at school!)

Hers was a lonely and blissful childhood belonging wholly to her father. Once when Emma, who took pride in distributing largesse in the shape of cakes and puddings to a group of old women near her home, had left her alone outside the cottage of old Mrs Caithey, the very ancient lady had patted her curls and mumbled something about a pretty mite and a poor motherless little creature. How incensed Ruth had been! Not waiting for Emma to reappear she had run all the way home like a fury to find her father, and it took all his persuasiveness and tact to dissuade her from dragging him back to the cottage at once and showing him to Emma's cronies. Showing them this perfect being and stopping once for all their silly woman's-chatter about poor and motherless.

Unlike most children who have lost their mothers at birth she had felt little desire to hear her mother spoken of, or explained to her, or described. Her father sufficed. Love and passion beyond her years were in the dreams she wrapped him in. He was in turn all the heroes of her favourite legends. It was all she could do sometimes on seeing him return from the town or from a visit, to keep from rushing out to him and crying: O *why* did you tell Polyphemus your *name?* I've been so *anxious* about you. And did you kill the Minotaur? And rout the Danes? And meet the Great Khan face to face? And defy the Tzar of all the Russias?

As they strode together in the grey winter afternoons over the cliffs toward Barton she would invest him with the magic of Wodan, his beard moving in the sea winds and his old black felt hat over his bartered eye, and she would ask him Why father this and Why father that, knowing that the god of wisdom himself was answering her.

The day on which she came to the story of Pallas-Athene springing from the forehead of Zeus her father, was one of extreme emotional content for her. She recognised it at once, this divine symbol of the unity existing between her father and herself. She read and re-read, heart hammering her ribs, eyes round as croquet balls, a smile on her lips, very happy. Everything then tended towards the deification of this rare father! They too recognised him, these divine beings from whom he sprang! Thus and therefore was she born. And secretly studying her father's high and tolerant brow she found the theory not only feasible, but wise and perfect.

Absurd then to expect gratitude when so much had died with her father and in a trance she had been taken away and in a trance had met and married and exchanged twenty years of adoration and constant and satisfying companionship and used and simple rooms and a flowery untidy garden with its beloved orchard and one stubborn old man who had his own way in the kitchen garden no matter what his cranky *maa*ster said and a stern old woman to look after them both, for this cumbersome imposing mansion, grey, lichened, terraced, beautiful in so many ways, pretentious and uncomfortable in so many more, filled with the come-and-go of servants and strangers meaning little, and set on a stretch of land which after two years upon it she was still ignorant as to where it began or ended. Absurd then to resent such casual acceptance by one who not only had never possessed, but had never been instructed in the decent attitudes of mind connected with possession.

She could not help feeling rather as the very young feel when gazing down in to their bowl of breakfast porridge (sugarless again this morning for some excellent if secret reason) they are told not only to eat it up quickly now, but to remember all the poor and homeless children who have no such porridge to come down to in the morning. Well then give them my porridge. Please give them my porridge. Give them all the porridge they want, but do not ask me to share it with them. Let them strut about proud places without beginning or end and strut through the formal pageantry of dead things and dead people, renewing themselves only in ghostly memories of these ghostly selves, which leaves them smiling politely down the centuries, bewildered as the nymph with her features erased as it were by a green-dipped finger. And give them also the Hungerford nose and the Stanner eye; particularly the Stanner eye. For Stephen's mother, as is known, having been a Stanner had brought the Stanner eye to the Hungerford nose: an impregnable alliance. Had not Ruth with a grave patience (which made his mother sometimes wonder whether, after all, there might not be, if not gratitude, at least awe?) listened so often to the serious apportioning of the Eye of the one side and the Nose of the other to those about to be, to those who were, to those who had been? And looked in those large smoke-grey eyes in their grey corrugated setting and tried hard to believe; and loyally tried also not to wonder whether Stephen's nose were not a shade too long and the nostrils a shade too wide for all the moral and physical distinction claimed for it.

The large and known Gainsborough canvas of Miss Thalia Stanner which hangs in the National Gallery (Room VI) is an excellent record of the Stanner eye. A pleasant and elegant young person Miss Thalia, not unlike a pink satin bolster held negligently together by silvery ribbons, the invitation of whose warm and audacious bosom is suddenly and surprisingly withdrawn by the meagre thread of those smiling lips and, above, the large and wintry Stanner eye mist-grey and exquisitely set; eyes which could tear the heart could they weep and irradiate it could they laugh, and are lost, irrevocably lost, by their seeming unawareness of all but themselves and that at which they gaze. As chance wills it, not far away, just round the corner of the next room in fact, fourth canvas on the left on entering, beside the small Romney study of Lady Hamilton vacant-eyed and mouth too far agape, is the Reynolds portrait of Rear-Admiral Sir Lawrence Addeley Hungerford, demonstrating singularly well the strength and weakness of the Hungerford nose. One smiles on first catching sight of that heavy paunched figure, ill-balanced by a face too large and a wig too small, and at the chubby hand thickly fingering the scroll of parchment which, can one doubt?, he has never so much as glanced at; and one is pondering how such facial glow and meaty splendour were matured and maintained in the days before naval seafaring had attained the comfort of a trans-atlantic luxury liner, when by lifting the eyelid one is made aware of the Hungerford nose, elongated, alive, ant-eaterish, setting at naught the ill-balanced wig and hefty paunch.

The Hungerford nose it will be admitted makes one pause. Even as it disappoints it excites. Here is a nose cast to found dynasties; active for scenting power; nervous for prying around Courts and hand-caressing-hand breathing what it has flaired into the ear of Popes. Too short for wisdom; too long for the wilful following of itself around unlit corners. Lamentably a thing of good and evil in equal parts and therefore valueless. In short, a treacherous wise and catholic nose, reduced by generations of ease and prosperity to being nothing more formidable than the touchstone of a small and tradition-sacred family on a small and tradition-sacred island.

Certainly it was not fair to them. They did not deserve this conspirator in their midst, outwardly quietly believing and quietly respectful; who yet recoiled from the humorous possibility of reproducing a Stanner eye as from reproducing a blind eye, and would as soon perpetuate Ganesha's swaying funnel as perpetuate the anachronistic Hungerford nozzle. You will not like it, said Ruth to the edge of flinty stone which could be seen in the distance half-hidden by labyrinths of yew-hedge, spacious towering single trees, old walls enclosing separate and tidy gardens, littering the ground which separated her from the house. You will not like it, and it will understand you as little as I do.

S he smiled at the thought of what they would think of it.
      After all, the world did not take so lightly to change now that centuries of religious thought and habit had accustomed it to the belief that man as he existed was the highest form of life god could create. She smiled, thinking of what Minos must have said on being presented with the infant Minotauros for which his wife had pursued her wild and milk-white bull across the woods and hills of Crete. At the river god and the muse with their litter of strange siren daughters, half-woman half-bird, half-woman half-fish. At the dolphined Tritons driving their golden chariots over the floor of the ocean, playing in the sunshine on the white surface of the seas. Was it not a proud day indeed when first the sounding of their conch-shells rocked the waters? And that nameless nymph who gave Hylas to Zeus and to Hermes (for this is a case of disputed paternity), did she not marvel at her first sight of those downy legs and upcurved eye and rejoice as later she was to rejoice and marvel at the shaggy haunches and tufted chin and listen for the sound of his shepherd's pipe of seven reeds and live to know the hills and groves and flowering oaks made sacred to him for ever. And Hera, that malignant and much-tried sister spouse of Zeus. What were her thoughts when the infant centaur burst from that cloud-image fashioned to deceive the lovelorn Ixion? (Was ever excuse of prim and faithless wife so transparent! Yet for Ixion's sake just as well, who knows, for surely a most formidable Royal Personage to love in the flesh.) Did Hera smile, grim sentinel of heaven, the day on which she gave the first centaur to the world and saw its still-soft opaque hoofs seek to adjust themselves to the earth? And in the rare intervals of her slayings and cruelties and jealous womanly treacheries and in her long days bereft of love, pause

to wonder at this new and unexpected being she had created? Did it evoke in her a sudden tenderness to watch him leaping and frisking on the grassy slopes of his mountain home, as he learned to plant his milky hoofs more firmly on the stubble of the mountain paths and stampede the herds in his mother's fields and race with them?

Did they play with their children? Who knows? Helplessness was not a virtue to the greeks. Immaturity not a condition that appealed to them.

What a sombre morose day. A grey day, cloud succeeding cloud in a grey sky under which even the new buds looked chilled and the grass seemed to find no warmth in the earth it clung to. Only the nymph smiled her green erased smile. Ruth remembered her father regretting the exploits of Herakles as having caused so much bad art among Hellenic sculptors. What of the naked young men in Arcady's sylvan streams and the post-Canova stone manipulators?

She was still tired and restless as she rose and made her way slowly to the house. Her head ached stubbornly. She wondered how she could avoid Dora, who would notice it at once.

Curious this solicitude in women, these tentacles of tenderness with which they seek to bind those near and dear to them. Was it a defensive weapon this inexhaustible fount of woman's sympathy, this tender interference, this insidious and perpetual warfare of subduing and conquering by dependence on their indispensability; and of making the strong relinquish to it their freedom and their will: as the pathos and helplessness of an infant is set as a trap for those on whom it depends for the continuance and necessities of its life? Was this then the secret dissatisfaction between man and woman this perpetual binding of the strong by the weak, the perpetual triumph of the binder over the bound, the easy unscrupulousness of the weak and the angry helplessness of the strong. Or was it that only woman understood woman: as only man understood man. And but rarely, as with father and myself, man and woman understand one another, and create the perfect human relationship?

Whatever it might be, useless to hope that her headache would escape her friend's vigilant eye and vigilant ministrations. And she was right; Dora came across to her a solicitous frown between her eyes. Where had she been all the afternoon, she had been so anxious; she looked pale, she looked cold, had she not a headache? she looked tired; did she not know that she must not strain herself especially these last weeks. All of which correct and simple statements were countered with a smile and a few correct and reassuring sentences; wishing she could respond more genuinely; wishing she did not resent this evident and unselfish desire to be of use and serve; wishing one did not envy for women that male matter-of-factness of summing up and dismissing that made for hardiness of mind as rough oats made for hardiness of bone.

She was displeased with herself for she was thoroughly ashamed of such rebellious critical moods. It was wrong that she should watch unmoved but for an external politeness, a smile correctly adjusted, a word correctly placed, these ministrations for one's comfort. It was in moments such as that that she would come again to the desire to fathom whatever bound Dora to her with such an urge, such an intensity; almost with the implacability of enmity. A certain wilful helplessness in her appearance, an answering to Dora's need to protect and dominate; who insisted on the very animals about her being docile and grateful: which may account for her dislike of cats, thought Ruth, who adored them. Stephen too was bound to her through this protective need, evoking gratitude, projecting on a lesser and unhappier being the full splendour of one's goodness. She had been sick and heavy with her sorrow and loss when first they met; and what man can resist unhappiness in a woman? Be sad that I may be gay. The giving which is more than the receiving. How otherwise had Stephen gone against his own and his mother's prejudices, and accepted the weariness of her perpetual disapproval and disappointment?

What warm safety in the sound of tea-things moved and the stir of voices (she remembered that she had left her book beside the pond) and fireglow leaping in silver and walnut and touching to reality dark tapestry foliage and umber smiles in faded portraits and Dora's generous and finely drawn head bent over it all, smiling.

And in that gesture, in that familiar half-smile of abnegation and triumph which hovers about women's lips, menacing, indelible, Ruth was aware of the world as the victim of woman's ineradicable possessiveness; that emotional maternal substance which women ooze as a form of adhesive plaster by which mankind is held together, and is decaying.

The nurse, that mixture of servility and condescension, had arrived. She began at once on her triumphs.

Nurse Gunn. (Putting aside her book, taking the plate on her lap and detaching a grape, Ruth smiled down the years at Nurse Gunn.) An ominous-sounding name but not inappropriate. Direct, ruthless, single-purposed, with a certain metallic imagery suggesting power and action. Death one was assured had here a worthy opponent. One felt he would remember her. One understood he could not ignore her. Above, behind, beneath, about, each bed that Nurse Gunn succoured lurked the Dread Form behaving not unlike Sir Henry Irving in his more tempestuous moments. A simple tenet and an effective one seeing that it put Nurse Gunn on the defensive, and Nurse Gunn on the defensive moved with the wrath of the Lord in her step and the lightning of the righteous in her hand. Helmeted, collared, a vast shining iridescent and bulging breastplate buckled to a twenty-two-inch waistband, and shaking her thermometer as Blake's angels shook their spears; and more effectively.

When Nurse Gunn fought she won. When Nurse Gunn did not win it was because she had been called in too late. Her prowess in snatching corpses from under Death's hollow nose must have been trying in the extreme to that hitherto omniscient gentleman, if only that her manner so lacked respect, so wanted dignity. His swift and icy step was not, it seemed, to Nurse Gunn what it was to the rest of mankind: an utter darkness, an end to all, a dread which words cannot compass and thought dare not. Here was no silent prayer, no secret apprehension, no momentary doubt. Nothing of the frail acolyte and wrestling devil. No wan saint and high-breasted fleshly lady. No mercy-begging Magdalen curtained within her own hair. But a cool tra-la-la and away, a hide-and-seek-and-saw-you-first, a dash of something cool on the near-corpse's damp brow, a now-just-one-leetle-sip-more, a burning tea-spoon pressed to a reviving lip, a that's-right, that's-better on a gay soprano note. And Death was being handed his hat in the hall. Leaving the house with the efficient smiling doctor. Good day, Sir. Good day.

Foiled! Foiled again. And by that bouncing merry little woman with the large simplified face of a crab and the incredibly small mouth which when opened seemed full of rice, overflowing and retained with difficulty.

Those privileged to listen to the chivalric, frequent, withal-modest accounts of these combats became positively afraid of dying on Nurse Gunn's hands, so sure were they that Death on ultimately taking possession must make one pay dearly for such victories. Could such matters be smiled away? One could begin with a tactful but not obse-quious: how delightful to meet you at last. Of course I never quite believed those naïve, those quite too amusing. . . . One could not expect Nurse Gunn to come to the rescue by playing Sydney Smith to the worsted and aggrieved schoolmaster who must be off: I pray, Doctor, do not endorse my sins on their backs. Was she not too busy endorsing her triumphs almost as ruthlessly?

In fairness to Nurse Gunn it must be told that in her presence her patients thought but rarely of Death. There was about her a resolution which made them understand that even should the unexpected happen and one departed and arrived, Saint Peter would extend an apologetic hand and say: Ah no, dear lady. Not just yet. There has been a mistake. Nurse Gunn wants you back.

Mischievous as children they played Nurse Gunn as a game. The choice was embarrassing. One could have Nurse Gunn and Lady Titherley Paulton. Or Nurse Gunn and Dr Bonnington Hargreaves. Or Nurse Gunn and the mother of Lady Alberta Dimming whose maternal ardour encroached on certain professional duties until an exasperated Nurse Gunn stood confronting Sir Jasper Rivington: Unless I am left in complete control of my patient, Sir Jasper, I cannot. She seemed always to have been bearing down on eminent obstetrical surgeons and issuing ultimata. There still remained after all these years that favourite portrait of herself pale, authoritative, white-lipped, amazonian, moving firmly yet noiselessly over the heavy carpet towards Sir Angus McHugh (The Royal Accoucheur, emphasised Nurse Gunn) most reputed obstetrician in two centuries. Sir Angus you must operate. At once. My duty. Mrs Sibthorpe Hepplethwaite (the Norfolk Hepplethwaites) lived. But for you, she said. She knew that I had, well, not ordered, but, well, insisted. Lived, rare bloom in the herbaceous border of important cases flowering perennially down the fringes of Nurse Gunn's career and in her patients' memories.

S he had been filled with a comic dismay. What malignant or humorous fate could have dropped this solid talkative mass of all that she did not want to encounter or be reminded of into the midst of her exacting and arbitrary urge on the threshold of its fulfilment? She had found herself, a child again, weedling her new tyrant into allowing her to leave the house; had had to cajole for permission to walk five minutes alone in the grounds.

—Who will rid me of this turbulent priestess, she had cried in mock alarm, running into her in every doorway. Useless. Nurse Gunn inspired a degree of awe and obedience that a chief inquisitor might well have envied. Many a time she could almost have cried with vexation at seeing these last days of such intense and urgent purport intruded on; their peace, so necessary to her just now, broken in upon and shattered. For a moment it even occurred to her that these meetings were deliberate; that she was being watched. That the inescapableness of Nurse Gunn was a plot. She dismissed this as absurd and as a sign of morbid pre-occupation: although inevitably she had been right. It never occurred to her that she was every bit as unreal to Nurse Gunn as Nurse Gunn was to her. Or that Nurse Gunn after a conversation with Dr Mason had been more than confirmed in her early impression. Such a singular young woman, who seemed to have no idea at all of what was happening to her and had asked none of the usual questions. Asked no questions at all in fact, and stared in comically frightened and surprised manner if the subject was broached. Queer, said Nurse Gunn. And deep.

While Nurse Gunn was being shocked by this discovery, Ruth made one of her own. That not only had Nurse Gunn's patients all been brave and noble but that all the children she had helped into the world had been dear and beautiful. It would seem she could not bring herself to form the word child without the qualifying dear and beautiful. Such a beautiful child. Such a beautiful boy and such a dear little girl. Boys were always beautiful; girls always dear and little.

Decidedly God might have found a nicer way. Why had He been so masculine in His disregard for the acute sensitiveness that He might surely have understood, had He given it thought, a woman feels at the culmination, at the anticlimax? One understood that fresh from creating mountains and releasing torrents; but He might at least have made it a private matter; quick, secret, and alone. It was inexcusable. It was obvious that He had had no woman to advise Him on the subject. He was directly responsible for the presence of Nurse Gunn! Knowing how absurd she was being, Ruth still could not help feeling it as the supreme humiliation and absurdity that one must deliver oneself into the hands of total strangers at the most weird and aweful moment of one's life: and it hurt her as something physical that others should first see and handle the new and strange being which she had brought to perfection in her body.

And all at once it seemed equally wrong to her to bear her child in a bed. Especially in this heavy portentous canopied tomb of a bed with its sly and hearty boast of the loves and births and deaths which had filled its capacious and elaborate lap for the last three hundred years. Used.

Worn out. Old. Stale with stale memories of repeated and familiar sights. How had it happened that every thing vital had been reduced to the limits of four walls, bringing shame and fear with them? One should be born on hills, on clouds, near streams, in woods, on open and pleasant spaces. Civilisation. Fear of unsheltered spaces. Too many walls inside which things were performed in fear and shame.

She grew so easily tired and restless indoors. They would not let her go to her woods now, nor beyond a stone's-throw of the house. (Then Stephen shall throw a stone for me Ruth had insisted slyly, losing patience; leading him to the window and pointing in the direction in which she wanted to go, and Stephen to her amazement and delight had thrown a stone which no one saw fall. Even then, for all the fun and chaffing it had caused, they would not let her go after it.) They feared for her. Ever since he had died she seemed to have been surrounded by people who feared for her; and yet she had no fear for herself or the new thing her mind had perfected, and which her body would soon reject.

The Apollo-image, that at least had been a wise direction of consciousness; yet, there again, Apollo, with Socrates on the potter's ware at their very door! Still, there was something adequately wise and noble in such an impersonal choice as beauty: which was more than could be said for the monstrous fetish of the Family which women had since created for themselves. Shoemaker no higher than the shoe. Woman no further than your immediate environment. To fail to create an Apollo was at worst a dignified defeat: to succeed in getting a family likeness at best a doubtful triumph. Look! his father's nose. The blue of his mother's eye. Do you not think that this is a perfect imitation of myself, of us, of my great-grandfather, of his mother's mother's mother, of everything that has been in the Family since its inception?

The monstrous conceit that birth was limited to the reproduction of imperfections hallowed by their association with oneself! Where was man's humility, his sense of the ridiculous? Bred his beasts in fear and reverence; himself as an after-thought; clipped ears and docked tails; paid stud fees that would keep a regiment in food and drink for half a year; who could not see a petal too long red without worrying it to purple. Was this then why man had ceased to evolve: as though a doubtful perfection had been attained? And having ceased to evolve had fallen back on invention: a crutch for an able leg?

Was it not exasperating the ineffectiveness of man? Take for instance all this talk raging around flying. Were they not beside themselves just now, incredulous, eager, partisans, sceptics? Would it one day be possible to remain in the air for two entire hours? Or fly above long stretches of water? A joke in poor taste. A madman's hallucination. Actually man was to attempt to float on the air in a box of a machine with wings to bear it up? A box with wings! And they were proud of it or angry at it and one and all fearful of it.

Why, man had dreamt of wings since the moment he first, with shaded eyes, stared at something swift and purposeful flashing high above his head through space, and grown sad (for there is no sight more melancholy than that of birds winging across skies, grave arrows from some celestial bow) at the knowledge of his two stationary feet: on earth, in earth, of earth; his heart and eyes taking the flight his feet could not follow. Who knew in what first dawn this urge came to man? (He would have known. He would have told me, thought Ruth.) The earliest Art had traces of it; stiff broad feathery boards rising from shoulder blades; some winged their beasts; others their gods; others their victories; all, their supermen.

Always this thought of wings lifting man to godhead. Knowing their lack, sensing their insufficiency, content to imagine their desires instead of creating them! Their little box with wings attached was nothing: was less than nothing, poor travesty of man's first awe! Women could have shown them that. Women could have shown them how wings are made had they taken heed and used wisely the centuries of thought and prayer. What Leonardo had dared dream woman could have dared achieve. Piglierà il volo il grande uccello . . . empiendo l'universo di stupore, empiendo di sua fama tutte le scritture e gloria eterna al loco dove nacque. . . . Hers the nest in which to hatch that dream and people those skies. Vagliami il lungo studio e il grande amore! Those were words to emboss in brave lettering on the banner of one's soul! Swiftness of leg should have bred hoofs; swiftness of thought wings; swiftness of mechanical labour a Siva-like many-handedness. Only thus in its never-ending combinations should man have achieved that which he desired and envied; have evolved instead of atrophied, and been born new instead of old; new, strange, and different. (So that there would always have been such fun in it, as she put it to herself.)

Without this knowledge of something new and rare to sustain her she would still have been as unreconciled and appalled as in the first bitter weeks of her pregnancy. She spent the last few days in an exaltation bordering at moments on frenzy. Enclosed within herself as she had been since her father's death, her sense of his loss was most acute now that all that she had since become cried out to him to be near her now when most she needed him. That apart she was emptied of all emotion save a sense of boundless serenity and power. She had no misgivings and no fears. She felt abundantly strong and eager. She thought of the dreams and legends of her youth and knew that no child conceived and sired as she had been could give birth to a thing commonplace or usual. As she had made no specific demands, had projected no definite mind-image, she could not anticipate. Nor did she desire to. How often later she was to reiterate this in moments of half-hearted self-justification and derive some measure of comfort from it!

She bore her child on the evening of June 5, 1907, after several hours of prolonged pain in which she had the curious and appalling impression of being burned alive. As she sank in a heavy stupor of relief and tiredness she seemed to catch the echo of a distant voice murmuring: such a beautiful boy. But that might have been a dream. She laughed weakly.

Instead of a cool and normal awakening she woke with fever and grew worse as the morning wore on. For almost a month she was ill; often delirious; rarely altogether conscious of what was happening about her or what had become of her. But by the first week in July she was being propped up on her pillows aware of a wealth of pale summer flowers about her, as soft movements from the open windows bore their presence to her in sudden waves of flower-incense.

Everyone about her was very quiet and gentle. She would have thought them almost sad had she been able to gather her thoughts together with any sureness. But she was tired. She had had a child; that was why she had been ill. From a dense bundle of ribbon and lace, which became so heavy when placed in her arms that, startled, she could not hold it, peered a nebulous round face, a sparse fluff covering its minute veined skull. Two grey eyes widely spaced and set stared at her and stared. Two fists of a surprising minute perfection, clenched themselves. They told her it was a boy and, still startled, she was astonished and delighted at its winsome and minute perfection.

—Is he not beautiful? hazarded Ruth. Everyone agreed with her, gently and kindly. She was growing strong again. Something troubled and escaped her, as with children who turn suddenly, warily, and leap in the very centre of their shadow only to find it once more ahead of them, intangible, tormenting.

Late one afternoon, half-waking from a short troubled sleep, she heard a woman's voice saying mournfully, distinctly: but later Nurse he may walk? and a woman's voice deferential but decided: O no. There is no question of that. You can see for yourself that that . . .

She must have made some movement or sound for the voices ceased and some-one stood beside her bed. She asked to see her child. When it was brought and she had asked them to undress it, unwrap it, and they hesitated saying something vague about the chill and not yet being too strong, she began with calm and steady fingers untying the innumerable ribbons that held him together. The child made no sound. He seemed in no way to resent his stripping; seemed indeed hardly aware of it. Hastily windows were being shut and gentle remonstrances continued, as though sudden noise could in some way relieve the tension.

He was beautifully whole and finished; except for his feet. They hung loose and shapeless from the ankle, soft loose pads of waxen flesh. She stared at them unable to bring herself to take them in her hand or touch them. She knew without knowing how she knew that such a newly created being gathers itself together in its feet, grasps with them, beats at the air with them, eagerly draws them in in small soft folds, and with all the hunger of its new-found energy shoots them out again, bending them, curving them, waving them to the rhythm of its new-struggling animal restlessness. She knew that this restlessness continually washing over him in a wave should be gathering him in an ebb and flow of folds and wrinkles. Knowing this she raised her eyes from the loose formless pads of waxen flesh that were his feet to his impassive infant face in which two light eyes widely spaced and set stared at her and stared; and this time she understood the vacant fixity of his infant stare and his utter soundlessness and immobility.

S he was sobered and appalled. It was terrible to her. It was as though in a drunken stupor one man had hit another, and they came and said to him: he is dead.

A t the foot of the hillock round which Graziella had vanished something heavy and black was moving among the vines. Padre Antonio punctual to the minute was returning from the seminary at Foria Ponte. And at exactly this moment of each afternoon (was it for this she sat there?) she would hear again the crash of Uller's fist on the stone edge of the balcony, see a palette knife describing circles in the direction of the approaching priest, catch the echo of a voice thundering in ill-natured contempt: here comes God's beetle.

A dull beating of muffled drums, a grinding wail not unlike that of a rabbit snared, the gathering murmur of threats: the distant thunder heralding the coming storm of hoofs and blows that would crash past the house now that the men had started for home and those making for Sant' Anna branched off the main road and took the steep path past the house leading to the hills. Here began the ascent and here the place to make the beasts understand that there was work to be done, and a good stick was of the company to ensure its doing.

At first for a very long time on hearing the warning rumble Ruth would fly to the back of the house, to the long stone kitchen where Lisetta at this hour was busy over her charcoal fire, to hide herself and be out of hearing when the storm broke. She could not bear the shrill curses and crackling whips and heavy buttock-blows as the beasts tore by, panic in their hoofs.

—How can they be so cruel! She would stammer to Lisetta, holding her hands over her eyes, aghast at the pleasure it would have given her to rush out in the road, wrest the sticks from the men and bring them down on their own backs, thrashing them down on to the ground, striking them heavily about the eyes and face as in their slyer moments they struck their beasts.

—Macchè, macchè, who is cruel? Do you not see how hard they work themselves? Five times as hard as they can ever get their beasts to work. Pity the men, said Lisetta dismissing it impatiently; it is sadder to be the tamer than the lion.

In time she came also to see it in its truer light and to justify the blows by the prodigious display of sustained energy the men put up daily, year in year out. But even now at times she could still feel the blows on her own back, and could still dread their muted approach as acutely as on hearing it for the first time. The logic of the thing she understood. Crude nature against crude nature was their affair, with a turn of the quick head and a spit true-aimed over the shoulder. It was not easy to regard one's beast in heroic light with one's own feet thick with blisters, and one's own back aching under a load almost as heavy and a march every bit as long. Then why should the sight of a man sweating under a load too large for him arouse in her less pity than the sight of a beast overladen and the sound of blows and galloping hoofs?

Why should the cry of the little goat tied with the ridiculously thick rope to the wall of the house in the hollow which she overlooked, weigh on her heart with a sense of injustice and cruelty? He began crying as the sun went down and continued well into the night: such reproach in his tremulous bleat. Earlier in the week she had noticed him tossing his legs about sideways in a young drunken leggy run; out of tune, out of time. They had hung his food, some strings of vine and laurel leaves around his neck; and there he tossed, fresh from some Pompeian fresco, very lost, very appealing. Some-one was sick in the house: the extra cup of milk was needed. Hitched to the wall with his mother answering him at intervals from the other side of it, he threw out his sad little stutter of self-pity. He would complain: he insisted on complaining. Now and again there came the banging of a door and an angry sound and then a scurry of hoofs. A short pause and away he went echoing through the night silence. One could not walk into another's house and say: here is the fraction of a penny with which to buy that extra cup of milk of which he robs his mother. And Ruth who also could be lost in something near to panic when night fell, would lean alert in her chair or lie awake on her bed reading in his silly young shivery bleats so very much more than there was to them.

Yet the sound of Giovina crying, the never-ending irritable drone of a tired child, awoke in her only acute vexation and dislike.

She could no more explain her attitude than understand theirs. Why they picked up and swung kittens by their hind legs. Or put large birds in small cages. Or how it had been possible for Graziella, herself large and proud with child, to shoot out a foot slyly under the table and jab at the heavy belly of the thin grey cat prowling around warily for scraps.

The last evening was like the first. The afternoon would break imperceptibly between the sly-faced gentle goats swinging down the saracen road. The women and children moving well-wards. The officious shriek of the passenger boat. The bells of San Soccorso (wherein hung the sinister black Christ in his barbaric crimson robe and golden turban, soiled now but horrible, a real idol. The saraceni threw it in the sea and when it came out it was that colour. But the turban? The eastern robe? That all came out of the water too. But how? Ah, well, the saints alone could answer that.) rocking the air with shrill and monotonous clamour. On the edge of the Bay the gathering clouds preparing for an Ascension. God's beetle appearing among the vines, stopping a moment in full view of the balcony to mop his head with a large blue handkerchief and look up, deliberately surprising himself at the sight of her, and passing the time of day. The thud of hoofs flying past the house and dwindling to their first vagueness and out of hearing. The bats rushing past at which the children threw pieces of light-coloured rag loaded with stones or earth to bring them low, scattering as they swooped. A settling back into the evening quiet in a muted orchestration of scent and sound. The pale long ethereal strips of maize glowing in the gradual dusk like tall headless lilies. The dark pinewoods blurred to the consistency of wet moss. The darkening hilly background of the coast, crisp, one-dimensional. Strings of light appearing on the horizon, drawing nearer at intervals as the island lit up. Little Maria creeping on the veranda and squatting on her haunches in a corner, her pale candle-grease face translucent in the shadow. The sound of sudden increased activity below and a voice crying: *Signor'* v-i-e-n-, *vien'mangiar'*.

Down the stone steps of the balcony she would go, the day's papers or a book under an arm, through to the back of the house, across the long stone kitchen, out on to the vine-thatched *terrazza* where Lisetta's modest *ristorante al mare* looked out from its rocky eminence over the narrow strip of sandy beach and the long stretch of water; the misty outer edges of which now showed pin-pricks of light near Gaeta.

Since her first sight of it Ruth had loved this terrace on the sea and had chosen her place at the far edge of it, opposite the narrow path cut in the rock by which the children, the fishermen, and anyone belonging to the house, climbed up from the beach. At night it was all a grave smoky blue in which the terrace, the sands, the sea, left the sky only where the stars began. On her table a lamp burned. Lisetta was always urging on her more light, was always repeating that the electric light from the house would be extended to the terrace. But she would have none of it. She loved her lamp. Any suggestion or attempt to alter or displace things as she knew them always upset her. She liked what she called her blindman's ways; her ability to find anything with her eyes shut.

At night at the centre-table the men played cards. A candle lighting one side of their sun-dried faces in strong Ribera effect cast heavy shadows down their long spanish noses; gouging out their eyes, hollowing their lean cheeks, throwing into relief their fine white teeth as they moved their mouths now and then in a half-laugh and a short jerk of the head. At their elbows the tumblers of heady scented Forian wine (which the outside world knows ill and overmuch-handled as Lacrimæ Christi) caught the candle's eye and shone like dull topaz lamps about the rough wine-spilled table. They rarely laughed outright or made much noise: as though in emerging from their shadow-selves they must dissolve on the common air. After the perfunctory evening greeting to the eccentric englishwoman they ignored her; unless a newcomer with them had just heard her story and must take long under-eyelid looks at her until, his curiosity sated, he could ignore her with the rest.

A sight of which she never tired. Every night would find them in the same positions, in the same light, at the same game. Whether the faces of the players were the same was of no importance: there could be only young or old versions of the one theme. A few drinking-boys' heads, a few Spagnoletto saints regretting their desert-fasts emaciation, sat together at an inn table and discovered that wine was good and that they were by no means as saintly as they had supposed; which made them jerk their heads at intervals and bare their teeth. Such was her idea of art: a pretty trick of ready-made shadow and a ready-made masterpiece ready to the artist's brush. It pleased her. (She had tried to make Uller paint them and had been surprised and silenced by the vehemence with which he had cursed the whole damned School, shouting loudly for electric light: the salvation of Art. Of the world seeing that it let the sun shine all night, and only by light could one paint. For paint is colour: not excrement. And now its torch had been handed to night. Aired, exposed the darkness and rubbish accumulated through centuries of candlelight. Ordered Lisetta to inform him immediately why she pandered to the fifth-rate taste of genteel englishwomen and continued upholding the barbarous and insanitary customs of her ancestors. Told her to tie strings of tri-colour lights along the vines and walls as all patriotic italian inn-keepers should. And the music? Where was the gramophone? None of your tremoloing brigands. If he wanted to return to Sorrento, shouted Uller flushed with the sound of himself and as usual at his most loud and effective when he had succeeded in making her face retire within itself as it were, drop down its curtains, dissociate itself completely before the handful of italians from his street-boy rudenesses, if he wanted to return to Sorrento he'd make up his own mind about it and not be driven there to escape demented guitarists trying their moonlight-and-napoli aphrodisiac on sluggish tourists. Rows of red white and green lights glaring down in hard icy stare on the tables and a gramophone blaring any popular tune of the moment: and let the whole island in to caper to it and drive the *tenebrosi* and their sham picturesque that quickened the heartbeats of english spinsters back to the darkness of the Michelangelos (the curse of art, that man!) let loose over europe, and from which, thank God, they were slowly but at last emerging.)

Small green lizards, elegant miniature crocodiles, darted after flies on the evening walls. From where she sat she could see the full uddery bladders gleaming through the darkness of the kitchen, strung among the strings of garlic and sausage hanging from the heavy whitewashed beams, richly golden as old amber or polished ivory of great age.

I n such manner from first to last night fell for her. Each incident tallied: except that the Concettas or Giovannis or Graziellas or any other of the innumerable children about the place, grew and made way for the Giovannas the Peppes the Marias to bring the offering of their small candle-grease faces to glow in the shadow; except that Uller had come, had gone; except that the sun had not exhausted its many gracious or angry ways of retiring; nor the moon of appearing; nor the clouds of transforming themselves into the likeliest pattern to harmonise with these beginnings and endings, these departures and arrivals.

Remained the evening meal to be eaten, after which Lisetta, bringing herself the coffee to the table, would fetch her sewing or embroidery or a small heap of those very clean very coarse table-napkins she had all but respun with her darning, and rest herself for an hour or so: an indispensable item of the evening ritual. The two women talked together in low friendly voices. Ruth read aloud extracts from the day's papers. Again Lisetta was surprised at everything. Still surprised at everything. Especially did she like to hear about the road accidents. Again they appalled and delighted her. Still appalled and delighted her, although now they were so frequent and so similar with their same number of motor-cars running into the same number of pedestrians and the same number of pedestrians running under the same number of motor-cars, that that alone should have cooled Lisetta's ardour and pleasure. On the contrary they grew on what they fed: so that by now only a really ruthless train-smash could distract her attention from man and machine in conflict: and what followed for the man. And Ruth read on and on, prolonging the agony for Lisetta and for herself. A treat for Lisetta; a respite for herself.

For after that the evening was at an end and she must go up to the room where Richard slept. Came the scene for which the whole evening had set itself. She had been waiting for this. As something she dared not finger or look at it had lain on the floor of her mind while the sky went through its nightly performance, the children and passers-by ranged themselves in their order, the orchestration of sound and colour swelled and diminished, the men played cards during the interval, she herself going through her leading part among them all, taking her cue with easy familiarity about the shadow stage with its shadow background. And it was not only the evening that passed in preparation for it. That was an untrue and ineffectual evasion. In a sense the whole day was a preparation. The whole night. Waking and sleeping was a preparation. Eating, reading, watching was a preparation. The thing was inescapable. No sooner did she leave him than she was preparing herself to see him again.

Not that she did not see him in the daytime. She did, seeing that he was bound to be around the corner if one turned it. But that mattered little. In the daytime he meant little to her. He was but one of the many players among whom she also moved. In the daytime she could endure him because in the light he did not reproach her. In the light he was not hers. He did not belong especially to her. He might belong to anyone; to whoever was with him and attending him at the moment. Not more to her than to anyone else. All took their share in him. In the daylight he had no claim on her. Or comparatively small claim. For in the day she was distracted and impersonal. The daylight saved her. The daylight always saved her. And that was why when it began to fail, when it began gradually to give way to darkness she became precise in her movements, as though she would fall, knowing them as a sleepwalker knows doors and stairs and passes them with safety and sureness. Until the moment came for her to leave the table and find herself in his room, awake.

She thought it was only as night fell that such preparation had been shaping itself at the back of her mind. She had feared and put it from her all the day. But she did not know this. Only at night it was no longer possible to ignore it and so she was afraid of the night. When night fell she died utterly. She was afraid. She was wretched. Lately she had come to fear the night as an unhappy man fears sleep for the recurring nightmare that must come with it. At times she could have howled with fear like a child waking from an ugly dream and aware that reality may be but the continuance of it. Because her soul was sick: and only robust souls can treat night with indifference and connect it with the rotations of the earth, and pretend that it is no stranger than the day.

Each night she went to her son's room to wish him good-night and see that he was comfortable, and bend over him as a woman bends over her child and watches its sleeping face. Or rather seeing that it was manifestly absurd for her to wish him good-night or for her to take delight in his quiescent face, she went each night to her son's room mentally wringing her Macbethan hands which not all the perfumes of arabia etc. But Lady Macbeth, it had once occurred to her in one of those moments when she could stir up a certain grim laughter at the folly of her self-imposed and never-ending penance, at the useless martyrdom which she had taken upon herself in a moment of fervour and repentance, Lady Macbeth did not have to live with the corpse. Decidedly Lady Macbeth did not have to live with the corpse. And she would writhe with dry laughter at the thought of the Macbeths with an unshakeoffable Banquo planted at their table, obstinately standing his ghostly ground and stubbornly fixing them with his blood-caked eye over their porringers.

They would have grown used to it. Custom stales. Custom would have dulled the fire in Banquo's eye and the remorse in his hosts' hearts. A few more years and they would scarcely have looked over the edge of their bowls to see if it were fixing them. And had it been they'd have yawned in it, the grotesque unwinking carnival eye with red-stuff on it!

Not so with Ruth who had had no legend to bring her to life or relieve her of it and of her corpse and its responsibility. So that she had had to learn her lesson: that tomorrow always comes. Only in youth can one believe that one will die in the night. That mercifully no day will seek one out. That one will sleep for ever in one's pain, nursed on the sleep-sea on which, for the eternity of a few kind hours, one sinks. But tomorrow always comes. The day returns. Too soon: but returns. And when at last one accepts this adolescence has been left behind: though one is seventy.

S he had not always felt this about going up to see him and say good-night. In the beginning it had been a comparatively easy, almost a natural, task. Even when Uller was there her attitude had not changed. She had always been somewhat afraid of the darkness which falls with such remorseless certainty. Only recently had it become a menace. Only recently had she become aware of how very much she dreaded her nocturnal visits to her son. Possibly the dread had always been there in a half-hearted way, but now it was as though being tired of her long vigil with herself she had transferred it to a horror of the thing responsible for it. Which was absurd, for she alone was responsible for it. She had lived a long time with her own guilt. Possibly she was tiring of it. Possibly she was thinking that perhaps she had paid. Not in full, but in great part: anyway, enough. Lately she had taken to insisting to herself that as he did not know her when she came, or know that she came; and that therefore as he did not know her. . . . She had fallen as far from grace as that! Coward, coward, she said. And she knew it and despised herself and was restless. Lately she had grown restless. But she went upstairs at night just the same.

That measure of calm and quiescence which so many years had built up was gone. Gone suddenly: but why? Outwardly nothing had altered. Each day for twenty-two years had been much the same, passing out down the road with the smooth gentle-faced goats. She herself noticed no change. Certainly no regrets. Put back the clock twenty-two years and she would have done the same thing again. She would have accepted the monstrous thing that she had done and taken the consequences. Certainly she had no regrets. She was being suddenly confronted with something much more difficult to handle: doubts.

During his childhood's years it had all been so much more difficult for her to realise. Or rather so much more easy to ignore. And of course the glamour of the thing was still on her. Through all the horror at what she had done the glamour was there. Was (who knows?) still there. Put back the clock twenty-three years and she would still do very much the same thing. She would still try. She still thought much about mankind as she had thought then. Even though with years her ideas had altered about many things and she knew that she had been wrong and foolishly young and romantic and trustful. Though she knew that there is but one purpose in life. Man woman and child and child and child. Woman and child. Wash child, wash corpse. That was all there was to it. That was all there should be to it. Could be to it. Woman from the neck downward. Man from the neck downward and upward, as he chose. But for woman no choice. I think, Stephen. I think. I think I carry my womb in my forehead. And she did. And still did. And always would. Because some there are whose souls are more pregnant than their bodies. No, Socrates. And no one has ever thought of applying that to women, because women, Dora. From the neck down, breasts and thighs and pelvic bone. And for head an enlarged heart. A fatty noble heart swollen with appropriate emotions.

Faced with his useless feet and staring silence she had known at once that she was wrong. And even had she not known it, that was soon learned in this land of old women and babies. She knew very well how far from grace she had fallen. But what if she had succeeded? She could still wonder about that at the back of her wilful half-repentant heart. Half-repentant: repenting the consequences and not the cause, which is hardly a repentance at all.

For she still found it difficult to believe that man as he existed was the highest form of life. She still could not bring herself to see that because man questioned and concluded he was to be placed higher than animals who did not (to human knowledge) leave their doubts on death, on life, on gods, for posterity to ponder. She still found the very fact of man's arrogant will-to-know against him. Wild creatures contained their answer within themselves. They were complete unto themselves: their completeness was their answer.

The highest? Certainly the most stupid, the most destructive. No animal destroyed itself so willingly and so conscientiously as man. And yet the most afraid of death!

Uller had once told her that only two kinds of beings are indispensable: the peasant and the artist: the body and the soul: the bread and the wine. She was more and more inclined to the belief that only one of these was indispensable: the peasant, the body, the bread. Leave the drunken soul to its mischief; let it lie fallow a while and give bread and water a chance.

She could still think with distaste of mankind being born into a world not new and having to adapt itself to theories and habits made to fit it by others. How old, how nearly rotten with age seemed man's world. Hourly on its crust swarmed new life. New life appeared on the worn-out world and the worn-out world closed in.

And his children what were they? His challenge to Death. His defeat of death. His root which must not wither. His right to life by proxy. What he cannot achieve his children shall achieve. His work lies unfinished: never mind, his children shall bring it to completion. Safely, safely to completion. They were born only to bring to completion that which he had had to leave incomplete; and was presumably worth completing.

But she had not wanted, and did not want, to live by proxy. (Cook's Tourists in their own lives, had said Uller.) To her a child must be something complete within itself, without a why or a thank-you or a perhaps. She had asked of life a new form. A being who would have escaped the worn-out form and order of life. As other women ask deified parodies of their lovers or husbands; or like music and hope it will perform on a piano; or follow the family tradition of being a lawyer, a judge, a gentleman, a greengrocer; an engine-driver is the father merely a porter; a baronet is the paternal parent a mere industrialist. She still could find it strange that what man conceives in stone and colour and sound he cannot conceive in flesh and blood. So much for the drunken-soul of him!

Enough of the drunken-soul and its mischief. Out they rush with a wail into a worn-out world. The worn-out world closes in on the new life. And by the time the new life has freed itself (if it ever really does) it has acquired the prison garb and the prison habits. So that it cannot be free. It can never be free. Freedom is not for the new thing on the musty-smelling earth. The new thing will continue living its second nature. Always on its acquired habits.

She could still wonder at this at the back of her wilful half-repentant heart. That was the core of her. That was the drunken-soul core of her which she had plucked out and finished with at twenty-two; the mirage she could still see at times, though she no longer looked for it. For now she believed in the body and the bread. Wash child, wash corpse. Let man look to his own salvation. For woman it lay from the neck downward; breasts and thighs and pelvic bone. And for head the ever-enlarging heart. The fatty ever-noble heart swollen with appropriate emotions.

The darkness had not always been a menace to her. She had not always been afraid of going to his room at night. She had bent over him with becoming enough grace, as a child. But now he was no longer a child, and she had grown restless and tired and even rebellious. Not a little tired of it all.

It was now his turn to reproach her. She told herself that now that he was a man he reproached her, though she knew that he could no more do so now than on the day he was born. It was merely the morbid attitude of mind towards things large or small. Between killing a cat or an ox. The result is the same, but the one seems so much more unpleasant and brutal than the other.

She felt that everything had been repented of and in some measure expiated; and been turned to the calm that is or should be the reward of long habit and uneventfulness. And now it seemed as if the struggle must be taken up again, as though she had not finished it long ago and was entitled to her reward and rest. She had the right, she felt, to desire not to be disturbed.

So absorbed had she been in the years of attainment of her gradual peace that it had taken a dream to make her aware that he was a man. Uller told her that her son was now a man; and she had replied with that curious casual acceptance of dreams: yes, Richard is now a man. They were standing in the piazza and it was very hot. They stood together in heavy heat without shade. Uller kept looking over his shoulder with such persistence that she lost patience and said: one would say that your head was turned back to front. And Uller said: so it is. And so it was. So she went round to the back of him to talk. His face was not at all the face she remembered him to have had: but she knew his strong handsome hands which he now held joined as though in prayer as they talked. As they stood talking (she couldn't remember what was said) they became aware of Richard stalking them with an idiotic concentrated malice: darting about on the points of his toes from tree to tree and along the wall of the house opposite: focussing them with an awful intent with his long eyes, cool as water. They began fussing about in a sort of half-panic to avoid him and ran down a street leading off the piazza, dark with shadow. There he was at the bottom of it, waiting for them. They turned back and ran and ran and then she was in a carriage, an old enclosed carriage, something like an old London cab, which smelt rather unpleasant. She looked out of the window in the blinding light and saw that they were climbing a narrow steep path beside the sea, up and up a long rocky path. She was relieved. It was much too hot to run.

She heard some-one panting in her ears, although no one was in sight. Pant pant pant. Some-one was toiling after them, making a terrible effort in the sunshine to reach them. Higher and higher they climbed.

And then the coachman suddenly stopped for his horse's convenience. It went on and on; a fountain of horse inundating the road. The horse standing taut and slowly taking on the grey-green surface quality of stone. The coachman's back relaxed in a first attitude of sleep. This was awful. She leaned forward and with a weak hand shook the man's shoulder. His coat was so hot that she tore her hand away. The palm and fingers were lined with small white blisters; but she felt no pain. She opened her mouth to speak and her voice would not come; so she went quite close to the man's ear and seemed to pour her words in it with great and careful effort. Quickly, she said. We have no time to waste. Be quick. PLEASE BE VERY QUICK. She must be shouting now. She grinned at the ear, her mouth wide and set. I must be very gracious to him, she thought. She thought: now the road will be muddy and difficult to follow. He will slip and drown. And yet she knew that it was not so. Pant pant pant. The horse must be finding it difficult to climb the hill, she thought. And again she knew that it was not so. Her ears were filled with the heaving raucous breaths. He was gaining on them. Again she thought: it is the horse. And then felt the breath on her neck: a sudden hot jet running down her neck, thick and slimy. She shivered her head and turned to the window, and there was his face looking indescribably foolish and malignant, hardly larger than an apple, lolling to the right of the handle.

She was surprised, but not yet afraid. Then she saw that she was alone in the carriage and she thought: Hans has left me, and felt tears on her cheeks. Pant pant pant. The sound filled the carriage and with it the heavy dragging of feet. How tired he must be, she thought listening to the leaden dragging steps, and feeling an infinity of sadness for all who were tired. So much tiredness, she felt, saddened her. She wept a little, noiselessly, pleased that she could weep without noise.

And then quite slowly the head began to grow. It balanced itself on the projecting celluloid stick handle and with a fixed and horrible intensity grew steadily larger and larger. And as it grew she crouched. She found herself fighting to make herself smaller and flatten herself against the far side of the carriage to give it space. The panting became louder than ever and the feet dragged themselves with frightful, heavy menace. The head was now enormous: and as it swelled it slowly turned a nauseating purply brown colour. Its eyes were shut, but she felt that they saw her, had found out exactly where she crouched. And now she was frightened. She made a sudden agonising and futile effort to huddle out of sight. But by now the head had swollen to such dimensions that it filled the carriage window on all sides with its purply brown pulp. She smelt a sour decaying smell; a putrid smell of meat and excrement. She saw large drops of sweat oozing from the forehead and upper lip. It was swelling so rapidly that now it spread over the edges of the window and the frame gripped it painfully at the neck and skull as its colour darkened steadily. The windowframe creaked under the pressure of the monstrous swelling head which now took up more than half the carriage. Suddenly a look of indescribable agony came over its face; and then a sudden relief. And then without opening the eyes or relaxing a muscle, it quivered horribly at the window, wrenched itself free, heaved in a last supreme effort to reach her, and fell with a ghastly and deliberate clatter at her feet. She could not get them away in time and felt them wet and sticky with blood. And looking down at her feet she saw the eyes slowly open and look for her.

Lisetta was at her bedside. In the absurd kimono which she had discarded so many years ago. The silks frayed, the colours dead. Lisetta was holding her hand. Such screams! Mother of God, they froze the stomach. Ruth sat bathed in sweat. She clung to Lisetta's hand stupefied by the sudden light. She put up her hand to ease her hair away from her neck, and then at the ears and temples. At the roots it was wet and clotted.

Ho avuto un sogno. She ran her outstretched fingers through the wet roots of her hair, looking up at Lisetta so hardy and reassuring, smiling down at her a good reassuring grin of good-fellowship of the whole face; warming her slowly back to life. Non mi lasciare; non mi lasciare sola! Ho tanta paura. . . .

But Lisetta did leave her now that she was propped on her pillows, her hair newly brushed and plaited, to go to the kitchen and make some strong coffee. Ruth sat up, still and surprised, relaxed after the awful experience of the dream tension, and feeling physically weak.

It was nearly four o'clock. The sky was luminous with a fresh wash of pale colour; the dawn was breaking. She looked long at the sky which promised Lisetta so much. She sat still and surprised as though she had been rescued from sudden and brutal death. Rescued too late. She felt that she had died and been brought back to life. Late and unwillingly. Yet how good to lie back and take long looks around the familiar room, embracing it gratefully with the mind's eye, reassured and on the whole grateful, though physically weak as after a long illness.

Lisetta came back with the coffee and a dish of fruit. She said that Maria was afraid that she must be badly hurt to cry like that. Hurt? She thinks, explained Lisetta, that you fell out of bed. Which was just what was needed. She laughed till there were tears on her cheeks.

So that now she was obsessed with the thought that he reproached her. She knew that he could not do so, yet the obsession remained. More, it strengthened. How it came to her first she could not tell. It suddenly seemed right and natural that now that he was a man he should reproach her. So she grew restless and not a little tired of it all, feeling that she had paid, not in full, of course, but in great part. Almost enough. She did not want to begin again; how could she? She had been so intent on hoarding some measure of calm through the years which she voluntarily had dedicated to him. Now such calm was beginning to fail her, and she did not want to begin again. She had built up her calm of mind and body through twenty years and from much effort. It was a mistake, the years said, but it was long ago. It means little. It is forgotten. And here she was at the end of it all with her heart suddenly as feverish as a girl's; and no stronger.

In the immediate fervour of repentance following on what she had done, she had taken on herself the expiation of her sin. She had allowed no one to shoulder her burden for her: nor herself to shelve it. Which would not have been difficult, and far more pleasant. Cruel and selfish she had been. Had ridden rough-shod over everyone. They ceased once more to exist for her. The fervour of repentance was on her; she must expiate. And no one existed for her but her child and herself: herself only as an instrument of service. In such a state of mental fervour and will-to-sacrifice nothing could turn her from her purpose. She set and hardened to a state of maniacal rigidity of purpose, that daemonic rigidity of female purpose seen in female saints and poisoners. She could have passed through barred windows and iron-clamped doors. No prison had been devised that could hold her. She knew it and died to everything around her; lived only in the adamantine purpose of her female will.

She told Stephen the truth. That was part of the expiation, and his due. He did not believe her. How could he? I did this, she said. It is my fault. I willed it. I am responsible.

He was full of pity for her. His mind still could not compass the full extent of the misfortune that had suddenly come their way; and as though the thing in itself were not enough but she must needs take it thus. So she became cunning. Hard and cunning. Once her confession made she never again referred to her share in the matter. She let him think what he could not help thinking: exactly what they were all thinking. That this wild desire of hers to take the child away, abroad, anywhere, herself alone with it, her life given to it, was something rather sad and beautiful; was touching and beautiful. Wrong, ridiculous, but touching and beautiful. To be resisted as something which she would (must) eventually see when finally restored to health; when time had healed; for the unreasonable and useless thing it was. But in her heart she despised him. Despised his maudlin pity-offering: his gathering-together of all the sentiments proper to the occasion. All the correct gentlemanly sentiments which could most humiliate her in her pride; turning her fine courage to the delirium of a sick and disappointed woman.

As though she would be making this gift of herself to an accident! Was not this very desire for expiation the outcome of her guilt: and its proof? What had had accident to do with her? A fall? A throw back? A pre-natal impression. Would these have lighted the candle in her heart that not all the days of her life would put out? To how many women did that happen! How many children of good birth were to be found shut away in private homes, thrown aside, discarded in asylums; out of sight and mind and dutifully attended by all the comfort and neglect which money can buy. Could she not also have sent it away; placed it conveniently from sight; hidden it in the many rooms unused or seen; bought aid and ease for it and paid others to keep it from her sight for ever? Did they then find it so easy, this thing which she was doing, that she would do it for another's guilt?

Do not admit your guilt: cover it up, as a dog covers its dirt: let all be as it was. But she could not. She felt too deeply her share in the tragedy. Had the penalty been death she would have died. So she took her child away: ostensibly for a sufficient period of time in which to regain her health. But she knew she would not return. She left her Eden only too willingly; indeed had to struggle to get beyond the gates. She was surprised at Eve, hiding her face in her arms and weeping. The relief was immediate. She had been very hard and definite in her refusal to accept an allowance of money. This was her business. She had her small yearly income of a few hundreds; her own money; her father's money. It more than sufficed them. Outwardly she was numb. Nothing seemed to reach her. Her eyes remained bright and speechless.

Lisetta undressing him for the first time, unfolding the quiescent elegant bundle with the slow beautiful natural joy of the italian woman before the child, had given a high sudden cry, and Ruth had felt her heart tremble as she stood colouring with shame looking where Lisetta looked. The italian woman's sharp accusing cry as she stood with the small white sock in her hand: the soft first-shoe which some women lay secretly aside with a few toys and perhaps a letter or two. She had been told by one of the nurses that the child had come from her without a cry. That first lusty yell of relief a new-born creature gives at finding the struggle over, had not been given. He had made no sound. She remembered that now, and she was glad that she had left her safe Eden.

Had fought her way out of it to this sudden protesting cry. To the angry accusing cry which he had not been able to make and unknowing had found some-one to make for him. She was glad of it as she stood red with shame before the italian woman. But she did not expose herself again. She did not say: I did that. Never again. Not even to Uller did she say: I did that. He was puzzled as to whether it was a premature birth; or the result of an impression during pregnancy; or heredity; or an attempt at abortion: and rather favoured the last. She so evidently was not what is called a maternal woman. She showed little trace of affection for the child, though attentive to it in that she would sit beside it for hours on end and was restless until she knew with whom it was and where. She stitched away, embroidered, learned to knit, seemingly more to distract herself or pass the time away than because she was interested in what she was doing. He could never recall hearing her speak of it. Indeed there seemed to be some kind of tacit agreement among those about her that he was not to be mentioned.

Uller having suffered much from the maternal ardour of woman liked and approved her attitude, surprised that any woman could resist the temptation to impose her will with deadly and possessive female purpose on what morally and maternally and legally speaking was hers. He could not know that she felt no such temptation: having imposed her will.

H e was nearly seven when Uller came to spend the June and July of 1913 on the island, and was still in the wheelbarrow-cum-bench-on-wheels of local manufacture and design. But later she ordered for him one of those gay painted wheeled carts from Castellamare: absurdly gay, primitive, and exotic with a profusion of reds and yellows, and a strangely-staring saint reliving his sad bright life about the panels.

What a char for my Bacchus, she thought grimly the first time she saw him seated in it, the children quarrelling among themselves as to who should push it on its first journey. She found that the wheels were too high, coming almost to the rim of the cart, and she was anxious (O exquisite irony) for his hands which he trailed over the sides; and the children came to learn that their first duty before starting was to see that his hands were inside the cart.

It seemed to her he had liked his new cart. He seemed never to tire

of staring at the bright-coloured patterns. He liked bright colours. Any
new bright pattern could hold his attention for hours. He would lie
watching Uller at his easel with a catlike intensity of concentration,
following the ladling on of colour (for to Ruth, used to the discretion of
the English School which she admired, and the sobriety of the more
soberly respectable Old Masters, Uller seemed to pat and plaster his
colour on the canvas with a trowel. More like a master-mason than an
academician, was her secret comment), and the movement of Uller's
yellow-sleeved shirt. Uller had a circus-tent taste in shirts. Richard
stared and stared and seemed to approve them. Any thing bright or
shining he watched with the same feline intensity: and at times made
sounds and sighs. Curious sounds they were, sometimes sharp and
sudden, sometimes long and throaty: conveying whatever one read in
them. But such, with that stare of hard concentration, that will-to-
know look that came in his eyes, his brows drawn down and tense, that
she would suddenly feel that only speech and movement were lacking,
and that he was not. Not.

For instance his way of balancing himself on a chair and propelling
himself strongly and safely about the terrazza. He had found that out
for himself by accident. He was about seventeen at the time. While
arranging the pillows and rugs on his painted cart they usually lifted
him on to the bed or lowered him to the floor. For some reason this
day, no bed being near, they placed him on a chair. His long legs
touched the floor and swung against the chair legs. It was the first time
he had ever been placed on a chair. In the unexpected freedom of his
hanging legs he began, it seems, to rock his body. It was a slow hesitating movement without strength or consciousness. He rocked his body
slowly and carefully. Then apparently gaining confidence he accelerated
the movement, and with the gathering strength of the movement the
chair began rocking also. All at once the chair moved forward slowly,
jerking from side to side. Suddenly he stopped moving his legs; paused;
and just as suddenly began again. He appeared to understand that the
chair was moving at his will. At any rate he understood that the chair
was moving. To the onlookers it was clear that he was willing it. The
control came directly from his body: from the base of his spine and his
back which were pressed against the back of the chair. Sitting there
with his loosely hanging legs and stiffened back some sudden instinct of
self-preservation seemed to be working in him. He swung his legs and
stiffened his back and spine and the chair moved. He stopped: the chair
stopped. So he moved on again.

They set up a clamour and a cry and ran to fetch her. A miracle! *Signor'* vien'—vien'-veder'. Un miracolo! Mother of God to have seen the day! And there he was stumping about the room on his chair: jerking slowly from side to side; the legs of the chair advancing slowly carefully, controlled by the mechanism of his spine and back. It was a strange and unreal sight. No wonder they thought it a miracle. It was so nearly a walk. It was as though by some divine dispensation he had been given the nerves, the spine, the haunch sinews of an acrobat, and the sudden decision and power to use them to advantage. His sense of balance alone was astonishing. The moment was tense with a certain macabre unreality and quite unforgettable. Herself in the centre of the doorway crowded with familiar figures whom in the excitement of the moment she could no longer distinguish, nor the many sounds and signs they made, watching avid open-mouthed this surprising acrobatic performance by something, by some-one who had not, to anyone's knowledge, sat upright in his life. A miracle indeed! How not? By what divine accident had he been placed this day on a chair instead of the usual bed or floor? What divine dispensation had come to his aid with the nerves and spine of an acrobat, and the sudden power to seize and use them? It was obvious and simple enough to be uncanny. Leave him, she said, to the exclamatory and awestruck household. Do not disturb him. Let him learn.

On and on he went. Rock, rock, left, right, this way, that way, advancing, retreating, avoiding, choosing his path. Slowly steadily monotonously surely. But how soon they had grown used to their miracle! By now they had almost forgotten that it had not always been so; such a familiar sight as he now was, rock-rocking his way about the house. He used it for all purposes, except for the sands or when the children went to the Pineta to gather pine needles or play, or went any distance from home and wanted to take him with them. Then they still used his painted cart, now in its third new coat, the same profusion of reds and yellows, the same tribulations of the same brightly staring saint on the panels.

No wonder she now felt that he reproached her his twenty-two years of uselessness. His one assertion of will his rock-rocking about the house; a blind vindictive man's stick beat-beating on the tiled floor for her ears.

Yesterday in the late afternoon on the point of going to the town she had come on him unexpectedly on the terrazza. With a swift preoccupied movement she came through the open doors. There he sat looking at nothing. The sudden unexpected movement must have frightened him for as she was about to pass he gave a high sudden laugh: like a shriek, a sob, a guffaw; something obscene and startling. She too was almost angrily startled. About to pass him she paused. She thought she detected something unusual, almost personal, almost angry in the sound, so unlike his usual shouts and noises. She stopped dead in front of him. Clearly her imagination was playing havoc with her nerves. However it was, she had the strong impression that it was not his usual cry. That he recognised her. She felt that he was speaking to her. So she stood quite still and on an impulse, thinking that it might please him, might reach him, she did a dreadful thing. She stood still and throwing back her face she imitated his cry, shrill and hollow and sustained: imitated it on the whole very convincingly. It was the first time she had ever done such a thing. Perhaps, she thought, I have found his way of speech. But the sound hung in the air too long. It laughed the last. It mocked her. Immediately it was made she knew that it was useless. The echo mocked her, leaving her ridiculous and shamed.

A look sly and alert came in his face. He listened. Obviously he was surprised. His mouth opened as though to make another of his sudden animal sounds, but he made none. Instead he gathered his forehead in a knot between his eyebrows, and his grey eyes, speechless, almost transparent, stared at her face, at her mouth, stared and stared from the one to the other with a wild surprised intensity. Was he waiting for her to repeat the sound? If he was she was incapable of doing so. Was it fear or menace in that fixed grotesque stare behind which he seemed to be gathering himself together to spring at her, or leap away?

She began to tremble slightly as she often found herself trembling in moments when he was not merely a thing dumb, pitiful, deformed, but something evil, monstrous, and unreal into whose power she had delivered herself. He knows! he knows! scrunched her feet over the stony path as she hurried away, going to the town the steeper and more tiring way rather than pass in front of him. Run away, scrunched her feet. Run away. Cain his own accuser. Whenever he stared full at her with that strained intense mesmeric look her heart trembled with the thought: he knows.

At such times had he suddenly spoken and accused her she would not have found it strange. She would have known even the words; she had been expecting them too long. She might even have been relieved. Which was absurd. He stared in exactly the same way at Lisetta, Pasquale, Maria, Concetta, the bowl of noci, the goats, the half-open door, the lizards on the evening walls, Mario plaiting his tight scarlet ropes of tomatoes, the mad high fiddling of the cicala, the crimson and emerald pepperoni lying about the tables, the wine-stained cloth, the coloured discs of the inlaid floor; any and every familiar sight of which, through some momentary trick of attention, he seemed suddenly aware for the first time.

He slept, and she was relieved and stood longer than usual looking down at his pale-coloured hair damp on his forehead, his curved eyelashes resting on his cheeks, soft eyelashes of a young and appealing woman; his well-cut nose, fine-nostrilled. Uller had once told her that she had the too-thin high nostrils of the fanatic. Richard had them also; asleep they gave his thin face a look of tension, almost of severity. His head thrown back on the pillow lay half out of the bed; his left shoulder lay across the edge of the bed; his left hand touched the floor. She did not lift him back for fear of waking him. But turned out the light and went out on the stone balcony that joined the house from end to end, and leaning on the stone edge of the balustrade wondered why strong and active beings are sad in sleep, nullified, emptied of all that which gives them reality, the husk of their own eagerness and pulsation: so that one cannot look on them asleep without pity; whereas weak and empty beings achieve in sleep a certain static unity, a borrowed strength, a certain three-dimensional reality that is not their own: as though in quiescence, in complete abandon, they were fulfilled, and serene and harmonious may no longer be pitied.

The moon lay sideways, effaced; a pale shell lying in ripples of blue sand. A wash of milky stars was on the dark surface of the sky. It was August, the month of shooting stars, often standing there she had counted as many as thirty within the hour, which reminded her always of Ibsen's remark on first seeing Milan Cathedral: the man who made that could make moons in his spare time and toss them into space! Below her the green vine-forest disappeared in a swaying movement of dark reeds waving darkly and tortuously on the floor of the sea and seen through heavy water. The heavy suction-sound of the sea was in it; sucking in, swallowing up, no traces left. Everything as it was; as though it had not been. It was like the dreadful sound of a bucket being thrown down into a well, a sound to which she still could not grow used. It was like death.

Strange that she should fear night who had no fear of death. Night fell so heavily, so inexorably on the earth: on her earth. How could one help fearing it? It was beyond all argument; beyond question. Nothing of this dark threatening-angel business about death. On the contrary it was clear-outlined and intelligible to her, just as night was dark and unreal to her. Night, like birth, was a wearisome, unfinished, repetitive business, whereas death was clean and final. She had not a particle of fear of death. And not because she expected some reward in a mythical hereafter. She found no comfort whatsoever in the many popular forms of belief in survival after death: so very much the coward's way out. The secret door one keeps ready.

Of course as a child she had seen Heaven as a vast very pretty mother-of-pearly domed hall, a sort of ducal ballroom magnified exceedingly, with golden gates and golden floors which would be slippery and difficult to walk on, though nice to slide on (but would one be allowed to slide on Heaven's floor?) and a great many carved and high-backed golden chairs with elderly people sitting on them; and at the end on a throne was God with his long grey beard (but very *very* kind to *every*-one), and the grey dove over his head and a great deal of golden light rayed from his head, and Jesus and his Mother and all the Disciples, and Latimer and Ridley and Sir Thomas More, and a great many plump Bishops and Deans and vicars and old ladies, and all the poor people now prettily dressed and smiling, and all the sick people now healed and pleased, and many beautiful angels and a great deal of music, and everyone singing; all the time singing and sitting very straight on golden chairs with high carved backs.

Followed inevitably the age when it seemed so much more real and worthy to go where all the wicked and interesting people went. The time when grew the suspicion that those glorious creatures, so passionate, or gay, or wise, or cruel, that the dun world could not forget them, deny them as it would!, would not have been at all at their ease among the Bishops and old ladies.

I t would be good to be buried under a tree, she had said, that after-noon on which they walked together above Barano. To be reborn each year in its sap and renewed in its bloom. That was the only form of perpetuity she could believe in.

One dies in a room, on a chair, on a bed, and one leaves a certain part of one's self in that chair or bed for ever. Nothing can ever wholly cleanse them of that influence: of what one has dissolved into. . . . Even when dismantled, broken up: there one is still in the bits and pieces: will always be. That is immortality. Manure the earth; fade out on the air. That is why it was so horrible going down to the earth in boxes. Not letting one have the earth and its action about one: coldly and tightly about one. It makes life so flippant, so negligible. To deny one's body to the earth and all that flows and flowers from it. Being respectable to the very end! The pretty box might keep the grave-worms out.

She could imagine if some-one she loved intensely came to die before her, burying them under a vine and each year when they flowered and came to fruition eating the grapes or having them pressed into wine. She said wine because everything is vine here in the South. But at home (why should she have said home? She corrected herself) in the North she would choose an apple or cherry tree. First the sharp staccato of new leaves and then those hard incredibly green buds, and then the morning on which one goes to the window, goes as though one were expecting nothing unusual, and it is as though the tree sang with steely blossom, so clean, so full of hope and promise, and then cherries like blood and rough apples like flesh. Of a person one loves that would be beautiful, she thought: for both. For the dead and for the living. I would like to flower and come again in the same way to the person who loved me sufficiently to want me to renew myself for them yearly. . . .

How strange and irrational we are, she said, going through an outworn symbol of drinking the blood of Christ whom we have never known; never fully understood or realised as a real person; who has been rather thrust upon one from childhood. A certain hallowed cannibalism. He had the right idea, of course. But only to the few. Only to the very few. Only to those who had known and loved him: and to whom he offered it. One could imagine him being very tired of it all when he thinks of the millions and millions . . . being thoroughly ashamed at having been made the refuge of the weak-minded. Or was it rather the weapon of the strong-minded?

Exactly. That he could understand. He felt like that whenever he saw a violinist or a singer or a pianist, or what they call a famous musician, bowing and scraping and thoroughly pleased with himself before the shouts and the thunder. He never looks around his audience to see their faces! He, Uller, wanted to jump on his chair and shout: Look at them first! Don't thank them till you've seen them! Had she noticed how musicians and priests get the most imbecile-looking audiences? Concert halls and churches filled with people with their mouths open and nothing behind their eyes but tear ducts? Why should Christ be more squeamish than Caruso or Paderewski? Judge a man by his friends! Then God be praised that an artist can't see his admirers!

And he was off and away chasing his musicians. How he loathed them all! And music. Especially Wagner. He called it Jew-sound. Thick and rich and unsimple. And if one ventured Scarlatti or Bach he said spinet-sound: a hammer on a nail and a piece of wire. He said music was a drug: as potent as religion and almost as pernicious. He called music auricular self-abuse. He said a singer or a violinist or a pianist was a well-trained acrobat without the acrobat's courage. He could perform without endangering his life. He could land on a wrong note without breaking his neck.

And their conceit! Was there a set of people in the world so eaten with conceit? The greatest painter alive hadn't the conceit of the smallest singer or meanest fiddler. And what was it all but a mixture of stubbornness and capacity to stay put. An unfair trick. A digital tongue-twister, as it were. A swim swan over the sea swim swan swim swim swan back to me well swum swan, in all its alphabetic variations, and when they had it pat they ran and declaimed it in public, and everyone thought it wo-o-nderful knowing how much sitting and tongue-twisting it had taken to achieve.

—I like my acrobats in pink tights and spangles, said Uller.

(Thoughts on death. . . . Wiser perhaps to keep such things to oneself.)

Priests and musicians: how he hated them! The two forms of drunkenness he hated most. What a relief to meet an honest drink-sodden man, decently drunk out of a glass!

—This from an artist.

But not a drunken one. He could explain the wherefore of each of his brush strokes. His compositions were mathematical problems correctly resolved. As clear and as difficult. Nothing drunken there.

Yet watch him at work with that mason's trowel of his. All that which to her was static, the stretch of hot white sea, the sands thick and heavy with heat, the cypresses hanging high above them in the cemetery, at the very edge of that formidable yellow rock once a moorish stronghold—static, dazed with heat, held erect and leaning on it: was to him nothing short of an eruption. His cypresses were agitated as a wave, wilful, tormented. Ugly, she thought.

—I do not see it like that, she once said, looking up from her book.

Apparently no one saw it like that or he would give up painting. Also, she did not see it at all. She, as indeed most people, saw only what she had been taught to see.

He never spoke to her of his work after once listening to her opinion. Not so much that she was a woman as that she was an englishwoman. It simply was not in the blood. How can the english appreciate art when they cannot appreciate women or food? You're wrong, he would say and turn away and the conversation was ended. His shoulders said Go away and don't annoy me, silly creature. Oh oh oh. She would walk away trembling at his insolence. She who had been thought unusually daring for her admiration of Whistler! *Whistler?* WHISTLER? Ought to have provoked a japanese war. International complications for botched spy-work! But you have Turner, you english. TURNER. Turner at seventy. What do you want with Whistler? Aren't there a hundred thousand Whistlers?

She had always thought that artists were gentle-spoken creatures, diffident, silent. She had once, shortly after her marriage, sat next to Mr Sargent at a small informal most-agreeable dinner-party, and had found him monosyllabic to the point of embarrassment. It was apparently his usual manner. And then dear Sir Edward Paston, with his white-maned Arthurian head, who had admired her profile and colouring so discreetly yet so warmly that there had been talk of sittings, but that they had left for the country almost immediately. How gentle and wise, how infinitely lovable he had been! Artists were gentle-spoken creatures, diffident silent. Those whom she remembered had been like that. She told him so.

Really, he was very patient with her.

With an uneasy tongue, parched and thirsty in its ceaseless promethean vigil, Vesuvius licked at the night air; its red tongue flickering, retiring, leaping hotly out again. An ugly thing by night Vesuvius. A dual personality if ever there was one. What a man thinks and what he says. The safe work-a-day world he creates for himself: the night world rising out of him in dreams from depths he dare not fathom. By day decorative and peaceful-seeming, receding in its waves of pale smoke into the blue crumpled background of the hilly coast. By night menacing and cruel: a man-made cruelty. Man-made in his own tortured image. A tentative hell. Probably an Inquisitorial toy

left there by the dark-souled spaniards who knew so well the arts by
which christianity could be turned to a Black Mass. The stench of its
blood and smoke still rising to the night sky from its parched and restless throat. A flame on an altar on which a body lies, naked, mutilated,
worshipped by the meek-old and men-women, and women women
and women. Who must weep and fondle. And at its feet the ashes of
what must have been, Athens excepted, the most exquisitely civilised
and the loveliest city in the western world: sun-coloured, sun-fused,
pagan. Tourists blister their feet on its pavements. The hire of a parasol
costs three lire.

From far a thin sweet voice, young and pointed:

> cu' sti ccrucette d'oro
> e' sti rruselle 'mpietto. . . .

came drawn across the darkness like a fine chalk line across a blackboard

> nun date cchiú arricietto
> a chi ve vo' guardá!. . . .

and a woman's high nasal cry (every male on the island killed and every
female from the age of ten given to the conquering spaniard, and
Vittoria Colonna living on solitary splendour and occasional verse in
the castel') a spanish voice curling upward from an open throat, rough
wine from a wineskin: Giannin' . . . vien' . . . su . . . su . . .a' capit'? A
door or window fastened noisily and abruptly.

From below, from somewhere at the back of the house, came the
frightened scream of a child and then a long-drawn settled howl. One
of the innumerable (innumerable-seeming though four in all) children
of Lisetta's sister-in-law Giulia (Peppe probably), falling out of bed. As
many as could be got in the bed and the least skilful falling out. Ask the
reason for the cries the following morning and a gay shrugging: e
Peppe . . . è cascato a terra. . . . Peppe's average was five falls a week.

There's your true peasant the world over. Knows the last farthing to
be dug from the earth or pulled from the tree. But do not ask him to put
that farthing on a mattress to keep his children from falling out of bed,
no matter how much the earth and tree have yielded him. For God
protects gli innocenti. The little innocents fall from bed and are never
hurt. A grown man, yes. A man may be very gravely hurt in falling
from bed: but never a little child. Why? How can one ask? Because
God protects the innocent, Signora. The innocent may fall from bed:

God sees to it that they are not hurt. He may even push them out to show that they will not be hurt. For who would hurt a child, Signora? There she was sleeping between the wall and me . . . and there . . . right on her head, Signora. (Giovina jumps her small arms in the air, agitates her tiny hands, never meeting them though seemingly attempting to, and stares from her mother's arms with round pebbly eyes.)

Only the other day in Portici a baby fell out of a top-floor window (but you must have read of it too, Signora?) unhurt. Not even a bruise to mark the place it fell. For God protects the innocent. And if a man has children, Signora, God looks after him and he prospers.

He prospers. His children will work for him from the moment they can carry a bundle on their small heads or wield a stick on the ass's rump, or put up enough emulative noise to frighten it forward, or dig or fetch or carry or wash or spin or care-for or stand by to await orders. He prospers: and the woman in accepting the yearly child has found the means of keeping his favour and of being well treated and of being regarded as necessary. He prospers: for the more children the more unpaid servants: the more grandchildren the more security.

Five times of a morning under a fierce sun—she had caught herself counting them—had Maria taken her bone-thin nine-years-old legs the steep climb backwards and forwards on errands to the beach, the town, and up and down the flight of steps leading to the upper rooms with water-jugs and anything forgotten or suddenly remembered and immediately wanted. How immediately things were wanted! Mari . . . a. Mari . . . a . . . and her stubborn bit of tallowy face would emerge from nowhere and her bone-thin unwilling legs were on the stairs.

Going to her room the other day in the early afternoon she had found Maria squatting behind the door. Mari . . . a. Mari . . . a pealed through and around the house. Calling calling, angrily, persuasively, again angrily, impatiently, and cuckoo-pitched in various distances at once. But Maria continued squatting where she was found. Up went her finger to her lips. Not a pleading gesture but authoritative, severe, darkly menacing, her eyes very wide and black and stubborn. Such a flame of fury and defiance seemed to have burnt her to her bony brownness! A wiry angry dark little animal ready with nails and teeth. Only her brown feet were soft and gentle and childlike; such sad, tender feet with the beautiful even toes of the barefoot mediterranean child. Small bedouin in her one dusty garment. Black-streaked arab hair and beads of fine white lice on her black hair threads.

Twice Ruth had tried washing it: had brought her a brush and comb and parted it on this side; down the middle; combed it this way and that; put a bow here, taken it off there; plaited it in two thin whiplike plaits. And given it up in despair. The comb dug the earth; the brush had lost its handle when thrown at the stray dog seen near the chickens; the ropy hair hung again over Maria's eyes and the white beads gathered.

So she had had to give up trying to inculcate some sense of personal pride in her; talking to her of cleanliness, bribing her with gifts of coloured beads, a colour-bordered handkerchief, a little silver chained bracelet, and sweets. She had soon given up trying, and paid no more attention to her than to the other children. Yet she resented her failure. Had she been an english child she could have taught her to read or draw or play. She would have brought children's books and read to her; set her small tasks to puzzle over, if only for the sake of doing something with herself and amusing the child. But Maria was not amused. For days the child would avoid her, seemingly planning some subtle imaginary revenge; would snatch at the handkerchief or the beads with a nasty grin round her tight little mouth and make off round the nearest wall, still leering. Detached and defiant and all her own, her small savage heart unconquered.

And towards her Ruth alternated a complete indifference and intense exasperation. Little animal without soul! Towards herself contempt: was she seeking something to graft herself on, to possess? Why this thrusting of souls, of consciousness, on people and things? Maria remained detached and defiant and all her own; quite savage and contemptuous. A hateful child from a northern view. But she was right. O she was right. Cats have this same quality. Watch them walk away dark and ungettable for all the stroking and milk in the saucer. Monkeys have not this detached untouchable quality. They are merely mischievous in a sentimental way. Everything is written on their faces. But mediterranean children are not monkey children but cat children. Don't stroke them and you won't get scratched. So she left Maria to her one garment and beaded hair.

It had been the same when trying to teach (to her recurring shame) the first batch of children to say thank you. (That was many years ago. Nowadays she could hardly believe that there had been a time when she had found it necessary for a Forian child to say thank you when offered anything!) Keeping very near to the table in the hope of a fig or a slice of melon or a glass of wine with ice bobbing in it.

What do you say? Nothing. Snatch it and away and eat it out of sight and beyond recall. Yet with Giovanni she had persisted because he was sturdy and beautiful in his four years and months, and warmed through to an even brown and always naked; and also because beauty is hypnotic. Lisetta said that she put a shirt on Giovanni every morning but he was rarely anything but naked. Now and then he could be seen carrying something in his hand which looked like a shirt: carrying it at arm's-length. A compromise. It was wiser to let him strip himself. When told to keep his frock on he tore it straight up the front and there he was with two sleeves and two side flaps, as naked as ever and less comfortable.

Here you are, Giovanni: what do you say? Giovanni clutched at the cake and was stumping off but for a firm hand reached out to catch his arm in time. What do you say? And Giovanni would stand squarely planted and would stare at the cake, at the strange woman, at the sky, and finally say Signor' (which was doubtless what she had been expecting) and run off. Or he would say "Giovann' " that being a word he knew. He knew few words: and what did she want with him at all?

And once as he stood staring at her, straining to be off, Antonio his elder by three years, two enormous black eyes heavily lashed and lustrous, a narrow spanish face, thinly made, finely jointed and elegant as a young page (El Greco's son, Uller called him) as yellow and thin as Giovanni was baked and strongly planted, brought out in a snarl: ma ha *detto* buon giorno. He spat it at her. He *said* good day: now leave him alone. He was right, of course. The dark spot in the elder brother had found her out, snarling at her to leave alone that which did not belong to her and did not wish to.

How Uller had laughed and remarked on the activities of the english missionary service abroad! taking himself and his painting material off to the Pineta. She had watched him pass down through the vineyard with the naked taciturn Giovanni who clutched in his brown hand three fresh green figs, his little heels planted firmly in the dust. His brown serious strength made her sigh. He seemed to have grown gravely from the earth he planted himself on so securely and possessively. His small spine was like a rope of vine knotted and unbreakable. There was something of the same bloom and perfume on his skin as on an unpicked cluster of grapes. And strangely enough when Uller painted him—finally after the innumerable sketches he was always making—squatting there naked on the stones, he had painted him blue against the blue sky, among blue leaves, on blue stones. It was all quite absurd, of course; even ridiculous. No one was blue; a sky might be, but leaves were green and stones were grey and the naked child was brown. And yet for all its absurdity he had caught the browny-blue bloom which Giovanni gave off like a fruit, even though he had painted him bluer than the skyey background, or any sky that ever shone for that matter. Was it blue or purple? Still more unusual, Uller had declared himself satisfied with the work.

Now both Antonio and Giovanni were in America: had been for the last ten years and were sending money home as would their children and grandchildren: for God prospers the man with many children. Prospers him especially if they are in the americas. It was everywhere on the island the same. Not a family but had a son in the americas or one ready to go or one preparing to go as soon as his military service was done with. All were going. All were preparing to go. All were eating their hearts out because they could not go. Everywhere notices of steamship sailings and snatches of american-english. For they returned and built large ungainly villas and were called americanos.

Now everything wanted was called for partly from heaven but largely from America. At Piedimonti the church of Monte Vergine was being almost entirely rebuilt after having been in a state of dangerous decay for years. The glittering campanile new-tiled; new bells cast and clattering. Heaven had been warned about it for more years than were counted, but it was not until some devout mind remembered the americas that anything was done about it. Now the money was being sent home to mother weekly from every son of the parish and the Madonna had as steady and proud a house as she could wish for.

When that old brigand Mazzello returned from America with the proceeds of his rum-running activities and bought the handsome green-and-red-painted barca—which can be seen any day in the porto laden with its wine barrels and onions and melons for the peaceful and sleepy trip from Naples to Foria Ponte, though sometimes going as far afield as Livorno—he flew the american flag in gratitude. And there it waves symbol of good fortune and plenty, the envy and admiration of all. A man may return to his own country but his heart remains where his money was made.

And the corruption was everywhere. The malignant cancer which decays and lops off a man from his earth, and for which there is no cure. Stony ground where forests stood and sandy wastes where was pasture land and fruit-bearing trees. The uprooted gaining clean and useless hands and neat town-grey faces.

Once when she had questioned his curled seas and tormented trees and strangely-limbed-and-coloured children, Uller had said: Unless a thing is three times removed from nature it is not art.

Be that as it might. Certainly a man three times removed from nature was no longer a man. And they were all doing it. Removing themselves from the earth unto the third generation, and the lunacy and childbed-death statistic beings visited on them as a form of removal tax. Going into shops and workrooms and the envied few returning with dollar-conscious grins round their mouths and littering the country with ugly villas, smugly entrenched behind the envied title of americanos.

Had not he himself said: in another year or so I shall go to America. Either of them. Preferably South. Europe is dying, already gangrened and fly-blown. A decaying deposit of century on century.

It told on him being born to the somnolence of a canal-gazing, bier-halle, Ritter und Thurm, timbered house lurching against timbered house in the unsober medieval picturesqueness of Strasbourg. He said: a house built especially for oneself is better than an old house built for others and in which one is compelled to live. It may be the same with countries. Anyway, in a couple of years when he had put together enough work he'd find it out for himself. And whatever he was to find, he said, it would not be a corpse.

Of course the sun had really done more for her than anything else. Much that she attributed to time or habit or to her own inner struggle was the sun seeking her out, dissolving the darkness, the sense of doom and guilt that was like a poisonous drug of slow action. She told herself not without bitterness: I seem born to hide. But the sun did a great deal for her in searching her out and extracting the poison and dissolving the dark anger-spots. Before the sun's strength the action of her willed bitterness was powerless. Doing for her what Uller had said electric light was doing for the world; flooding the dark corners; turning the brave light of reason on the over-accumulated and over-revered débris of centuries. In time she came to lie back and watch it all, and in the light of the sun to see much not formerly visible; although she was dead and did not really belong and seemed to be resting there: a stage on a journey she was never conscious of desiring to complete; and which taken all in all could be only death. An unusual woman; taking little interest in the company in the thoughts in the doings of other people. She was restless now because he reproached her and seemed to menace her, so that it all came back to her again the first sense of guilt and shame. Much of it the result of living alone with him for so long. Perhaps, she thought, it is because there is no one whom I love. But who was there for her to love? She did not love easily, and he whom she had loved had left her years and years ago, and she had lost masses of her beautiful and shadowy hair, and had married without really wanting to but because a woman needs warmth and a fireside and protection.

And the action of the sun went on and on. She had been bitter and unhappy, though perhaps not altogether as bitter and as unhappy as she believed herself to have been. Who is? And she had gained quiet and a certain measure of satisfaction. Mostly the action of the sun on the skin, and intense blue light of sea and sky on the eye: though she put it down to an inner struggle that was perhaps a little more Laocoönean in retrospect than it had been. In the sunlight black spots dissolve in the consciousness as before the eyes. In the sun the struggle and the chaos adjust themselves in sleep. Take from a cold climate a man intending to commit suicide and place him in the sun and the intention will be sublimated to a quiescent fatalism. In the light of the sun it simply isn't worth it. (In which one gains the doubtful advantage of being numb without being dead.)

At first it had taken her by surprise. She had never imagined that a sun could be so hot nor shine so long; nor skies be so enduringly blue and cloudless. Her eyes ached alarmingly. Her head hurt with attacks of mild sunstroke from the reflected light. She felt like a candle in the sun, wilted, grew white-faced and scarcely touched her food.

The Hour of the Damned Souls, the name by which the natives knew the early hours of the afternoon, she found no exaggeration. Everywhere the heavy powdery dust lifting in clouds only to settle more greyly and heavily. Flowery grey dust in the bushy hair of the islanders: hair rayed from low foreheads in wiry bushes and held down by a thread of osier root so as to free the eyes: as with the youths in the greek statuary where it is mistaken for beauty or effeminacy, and is mere utility. Warm grey dust on everything. Grey-powdered feet; eyelashes grey with dust; grey vines; grey cacti; grey carts; grey leaves; grey dust smeared thickly on the billowing road-bordering walls in which the small stones rose and fell in cobbled rhythm.

Everywhere flies in angular flight. Restless dogs worried by flies. The hammer hammer hammer of asses and mules kicking the cobbles. The long white dusty roads that ate at the eyes, and walls glowing in the heat like naked sword-blades held to the eyes. Splayed green leaves luminous against the sky. All form all colour petrified in the brasier-glow of intense light. Fig trees hanging their long flat hands in purple shadows. Stone-coloured lizards motionless on lizard-coloured stones.

And never a soul in sight. On the spangled surface of the sea a sail leaning toward its phantom self. At this hour she was not so much alone as lying above the world in the detached isolation of an island; mindless before the tranced Blakeian unreality of lying in island space and mattering not at all. Lost on the rim of a crater; on the small upthrust-ledge of volcanic rock. At any moment thrust down again to the floor of the sea. As far as sight could reach only the steely setting of blue water and the tranced passionless suspension between heaven and earth.

N eedless to say, singly and in groups and on whatever pretext offered itself all the de Chiara offshoots and their friends had descended on Lisetta to have their look at her; and having stared carefully and well, and decided that it was sad to be mad so young and asked Lisetta whether she had any religion, the women peered at the sleeping boy and professed themselves astonished at every detail of its infant face; and went away with exasperation in their hearts, envying Lisetta her windfall. Having a mad foreign woman in the house was equivalent to having three sons in the americas: three sons doing well.

She had allowed herself to be stared at and commented upon, both because she could not stop them doing so, and because she had no feelings on the matter. It was Lisetta's triumph and it was difficult to grudge her her evident pleasure in being questioned and cross-questioned and sending them away half-answered; their heads full of difficult arithmetic and comparisons between hard work and the ease of having a mad foreigner on one's hands for life.

She listened and understood scarcely a word. Except that once hearing the words fiasco di vino she had become red and hot and moved away thinking that they had called her child a divine fiasco, instead of innocently calling for another bottle of wine.

But now from having lived among them long she had become almost a legend and quite negligible. Recently taking her afternoon siesta as usual on the veranda alcove facing her room she had seen a group of tourists staring up at her and pointing her out among themselves. They had evidently come especially from the porto to have their look at her. It was Giulia. She knew it. Giulia, Lisetta's sister-in-law, eternally the war-widow, eternally-the-mother, loathing her charity and despising herself and its donors, attaching herself to it like a leech; servile and arrogant and entrenched; two large unsteady melons stuffed in the front and the back of her; and arms and legs of equal thickness. One of those heavy yellowish-white women whom the lithe arabs prize so highly, and Naples and the coast abound in.

For the first time in all their years together Ruth spoke angrily to Lisetta. But she was not a tourist attraction. She was not one of the sights of the island. And having been turned into one she would leave the island as soon as her packing was finished. But Lisetta with a clatter of words and upraised hands was angrier still. Her nursling, her turtle dove, the english signora had been offended. She knew who was to blame. And on and on the two women clattered at each other in the kitchen, their voices pitched to the high grinding of an unoiled axle of an old cart-wheel. Giulia denying, admitting, cajoling, menacing, losing control of the bile stored in years of real and imaginary humilia- tion, calling on her children to prepare to tramp the roads and beg their bread now that they were homeless, foodless, without pillows for their heads or covering of any sort, for God is on the side of the rich and arrogant and has no pity for the widow and her fatherless children; and having worked the children up to various degrees of tears and variously pitched howls, burst into tears herself, calling and sobbing and rolling her eyes upwards and round, her tightly buttoned melons heaving perilously. Of course there were apologies and appeals and absurdly dramatic and biblical references to fatherless and starving little ones. Poor Giulia had had a shock. She had accused Lisetta of putting a strange woman before her own flesh and blood; of being more fond of her than of her own family. Which was probably much more true than ever Giulia in her anger realised, and certainly was not the safe appeal the widow had hoped. Perhaps Lisetta would as soon have turned her own daughters out of doors as seen Ruth go. Doubtless a judicious blending of affection and interest: but on the whole affection upper- most. Lisetta liked having her about; liked looking at her; liked looking up at her. Found her pleasure in serving her. Why or how she could not say: her need was stronger than any reason she could give for it. Her mad one had become indispensable to her. Giulia certainly had had a shock.

But Andrea, brother of Lisetta's husband, Mario, was altogether a delight. Ruth took Uller up to see him, right up beyond the Pilastri to the grey arab house with the worn outer stairway leading to the first floor and flat roof: within the room so dark that one asked if a prison were more forbidding. And in one corner of the long room where a table was vaguely outlined with a few plates and mugs, and a narrow barred opening high up in the wall filtering her some rays of light, Amalia his eldest daughter sat working at the loom day in day out and one wondered how she knew when it was night.

There was Andrea fixing the rat traps among his vines, shirtless, his trousers belted low on his thighs, balancing himself on his heels, walking with the roll of his thighs and buttocks like a small and friendly ape. All around him among the vines and fruit trees dodged his eight, or was it twelve?, children (one was always meeting another of Andrea's children) making of his paternity a gypsy encampment, gypsy-coloured, gypsy-garmented, barefooted and shy as wood creatures. From a distance they trailed after their father, stalking him.

He, back on his heels, laughed and talked and mimed and explained: the one person on the island except Lisetta who laughed from the heart and not the teeth, she always thought. Andrea was lively and mischievous and turning grey; a reddish gleam in his brown skin and grey-marbled eyes. He took them round to see the new traps and the gun placed in position over the water-cistern, full of his grievance against his rats, and the damage they were causing, and, of course, the further taxes on wine and the lack of last winter's frost. If only the brutes (and this year they were twice as large as any rabbit he had ever known!) would only content themselves with one bunch and have done with it: but no, they must go from one to the other nibbling, nibbling. No rat gnawed more than one grape from a cluster but picked and chose and ruined as many as he could, which was pleasant if they were your grapes.

Taking a handful of nuts from his pocket he cracked them between his teeth and held them out to them; and then Ruth made him take Uller to the corner of the vineyard where in an egyptian tomb of a square stone hut were the two long deep stone cisterns, vast stone troughs where the men trod the grapes, leaping in up to the armpits in a frenzy of sweat and singing. The women having brought the grapes in the long plaited baskets, watching and singing but taking no active part in it all. You couldn't let a woman tread the grapes or the wine would be sour and unsaleable. Why? Because it always had been so: who would drink wine that a woman trod? Andrea spat. It was a man's job and a man's drink. Not that there was much music and festa about the business now; it was just a work to be done and done well and quickly. But there had been a time, long years ago, in his youth, when it was a matter for frenzy and wild music and songs sung that were heard only on that day of the year, and the zampognari came and there was more feasting and laughter than at a dozen weddings. But now the youths of the place were a poor lot; the flower of them scattered on the mainland and in foreign cities. And taking a jug which stood under one of the enormous barrels, Andrea watched the yellow cloudy liquid pour in, took it in his hands, drank some himself first, and then handed the jug to Uller, who offered it first to Ruth, who saw the amazement in Andrea's round eye, knew what it meant and wouldn't have hurt his phallic pride for the world; and made Uller drink first and drank after him, though properly he should have passed it on to Domenicos, Andrea's son-in-law who stood by and the two men workers and then to the several male children: after which she came and the female children.

Up went the jug, child after child dipping its face in the opening and tilting it backwards. First thing in the morning before going to work with father, they drank the yellow clouded wine with their piece of earth-coloured bread broken from the loaf and stuffed with garlic. Drank the very dew from heaven where squeamish pale-faced youngsters the world over dipped their delicate noses in glasses of cold milk: cow-juice v. sun essence. And Andrea balanced on his heels, his hands in his belt called attention to himself as an example of wine-drinker: mother's-milk and wine the only liquids he'd known in his life, and was there a man like him on the island, or a hundred miles along the coast either way? Leaning back on his heels he rubbed his furred chest as though pleased with the feel of himself, and placed a hand on the matted, tasselled hair of his youngest child.

Mario, on the other hand, spoke little and shared the dark untouchable quality of the island soul. He would sit silent and shut-in seeming, plaiting his long scarlet garlands of small scarlet tomatoes which were hung like beautiful blood offerings on the walls of the house and about the poles which held the vine-trellis over the ristorante. Watching him hang his garlands with a care that was almost reverence was like surprising Abel preparing the first sacrificial fruit offerings for his altar. Mario's face was mapped and leathery, his eyes expressing nothing. He was a good twenty years older than Lisetta. Nor she nor his children paid him much attention. He was there and he was theirs; still useful in his way, though wracked with rheumatism.

Every morning after first standing up to his knees in the sea, motionless, pipe in mouth, he dug himself in the hot yellow sand. There he lay,
umbrella over his head, pipe in mouth, packed in sand to his thighs, his
trousers beside him in the shade; and after an hour's baking of his bones
he would dig himself out, brush the silky sand from his legs, get into his
trousers with a furtive peasant modesty and climb back for his midday
food and drink.

Mule-stubborn to the pitch of exasperation. It was he who placed
the poisoned leaves among the vines for the rats:.and the rabbits died.
Again and again and again; poison for the rats and dead rabbits. And he
wouldn't see it. It was his land and he could place poison for the rats
where and how he chose.

The one person he seemed to take any direct interest in or care much
about was Nicola, his son-in-law. Each evening they played cards
together against the other men while Pasquale sat watching from a near
chair, sulking with that sulkiness of old men aware that they have
outstayed their welcome; hanging his toothless stubbled head and
mumbling now and then some remark which no one could make out,
or troubled to.

Staring past Graziella bringing the wine would move the very old
man to remark on women. His own, he said, it had lasted him fifty-five
years. A good woman while it lasted. But dead now a long time. Femina
always dies first. She worries with the children and suffers much.

N icola under a tree peppering away in the air with a dreary
intensity. One solitary bird on the island and he must be after it.

Padre Antonio bending with heavy effort over Maria's waxen image
says that little girls who cannot place a hand on their rosaries at a
moment's notice are not regarded with much favour in heaven.

Poor man he might as well have spared his breath and the effort it cost
him doubling himself to fix Maria sternly with his solemn black ink-
spots; globulous, not over-clean. Once around the corner: the back of
the hand jerked three times from under her chin and her mouth pursed
to a button. That was Maria's opinion of that. The gesture clearly a trifle
exaggerated in a desire to impress the Signora but on the whole expres-
sive of her opinion of him. To be screamed at and boxed soundly on the
ears she understood; but to be bent over and have a few unsubstantiated
threats breathed on her face deserved the contempt it met with.

About him to Ruth there lingered always the flavour of Uller's contempt. How Uller had disliked the man on sight! His heavy-lipped
pendulous face and fatty well-being. Reminded him, he said, of his
moneylender in Paris. God's beetle. How he had baited the poor man
and been inexcusably rude and harsh to him, seizing any pretext to insult
him with a pleasure bordering on viciousness. It came to such a pass that
Padre Antonio could not bend down to pat Giovanni's cheek without
prompting a loud aside: Another male saint mauling a small child!

And when the priest (feeling it his duty to come to grips with the
unbeliever, the foreign devil sent to tempt himself and corrupt those he
guarded) had expounded and held forth and made all his known and
narrow defence of faith and human aspiration, Uller would bring his
fist on the table and tuning his voice to deliberate resonance and invitation, would ask: What faith? What perfection? And who decreed that
man should be other than what he was? A few inspired minds at intervals
of centuries had seen him clearly for the low animal he is and is meant
to be. And had refused to believe it. So they assumed that he must know
it himself and desire to be bettered. Rubbish. A man has certain functions to perform—and so long as he performs them adequately he is
alive.

—The indictment, said Uller, came from Christ Himself: feed my
sheep.

A sound judgment, that. As good as anything Solomon ever said. If
He had no illusions, Padre, why have you? But personally, much as he
admired Christ for much sound sense, on the whole he preferred
Buddha. If only that he had no father waiting for him in heaven. God!
how sick he was of people with fathers waiting to shoulder their burdens
and kill calves and make life generally warm and saltless!

Besides, christianity had been too long used as a political weapon
and as such must perish. How long, O Lord, how long before the
people outgrew their priests and caught-up their great men? The few
who came to them with messages which they read three hundred years
later and said with bated breath: The genius! The forerunner! Centuries
ahead of his time!

Stuff and nonsense and be damned. No great man had ever been
ahead of his time: his time had always been behind its great men. His
Time had always, like Savonarola's Army of Innocents, gathered in his
inventions of the devil and his printed heresies and his lewd pictures
and burned them on the little bonfire which they assumed was
Oblivion.

And walking to the shutters he flung them open releasing the hot radiant light which poured out into the darkened room in a shower of golddust, and shaking his fist at the sky bellowed: There is our true god, my dear Padre. And when *he* dies you may be quite sure we die with him.

The priest had departed chewing his lips. And Uller watching him from sight had hopped up and down in front of the window like a large ruddy baboon.

—You make yourself ridiculous teasing the unfortunate man, she had said, thinking kindly of the priest's distorted face. And to no effect. Why don't you throw stones like a schoolboy or stand behind the door and jump out on him?

—I will, said Uller, he'd understand that.

And with faith so with human conduct. Bringing his light to a blind man. Showering wisdom on this fool. Then leave him to himself, said Ruth, he does you no harm. But no: he must demolish, tear down, drop the bottom out of the man's world; though he could have spared the energy he put to it. His victim was secure: what was not writ in his breviary: was not.

Marriage. One would have thought that Padre Antonio had invented it, patented it, and popularised it.

—The Church, which lives on the people, and the State, which lives from the people, encourage a man to marry. A married man is a slave. He is a man in chains. You have him where you want him. He is easily punishable. He is good. He is docile. He will not easily leave his children. The State has perfect control over the married man. Should he revolt, his wife, his children, his field, his house are his hostages to the State. In him also the State has four or five potential soldiers: and no responsibility.

Marriage enslaves the man: but his slavery is perhaps less heavy to bear than the slavery of the woman. (Ruth settling back, smiled. She at any rate could listen to him with malicious pleasure.)

—Women are not virtuous. They are by nature more lascivious and uncontrolled than men. (Padre Antonio raised shoulders and hands as though the chastity of the Blessed Virgin Herself had been in question.) Now when a man is given the right over a woman by the State and the Church he has the right and power to keep that woman in slavery. No man may approach her. She may go nowhere without his sanction and knowledge and in a few years her youth and desirability are past. The woman has been destroyed: the man's freedom has been destroyed. But it is doubly hard on the woman.

—A brothel protected by the State suffices for the man. He need not sin. He may not want to. But the fact remains that he may should he want to. He has, therefore, mental freedom. He knows that should he desire he may gratify. This mental satisfaction gives him an illusion of freedom. Meanwhile the woman has been several times blown out like a balloon: nobody desires or covets her. She has neither mental nor physical freedom. She is either carrying a child inside her or children are clinging to her skirts. No man can desire physically a woman large with child. Except to the artist a woman with her belly magnificently full is not a thing of beauty. Even you will admit, Padre, that a woman large with child is hardly an aphrodisiac.

The priest's eyes narrowed; how he hated the man!

—You may say that she may be unfaithful to her husband if she chooses. But the curious thing is that she rarely chooses. I speak of the average man and average woman. In fiction, yes. But it is extraordinarily difficult in life to find a woman who is unfaithful to her husband, or wants to be. On the contrary she is viciously, narrowly and furiously faithful to him. And by the time she has decided to be unfaithful, neglected and unable to please him, she is not wanted by other men.

—Always the people run for the State rather than the State for the people. The Church and the State. The Few: devising their splendid sacred laws to keep the rabble tamed. The Church-State the owner; the shepherd counting his sheep, feeding them, protecting them until the time comes for slaughtering them. So don't talk, Padre, about the godhead in man as though man had anything to attain or could be bettered. A man has certain functions to perform and as long as he performs them adequately he is alive. No more and no less. Christ called them sheep. They were sheep before he noticed it. They are the same sheep today.

Uller said that the root of the slavery of mankind was marriage.

And it never occurred to the baited priest, woman without woman-wit, to assure his lecturer a little pointedly that he spoke as a married man. Even as a much-married man. Which it was obvious that he was, loathing his wife and loving his two children. Or having loved them once. Now in a sense they were no longer his. A man's children are his own for so short a time. And he saw them rarely. At most once in two years; and each time they became more and more like two bright strange birds settling a moment on his hand or shoulder and flying unconcernedly away.

Again and again he spoke to her of his children. His face would grow hot with the strain of a certain comic innocence and fun. He would forget that he had told her the story several times; and each time had told it with the same precision, the same emphasis, the same surprise and the same laughter, in which the father assured himself that he had once had children. So she would stand with him again beside the goldfish bowl under which his youngest child had stood and called: O father, come quick and see! They are waving their little hands!

But it was the stories of his eldest child whom he had tried to teach to draw which pleased him most. Who when given a bell to copy would draw in the tongue. Why? Because it was there inside. But one could not see it. No: but it was there and if it was not drawn the bell could not ring. The same with a cup of flowers: drawing them inside the cup, on its face, as it were, and not growing from out its rim as they should have been. And asked the reason he argued that the flowers were inside in the water, and that if you drew them out they were no longer in the cup but in the air, and that could not be. And if given a box with lettering or a design on it to copy he would draw the box neat and bare and place the lettering or design apart, beside the box. Why? Because otherwise people would think the lettering or design was shut-up inside the box, which would be quite wrong.

You see how right he was? You see the clear rational workings of a child's mind? Extraordinary. Extraordinary. And only just five.

And one day he had taken a sheet of paper to draw where his house stood, and said: And then you come to the end here and you go down a long road; and had drawn with much care one long wriggley line right across the page. O but it is a much longer road than that, isn't it father? May I have another sheet of paper? And you go on and on down the road. Another line drawn with much care and anything but straight right to the very edge of the paper. O but we haven't come to the house yet! Another sheet of paper, another slow careful line: and still not there yet. What an interminable road it must have seemed to the small Johann! Six more sheets of paper before he finally reached home; and when he got there it had become larger than a church with a belfry and a bell, and a stork wheel to top it all.

And one day the child had come to him and said: Father please open your mouth . . . wider . . . still wider. I want to see your heart.

B eside the dark effaced islanders Uller was like a fistful of straw
held to the sun. And it was just that pale luminous solid-fleshed
german-curved thigh and buttock quality that one was not sure of;
so inefficient seeming beside the subtly jointed bone-thin effortless
strength of the small island men. Instead of turning brown he blistered
red; in itself discordant and comic, and giving his easy-going blond
largeness an air of a well-fed prize entrant at a baby show. But, as he
said himself, he had it under the hat. His mental outlook his father's, a
French-Alsatian, whom he had lost when he was ten years old. His
bones and colouring those of his square heavy-breasted german mother
who had wanted him for the priesthood; who had beaten and bruised
him with her fleshy boxer fists; who had broken and ground down
those first packets of coloured chalk bought after weeks of planning;
who had burned his first drawings before his eyes, holding him down
by the neck like a rat, like a house dog that has misbehaved on the mat;
who from his store of memories made him once describe the navel cord
as more deadly than the hangman's rope.

He said things which in her world simply were not said, were not
thought: but she had lived too long out of any world to care what was
said or thought. And it was exactly in this that he was new and stimulat-
ing and stood for something she had never known in an atmosphere of
narrow gentility and insularity which is so dully and ineradicably
County and the Services; and to which she had been a rebel, the
stimulus of her father ever uppermost in her mind. In which sense Uller
pleasantly was not a gentleman: having come to his own conclusions:
having tramped most of Europe's capitals since the day of his sixteenth
birthday on which he walked from his home and slept in their doorways;
stayed behind when the others left to gulp the worked and charcoaled
bread left on their easels and steal whatever lay about, choosing always,
with youth's justice, the overstocked boxes of the wealthier students,
here a brush, there a tube of paint; having grown skilled in the many
devices whereby such necessities as drink, food and women can be had
at another's expense; finding the world a decent enough place on
receiving the charity of a few francs for his canvases; having risen by
such steps to the notoriety of a few art-show scandals to the privilege of
having the discerning Brothers Grünheim store away his canvases in
their Paris cellars against the possibility of his early death.

And so here she was after all these years repeating his words; still
pondering much that he had told her. Was it then true after all that
women were but the receptacles for man's thought and children? Only

that which he placed within her could be hers; her consciousness and life derived only from him. An acrid-tasting pill. Yet here she was still conscious of him; still finding her pleasure in remembering and repeating him and giving him shadowy life beside her.

He had never explained, or shown diffidence, or understood that there were things which one does not discuss; and which troubled her. As when he told her that his sister was the first woman he had loved. One day he saw his mother beat her, striking her heavily across the face and head, and heard her cry out. And all at once he loved her. Love came up in him like sudden tears. Passionate love, making him aware of himself. For many years he could not believe that there lived anyone more beautiful, more dear, than this girl who had their father's long gentle face and calm movements. She had nursed him through a schoolboy attack of chicken-pox. It remained one of the happiest memories of his life. How he had tried to become ill again! Calling on boys who were said to have measles: taking off his coat in winter to catch cold. Alas, he had his mother's bones and death-defying constitution!

When the time came he confided to her his plans of escape; but she would not come with him to Paris. She did not share his need to see the rest of the world. She cried; she feared for him; but she did not try to restrain him. His first lesson in womanly caution. He was shocked, but he forgave her once he got to Paris and the problems of art and food engrossed him. The day he became rich and famous he would go back and fetch her; not knowing that when next he saw her they would be married to different people; she absorbed in her first child, a boy whom she called Hans, and very sisterly and benign. Yet even today he would become excited and happy as a schoolboy at the thought that he was to see her soon. And this though she understood him not at all. Not at all. Found him strange and restless and not altogether a family asset. It troubled Ruth; but the story of the drowning man pleased and excited her.

As a boy he was standing on the bridge near the washerwomen's floats, near the Quai St Jean, as one comes up the road from the Grande Rue, gazing down into the water, when he realised that what he had at first mistaken for a dog or a piece of driftwood was a man going down for the second time. Appalled he threw off his coat and flung his leg over the bridge to leap after him. He was a strong swimmer. Yet just as he hoisted himself to the bridge to bring over his other leg he thought: suppose this man does not want to be rescued? And he sat there and thought it out. In a flash, as one thinks at such moments. He was only

fifteen at the time but thoughts of suicide were not new to him and here
was an unhappy man. A man doing what he had sometimes thought of
doing. He remembered thinking: Perhaps, poor fellow, he had only
just so much courage. If I rescue him he may not dare again, and I shall
have his misery on my soul. So instead of leaping in he sat and waited
for the drowning man to reappear. And when he did he must have
guessed the boy's thoughts for he nodded; showed his teeth in a smile;
waved a feeble hand and went down. The boy put on his coat and went
home, smiling also.

He was amused at her attitude.

—Women as a rule loathe the story: and loathe me ever after.

But she liked it; liked its power and ruthlessness. It was good to let
die a man who chose to die. Good to let people go their own way with a
male remorselessness beyond female comprehension and pity. She
liked it and it frightened her. It was just in that that he was a stranger to
her. That woman-what-have-I-to-do-with-thee? male impersonality.
In women it was different. Then when she would expect him at the
beach, at the Pineta for the walk or picnic they had agreed on the day
before, and he did not come and had forgotten utterly, she would know
that it was deliberate. That it was calculated. Women forget nothing:
they act only deliberately. But with him it was indifference: to her, to
time, to common courtesy. Something impersonal to which she could
not reach. And which shocked her more, for a woman is most shocked
by the impersonal. That appalling male indifference which means
simply indifference. That she could not cope with.

But woman, as he said, was but one need. It was not true that woman
was man's most urgent need. In civilisation there is no hunger and no
fear as it was first understood. Therefore woman happens to be the
need nearest to us and we can take advantage of it.

Woman (he said) was but a limited influence in a man's life. Of
course there was mother-love and patriotism which in the patriotic
figurehead was always (had she noticed?) a brawny, open-mouthed,
shouting woman in whom men saw again the bullying wife or mother:
so that they were hypnotised into obeying: collectively awed by the
presence of this open-mouthed arm-raised female; and marriage.

Yet when a man looked back on his life to count its pleasant inter-
ludes, his memory lighted first of all on his school and student days and
the solitary years of his early struggles: periods when, shaping himself,
he lived his own male life beyond and outside woman's influence.
Perhaps the only free days a man lived. In that hour, beyond wife or

mother or child or mistress, a man would choose his friend as having given him the more complete and lasting satisfaction: the give and take of free human intercourse, which is not between man and woman.

In that hour he himself would choose Nasetkin. She hesitated, yet could not keep from saying: and I, my father. Which, as he said, came to much the same thing.

Uller had all the continental contempt for the english. That his remarks might offend her never entered his mind. He never understood that she should care. Why should she? It was not a personal matter. It was simply german discipline and french logic united in contempt of a complacent and mentally lazy people.

They must have been amusing in england, he and Nasetkin, with their few selected canvases tied together with string with which to conquer London, having decided (finally) that Paris was hopeless unless one were an artist for wealthy prostitutes.

He told her about that as they walked back from Castola, the evening settling in uniform tepid blue and shadow. Women bearing heavy loads on their heads rustled past them in the dust like harmless grass snakes. Children with water-jugs slid by, singing with the shrill pointed voices of young cats. Cat-sound, cat-calling, which must surely have been the first human sound, anticipating speech? Now and again as though in answer to each other came a prolonged retching he-haw he-haw-haw-haw-haw . . . w . . . h-a-a-a-a-a-aq, dying in foolish and unprofitable lament. A parody of love, said Uller; a vocal satire on the culmination of passion.

At intervals along the cool shadow-gathering road they would walk into a wave of warm heavy air. It came grimly from under their feet. Reminding them, they agreed, after the manner of copy-book maxims or sermons in stone that All must Live as though About to Die, or that in the Midst of Life one is in Death, or that Although the Sun shines the Clouds are Gathering, and There is Always a Volcano underfoot. Which by some mental deviation she did not follow reminded him of england.

Needless to say they were back within a week. Nasetkin describing hilariously at the first glass and tearfully at the last how englishwomen wore thick flannel underwear, and never. Never. Was it believable? The barbarians. While he himself principally remembered that the rain was the wettest he had ever known, and that if one wanted a drink one went and stood up in a dark stale-smelling place where they sold nothing but port or whisky or a thick sticky beer which seemed brewed from putrid barley.

The main characteristic of the english, he considered, taking it all in all, was laughter. Chiefly at the expense of the foreigner. But on the whole at anything new or unusual. (From which she gathered that the few select canvases tied with string had not been handled with the respect due to them.)

He would even call laughter their national defence. It defended them against onslaughts of the mind. But fortunately for them the mis-trusted foreigner did sometimes get past and beyond the defences, and, for their own good and after much resistance, showed them that there were other ways of using civilisation than drowning it in their tea-cups.

She must not think that he spoke idly or without giving full thought to the subject: but could she deny that it was these despised foreigners who had taught the english all that they knew? Did they not depend on the foreigner for the refinements of life as they depended for food? Allow no food-ships into england and in a month she would be physi-cally starved. Allow no foreigner and she would be artistically starved. Until the foreigner came she had lived by bread alone. Were they not the one people in the world ignorant of what to eat, drink, or think? That this was true was proved by the fact that only those english who lived abroad or travelled much were fit to associate with. Once beyond the parochial confines of their narrow island space they became human (he thought) beyond recognition.

And what had the rest of the world to envy them except their capacity for believing any lie provided it was pleasant. Why? Because they were mentally lazy. That was why they mistrusted the french and mocked at the german thoroughness and love of knowledge as an end in itself. That was why they liked everything to be what they called: straight-forward. No thinking; no knowledge of foreign languages; no desire to try and understand new problems and developments. It was so much easier and quicker to laugh. Which made other nations regard them as hypocrites. Untrue, unfair. It was merely a certain rustic straw-sucking simplicity in the midst of a complicated and exacting civilisation.

To the english a pictorial flower of civilisation is a hunting-field or a garden party, remarked Uller to the evening sky. And one must know everyone there. Whom one does not know one ignores. An english-man's greatest sin is not murder or rape or incest. Such vulgar passionate offences. No. It is wearing an incorrectly coloured tie with the wrong cut of coat; or having to admit that he is not a gentleman never having been to Eton; or that he has not sufficient money in his pocket to pay for his meal. That is as far as an englishman's soul's embarrassment can go.

On the continent (it seemed) a man looking at his fellow thinks: I am as good as you. In england a man looking at man thinks: thank god I am not as impossible as you. His pleasure is not in looking up but in looking down. A sly servile movement. The trait of a servant.

Not that he did not like the english. He was beyond racial prejudice of any kind. She must not think that because one understood a nation's faults one did not also recognise its virtues. Besides some of his best friends were englishmen. And he had told them what he thought of them as a whole every whit as freely as he spoke to her now.

—No doubt you astonished them.

—You cannot astonish an englishman, said Uller drily. You can only shock him.

He made many sketches of her and finally painted her in her worn island clothes with Giovanni on her lap. Giovanni naked, pugnaciously naked and glowing like a goblet of heavy dark wine, the weight of the sun through thick leaves. She told him little or nothing about herself and as he preferred talking of himself he did not care sufficiently to press for confidences withheld. How he roared with laughter when told that in this case Hungerford was pronounced Hun'ard! But what, after all, when he had finished, did it matter? he asked. Creed, nationality, blood, how little they had to do with it all when one thought it out. That was what one could definitely admire about Christ: His getting beyond patriotism and nationality and preaching the brotherhood of man, which takes no account of colour, blood-tie, creed. The brotherhood of man: that was all He had meant in bidding them spread His message over the world. And that was, of course, the one part of His message they had taken such care not to spread!

The only possible brotherhood of man was the brotherhood of mind and trade. People with similar thoughts recognise each other the world over. The miner from Wales would recognise, understand, know instantly, the miner from North America, from Mexico, from Africa. The local grocer from a Berlin suburb is one with the local grocer from any white or coloured townlet. The architect only can grasp the problems of his fellow architect. The gambler—the gambler. The idle rich idles with his wealthy fellow. Those who speak the language of the brain or soul answer to that same brain or soul in another. Pick up any man, of any colour, of any creed, in any trade, in one corner of the earth and place him beside another man, of opposite colour and opposite creed, in the same trade at the other corner of the earth, and those two men will meet on the same ground: will know each other's problems: will be brothers: will talk together immediately in the language of work and common interest.

To Lisetta she had said that she would do her usual shopping and might then be going to Castellammare to see about that cart they had discussed. She might be away for a night or two. And might even spend some time at Sorrento. She was tired, of what precisely she could not say, but she had a sudden longing for change.

She went down to the beach with the rest of the household, watched him climb into Vincenzo's boat with the peasants and their parcels and melons and baskets of fruit, and be rowed out to the *Virgilio* blowing an apoplectic little whistle, advising them to be quick about it.

He was visiting Florence on the way home. He had said: I shall be back in Naples on the 18th. Had said where he would stay and at what hour he would arrive. They could go to Ravello; anywhere; Rome, Viterbo: he left her the choice. She would be there? That was all. Yes, she would be there because she liked his way of asking; of keeping it down to the level of the commonplace.

She took the midday boat. The *Virgilio* blew its apoplectic little whistle for her also, just as she was being handed up to the large man with the ropes, hanging his face like a harvest moon over the water, to see what more there was to come. Some-one was waving from the house. From far she watched Nicola, apish and alert, leaping about the hot sands, gathering in the red-brown fishing nets.

What to do with the few hours left to her? She was restless and undecided and must compose herself. She turned from the torrid seething streets whose noise usually delighted her to the cool of la villa. Through an opening in the heavily clustered trees she saw the idling carriages and the carts musical with bells and high silver trappings and scarlet tassels clattering along the white road bordering the intensely blue sea, towards the rocky outline of the Castel del Ovo.

She sat beneath the twisted uneasy olive trees watching a group of workmen working at a flower bed, and children playing in the sandy dust-white path. At intervals a child's scream filled the vaulted branches with echo. Now and again an older child picked up a younger one, held it tightly with passionate play against its breast, kissed its face again and again, and released it, struggling. Little boys were obstreperous. Little girls seemed to have vowed away their lives to the unbuttoning of their small brothers.

Later an elderly man joined her on the bench, staring in an uneasy way at her upheld profile. After a while with his stick he began tracing in the dust the outline of a shield with armorial bearings. He drew slowly, with care and flourish. She knew that it was meant for her. The ageing aristocrat-professor, reduced, deposed, unable to forget. All hanging out of the tops of their medieval towers, tapestry-wise, shaking fists at their neighbours. At one time (she remembered reading) there were three hundred of these towers with fist-shaking aristocrats leaning from their tops, in Lucca alone: but this was too much even for the insignia-loving italians, so they pulled down all but the twenty or so remaining today. And here was one of them, as it were, shaking his fist on the ground. She knew exactly what she would hear by showing an interest in his solemn dust scrapings. But today she was incurious and unconcerned. Besides, she felt that nothing he could tell her would be as interesting as the thing he did not tell. So after waiting, waiting, contemplating it in studied sadness, chin on stick, he made a quick impatient movement, thrust the toe and heel of his boot all over it, rose and walked away. He was offended; he made her feel as though she had struck a blow. She watched him walk stiffly, primly away in laborious search with the back of his head, with his very coat-tails, for another bench, another dusty design, a more discriminating spectator.

She sat on and on looking at what was happening around her; and then quite suddenly she too stood up and turned away. She walked quickly away from the bench towards the street. She did not want. She just did not want. Suddenly, she had no desire. She walked out of the gardens and hailed a carrozzella. There were exactly twenty minutes in which to get to the Cumana and catch the last boat from Baia. The carriage bumped noisily over the stones and she sat stiff-backed and purposeful, devoid of feeling. She did not want. Again it had been mental, as sensation came to her. And even had she missed passion in her life, which she had, now that it was offered her she did not want it.

Suddenly, like that; making her get up and leave the giardini and hurry to catch the last boat. Later in Foria it would be otherwise. In thought he would come to her again. Thinking, she might regret, often. She would not forget. He took place beside her father: part of her life. She did not feel that she would belong more to him by possessing him. She drew back from the thought of contact; half-willing, unable. Later, much later, she might understand why she had turned away so abruptly from the shouting children and the men at work over the flower bed. She would magnify it, worry it. A person, an episode, ridiculous, inconsequent, could remain with her rehearsed and reënacted for years. She could not help it, whose whole life had been but a struggle to accept and dismiss. And soon, when it was too late, perhaps because it was too late, she would be curiosity itself and regret, unnerved. And he would be real again and have some quality of the sun about him: the cold northern sun or a large white star. But just now sitting stiff-backed and devoid of feeling as the horse toiled up the steep Via di Toledo to her last train, he seemed not more than a large overpowering man, far too talkative and self-assertive and ill-mannered; and not a little heavy-fleshed for a lover. Yet she could not rid herself of the feeling that in betraying him she had betrayed herself. Yes, she had said she would be there.

Hearing the crowing of the ship's whistle she wanted nothing so much as to go out and weep; so irresolute she was, as a nun about to break her vows and unable to do so.

N ow Padre Antonio could return to the patting of childish heads and reassume the authority of his threadbare soutane. Maria need no longer tiptoe across the flat roof in jealous stealth, her hands loaded with pieces of rock to throw at her brothers dismissed from their sittings. She herself could return to the solitude from which she had been unwillingly roused. Now nothing could trouble her more. Lisetta had promised that no other guests would be accepted.

She was glad to settle back once more and see the clouds rise like swans unfurled from the heights of Vomero, catching the sun's last look and bearing it to her. It even seemed that, idling on the stairs and parapet, the two pigeons, white as the Holy Ghost, regained their innocence and once more entered an earthly paradise. (Leda, as he had said, was a woman too easily satisfied.) As he had said. As he had once remarked. At all moments of the day he said or he once remarked. Yet it was good to be alone again. Like a blade thrust in her in some drama of passion she grasped the handle of her solitude, pressing it to her with no regrets. It satisfied to tears. Sufficient as lines taken at random from Landor.

Long long ago she had felt it in her, when always the cliffs must be bare, the road reaching out to the edge of the moor, deserted; where her eye looked out over it all only her eye must look. Possessing only where none shared. Her view and her sky. By whose right? But there it was. A few trespassers on her road, a movement on her cliff, and she would turn away her eyes and feel like crying, small though she was, her arm hung up to his hand. He looked, too. Together they looked across at the Isle of Wight lying like a whale on the water, ready to sink slowly and without sound. Together they looked: the only person with whom she had looked as one.

Now once again she could walk on the earth alone. Walk by the sea alone. Walk to the Pineta, over the red stubble lit with shadow, umber stubble and pine needles and mounds of grey-black volcanic stone, and peeled mosaic of tree trunks; and sit on the ground under pines rising to intense silvery cloud-puffs bound together by red sinews; alone. It made her feel light and unreal and transparent, this belonging again to herself; of being one with the orchestration of scent and sound: blend of incense and manure: heaven and earth. As she looked back at the sky through the spread filigree of branches, she thought how Time, the sadist, held no terrors for her. That is given as compensation, it seems, to the lonely of heart. What happened to the earth, she felt, must happen to her seeing that there she would sit will-less and wait for it to happen.

Six years now. She hoped they had forgotten her; and doubted it. She thought with horror of living on in the thoughts of others. To be living on in thoughts which never rise to the surface of the face. Eyes and eyes letting nothing through and behind them those thoughts in which, against one's will, one was imprisoned. Even the escaping dead were not allowed their oblivion in these thoughts going on and on behind shuttered eyes. Embalmed in speechless eyes; thoughts endlessly spinning the shrouds of their dead; more contaminating than earthworms. She did not want to be contaminated by their thoughts. To escape she had brought her child away, that together they might be free of the thoughts of others. She did not want aspects of herself lying like a half-read letter on the floor of other people's minds. She hoped she was forgotten as the dead forget with grave-worms behind their eyes for thought.

So, to cheat herself, she assumed that she was forgotten. She too in time must forget everything that had been. In oblivion, she knew, lay freedom. Who chose to die must be allowed to die, though one's coat were being jerked off, and one leg was already half over the parapet.

He wrote to her little more than a year later, at the end of November, 1914. What the mind took in of it and made its own would have to wait, she knew it looking down in a frown at the words as though willing them to regain their distinct outline and lie straight again across the page, for the worms to erase. *You who have wisdom but no peace. . . . my wife eager as other wives for the sacrifice. . . . excited by papa's brave uniform. . . .* How horrible it was, his letter! It was that shuddering sound which she still could not grow used to, of the bucket plunging down down down into the well and striking the water at last with a drowning cry as the heart, released, dropped in the breast. What had he to do with it all, this mean commercial débâcle? He could not fight. He could not kill. And at the thought he cried out to her. He abandoned himself as a child crying at the night. He held out his hands. *A vagabond, a stranger to you, wrapped in loneliness, sat down one winter's night to rest and cry a moment.*

For it seemed that he had missed her: had missed her as a sail misses the wind: a seed the soil: a shepherd boy a crown: a greek horse, wings.

War came to Foria in a few restrictions; from far a passing battle-ship; an airplane sighted. Later the women and boys replaced a few men in the vineyards and at the ports; and much more money was asked for the fruit and vegetables sent to the mainland. Now and then a search would be made of the house, the carabinieri, concluded and assertive, kicking open doors with the toes of their boots; so many were the students from the Naples schools evading service by taking refuge in the woods and vineyards.

Suspended in island space she watched it all, knowing she could do nothing with herself that would prevent or alleviate one drop of suffer-ing or blood. It seemed a matter of hundreds of thousands of tons of high explosives against hundreds of thousands of men who had nothing whatsoever against each other, and were being ladled, thrown-in, fed into the slaughter with such a lip-service of brave-sounding finality as to turn the onlooker to stone: to something tearless and without sound, so cold, so premeditated, so inexorable was the hourly slaughter of men who had nothing whatsoever against each other. At first it did seem that at any moment something must happen; that some monstrous retribution was about to be visited on them. Any day now the earth must open, swallow, and have done with it. Or be rushed madly whirling through space to strike the throne of God itself and there crumble to a small grey dust such as is retrieved for urn burial after the ordeal by fire.

Why scramble to stick one finger more in the hell's broth? Already enough were treating it as a giant picnic: not a little dangerous but great fun, great fun. Awful it was to stand there weeping for the world, weeping for the folly of it all, for the foolish people, the foolish foolish people who were being ladled, rained into it in their hundreds of thousands, so that one could hear the grind and thud of the machinery as it caught, ripped up and threw away before one could warn them (standing there, looking toward the mainland; having no right at all to all these tears at the world's death). For no voice could pierce the thud-thudding of machinery. Enough. Stop. One moment only. O stop one moment only and think! And then when at last it had to stop, then tears were turned to laughter. For one had to laugh if one read carefully but not too seriously (for surely they were not meant to be taken too seriously?) the solemn nobly chosen words which were being hung about the brows of elderly born leaders of men by elderly born leaders of men (of those remaining of course) around oblong and horse-shoe shaped tables, among nobly hollowed inkwells and reverently struck pens, and prancing gilt pilastres and carved and ornamental mirrors: all in the very best period of a gypsy's vision of the Almighty's personal caravan.

How he went to the war she did not know. Official news was scarce. No english newspapers were to be had. But she felt it would be all very clean and smiling and neat and dutiful; and it was sad to think of things dark, such as blood and dirt and suffering, coming the way of one so clean and dutiful and believing in it all whole-heartedly; and capable of beautiful heroisms and sacrifices beyond human conception because of this unalterable cleanliness and belief. Not for him the sudden cry in the night, the sense of futility, the anger at being dressed up to aim death at one's fellow-men. For him the correct, the fortunate attitude which clothed him in an added armour of valour and strength. Lord! what then lies behind the eye of man that can so alter the perspective of his soul as to bring to one courage and decision and to the next anger and futility? A vagabond, a stranger to you, sat down one winter's night: and there he was somewhere on the mainland, loathing it, cursing it, being bitter and ineffectual to tears; and caught up and ladled in indifferently with all who died at peace knowing now a mother, a sister, one's growing children, wives, young women whose warmed faces smiled in breast pockets above Love and To My, a cottage, many acres, a room, whatever space theirs in which to place their own: protected. And there he was in a german uniform whereas if he had any pride in nationality at all, which was doubtful, it lay in the fact that for all his square bones and blondness he stressed the french blood in him, no matter to whom the strip Alsace-Lorraine belonged at the time of his arrival on it.

Like a watcher from another world she would stand and look across at the mainland, stopping short in her walk to realise, to try to grasp, that the sun shone over all, or rain fell, and the year went through its gestation, birth, and death, and nothing was changed, not one single leaf its colour or wave its way in response to the monstrous happenings across a small strip of water. The earth cared not at all. Then the mechanism of its changes became awful to her. No more was she impressed by the grand manner of the sun working its will on the earth. Purpose and dignity (so childish she became, standing there, feeling how terribly it all mattered) seemed to have left it; remained a slow blindfolded mule moving endlessly round and round and round the waterwheel, stubborn, undeviating, fettered. The earth then was not for man, but man (what a harvest he was garnering now!) was for the earth. The earth caring not at all.

Nor for that matter, she thought, roused by the sudden sound of footsteps, did Padre Antonio, ascending in priestly leisure the path to the cemetery and engrossed in his breviary as though it were the very latest news.

All of which was long ago. So long ago, she thought, settling the cushions more comfortably behind her head, that she had become a legend in some sort, and a group of tourists had recently come to stare openly at her, and now and then (did she turn suddenly aside in the street from a stall or a window) she would surprise whispers in her direction and nodding heads: so strange it was for a woman living on day after day and year after year and unable, if questioned suddenly, to find a reason. I never see a greek statue, he once said, without being grateful to Time for knocking off its head and arms. That was it. A statue without a head. Or was she not rather a head without a statue? A head, she decided, going back many years and remembering, a head without its statue.

Brave and serious her head; a little severe perhaps, judged by certain standards, but with a definite calm speechlessness of stone about it. A head, as he looked up suddenly at her unseeing upheld profile against the sky, that would sit well on the Victory of Samothrace: though he anathematised greek art and Michelangelo (pollution of the world, that man) there being no one, no one but his god Orcagna; and of course Pieter Breughel the elder; and a man whose name she could not remember who was, or had been, a clerk in a bank, or a customs official, and whom he had known in Paris; showing her most curious pictures of his work: one especially, a tiger leaping at an arab on horse-back (was that it?) in a jungle undergrowth cut in sabre-strokes, and telling her contemptuously (for she *could* not see) that it was one of the few pictures in the world that mattered. Though he loathed greek sculptural art, swearing by his egyptians and chinese, still her head (seen at this moment) would sit well on the Victory of Samothrace, the only one of them he could stand, who was in his bones in a sense. The Louvre's fault: the stupendous stage management of her, as one advances toward her hardly daring to place one foot before the other (with tears in the eyes for one is sixteen and has left home for this) coming to meet one on brave uplifted wings. And though later one loathed them all, their dianas and crouching venuses and soft-bellied youths, She remained: the headless woman. And later how right it seemed: there to accept man not to question him and complicate a simple and necessary act. Off, off with their heads! That was what men felt in their bones; the perfect, the headless woman. And there worshipped. Like that should she come to meet one on brave wings outspread: but headless, headless. He was amazed at how well her head (at this moment, at this angle, angles and moments having much to do with the conduct of emotions) would fit: so brave and sightless it looked upheld on its neck-column.

Of which she was to know nothing for that was the morning Teresa Fusco's husband was drowned and he had behaved so disgracefully—

with such a deliberate childish rudeness—that she became speechless
and withdrawn with dislike of him. He had so clearly no intention of
leaving the widow to the enjoyment of her hour. One and a half litres
of strong wine Michele Fusco drank before going in the water and had
dropped like a stone. Yet why? He was a strong sixty-four and had
drunk his litre and a half before going in the water for the last fifty
years. Yet this morning in he went and dropped like a stone before the
children could reach him. That was at ten o'clock. By eleven Teresa
was already at the beach. Carved in some dark and ancient wood, her
island clothes wrapped tightly round her body and head, she sat on the
last step of the terrazza, rocking to and fro. A bodyguard of women
closed her in; a few children stood staring near their mothers. The
widow moaned and rocked herself. She wanted to take him home, she
cried. She wanted to take him home. But she must not, they murmured,
the doctor must see him first. The dead man lay covered by a sheet.
Why did the doctor not come? She wanted to take him home, she
moaned, rocking her thin body, holding it in her arms and swaying.
Now and again the women bent slightly forward and moaned with her.
They drew out the sound, seemingly spinning their grief. Feeling her
sorrow truly shared, the widow would make short sharp cries. Aia, she
cried. Aia, aia, aia, aia, aia, which was the pattern pricked out in relief.
Still, her eyes remained dry. How could water, she left one wondering,
ooze from something so dark-dried and withered? I want to take him
home, she said. And just then Uller began chasing Antonio in and out of
the tables. Immediately the centre shifted from the mourners to the
man laughing with the child. It was altogether a disgraceful performance. No, no, said his laughter, not so much fun for widows, if I can
prevent it; and he set about it with a vengeance. He knew, his attitude
proclaimed, that she was enjoying herself. Nasty old charlatan. Very
well, he sided with the husband. Soon it became a mimic and foolish
battle between husband and wife. He took the initiative by making a
louder noise. He knocked over a chair and shooed the cats back into the
house, and tickled Antonio till the boy rolled on the floor yelling and
kicking. You had better take a photograph of them, he shouted at her,
or shall I paint them for you? he is doing this for me, she told herself,
trying not to show how angry she felt. He is nothing but an obstreperous
child prancing before its mother. For it angered him most to see her
standing there taking it all seriously. A few tears, a moan, some-one
dead: and there you had it, the imbecile sisterhood of women. What
they called sympathy: and immediately it flowed from them this pity,

like. Yes, like that. How impatient, how unclean women made one feel with their communal ready sympathy and will-to-weep.

Below, the widow was trying to recapture the attention of her bodyguard by louder groans and longer cries, but it was difficult to pierce the clatter of overturned chairs and rushing feet and of Antonio's suppressed giggles, for he had been told from the house to stop his noise. So she ceased moaning and sat taut and silent staring at the sea. The women refused to look up so angry they were, resenting it more than the death itself.

For my sake, she said to him finally, the noise having become something of an anti-climax, knowing how their anger included her. These people . . . (she looked down at the women's averted, closed faces: no, she could not say love or like or want) . . . these people respect me. He pretended to take no notice, but shortly afterwards he went indoors. Below they knew (and she knew that they knew) that she had asked him to be quiet and he had gone indoors and would make no more noise. The widow knew it instantly. It was absurd the way even the back of her head knew that the noise had ceased. Still, she waited before reassuming her sorrow. She waited perhaps six minutes. Then she began again. I want to take him home, she moaned. The tension relaxed, her bodyguard bent toward her once again. Aia, aia, she cried. Aia.

He was wrong to disturb them, she thought, if only artistically. For the mourning group, fitted there at the foot of the stairs, had an extraordinary Pietà rhythm. It assumed that sorrow-laden and tortured unity of a Crivelli Deposition. Mary, dried and withered under fierce suns, and her women (she felt) must have mourned Christ with much the same sounds and attitudes. It gave the whole a strangely impressive significance. The dead man could not have asked a more solemn keening. What does it matter, she felt, whether the widow is serious or not?

A carabiniere arrived; stood talking at a distance and nodding his head. They pointed the widow out to him: she was fixing him from far with her birdlike eyes. I want to take him home, she wailed to him. They told him what she had said. He shrugged his shoulders. Some-one brought out a chair and he sat down under the awning near the corpse, staring at the sheet. By now the women were growing so angry and impatient that several were in real tears. Where was the doctor? people were asking. What right had he to take two hours to drive from Castoli when it could be walked in twenty minutes?

At last well past noon the enormous black-bearded corsair of a doctor arrived; took no notice at all of what was said to him; took out a note-book, wrote in it, threw back the sheet, bent over the body, tapped, untied the bathing drawers: was quite useless but impressive. Against the white sheet the dead man lay like a mummy, as dark and as dried, his cheeks sucked in the hole of his mouth. The carabiniere, now less important, rose and said they could take the man away. Wound in the sheet they lifted him on the stretcher and carried him across the sands; the widow walking directly behind with bent head and holding a darkly angular hand across her face.

S ix o'clock. Curious the power of these bells to soothe or irritate. Either they set up a prolonged and angry farmyard cackling, or imitated the useless screech and crow of the women at the fountains for their turn, or cried out like lost and frightened children, or pealed with mock joy as for an old man's wedding. This evening San Soccorso shook out the hour in motes of sound incredibly pure and cold. I must remember Graziella's coat on Thursday, she thought.

It was a pleasant clear-eyed October (eager restless month which she preferred to them all) but already the sun was colder and the winds treacherous. Graziella, she reflected, must be protected against them. But must she? Why protected? And against what? Did it matter to any-one but herself (come, admit) whether Graziella were dressed in furs or packing-paper? Was she not, with that inborn climatic sentimentality which causes old ladies to leave their fortunes for the upkeep of free-born cats and undesirable dogs, making another mystery of the commonplace? Admit that the girl herself attached neither mental nor physical importance to the thing. Graziella was suddenly and instinctively proud of herself: and proud of the envy her swelling out-thrust body caused among the women as she passed, her head set well back, and with something of her mother's slow Ionic smile on her mouth. As thanks offering to the many-breasted Diana, twin-horns of the new moon, she wanted her silver offering. Which was to be the first of many: the Madonna would see to that! Nothing more.

Nothing of that mystic entrailless joy, that frail byzantinian hand-crossed expectation which culminated and died in Fra Angelico's cell, to be reborn again of Raphael as a comely rounded wench filled full with milk and sap. (Women in eastern art, as he had said, serving to suggest the unapproachable: in western art to remind one of one's

mistress.) The woman's saint, this vacant-looking woman modelled to
Raphael's taste with the plump child on her arm, above the light
burning in every home, in every shop, on every street corner. How
tired one grew of the tyranny of her placid mammiferous charm!
Nothing here to turn maternity into a folly or a martyrdom (except
those Seven Swords because her son did not want her). What have I to
do with thee? he asked. And is punished by remaining ever helpless and
small and plump in her strong maternal embrace: woman worshipped.
(Had ever man in the grimmest stories of mythology, pondered Ruth, a
more difficult punishment to bear?) Occasionally doubts pierced her
woman's heart with Seven Swords, leaving her ennobled and more
comely and acceptable than ever.

She had to admit that it was altogether ridiculous of her to sit worrying (with a ladylike mystic sentimentality) as to whether the girl was
hot or cold whichever way the wind blew, or dropped her child behind
a hedge or in a bed; when the girl herself was as indifferent to it all as
God Himself breathing on His handful of earth and waiting (probably
with His eyes shut) to see what He would bring Himself.

She thought of Lisetta's slow Ionic smile: that slow secretive smile
lifting the edges of the lips and troubling the eyes an instant. It rarely
came now: she had a kindly open laugh: but Ruth had surprised it on
her many a time when she was young. Now in certain moments her
daughter had it. It was unconscious, of course: and brief. Therein lay its
arresting quality of wonder: (for could anyone, considered Ruth, be
more empty-headed than Graziella?) And children, very young children, have it: and therein lies *their* charm. It comes before speech in
some whole and mysterious way: infusing them with sudden reality and
beauty as they lie staring at space. Which was why it was so beautiful to
watch an infant smile. Smiling without words or spoken humour; with
no need for a cultivated taste in buffoonery or the ridiculous. How far
away one was from it all! Used up and old beyond recall one felt before
the sight of a child making its own joy because of a texture, a soft hand,
a silky sleeve, a sound, a colour. But with the coming of speech they
lost it; as though by an added faculty of expression they weakened that
of sensation: and nothing was left to wonder at but the commonplace.

Concetta certainly was without it. A fine large girl cut all in one, as it
were, from a block of dark-coloured stone: the whites of her eyes and
teeth all that had escaped the sun when it burnt her up in its prolonged
splendour. For her mother Concetta worked as hard as a grown man;
she swam like a fish; she was more devout than any novice. She prayed

with pleasure and attended every Mass. From the age of ten she had been burning candles and wearing out her knees to Santa Restituta to help her to get to a favourite uncle and aunt in South America and work there: work hard and send money home like her brothers, and not miss, as she herself put it, all that was happening "outside."

She would bring Graziella's coat next Thursday (though admitting all the arguments against it!) and finish Concetta's jersey by tomorrow evening. She frowned thinking how she could have got the wool more quickly by going to the town for it herself; and with a presentiment that Graziella would come back empty-handed pretending that it had been impossible to find.

But she was to forget all about the red woolen jersey because before Graziella could get back from the town the letter came from Strathwick, Strathwick and Strathwick, & Goode, informing her that as her husband had made no alteration to his first will beyond a few recent personal bequests, they would be glad to have her instructions regarding the property and desired to assure her of their loyal and continued services in her interests, and coöperation in whatever plans she should decide on.

I must go back, she thought immediately. I must go back. She felt like a lady in a ballad. My husband is dead, is dead. And I must hame, must hame. Surprised: but more because it seemed unusually real than because it was unexpected. She was surprised and excited in a calm unreal way. It was as though waking from a long trance she had crossed the room and looked in the mirror and the mirror lay in bits and she must float away down the stream on a boat and the spell was broken. Was she glad? She could not be sure. Yet she felt that she had been waiting for this summons to return.

She decided on the four-o'clock boat for Naples, catching the seven something for Rome, changing immediately for Milan. And before going went to say good-bye to him. She found him lying asleep on the sand in the shadow of a rock where the children had left him.

To the end of life, it seems, one may find oneself looking at familiar things for the first time. Asleep and dressed and in the sunlight, and perhaps because she was leaving him and was to be free of him for the first time, she found him unusually interesting to look at with his fine thin nostrils and well-shaped mouth and the long silky eyelashes of an attractive woman. His shirt was open and the fairish brown hair on his breasts caught lights from the sun and shone like coarse silk. His bare throat was brown as were his hands, long thin-fingered hands like hers:

not a man's hands at all, she thought, contracting her brows. He held no menace for her. Dead he might look as he looked now. But should he open his eyes he might smile and speak to her, and jump up and insist on seeing her to the boat. (O why did you tell Polyphemus your *name?* I've been so anxious about you!) Is it possible, she thought walking away, that he will not know that I am gone? For that matter had he ever known that she was there? Whole he looked lying there in the shadow of the rock: whole and good to look on. How well he looked! Who, seeing him asleep, could believe? At that moment and for the first time it occurred to her how proud a woman she might have been. But he was rootless, null, unproductive: therefore not a living being at all. And all of her contriving. To punish her he would not know that she was gone.

Lisetta kissed her hand: there were tears in her eyes.

Night fell quickly and blotted out the vines and farmsteads and mulberry garlands holding hands from tree to tree, as the train sped toward Rome. Moon and stars were very bright and purposeful. The bold dark outline of the hills against the pale intense moonlight gave an eerie impression of a cavern opened suddenly under the sky. As though, as she sat there looking from the window, the bottom had dropped out of the heavens.

S he woke and looked out on Tuscany. It was early: barely five o'clock.

The light alone was as nothing she had ever seen or imagined. Calm, limpid, and emptied of all colour. The grey-blue olive trees broke from the Tuscan earth in ghostly waterfalls. The very cypresses pointed their fingers gently as from a Holy Hand. She recalled his contemptuous dismissal of Tuscany: one is perpetually attending a Last Supper.

Yes, it was like that. The umber rising of the hills moulded with how gentle a thumb, and then smoothed by angels with mystic tender feet. No Titan ever strode across them or lay imprisoned beneath. Their very outlines were caressed. What an infinity of patience had gone to the making of this land, she marvelled. On the summit of each small hill a modest-gazing castle. Gentle campanili; a narrow silvered river; long dressed fields; and sorrowing cypresses in slow procession up the gently moulded hills. Infinitesimal cities sown on hillocks; the houses in their varnish of centuries so neatly fitted in the hollows; so eager; so stippled with brightness. And never an angry look. Sweet-sweet as a thrush song at dawn.

She remembered Uller's remark: baroque is a man who talks too loud and too long. And thought of the palatial arrogance of Naples. Its high-cast ceilings; its monstrous doorways breathing defiance; its colossal façades of tossed-up and floating stone. And with it went the ferocious southerner, round-shouldered, bull-necked. Even the southern houses, she reflected, had large mouths.

No trace here of the bravado of baroque. And all at once she knew what gave that look of warmth and friendliness. She must have known it at once. Once again she saw houses with roofs! Home! Roof—synonym of home. Friendly as thatch; as those brown-sagging roofs hung like fishing-nets over old and much-lived-in cottages. She must, she thought again, have known it at once. How long ago now since she had seen a roof? How far, how very far away it was from the sun-baked flat-roofed house which had become more real to her than her childhood's home.

The ascetic land: the land of Saint Francis, silver-green, even-coloured, cool. Its churches modest, its outline meek and smiling. Yet the earth's blood (she thought) is hot blood, is rich dark volcanic blood. No no. Frail and lovely though it was she was glad she had not stopped there on that adventurous journey south of long ago. She would not have found peace here, she felt, where peace was so orderly and even-breathed. Here in Tuscany all was beatific calm. Foria wild and dis-orderly was for ever drawing breath between one rage and another. No, no. After the first eye-filling wonder she regained her balance. Here I would have grown meek, she thought, resisting the spell. The limpid morning breeze would have condoned with her. The stippled green surface was too much of a caress. Rest on me it seemed to say. I bear all burdens. And in the end she would have emerged splendidly wronged and purified. No; Tuscany was best left to elderly water-colour enthusiasts, and to those incredible englishwomen abroad in gaunt raffia-trimmed hats and with large coloured beads around their necks, who look always an uncared-for thirty-seven.

When the train drew into Florence at something past six she could not resist the temptation. It would delay her: but who expected her? Who was there to expect her or know that she was coming? She had only herself to answer to. She could catch an afternoon train and leave Milan at midnight.

She was glad that she saw it first empty save for the people them-selves: carters, peasants, cleaners, workers on their way to work. Even so, and at its best, she was disappointed. It was neither one thing nor the other. Time was scattered about it in such disharmony as to make it neither past nor present. And it was definitely a woman city. Its face that of a woman smiling a sad and painted smile. Ineffectual and womanly, she thought, as its history: the not very serious warfare: the not very formidable priests: the pageantry of elegance and Madonna-worship: the respectability of its honest tradesmen and artist-craftsmen. Florence was ever the bourgeois of italian cities!

Once I should have loved all this, she thought, coming out on the Cathedral square unexpectedly. She felt cheated. She blamed Browning. For instance, his Giotto. Coloured sugar stick, she thought: and the Duomo. Coloured sugar stick, she thought again, resenting it, hurrying past the clanging trams. Were they never to be serious? For instance, that unruly heap of statuary in the Loggia which even her eye could see as irritating as it was out of place. And was that the David? He was right, she thought, who a moment since would no more have dared question Michelangelo than a child dares question god. That white giant, far far too white (she thought) against the dark grim-proportioned Signoria (a welcome male touch: the first so far) with his soft woman's belly and pensive face? Soft-bellied and white he stood like a naked woman in the serious setting of walls and cobbles dipped in the mellow dye of centuries. He had no business there. She knew it though seeing him for the first time, and yet for hundreds of years he had been allowed to stand without protest and cripple the beauty of the setting. But the Signoria was gorgeously serious. Good, too, the Palazzo Strozzi, and strong and angry-looking. How well a frown sits on a house, she thought, pleased. And now and then on suddenly turning aside one did come upon a mass of stone heavy and male and not built to house women-saints and courtesans.

Already by eight o'clock the congestion and noise so typical of Florence and more irritating and nerve-wrecking than anywhere else in Italy, were making themselves felt; and even the narrowest streets were alive with the coachmen's wild whip-cracking and bicycle-riders bearing down on pedestrians who took refuge in divine providence and sublime indifference. Escaping into the Piazza Santa Croce where Time has been least tampered with, she was doubly delighted because of its unexpectedness. And standing on the Ponte Vecchio looking now this way now that she admitted its charm, and leaned on the railings thinking that, after certain angles of Paris, this was probably the most familiar view in the world.

For the first time, leaning there, she heard english spoken. She picked them out from far: tweeds, mackintoshes over arm though the sky was radiant, coloured beads, long self-conscious strides and that look of cultivated indifference assumed by those english-speaking abroad to show the onlooker (always the onlooker, she thought) that this was neither new nor to be wondered at. It's a *great* mistake. Never tell them. Never say. So I said. Most comfortable, most, and only. Yes, I know. Yes. I know. Like it? No'bad. Ha. Ha ha ha. A'right. So I said. Never pay. My dear, do *you? Do* you? Yes. Ha ha. O yes. 'Right. Ha. O no O *no.* When an Italian says *that,* dear, it means.

Having been walked over the view was now somewhat bedraggled, as is the way with certain views and certain people. At a sound it had become a suburb of heaven. There was a voice that breath'd o'er Eden touch about it. A celestial garden city. We are full to capacity at the moment, she heard Saint Peter saying, looking up from the register and being helpful. Until the alterations are complete would you care to go to Florence? Charming spot. In a sense quite as pleasant. The same people and all that. And the views quite quite charming. You will like it there I feel sure.

The stern frown of the Pitti palace restored the balance. What character a house with a menace in it has, she thought, retracing her steps over the Ponte Vecchio and stopping to stare in a window of Art reproductions and Views. And there, to the side of the window, leaning against the reproduction in colour of a fresco-fragment by Nardo di Cione, a picture somehow familiar. I know that picture, she thought. And then stared again and lost thought of where or why she stood there. Giovanni stared back at her from stark blue-black eyes set in an incredibly blue face against an incredibly blue sky. She read Moderner Meister der Farbe. Das blaue Kind. The blue boy. Le garçonnet bleu. Vom elsässischen Maler: Hans Uller, 1884-1916.

So it was in the Tate Gallery. She would go there. Some-one then, something was there to meet her in London. It was a friendly thought. There must be other things of his. There must be books and reproductions. But these she would reserve: she would wait. She turned away from the window and into the maze of narrow streets, following where they led. What had guided her to Florence? Suppose she had not stopped: had reached Milan and not known, perhaps never known, that though Uller was dead Giovanni stared from the walls of a great gallery and made London no longer strange to her. They turned to stare at the tall brown-faced woman striding along smiling at the pavement.

She heard him say: genius is sanity. Genius is only sanity. Genius is common sense uncommonly used. Pick out the men of genius in the world and you have picked out the few sane men. Throw in certain grades and degrees of talent and men who excel at certain jobs. When the rest of mankind comes to die the only thing you can be sure of is that while they lived they helped fill the sewers. That was why, he said, the world's experience was always wasted and why the world repeated its mistakes. Only two people had ever profited from the lessons of the past: the artist and the scientist. The one understood beauty: the other truth.

And from that, apropos of nothing, he must tell her of Nasetkin's taste in women. He had to have them respectable and married. They were cleaner, he said. (Frenchwomen are best but not over-clean.) Wives of local mayors and minor deputies and officials, not too easy to get but once got most willing and yet needing none of the difficult wooing of unskilled virgins. Also, being a russian, Nasetkin liked to think that he brought pleasure into the lives of married women. Then would come such amorous incidents which he found so amusing as hardly to be able to begin for laughter, such as Nasetkin's wooing of the wife of the Maire of the . . . arrondissement, an enormous eighteen-stone creature fit for a circus tent; and how feeling that some heroic and decisive gesture was needed Nasetkin decided to lift her up and carry her to the divan in his manly arms and bumped and staggered about the room dragging the back part of her about the floor in a terrifying effort to lift her up, crashing into furniture edges and bouncing back and not daring to drop her for fear the divan wasn't there. All he knew was that every time she gave a shriek he had impaled some corner of her on the furniture. Until at last she found sufficient breath to hiss at him: no, it was not repeatable. And Nasetkin hurt and indignant panted back: and that also was not repeatable. At the time she had not thought it amusing, so shocked she was at the thought of anyone repeating such a story to her, and knowing that he repeated it only to shock her, miming with huge delight through the absurd comedy. He rocked, he roared with laughter! The englishwoman's fear of being treated as a woman!

Yet here she was laughing at the memory of it as she strode with amazon stride through the streets of the celestial suburb not caring where she went and walking straight into the mercato centrale filled with rich sounds of tuscan peasants calling attention to their wares, to the profusion of flat plaited baskets heavy with autumn fruits and leaves and making it a thing of sound and colour to hold the breath at.

Fruit and peasants again: how right they were! How purposeful and serious they looked. How unalterable it all was. And what a good smell it had, as she stood breathing it all in, full of gratitude to them and thinking how they, the people, had saved their city.

Leaving it she came into a piazzetta of no distinction but quiet and tree-bordered and with stone slabs of benches at intervals under the trees. She sat down. The morning had excited her, revived her, brought life back slowly in her veins. She had not felt the life around her so deeply for years, nor felt so free from care. She knew now that he was dead. She had always known it: but now she knew the year in which he died. Nearly fourteen years ago, and it was as yesterday! How the years had passed without her noticing them, as she sat there with the very best butter in her watch at an unreal ceaseless tea party with Richard and her father and Hans the unreal ceaseless guests. All at once it had become fourteen years and an eternity of time. Before she had known the date it was but yesterday. But it was all long ago.

She heard a cry and saw a small child of three standing between a quiet-looking tall woman and a man in working clothes. The woman was trying to distract the child's attention so that the man might reach his bicycle at the side of the road and ride away. They made a little game: the child followed it for a moment but always as the man reached his bicycle she turned and with a cry rushed at him. So he had to return and pretend that he did not want to go. He held the child in his arms and she clung to him and held on to his neck with her little hands. Then he put her down and again the cry was wrung from her. Ruth watched her contorted face and pitied her. All the passions were set on it. All jealousy, all despair was on the small contorted face and in the cry she gave. Finally the woman lifted her in her arms; and the man gave her a last kiss and ran to his machine and was off waving to her till he turned the corner. She struggled; she cried; she beat her little hands. Not more than three, thought Ruth. Passionate, despairing little thing! What would become of her, she wondered? What mistakes would she make?

The woman stood unperturbed smiling at the child's distress and stroking her soft tassels of honey-coloured hair.

—Was that her father? asked Ruth.

—No, said the mother. His wife nursed her while I was in hospital for nearly two years. He comes here to see her sometimes.

The woman took the child away to the other end of the square. The little creature came no higher than the stone benches, and now and then

Ruth would see a little head rise over a bench, still looking in the direction of the man who had fled on his bicycle.

She took a carrozza and drove to San Marco.

T he office boy gave it as his opinion that Mr Benjamin Strathwick was not tin. But he would go and make sure. No, Mr Benjamin was sow, but Mr Nathaniel was sin. Sin but engaged. Could she wait?

He was a nice small boy, quite clean. After handing her an evening paper he went back to the licking of stamps in a dark corner. She left the newspaper on her knees and sat staring into the tired-looking face. You'll 'ave to wait a long time for Mr Nathaniel, he called to her, they always 'as.

So (not to hurt the office boy's feelings) she opened the paper and found herself reading a ladylike tea-pale eulogy of foreign travel: the peculiar charm of Venice. After which she read an interview with a bishop headed: I believe in a Heaven for Dogs. After which she read an article in which a Dean was tolerant and clear-minded on Religious Intolerance. A small square was drawn on the page in which one read that the views herein expressed were brilliant, were startling, and would shed new light on a parlous subject and the editor took no responsibility. (From which she gathered that the value of being a clergyman in modern journalism was that one could write pale essays acceptable to the average man of moderate newspaper culture and win renown as a reactionary.) She was about to learn the moral the Bishop of London drew from the declining birthrate when a bell rang and the office boy wanted to be followed this way, please, and she was shaking hands with some-one thin and grey and incredibly tall, and then sitting down in a dusty and traditional leather chair in the dusty and traditional legal setting.

Just as one may come suddenly on one of those reed-voiced thin-necked curates who cannot be bettered, so outwardly Mr Nathaniel Strathwick was all that a solicitor of repute and long-standing should be, to the very finger tips upholding finger tips. With how dry a smile he uttered cold and amiable words of no consequence. With what precision of look and utterance he gave polite and meaningless remarks the authority of a legal decision. Three weeks? Ah, then she could no longer be considered a stranger, Mrs Rice-Hungerford. He used return and once more in England with such finality that she hastened to assure

him that she had come only for as short a stay as possible and was
returning almost at once. As soon, it seemed, as the business on which
she had come was settled. (Why, she wondered, should a human being
spread his fingers wide as a cat stretches a paw, and dance on their tips?)
Aah. It was both a sigh and a question. For a fraction of a second Mr
Nathaniel Strathwick sought to remember and allowed it to be seen
that he sought to remember. Exactly. The something queer, the something, exactly, about the young person his late client had married, let
me see, how many years would that be exactly?, against the family
wishes. Returning almost immediately? (Could it be that Mr Nathaniel
Strathwick was disappointed and displeased?)

And Sharvells? It seemed that after giving it much thought (which
was why she had postponed her visit until now) Sharvells was to
become the permanent home of a charitable institute which provided
holidays for London's slum children. Though the scheme was really
more comprehensive than that. It was to be a permanent all-the-year
round home for poor children who were weak or had been ill, and
especially for ill-treated children; at certain times of the year (they
were hoping to arrange) slum mothers could take their holidays with
their children. It had nothing to do with mentally defective children,
she hastened to explain, who were in no sense, she believed, worth
saving.

London on reacquaintance appeared a vast children's hospital. She
was appalled. (Now he has ceased dancing on his finger tips, she
thought.) For Mr Nathaniel Strathwick was quite overcome. He admitted as much. It was the last thing, he said, that he had expected to
hear. A sudden spark of pity struck in him for his late client who against
the family wishes had once married this eccentric woman sitting opposite him, staring him in the face with steady eyes. (Hard, thought Mr
Strathwick. Determined sort of woman. Difficult type of woman to deal
with. Not what one could call a womanly woman, thought Mr Strathwick who was usually most careful to get in first with any staring to be
done.) He used words such as heirloom and family (who *was* she exactly?
he cast about in his mind) and pride, and to his listener's astonishment,
touched on the matter of tradition and gave a short apologetic résumé
of dates and then stopped suddenly (would the woman never take her
eyes off his face?) and said that before this thing, before any irrevocable
step was taken, had she thought of selling Sharvells? He spoke of
commendable impulse, of the generosity responsible for such a (proposed) gift. But in these hard days of taxation it was not a wise or light

undertaking to throw away, he stressed the words throw away, both profit and property. (Again she noticed how an over-bred english voice can be a thing detached from the speaker: not rising warm and articulate from the lungs or even from the pit of the stomach, but emerging clipped and thin from the oval of the palate.) She caught the words hotel and golf-course. It seemed that the country had great need of golf-courses easy of access at week-ends. From no point of view (having always the interests of his clients at heart) could he assure her that the course she proposed taking was practicable. Such a scheme, he said, would involve a very great deal of money: a considerable part of which, he said, had already been swallowed in death duties.

There were the pictures, she said. She had been told, and had sought information for herself, that Gainsboroughs and Constables and the English School reached high prices just now. They could all go. Then there was the furniture. Most of the land beyond the woods could be sold. The tenants would be only too pleased to buy their own land. Whatever money coming to her under the will would remain as a yearly income for the running expenses (she had it seemed her own money which more than sufficed); the money from the sales could go to the necessary alterations to the place. It would not be expensive to run as the children would do practically all the work (under a new training scheme) their own gardening, producing their own food. The great thing was that the Society should have a home and headquarters and an income of its own, so as not to be entirely dependent on a precarious and reluctant charity.

But, said Mr Nathaniel Strathwick. But, said the intently staring woman, the spirit in which it was given mattered even more than the gift. The thing must be believed in by everyone. Most of all by those who drew up deeds and saw to contracts. She knew nothing of such things, but it was a work she believed in: had set her heart on. She had found that those with whom she had discussed and planned it, certain heads of the Society, those who were to be responsible for its running, were glad of it, were sure of its success: were enthusiasts. One did not want the legal advisers of a holiday home for poor children to sulk (nothing Uller ever said to Padre Antonio pierced so deeply as that unseemingly-used word of an eccentric woman pierced the senior partner of Strathwick, Strathwick and Strathwick, & Goode) to sulk because it was not an exclusive hotel or golf club. In such work people must be eager, said the eccentric woman as though she were referring to a sporting contest or a dancing troupe. They must be enthusiasts.

(Young people, she thought, watching his cold grey face controlled by some inner self-willed mechanism rather than by blood and muscle, with young alive teeth to smile down at them and young alive voices and with young healthy-looking flesh on their arms and cheeks.) He counselled her so strongly against it would it not be wiser for him to drop the matter and for her to go, she hesitated, perhaps to the Society's own? On which immediately Mr Nathaniel Strathwick smiled the disarming and helpless smile of one who has been in the wrong and is suddenly convinced of it and generously admits his error; and the scheme became laudable and of an assured success and an enterprise with which one might well be proud to be associated.

I n the sky a moon: round, solid, luminous. She crossed King's Bench Walk making for the Embankment. The evening was cold but unusually clear. Enormous coloured electric signs continually effacing themselves and trying again were powerless to detract from the beauty of the hurrying swollen river. On the South Side, thrust in irregular outline against the sky, massive blocks of dark warehouse walls lit suddenly by the glare of light, assumed the weird shape and colour of those burning backgrounds on which, in old pictures, Lot's wife looks back. She would walk, she decided, as far as Waterloo Bridge, to where Big Ben stared like a surprised and haughty owl. Weeks of sooty rain and dreary wetness made a walk an event to her.

She was growing used to London, but not reconciled. It still grated on her sense of beauty and fitness like an ill-timed laugh. She was still unable to believe the noise, the lack of air, the crowded come and go of roads and pavements. The shabby down-at-heel greyness everywhere surprised and dismayed her. Where then was that sense of spaciousness, of quiet beauty, or arched necks taut on their bearing reins, of green trees, of great squares more solemn than a cathedral close, which had remained with her through the years from her rare visits after her marriage. It was not so much the noise. She was used to noise. Nothing could be more noisy than Naples. (If it came to comparisons then the eight or ten women haggling over their wares in the piazzetta at Foria Ponte could reduce the most tumultuous London street to a whisper!) But there is such a thing as harmonious noise, integral part of sun and sky, and there is a grey monotonous clamour under torn and hesitating skies, hanging down over all like an old beggar woman's unkempt hair.

A vast children's hospital, she had said to that incredibly tall and leathery man who had stared at her from small restricted grey-blue eyes, hesitating whether to treat her as a lady or a lunatic for wishing to deprive the empire of a golf-course within easy reach. Is it useless? Will it help in any way? she wondered.

A tramcar hurtled past like a rocket. In depression sudden noise has an angry and menacing sound. She started as though, tearing past, some-one had screamed at her. Was the gift of Sharvells merely the gratification of an ill-considered and quixotic impulse? At most six hundred children at a time: from how many hundreds of thousands? And was it fair to lift them out of it for a week or month and throw them back again? Could she take that responsibility? And did it matter whether a few people more or less ate or did not eat, breathed or did not breathe? Doubt left her suddenly bitter and discouraged.

Had it always been like this? Which of us has altered, she wondered, coming on it with new and startled eyes: at its winter's worst, perhaps. She had no right (and no need) to notice such things having been driven straight to the discreet and exclusive hotel in Hans Crescent where people coming from the country looked neither grey-faced nor under-fed, and where one did not have to walk quickly, consciously using as little breath as possible, through narrow fœtid streets, as though the promiscuous herded millions in their interminable ribbons of dirty street had emptied themselves on the air and the passer-by must lunge through it as best he can. But she could not help seeing what was there to be seen, nor moving beyond that airy strip between Piccadilly and the few discreet squares of Kensington and Belgravia where the view was less drab and time-tarnished.

She could not help, behind the orderly and even-faced square seeing the mile of slum. She could not help, on turning aside suddenly from an elegant residential street, coming immediately on the rows of damp and stale-smelling public houses in their rows of damp and stale-smelling alleys. She saw the sour-smelling unkempt blowsy peacock-voiced women, the hollow-faced men unfitted for their work, the hordes of ill-clad pale children sitting for hours on the cold evil-smelling pavements. Unhealthy and rotten like soaked stumps of dead trees. She saw the hordes of mutilated beggars; heard the tuneless voices of myriad street singers; saw the stones covered with the ghostly trees and water-falls of a thousand pavement artists.

And was indifferent to none of it. (Lord! what then lies behind the eye of man that can so alter the perspective of his soul as to bring to the one courage and decision and to the next anger and futility?) What did the reverse side of the moon matter that she should be for ever trying to stuff it in her pocket? Was she not being unfair? Because streets were smoked out with petrol fumes and alive with motor horns where she remembered the tang of horse dung and the trimly beaten measure of slow-stepping carriage horses; or because, coming from years under a vast and luminous sky and colour and plenty and people strong in their work and with warm-baked skins and naked strongly planted children with backbones like ropes of vine knotted and unbreakable, she found the air thick and unpalatable and hung like a piece of sodden grey cloth above the opening between squares and streets. What right had she to question what she saw? What exactly did she want? A feeling of bitterness and impatience came over her, as to one who sees a favourite child doing mean and unworthy acts. What then would she advise? Nothing, nothing, said Ruth avoiding a black shape advancing toward her with a drunkard's amiable concentration.

She sought but found none of the appropriate emotions. All her life like a wish laid on her she had missed appropriate emotions. Even as a child, and in the teeth of protest, the cuckoo's song had seemed to her immeasurably superior to anything the nightingale could offer. And now she wanted, she tried, to see World-Trade and Hub of the Universe and London's teeming masses and London's great army of workers, and saw nothing but herded millions rushing to their daily death entangled in the puppet string of civilisation: hunger their fear, respectability their reward.

Yesterday in an underground train sitting opposite an elderly man with three separate strings of red hair drawn across his brow and turning the leaves of his newspaper with a thin green hand, she had thought of how a story could be written of just such an elderly man who had lived (like this) all his life underground, in trains to and from work, in badly lit offices, in badly ventilated badly designed houses, in the grave, and one day in a book or in his newspaper he read of the life and habits of the mole. And the absurd little creature (look! there was his picture, he pointed, for his son) made him laugh and laugh and laugh.

When the elderly man stood up and went out leaving his newspaper on the seat, she thought: now he has forgotten his armour. For it did seem to her that the people she saw about her carried their newspapers much as their ancestors carried a shield. In uniform self-defence, it seemed, they travelled in the trains and omnibuses with their heads wrapped in the daily papers. The great narcotic, the Universal Opiate

for which the Londoner paid his daily tax to get himself out of embarrassment. Which protected his outward self on his way to work against
any man or woman who dare approach or look at him. Which he
clutched to protect his inner self from the fear of sudden doubt that in
his daily grind from nine in the morning to six in the evening, he might
not, after all who knows?, be doing a hard day's work; be pulling his
weight in the world; be doing a man's work; the nation's work; the
world's work.

And what more than anything was so sad about this dry-grin of
humanity, she thought, was to see them all being so splendidly brave
about nothing: about nothing at all.

F ear! How full of fear they were, the handful of people of leisurely
and secluded lives gathered together as though for mutual protection in the pleasant quiet of Hans Crescent. That, too, was new to her.
How it shocked one this sense of insecurity in people whose lives,
concluded and unalterable, had never known the meaning of change or
fear! It was as tangible a thing as the hopelessness of mean streets and
the worry on the faces of people hurrying to their work. Fear and
worry. They gave it off collectively as an aura.

Particularly the very ancient Lady Neuerheim with all the desolation
of decay about her, making of her a tiresome old woman. She had long
outstayed her welcome. She knew it. Her wealth and jewels stood for
much. She knew that also. Apparently she belonged to one of those
jewish diamond firms for whom the english took South Africa. She had
once been fabulously wealthy. But times were not what they were. So
she complained bitterly of supertax and death duties. A brave smile
hovered; everyone seemed to be awaiting her death to take possession
of her money. They visited her only to eat her food. She was upset to
tears at a newspaper gossip paragraph mentioning the pictures and
gems in her country-house collection. Every thief in Europe has read
about me today! she smiled bravely through thick glasses. As evening
came her fears lessened. The effort of outliving the crowded daylight
hours over, and one more victory won from Time, she could rest. She
would be seen, guided by a resigned and competent-looking com-
panion-secretary up the long dining-room, her white hair rayed with
jewels, jewels covering her yellowing hands and holding up her throat,
and of course the renowned pearls, wound and rewound, and even so

reaching almost to the hem of her skirt, as they appear in the Sargent portrait which she mentioned repeatedly.

—Ah Sargent! said Mrs Saffron Oake. I place them together: Sargent and Wagner. Two great souls inseparable. (And Siena. Ah Siena. Mrs Saffron Oake wished to die in Siena. Or when dead to be carried to Siena. But she must know Siena? Not know *Siena* after thirty years in Italy? Impossible not to know Siena. Everyone. Then just as soon as she returns she must visit Siena, said Mrs Saffron Oake, and tell her exactly what her first impressions were. Only the first impressions. All other impressions are useless, useless. I go by first impressions only; and they never fail me.)

But a nice woman. The least fearful of them all. (What need Mrs Saffron Oake fear while stands Siena?) Perfecting a technique of conversation which depended on asking questions and answering them herself; stampeding people into listening to her singing of *stornelli toscani* which, she delighted to recall, she had gathered herself during her Tuscan wanderings. A short lecture preceding each song. A Miss Templestone at the piano throws up a dust of notes. Mrs Saffron Oake thrusts her mouth in a protruding oval and from a hidden recess produces a sudden sound. Listening, marvelling, knowing that her approval is sought, that her twenty-two years in Italy are being evoked and sung to, puts down her coffee-cup, has not the heart, smiles, leans forward and applauds just so much more warmly than the rest. (I must be old, she thinks, admonishing herself. I have an old-womanish heart.) Mrs Saffron Oake smiles in her direction and is off and away producing more sounds from hidden recesses. But a nice woman, the least fearful of them all: having Siena.

Whereas Mrs Warburton Drury, not having Siena, but having three daughters "out" and not doing at all well (common knowledge) although at home in most of the houses that mattered, being related in varying degrees to all of them, and having been bridesmaids at any number of important weddings and being dowdy on enviable dress allowances, and the second girl talking everywhere of independence and earning one's own living these days: hated many things: miners out of work; anglo-catholics; jews; americans; fascists; that nasty-looking man Mussolini; the Labour Party; all people who had no Right to govern; and the modern tendency to regard marriage as a light and impermanent tie.

A Colonel Crispin Farr said: We should refuse to shake hands with the Russians until they apologise for killing the Tsar.

A Miss Bettine Ross who seemed to have neither artistic nor practical use, nodded vigorously.

A Major Farjeon Gorr wished to see every —— socialist hanged on Tower Hill with other blackguards such as Bernard Shaw and Trotsky; and would like to take the job on himself and see it well and properly done. (Why were elderly army men so blustering and bitter?)

A Miss Alberta Braithey turned her heavy autumnal face to the light and said to her, slowly and conclusively: I have never thought much of my face, you know. But there must be something in it as so many men have loved it.

—No, said Ruth replying to a direct question. I hardly agree. A million shorthand-typists remain a million shorthand-typists, but a million mothers can found a nation. The italian woman, as you say, is a born mother (though that is much a matter of olive oil and sunlight). The italian view of an englishwoman is an old maid who kisses cats and fondles dogs. The italian woman kicks the cat and beats the dog: but she caresses the child. It is much a matter of climate.

(—I nearly dayed of laughing, said Miss Templestone, later. To say a thing like that one must be made; quite made.)

—But *you,* said Joan Agnew rapturously. You're different. You're so original, you know. You're marvellous. And without trying, like all the rest of them. God, said Joan dabbing ungracefully with her cigarette ash, I wish I'd had you for a mother!

She was taking Joan to a play. The girl's version of herself was that she was sponging on a sister who had married money and had left a Shropshire vicarage with no intentions of returning until she hadn't a bean. So she was looking for a job. Did she know of one? Everybody works these days; all her friends were sharing lingerie or flower shops or being mannequins or "walking on" in revues or getting on the gossip pages of the daily papers. One must do *something* or life would be too damned dull.

Ruth liked her. She was shocked and impressed and amazed. This, then, was the modern girl the newspapers spoke so much about. Keen-eyed, fleshless, arrogant. She liked it. It was new to her. It had promise. Everywhere there was fear, a sense of danger, a sense of despair, a smell of decay: but the young women had a certain hard fleshless courage. They had promise. It was new to her and interesting.

On coming out of the theatre they saw a crowd gathered. From the hole in the centre came a small querulous voice: An' I don't want to die 'ere in the street. O my Gawd I don't want to die 'ere in the street. . . .

—What d'you make of it? said the girl placing her long elegant legs on the opposite seat as the taxi jerked forward.

She hoped that he would not have to die in the street, haunted by the simplicity of the man's appeal.

—I meant the play.

She went to too few plays to be a good judge. But she didn't like it. ·

—To me you all seem to be prying into other people's bedrooms. You have all an eye at the bedroom keyholes of the world. I don't like your idea of what you call sex. There is too much of it. It is an obsession or a disease. You turn love either into a wasting disease or a perpetual Chopin nocturne.

—Um, said the girl throwing a match out of the window. There's something in what you say. It is rather a dirty business. Tonight's papers say the Luff divorce cost over £50,000. Nasty, isn't it? As though it matters in whose bed one sleeps. . . .

There he glowed like mother-of-pearl in the strong sunlight! He stared back at her from stark blue-black eyes set in an incredibly blue face against an incredibly blue sky. She sat on the edge of the red-plush seat as she had sat on the edge of her bed that night in the Taverna, heavy with tears that would not be shed. Irresolute she sat, as a nun about to break her vows and unable to do so.

She knew that they were now valuable these tortured fierce-looking paintings which she had watched him at work upon and found so strange. And still found strange but for the grape-bloom glow on this child made of the earth he squatted on, and which she too had understood. Two thousand guineas for *The Modern Blue Boy,* as the newspapers called it: and a bargain, it appeared, bought from the Paris art dealers who had bought it directly from the artist for sixty pounds. He had asked one hundred.

A vagabond, a stranger to you! How little that had meant, then. How evenly the days had passed. How very simple things were. How little those who achieved it lived for posterity! She had gathered in the books about him. She could not recognise Uller in these pictures of him, any more than she could recognise her father in their pen-pictures of him. Those who came afterwards, in hearsay, in admiration, meant nothing: meant less than nothing. The stories of his life in Paris with Nasetkin were witty and amusing. Nasetkin was made much of to give colour to the rumour of their intimacy. His biographers puzzled and surmised about an italian woman he seemed to have met the year spent in Italy prior to the war. She was to be seen in several of his later canvases. In the large *Woman and Child* the naked child on her lap is again the Blue Boy. Was she the child's mother? At first: probably. Later: undoubtedly. A rather severe head, even-featured, serious, remote. It ran through his later sketches like a litany.

They were clever, condescending, awestruck. They made of him a braggart, overbearing, callous, which seemed to give him additional glamour in their eyes. They worshipped him from far as a form of human burning bush which none dared approach.

Sitting there staring at the blue distorted child she seemed to have been on a long journey and to be nearing home. Have I been a lonely woman? she asked. Have I repaid my debt? Or was there never a debt to repay but in her wilful mind?

Did it matter if one human creature more or less was born into the world crippled, insentient? It happened to the most honest people. People who loved their children. People who desired children; who waited for years; who hoped; made actual prayers. And then Nature played them just such a trick: sent them just such an answer. See, said Nature, see what I have reserved for you! But all that was beside the point. Without waiting, without wanting, she had played just such a trick on Nature. See, she had said, see what I am giving you! A line she had memorised from her lesson books as a child came back to her: *and the elephant said to the flea: don't push.*

What intricate, what appalling things one did with the few years of life given one! But *you,* you're different. And she had blushed. There was a novelty and a certain glamour about the new young woman: but was she altogether satisfying? Had she attained anything not previously attained? A certain independence and what she called self-expression. A following less efficiently and more loudly professions which men had followed for years as a matter of course. There was about her a look of impermanence difficult to classify. A look of today. Something momentary. She would grow old and leave the world exactly as she found it.

You, you're different! How often had that been held against her? How she herself had reproached this very difference, this difficulty to take for granted, to produce appropriate emotions on their appropriate occasions, leaving her lonely as an invert. For surely (she thought) it was a form of mental inversion this loneliness of hers among her fellow-creatures; her desolate belief only in the few and fear of the many; her lack of hope; her sense of the purposelessness of it all. But times change. Now one not only might but one was expected to be different. What they called being different had an especial social value. It acted on others as a charm. She was shocked. She could not understand. Now, it seemed, the emancipated woman wanted no children. Women kept their figures and their jobs; besides, motor-cars (said Joan) were less expensive. How monstrous! she thought, understanding not at all. How mean. She hurried away from the blue Giovann' in his setting of radiant sky. She would return, soon; but she must go now.

Outside a steely rain fell in long detached needles. In the wet deserted street a solitary policeman in a rain-lacquered cape stood staring at the river. It was cold and wet but she must walk, she felt. Grey and black and black and grey and again grey and again black. She passed through it all as through a cloud, seeing nothing but opaque grey and solid black. People lived in this solid black: breathed soaked-in this opaque grey. She passed through the squalor of Westminster. Narrow streets leading out of and into narrow streets, and on each the same cold and desolate face. A grey mould covered everything.

She walked on through her cloud. She was startled by the sudden thought that had she lived among it all these years she would have noticed nothing. A blue expanse of sky had done that for her. Times without number she would have been driven through such streets, less alive than the blind man in the doorway, cap in hand. (He spat on the coin and bit it. Why did he not wear his hat, and trust to his placard on such a day? People don't like it, he said. They likes a man to be cawld and ter look it, afor' they gives 'im anything. They likes ter see yer fair dyin' for their copper. Thenk yew kindly lidy. Thenk yew. Thenk yew.)

And he? What would he have become in the protected ease among those fortunate few who, like himself, were lifted above such desolate reality? Suddenly she saw him lying asleep in the shade of the rock on the hot yellow sand under a cloudless sky.

In Trafalgar Square a procession of unemployed was passing. Traffic was held up; the people waited. The men, it seemed, were from the distressed areas of the North; were from the closed steel and iron works; were miners from Wales; were dockers from the Clyde. They had gathered in the North and had come down on foot with their banners and their massed appeal to protest. The men were soaked and shivering. Their faces were a uniform grey and haggard and emptied of

all expression save hunger and weariness. Their heads drooped forward
on their necks. They shuffled past, unsubstantial as ghosts. At intervals
mounted police in lacquered capes rode beside them, but paying scarce
attention to them, so worn and spiritless they were.

Again she had a sight of him lying in the shade of the rock on the hot
yellow sand under a blue outstretched sky. How she had feared him!
How long now, she wondered, had she feared him, imagining his
reproach? What then was the more culpable: physical or mental
insentience? To be unable to understand or to refuse? She thought of
the squalor, the grey faces, of blind men standing with uncovered heads
because others liked to see them cold, of the dreariness of poverty, the
dreariness of gentility, the limited outlook of the one, the limited outlook of the other, the decaying world closing in on the new life, and
everywhere people being so splendidly brave about nothing, about
nothing at all. What could she, she asked, what could she have told
him?

There was a movement and sudden noise and a sound of angry voices.
A policeman was speaking to one of the men. The man answered. The
policeman made a menacing movement with his arm. He was threatening to strike the man. To her surprise she began to tremble; she was not
certain but had the impression that her teeth were chattering. He must
not strike, she thought. She must cry out. It could not be that such a
wraith of a man, such a grey hollow thing, should be struck a blow, a
well-fed hearty blow, for a mere interchange of words. The people
around, those standing near him, she thought foolishly, would not
allow it. At last the policeman relaxed his arm. He shouted something
at the man. The man cursed under his breath, as the policeman turned
away. She ceased trembling.

Perhaps, she thought, if they could accept death this collective fear,
this smell of decay, would leave them. How clean (she thought) how
final death. To have lived and to die. How complete, how wise the man
(she thought) who having lived can meet death carelessly, knowing it
final. She remembered how worn and tired the earth looks after the
harvest and before the winter sleep; and with what zest the trees and
vines flung off their brown and brittle leaves. And then remembered
the musty fruit on barrows, or scarce and unvaried behind plate glass,
which those who sold had done nothing to produce. She thought of
Andrea balanced on his heels, tilting the jug of yellow-clouded wine.
She saw again the market place in Florence. The earth: with what
dignity it invested man! With what generosity it repaid him his efforts

in its service. Perhaps she had lived too long among peasants to be patient with the town dweller. Allow them no heaven, she thought. Dreaming away their lives in the expectation of living another. How much happier those (she thought) deprived of the mirage of a heaven, and living one life and living it fully.

On and on the procession shuffled, the men a uniform grey, haggard and emptied of all expression save hunger and weariness. Unsubstantial as ghosts they shuffled wanly past. The traffic held up: the people waiting.

In the growing press of people gathered there to attend this grotesque Calvary, she stood tearless and detached watching humanity carrying its Cross: bent, beaten and anxious, and yet more innocent than Christ. She turned to the group nearest her on the pavement; warmly dressed, middle-class. The man looked carved: the woman dried: the child bled: the dog inflated.

She turned away, again wondering what she could have told him. But now she smiled. She no longer reproached herself.

FUGUE

Per il che si ha a notare, che gli uomini si debbono o vezzegiare o spegnere. . . .

Macchiavelli

(*Il Principe,* Capitolo III: "De' principati misti")

A night to lead minor poets down white roads to the sea.
He hurried over the network of cobbles, keeping close to houses so angular with age as to seem but the reflection of themselves in dark water. From its flute the fountain played a watery tune. Despite his cautious step the stones rang with a hard deliberate malice as though to give warning of his escape; yet he hurried on, down twists and turnings that led an irregular and unwilling way to the narrow river, to the Raben Tor, to the road beyond the ramparts.

On the bridge he paused, thinking not without humour that where others took such pains to outdistance enemies, his haste was but to escape from friends.

The river was like a live thinking mirror. On its surface trailed a luminous finger. Infinitely deep, chill, and distant it seemed, gathered in heavy soundless movement under the cold lunar fingering. Incredible that an accent of light should work such distortion on a face which by day was friendly and shining, passing through the village from the fields over reeds and brown pebbles and the shouting children's naked feet; the women kneeling at its rim slapping the shirts and linen in a passionate ritual of duty and cleanliness, to which the younger women sang and the old cackled with a certain featherless busyness.

But this was no moment to idle on bridges. He must get beyond the village, through the Raben Tor, and out to the lane between the vines, leading to the hills.

He had escaped the crowded room but not its memory. Still through the fog of tobacco smoke Madame's pomeranian, rat-eyed, rat-faced, a dog like an ugly and spoiled child, yap-yapped for sugar and attention; the few peasants at the far end of the Wynstub chuckled over their cards and called the score in their hearty Alsatian speech which is like having one's mouth full of *The Canterbury Tales;* and Simeon Fenn, the elegant and out-of-place, leaned his head against the wall not taking his eyes from Lorwich's face, to whom Otto was explaining: first we had the old French taxes, then came the German, and now come the new French taxes, and we pay all three. Can you blame the Autonomists?

—O wine, wine! cried Sebastian. Fertiliser of the mind! Aphrodisiac of the soul! (Lend me your pencil, Lavinia. I'll write that down.)

A querulous voice was refusing to believe that the marriage of D'Arcy and Elizabeth was ever consummated. And the impersonal sweating Karl of the round red face and uncomprehending blue eye, swung his jugs and bottles through the confusion of smoke and people.

Place your Italian on the soil, Christopher Lorwich was saying, and you have placed him rightly. Sow Italy with salt and the Italian will prove as undying as the Jew. You will find him in every corner of the earth keeping his albergo, making his wine and pasta, building the world's roads, digging the earth and seeing that there is fruit from it. He has that deathless sense of race and family.

Miss Reade was complaining to Otto that there was nothing, nothing, in the *Guides Bleus* but *guerre sanglante* and *une très belle église moderne.*

—So that now the only thing to do is to jump on Russia. (The portly French doctor having missed the last train back to Strasbourg, was gathering his short fingers in little bunches and shaking them. His voice was live and quarrelsome.) Then Russia is off: finished. And so are the hotheads and the two to four million unemployed wandering about in every country and making a cursed nuisance of themselves. So long as they ate up their own savings it was bearable. (The doctor smiled.) But now they would eat up ours. They menace. They dare to threaten. Our answer must be to get rid of them. So long as they leave us in peace what can it matter how many heads they break: or whose? And what can it matter to us how savagely they annihilate one another so long as they do it thoroughly and in the name of Honour, Liberty, and Truth?

—(O nectarous, O pellucid beer! sighed Sebastian. From thy foam how many an Aphrodite has been born!)

—And do not think that England will escape. (The doctor was growing angry with Lorwich.) Yes, yes: we know it cannot be. Nothing ever can be, where the English are concerned. The world will continue to be the Englishman's little ball, and he to be the modern Atlas carrying his golf-clubs on his back. But slowly, imperceptibly, it will happen, my friend, even to you. You English do all things slowly. You will be atheists and communists without having noticed it or knowing how it happened to you, and without having shed one drop of blood. You English evolve so slowly. You do not believe me? But why should you doubt? Did not Darwin evolve an Englishman out of a monkey?

A sharp and prolonged clapping as though the gods themselves approved came loudly from the skies.

—The storks! The storks! cried Miss Reade. The storks are back! And leaned from the window to watch them settle. It was then (with her back to him) that he had turned to see if the door were open, and with hardly a sound had stood up to make his escape. But Sebastian had seen him (trust Sebastian) and with a lewd and intimate leer had twisted his owlish face in a drunken wink; so that for a fraction of a second he had hesitated, impaled, as it were, on Sebastian's knowing wink; unsure whether to go forward or retreat and coldly angry with himself for trying to appear to be leaving the room unnoticed for a purpose.

And here he was already above the village. He looked down on it, warm within its walls and guarded by the three squat gates with their high conic towers.

How astrologic the gothic! Made at night, can one doubt?, by searching the skies. The huddled houses upheld each other like a troupe of mediæval beggars. Above them the swaying roofs advanced and retreated: those sweeping Alsatian roofs, argus-eyed. And at the corners the serene octagonal fountains piped their reedy tune. How cold and sufficient their slow measure. How distant Italy and the baroque, with its tyranny of prancing Tritons. How sober and how unsteady it all was. A sober fact told by a wavering tongue: the potato grafted to the vine.

She would come and look for him. Of that he had no doubt. When she had turned and found him gone and Sebastian had rounded off the wink with the witty remark. She would sit down and talk brightly and quickly about nothing at all, and then jump up snatching at her book and handbag. Sebastian would again be beerily facetious. Obsessed by her one thought she would not resent it. Probably she would laugh. She had no pride. Of course she would laugh, snatching her bag and book without pretence, and hurrying away. And what was the use of remonstrating with her? She had the ruthless and irritating logic of the child. She would probably say, greatly surprised: Well, why did you run away?

Or she would say, as she had often said: Pride. *Pride?* Surely one can always put *that* down and pick it up again.

Except that she never picked it up again; or so it seemed. I am. I want. I must. I will. And she would find him here. She would take the road he had taken with an instinct as sure as though she had placed her nose to the ground. She would stand where he stood now; and he would be treated to the small boy running away from his nurse, or the heartless trifler with outraged love. It would depend on her mood. And from the moment he had got outside the house, no, from the moment he had got up from the table, he had known she would pursue and overtake. One would have to run a little further than the Raben Tor to escape Lavinia Reade!

Even so it was foolish to place himself deliberately in her path, so he climbed the bank beside the road and continued walking, hidden by the vines spread in long orderly rows on the hill-side. He was aware of the lush dark green smell of evening and of the metallic ring the vine-leaves gave as they brushed past him; and, now, that the dark shape he had taken vaguely for someone approaching was but the Christ marking the boundary of another vineyard.

They were at every corner these Crosses, bearing their gaunt and sorrowing burdens. They were mostly worn and moss-grown; but here and there were newly painted in the gay toy-soldiery of scarlet and gold, looking for a while almost happy. But always wrong; always out of place. Their surroundings mocked and cast them off, this sudden frown on a pleasant face. The very air of the hills and the grins on the flat kind faces of the people called for a tippler and a wineskin, or Omar and his book and bottle, or the jovial Hotei and his shaking belly. But only row upon row of gaunt Christs sunning themselves at the corners of the vineyards and looking unutterably sad and tired and foolish.

In the evening light, detail-less, simplified to the intention, the Christ had an impressive and mournful dignity. In the night the field was His. The vines, their arms upheld, no longer mocked the tyranny of His obstinate and abiding melancholy. He hung there, absolute in loneliness, turning aside His drooping head.

O crux ave spes unica!

Harrion was near enough now to make out the larger words and also the date

1643

Gedenke, O herr . . . von diesem Kreuze . . . .
reumuthig . . . . . glauben betet . . . . erlangt . . . . .

Forty days Grace promised for four Our Fathers and five Hail Marys said kneeling at this spot. A long chain-letter to have started three hundred years since! He studied the averted head and hungry arms and looked down again at the moss-obliterated words. He ground the earth with the toe of his shoe, and felt himself growing angry. Yet he had passed it a hundred times and had no feelings on the subject. But now he could feel as something physical the slow anger rising up in him. God! do we not all die for our fellow-men? What is it all but a daily death for others? Do we not all stretch hungry arms and avert our faces; betray and accept betrayal; and light our indestructible little souls along the everlasting road—though Time itself prove but a moment in Eternity?

—O *please* (with curious precision he recalled the glee it had given him as a child to stammer his wicked and unfailing joke) O *please* don't cleave the Rock of Ages for *me!* And the slow colour darkening his mother's face that Sunday afternoon on which he had suddenly put down his spoon and fork and said seriously and with his mouth full: Well, I *do* think Jesus is conceited saying I am the Light of the World.

This consuming anger, this hatred possessing him a moment since: he who had finished with anger and such passionate beliefs. In the cold averted face the red colour darkened, and the hungry unloved arms, powerless at last, reached out to him.

But here came Miss Reade. Knowing that from where he stood she could not see him, he did not move and watched her as she came slowly and with a small hesitant step, keeping well to the middle of the road. Evidently she was not at ease wandering alone at so late an hour of the night. But he was neither sorry for her, nor angry, nor amused, but watched her as though he had not seen her before; impersonally, as one watches unseen a person unknown to one. And she came as though led to the foot of the slope from which he watched her, and stopped dead. She was looking beyond the village, down across the plain, where at set distances other such villages glowed like tight bunches of dark heather, and a few lights shone. She turned her head to look down the road she had come, and then back again following it into the distance.

It was no use going any further. There was no-one. She had mistaken the road, after all. Yet she stood there undecided, unwilling to admit defeat, and peered on into the distance. And all at once she raised her head in an abrupt defiant jerk and stared at the sky. She stood alone and without movement, staring long and steadily at the stars as though wondering to what conclusions they had come. By their light her face took on a luminous unreal surface-quality of stone. The glitter in her eye might have been tears. Then she looked down again; her face set and expressionless. She stared at her feet, and once more down the road, and then with an impatient movement turned on her heel and went back the way she had come.

He saw her smaller, smaller, and lost in shadow. But if one is indifferent one can at least be good-mannered. Why should he have deprived her of her triumph. What did it matter to him now whether she found him or not: and how greatly it mattered to her, this tall undaunted creature who carried his child inside her. The least he could do, Harrion decided, was to overtake her in the village and let her lead him back, obedient to heel, up the steps Zum Goldenen Lamm.

By taking the footpath instead of the road he was first in the village, and they met in a side street leading to the bridge. She walked past him, her head high. So he hurried after her, feeling he might as well see it through.

—How absurd you are, Lavinia, he said, having followed her down two more random turnings. You spend your entire evening searching for me and when we all but fall over one another you make yourself ridiculous by pretending I'm not there.

At which she had to stop.

—I was looking, said Miss Reade, for Sebastian. He is extremely drunk.

—And here he is, said Harrion. For they had reached the bridge.

And, indeed, there was Sebastian standing in a heavy trance swaying at the river. So much liquid and not in a glass seemed to him unnatural.

N ow that she was gone he drew a chair to the window and sat looking down on the Marktplatz.

Midnight was striking in sixteen unhurried strokes from the Gemeinehuss. Then from the church the heavy bells crashed with deafening clamour, and to each slow crash the lingering echo that is almost a sob. Ugly and prolonged, the sound swung above the houses like a monstrous noise-scattering censer and under it the pointed unsteady roofs slept a blue sentimental sleep to the fountain's placid rhythm. It ceased; leaving the night to a strained silence which two young priests broke, hurrying past, laughing together.

A moment since she had lit the darkened room like a torch: like a long static flame burning from the floor. Until she spoke. It was her clothes. A something scarlet and over it a straight mannish saffron-coloured dressing-gown suggesting a thing brave and foolhardy: a tongue of fire or the Spanish flag.

But neither her foolhardiness nor her child was of interest to him. From a height he looked down and saw her and was neither interested nor angry nor amused. The anæsthetic of indifference had been administered, it seemed, and under it he had died. So she glowed, she burned about him, announcing her bringing of new birth, yet could not warm him back to life. For he was released from the shell of himself. He who had lived so long among dead things and dead people was now one with them. He too shared their dead life: but knew his deadness. He was not, as they, spines upholding flesh, indifferent to all but their surrounding and immediate needs. An indifference of the will; a coldness of the mind. In detachment absolute he looked about him and knew himself dead among the dead. They, the other dead, believed themselves alive. They found in the movement of an arm or leg a proof of life. But he knew otherwise. Never again was he to need the wine of love or comradeship to make life palatable. But knew that only illness or sudden death could alter that which he was now; and that then this husk-like self would cease to be.

Once he, too, had believed in an after-life, and sightless in the night, in the inky hole of nothingness which is our glimpse into the grave, had leaned on his elbow crying: and shall one never rest? Is there no rest for me? Once tears had poured down his cheeks, he had felt so weak and abandoned to his fear that there might be an after-life.

Suppose one does not die? Suppose there is another life? Suppose they disturb one still and make one's spirit do idle and unprofitable things? Or make one's bloodless body spin through space? (O how d'you do, Mrs Odle-Heming? You spinning through space also? How pleasant is it not, spinning thus through other lives, for ever better, for ever higher?)

Then release is but a longer hell; then peace can never be; then is Death itself the final mockery: the savage jest of a vicious child.

Then why not fade away? Why not dissolve at last into perpetual astral movement and fade away through the ceiling carrying upward one's little lies and one's little goodnesses and one's tea-cup? A sudden thinning and transparence of the flesh: a slow dissolving and elongation on the air. An exit neat and sanitary and decorous. No funeral, no tears, no box, no decomposition, no flowers.

O so-and-so is gone. Have you heard? He faded away before our eyes. He was sitting there and (my dear, it's incredible!) he simply faded away. Up he went: up, up, up.

—How like Paul, Frances would say in her thin and level voice. Anything, *any*thing to annoy me.

For she would meet even Death correctly. Shod, gloved, and clothed as for a journey: inconvenient but unavoidable.

He smiled. For he was safe; borne away on the cold and fathomless sea of indifference which does not give up its dead.

At sixteen he fell in love with Christina Rossetti. He imagined her dark and silent and remote, dreaming ever above sundials, and tended by handmaidens from her brother's paintings. He walked with her across the Downs from Eastdene to Alfriston. He lay on his back, his arms stretched behind his head, feeling the earth breathe under him like some friendly green-furred beast.

She sat the grass as though it were a cloud. She floated there: strayed from the heavenly groves of Orcagna's *Trionfo,* her gown of blue brocade swirling beyond her feet. She sat with transparent hands folded on her lap, following with heavy eyes the lark's effeminate flight. She said: Paul, this I have written for you alone. And slowly unrolling a magnificent illuminated parchment, began with rich melancholy: *I took my heart in my hand, O my love, O my love.*

He must have fallen asleep and when he woke the sun had a chill evening look. He leapt up and set off at a great pace, jingling his hoard of pennies in his pockets. Usually their sound clothed him in the brightest and heaviest suit in the King's armoury and his iron step rang out on the castle courtyard, but now they sang the urgent song of tea and jam and watercress.

Yet he could never bring himself to read about her life; nor had he ever brought her to reality by learning how she lived and among whom. The sight and sound of her name was to him always Browning's dear dead woman. And when people said that there had been no woman poet and that there never could be, he still would say diffidently: there is Christina Rossetti.

He had said so to Lavinia Reade but Miss Reade had dismissed Christina with an abrupt: I dislike those who turn from man to God.

He was amused, for he had met Miss Reade but yesterday, and sixteen was long ago, and Selina had been dead a number of years, and it must have dawned in some other life that morning on which Frances had stepped from behind a burning-bush of lilac, the basket on her arm alight with daffodils, and his heart being young had seemed to break in several different places at once.

But though young not without promise. Indeed, not without achievement, having recently found God in a book of essays which sold 10,000 copies. Having found God in a blade of grass and in the babbling brook and early dew and in other such gentle manifestations of Nature as would ensure (his publishers noted and asked him to luncheon) its steady sale at each hallowed approach of Christmastide and Lent. And even at prize-giving a young tremulous hand might find itself clasping in tooled morocco, scarlet, inscribed, shining-edged: *The Ever-Winding Path.*

The Reverend Lindsay Cressall (writing from Belden, Hants) had been among his first and most urgent admirers: which explains how he came to be standing in the vicarage garden one morning in April. One of those April mornings so fresh, so green, so undiscovered, that one would not be surprised to find oneself covered in grass or patched with cloud or hung about with sky, so part of it one feels. So ardent, so deathless, so purposeful it seems, to be part of the earth's slow stirring to life.

Frances Cressall, the Vicar's third daughter, chose such a moment to emerge from a hedge of lilac, her gardening basket on her arm, her gardening gloves in one hand, and her gardening scissors in the other, engrossed in household thoughts of the familiarity of the butcher's boy with Rose, who was becoming almost insolent of late and who yesterday had sent the tea-cakes in burnt to a cinder: deliberately, of course; and because Prunella (her elder sister) indulged Rose beyond all limits of good discipline.

That afternoon they bicycled in to Christchurch together and Frances smiling gaily, hurried in and out of shops, and in the Priory they held hands beneath Shelley's monument and sighed, compelled to seriousness by the amount of marble on which the poet lay dying; and deciphered that plain stone slab let in the stone floor undated, as pain takes no heed of hour or season.

SALLY WILLIAMS DIED OF GRIEF

and together laughed at its nursery-rhyme simplicity, and particularly (running out to see if the bicycles were still there) at death and grief.

Finally they decided on South Kensington. One of those neat squares of neat houses; genteel of face; correct, column-upheld doorway; windows two by two and expressionless; and Frances indulged her taste, which was three parts Queen Anne, with something solid-coffered and Jacobean in the hall, and something flowery and Chippendale in the bedrooms. And where he was to learn that the flaming sword of Reason steps in only later and (as in the classic story) too late.

He had thought she would be lavish and beautiful in her giving but she was dull and conventional and ashamed. Uncleverly dull and conventional and ashamed, for it was noticeable. She repelled him by a dutiful submission more suited to a prayer meeting than a marriage bed. A Let us pray lingered on the air with the ghostly echo of a gabbled psalm and before her restrained submission he felt gross and brutal. But she was dutiful in all things, even in things one accepted as part of married life.

Inevitable that her heart should be graven with her household goods: she who had never known a room that was not shared by a grown or growing sister, nor a book nor a ribbon that was not the property of them all. An autopsy on a wife, Harrion had once thought (the early indiscretion of blades of grass and morning dews having been redeemed by years of editorship of a popular-cum-literary weekly) would reveal a dusting brush, a bright array of polished taps, a clock or two admirably precise: the whole culminating in a heart-shaped box of plain English walnut, or inlaid Sheraton, or a slab cut from the Dutch dresser on which how many housemaids had polished off their youth.

For he had learned also that maternity does not necessarily glorify a woman. Even were it not of itself already an ugly function, how un-beautiful they made it by their reluctant and difficult performance. He had been shocked by the unpleasant and unnatural thing it had seemed, the nursing home in which he had paced the hours away; the smell of ether, the forceps, the sense of death and pain. He did not altogether wonder that she seemed to bear him a grudge ever after: seemed secretly to resent it as an injustice against her.

To her intense dissatisfaction their first child was a girl. Possibly the maternal sense of possession (which sucks back the life it has given: which, whether one has loved or hated it, dominates one's days) is not wholly fulfilled in a girl, who, in the end, escapes the more easily and completely. Her not wanting the child made it the more his. He left her the boy, born two years later, partly knowing that she would allow no sharing and the thought of the unequal fight humiliated him, partly having now no need of it.

Ting-a-ling, ting-a-ling. She danced away in front of him ringing like a little bell. That was always his impression of her, that she rang out her own effortless joy as she danced across rooms and pavements. To him she came with everything. Passionate wilful little thing, after she had set her scene and sobbed herself out. She came, placed both elbows on his knees, looked up in his face. Tell me, father, what is it all knotted up inside my head when I'm wicked?

—She makes these scenes, Frances would say coldly, waiting to restore Selina to her nurse, for you to indulge her a little more. If that is possible.

And he would take Selina in his arms, which was like embracing grass, was like a field of buttercups, was newly turned earth. Her young flesh had the sweet clean smell of freshly cut grass.

Through her that April morning lived again. Those sharp eager facets of his soul which time had ground down and experience dulled, shone from her with the poignant gleam of innocence. The best in him, it seemed, though dead was not to die. Nor must it die in her. Let Frances expend her dusting brush and shining taps and inlaid Sheraton heart on her son. His dreams were strange dreams; his schemes had an odd and bitter flavour. For instance, courage. Of all things in life for her, he asked courage. He wanted her courageous; he wanted her brave, even foolhardy. He wanted her generous. He wanted her to give whole-heartedly of herself, her thoughts, her days. He wanted her to love; to love completely and irrationally. And give herself: when the urge came to her she must give herself, without thought, without regret. And be betrayed. And return to him (for to whom else should she turn?) bearing within her the burden of her love: wiser now and hurt, but with no regrets. And he would take her away, away from the outraged Queen Anne (three parts) and the flowery Sheraton bedrooms and the latest carpet-sweeper. South to lazy days under endless sun and watch the child bud and ripen and the life return to her face. For she must be brave and the life within her must not die but glow the more proudly.

It had never seemed quite real to him that when the end came he was not with her. But the telephone bell does not indicate by an altered ring whether its news be good or ill. Nor can one wing with one's desires, nor can one's body precede the lightning of one's thought. Only Frances doing her best to be brave: we must be glad, dear, there was no pain. The end was immediate. As, earlier, the driver of the lorry had stood stammering: It all comes so sudden-like.

He was left alone with her, with nothing but his thoughts of how impotent a thing this love that cannot bridge the bondage of distance, however short. How defenceless love, how inadequate, that not the width of the world can separate more surely than a street, a wall, another room. How powerless love that unless before one's eyes the beloved object does not exist; may call and one does not hear; dies, and a mile away one will be laughing.

How frail this thing on which his life had hung! His Dormouse dead.

Gone the threat of putting her in the tea-pot! And to-morrow being Sunday they were to have gone to the Zoo together to see the hippopotamus, her "sweet solid beast" which she preferred to them all; for she no longer searched as on the first day he had taken her, and back again, back again through every house, past each enclosure, until at last despairing, she had had to whisper: Father, no *unicorn?*

One is, it seems, but the impression one conveys. Nothing more. Only the impression one gives or one receives. All that she was was her impress; and that impress of her all that now remained. A solemn listening face, a field of buttercups, a sudden cry, a ringing of bells. All things that fade, are not renewed; grow dim, are not replaced; and life once good to live has lost its savour.

And then by accident he learned that on a last sudden sign of life she had opened her eyes and called to him. One of those things one is the better, perhaps, for not knowing. But it was not for that that Frances had kept it from him; and knowing this, she was never again quite real to him. So cold and secret his anger that she never guessed. Sensed a difference but never knew; never knew that in the hour of her treachery she, too, had died; but so completely as to leave no memory.

During the War women detached themselves from crowds, or hurried after him across streets, tight-lipped, purposeful: and his horde of feathers grew. Yet all his jingo leader-writing on the *Daily Flare* was more important to them, he often thought, than the one man he might be in a trench as target. And these human targets would they go so willingly to the slaughter if such as he ceased jingoism and Last Penny and Last Man-ing them? Sometimes he wondered did they believe it? But knew there was not one doubt from the breakfast tables of Berkeley Square to the breakfast tables of Belham. They read; they approved; and wrote thanking him for the hope and courage he renewed daily with the toast and marmalade.

He was much in demand at charity *fêtes* where smiling Duchesses raffled lace-and-taffeta cushions and the latest stage favourite kissed the highest bidder. I will give you a kiss and you shall give your life. The type of bargain (he would think grimly) a woman will always make. For he, too, sat upon the platform. There would be cheers, laughter, a loud smacking kiss, the favourite smiling in the direction of the press photographers, a flash, a sharp smell of magnesium; the favourite, clasping flowers, would sit down, and he would leap to his feet and in forceful and compelling voice say very much what he said each morning in print.

It sometimes happened during his tours of the country that here and there among his audiences a voice would ask a question, a question invariably beginning: And why aren't you? So the War Office put him in uniform, and Frances was no longer shamed and affronted as though the whole thing were an insult to herself. And reflected above her pools of tea no longer said quietly: You see, the War Office finds Paul too valuable. The uniform spoke for itself; and with more dignity.

As individual tragedy the War moved him not at all. The collective and incredible heroism of the men who fought: went out in the full-throated ardour of belief, went out again in good-humoured disillusionment, was a dimension of the human soul which neither words nor tears could reach or compass. But the I have given: I have lost: we are giving: we have lost, he saw for what it was. Saw also the dreary record of one mistake after another repeated with the same bravura, the same self-satisfaction, the same shouts, the same bloodshed, the same pomposity; and with a clear sense of what he was doing continued daily to renew the hope and courage of those who sat secure above their toast and marmalade.

Later he attended several Peace Conferences; and came back to find the editorship of a new popular-cum-literary weekly *Book-o-the-Week* abegging, and against the advice of all to whom he mentioned it, decided to accept the offer.

Book-o-the-Week is one of those entertaining and popular weeklies devoted to literature and the idiosyncrasies of the literati, ancient and modern; through which the mass may digest in more palatable form the crumbs from the tables of the erudite: bringing pleasure to the many and indigestion to the few.

Not that the indigestion of the few need be taken seriously. They well knew the value of a review in *Book-o-the-Week* as against a review in a purely literary paper such as, shall we say?, *The Rambler. The Rambler* whose circulation is sluggish: whose advertising is insufficient: whose remunerative rates are negligible. A few sparse political paragraphs, a few sparse initialled essays, a book review or two: from a friend to a friend. The few choice words, whose elegance cloaks their genteel lack of matter, which have been placed this week in *The Rambler* for the pleasure of seeing one's name in its correct setting, are re-written with more matter, more sense, and an almost indecent abandon for next month's *Book-o-the-Week*. *Book-o-the-Week* whose circulation is abundant, whose resources are inexhaustible; which, though not upon the tables of one's friends, carries one's name to that world at large (unrecognised but yet existing): carries also one's photograph. The spiritual weariness of the high-souled is ever dissipated by the sight of an adequate cheque; and the Editor once more casts his nacreous crumbs.

Harrion made few mistakes. He knew (despite our old-world and almost envious contempt of America) that a vulgar robustiousness is preferable to a stagnant gentility. He made his paper a financial and popular success as ably and impersonally as he had made the War palatable to those who could not do their thinking for themselves, and who accepted his assurance that it was as courageous to sit and wait as to fight, and that a blind or mutilated man is as nothing to a woman's anxious heart.

It is Lavinia Reade who described the poetess Eldra Litwell as: *grandmother of all the angels in a Flemish heaven: yet human enough to have the slightly supercilious air of the ducal nursery governess admitting of no familiarity.* And who wrote of her work: *She follows in the footsteps of Rimbaud and finds each footstep a valley.*

It was Lavinia Reade who brought him the essay on Tennyson in which in her opening sentence she said much that it had taken Mr Lytton Strachey an entire volume to say: *And on the throne a sulky pumpkin.*

Again it was Lavinia Reade who, on the news of D. H. Lawrence's death, startled the office by putting her head on her desk and weeping long and angrily. And later wrote: *It is all very Upper Reaches of the Thames, and Belgravia, and W.14; so composed, so joyless, so many. It was not merely that he saw clearly this mass unevolved. It was that, seeing clearly, he gave the impression of not being a gentleman. Recognition came at last with his least serious work: The Woman Who Rode Away. That the Woman Rode Away, one feels, had much to do with it. Had she merely walked away genteel curiosity would not have been aroused.*

There was about her work a certain rational madness more sure than any sanity. Which she herself would explain by: I never fish in tea-cups.

Yet it was exactly at such a party, one of those interminable literary parties at which these island tea-cup fishers sit boasting their catch or belittling the catch of others, that he had met her. Not that she herself was boasting or belittling. She was sitting alone in another room near the bookshelves hurrying through a large and latest *de luxe* edition, and as he came near she looked up and smiled and said: I've saved five guineas. I've been coveting this for weeks, and it isn't worth it!

He sat down. Perhaps he was glad to escape the raised and interpolating voices, the clatter of cups, the overcrowded discomfort, the sense of being a marked man among them. From far the whispered comment, and the approach, the quite unclever approach, of the bored and the serious, the lisping and the soulful, mentioning casual triumphs, inviting themselves to the office when no invitation was forthcoming: until he felt he must be wearing top-boots and an enormous button-hole, must be cracking an invisible whip, so neatly did the tame ponies prance through their mental paces and through their literary hoops.

Perhaps he liked the wide and eager smile with which she had greeted him; the scarlet frock: a frock a child would choose for best; the neat way her eye took in a page and turned to the next. And not once did she pose for him: neither aware of her legs, nor her nose, nor her hair, nor her hands. She read on, intent and unselfconscious. So he sat and waited and watched her.

As she closed the book and saw him still sitting there, looking at her, she laughed and said:

—If they *will* fish in tea-cups for thirty years what *can* they produce?

He was about to say, but she anticipated him and said quickly: No. I am here only to watch the fishing. I'm a journalist.

So they talked about journalism, which he gathered she detested. But was positively indignant when he said that on principle he disbelieved in all women journalists as they never got the news.

—Tell me, said Lavinia Reade. Do you know anyone who could have got that story out of Samson except Delilah?

So he asked her to come and see him at his office and she came bringing the absurd and irreverent essay on Tennyson. He said (it was a foregone conclusion) I cannot publish this, but. And then asked her to luncheon to talk it over.

It would be untrue to say of Lavinia Reade that she talked. It seemed she smiled and that the words which followed that smile were the articulate expression of its radiance. One felt visibly her abundant life and the bold rhythm of her blood. In her movements, in her words, in that long independent neck, in her silence, one felt the bold rhythm of her heart-beats. It was not merely her youth. Youth (as the advertisements insist) is but a matter of arteries. Youth is ungainly, brave with the bravado of ignorance and to the onlooker peculiarly dull. It was not merely her youth, for on a word, on a silence, she could seem all at once immeasurably old and versed in sorrow, and seeming to have wept through many lives as deeply as she laughed through this one. But unaware of it herself she gave an instant impression of courage, even of foolhardiness; and the bold rhythm of her blood was infectious.

There were more luncheons, and a few book reviews, and finally the offer of a staff job at a salary which made Miss Reade feel that life could play one enchanting tricks and that her uncertainties were over for a little while at least.

Her immediate impression was too unserious not to be resented in the office. A newcomer must be humble. A newcomer must not do with ease that which it has taken others long years of practice to achieve. Wisely other members of the staff, older, experienced, longer in service, resented Miss Reade's unconscious possession of every place she entered. So a few of them put their heads together and showed by their manner exactly what they thought of it all. But they were anticipating by several weeks. Lavinia Reade did not live with Harrion until at least two months after their first meeting. Even though he several times had been down to the flat in Chelsea overlooking the river, bringing with him books, and fruit, and gramophone records. Only to depart leaving Miss Reade staring at the gulls swaying above the water, and wondering why the human heart grows sad because a bird flies past a window and shows silver under the wing.

Possibly it would have continued being a matter of books and gramophone records but for the letter which came one day as she was giving him tea, and Miss Reade, thinking he knew all the gossip about M'Hugh, and Rollo the portrait-painter, and that great white slug of a creature Trinkovitch, the violinist, decided she might as well be hung for a sheep as a lamb, or simply didn't think at all, and looking at the snapshot cried: goodness, how large he's getting! And there in the long-grass of a Cornish field, a round little boy of about three, peeped from behind the heavy skirts of a great sturdy female grinning into the camera. There was not much to see of the little boy for a bunch of hair hung in one eye and the farmer's wife was so very large, but Miss Reade after looking at the picture intently, said: O bother. He's getting as dark and hairy as his father.

Harrion had stared with peculiar satisfaction at the picture. It excited him strangely that she had had lovers and this illegitimate child and that she sent money each week to this massive grinning female, and that with it all she was gay and untouched as a virgin, with a proudly set head and the strong bold rhythm of her heart-beats, which now seemed to him so urgent in their invitation. He sat there staring, staring in a heavy stupor of exultation, and at last heard himself saying something charming about the child. They laughed together; Miss Reade with a peculiar high gaiety, a rush of sound, an eager jet of escaping fear, knowing that the worst was over and she was safe, and would not stand, that afternoon, watching the indifferent gulls swaying above the river, which the barges ploughed with such stubborn energy.

S he could see no sense in leaving the office, but he insisted, and she was all obedience. It made it so furtive and she was not used to furtiveness in her love affairs. But he could not bear to see her sitting there before her desk. She must be waiting for him and he must come to her; and as it was the nearest he ever came to a declaration of love she humoured him and found pleasure in her disappointment.

So she sat dutifully and waited, trying not to finger the secret doubts in her mind, and distractedly reading the pages of books two or three times over, and looking up and saying aloud: I love him! I love him! Because it was essential to her to love the men with whom she slept (except of course Trinkovitch to whom she went to show Rollo that one might be discarded but not necessarily despairing, and who *was* a celebrity in his own way, after all, and really more unpleasant in retrospect than in fact).

And because it was so natural to her to love, asking only the opportunity: and each time with abundant zest and as though it were the first time such a thing had happened to her.

But never before had she sat dutifully waiting. And never a word of love. Perhaps it was beyond love this strange thing that had happened to her. It was rather awful the way he came into the room as though expecting her to be ready for him. And hardly an endearment. Afterwards she would lie in that obscene-looking scarlet bed of hers looking at the moon and stars on the absurd blue ceiling, and try not to understand how very different it all was. For it was horrible the way he held her down and consumed her. It was no longer a mutual act, but a thing dark and fearful which he performed despite himself. She thought at first it was because he was a man who had been long denied. But that phase was past and it continued like a war waged against a secret enemy.

It seemed a thing he did in fear and secrecy. Some dark forbidden thing, a thing avid, sinful, that he fought to shut out as he held her down, impaled; impaled on the drawn sword between man and woman; enmity eternal. Yet he seemed scarcely conscious of her. He drained her in this dark and secret way. And the result left her lost and impaled, so that she sat and waited for his return; a thing she had never done and could not have conceived herself ever doing. She would look up from the page she had re-read three times and say aloud, with her head thrown back: I love him! and feel warm and satisfied and proud with love, as she understood it. Almost her old self. She needed again this spoken day-lit assurance of normality.

But he would come back and the thing would begin again, like some unspeakable vice, some dance with death. And all day long she had been waiting for it. All day long she sat and waited. And when he did not come she felt leaden and bruised and resentful and loathed herself for what seemed more a morbid habit than love as she had known it.

Now the ebb and flow of her blood was not so swift and careless. Nor was the rhythm of her heart-beats so bold. The bright virginal look was becoming a little pinched and vicious. But he did not notice it, though she looked pale and used-up and rather ethereal, like a bewildered vicious child. She rarely went out. She would sit at the open window and revert to her old fancy of imagining lives for the people who idled beside the river and sat beneath the mottled plane trees. And would think disjointedly: I love him, I love him. Then all at once would feel resentful and held prisoner. She looked awful: awful. And he never noticed it! Like a fool, like a whore she ached and waited and allowed herself to be ploughed beyond her strength. He burnt her up and she stood it no better than Semelle stood it. And never once had he told her he needed her. Nothing for her. Only this rapt consuming fire of his which slowly and relentlessly extinguished hers.

So she sat at the window and waited, wondering was this what it meant: whom the gods love die young. Wondering was this how women waited in turret tops, bent above tapestry frames. But that could not be: for how gay and impudent they were! And only love fulfilled is gay and impudent. And going to the gramophone she put on: Belle Doëtte à sa fenestre se sied. And then: En revenant dedans les champs, Avons trouvé les blés si grands.

And called it education, the spread of gentility. So that no-one now waited in turret tops and was gay and impudent about it. For what heed takes genteel education of reeling and writhing and laughing and grief?

It was the shopping-hour and they hurried in their droves, all passionately clutching little paper bags of inexpensive silk stockings. And the
needle, too, was for other uses. The needle trilled

> . . . les blés si grands,
> La blanche épine florissante
> Devant Dieu. . . .

and Lavinia Reade trilled with it, for there are words born as a caress to
the soul whether it lies (officially) between the eyes or the breasts. La
blanche épine florissante devant Dieu! I want a garden, thought Lavinia
Reade, fingering the record gently and wondering would tears wash
away its song. I want to sit and wait in a garden. Every woman, she
thought, looking at the sullen unhurrying river and weeping bitterly,
should have a garden in which to sit and wait. So she sat down and
began a short story of some-one who wanted a garden in which to sit
and wait, and the afternoon was gone unnoticed.

In another such abnegation would have seemed to her unpardonable.
She would have protested and been full of theories. But the very
strangeness of the experience, the sense of guilt and immolation, the
troubled sense of its abnormality, was the measure of its fascination for
her. Secretly she was appalled at the resentful satisfaction she felt at
sitting and waiting; the sensual ease with which she assumed the rôle of
odalisque. So she stared at the printed page and said I love him! I love
him! as though to gloss with charm and familiarity the gross and the
unfathomable.

She wrote several short stories; unequal, diffused. She would read
them to him knowing them frankly bad, and be shocked by his easy
acceptance of each as a minor masterpiece. Indeed, his attitude to her
work had changed. Now he indulged her. He was good-natured about
it and pleasantly encouraging, as though she were playing with a new
and difficult toy by his especial consent. She had the impression that
soon he would correct the pages and add good conduct marks. So she
put them away in a drawer, unable to destroy that which had cost her so
much useless effort to produce; and to save herself from dying piecemeal of a pernicious mental anæmia (as she put it) insisted that he bring
her books to review. But they were uniformly artless and unreal, un-
flavoured, thoughtless; and she was uniformly irritated and impudent

about them, untroubled by qualms of conscience.

She was more troubled about her looks. Troubled also about her mood, which grew increasingly melancholy and resentful. She looked awful and still he did not notice. But Clare Sefton noticed. They ran at one another in the King's Road early one afternoon; Miss Reade under her friend's bold scrutiny carrying languidly the pose of love too well requited. She learned that she was rumoured to be in Italy: but not with whom, for opinion was divided. She learned that Simon Linsey was giving a party at his studio. And that M'Hugh had been asking for her; and that M'Hugh would be there. So she accepted and felt quite gay at parting. She must show M'Hugh her new look of a bewildered vicious child. Tired and languid and remote she would sit, wilting and bored, among the merry-makers; and would wear her most circumspect and spinsterish gown, for never is vice more alluring than when clothed in discretion.

Unfortunately by the evening the excitement of her plan, for which she alternately reproached and applauded herself, had brought the colour to her cheek and her eyes were quick and mischievous. So that Harrion arriving unexpectedly (to find her in a long black satin frock curling short tendrils of hair to a studied rebelliousness) saw her lively eyes and peremptorily asked where she was going, and not unnaturally assumed that the meeting was clandestine and desirable. She told him where she was going; knowing as she spoke that she would not be going yet continuing gravely to aggravate the tendrils of hair. She let him storm and reiterate for fully half an hour before kicking aside her high brocade slippers and pulling off the long tight frock, spoiling the curled masterpiece of a head. Astonished she stood listening to the crude and unreal arguments with which he fought. One would have thought she was about to compromise herself irrevocably. One would have thought it was her first illicit party and that she was caught as she escaped to it. She refused to believe that he was serious. Something about his anger struck her as unpleasant and curiously impersonal. When she had listened long enough to harsh and peremptory commands such as: I forbid you to be seen in such a place, she stopped him by the wintry irony of her voice: Quite. I know my place. Then burst into tears and said that she was tired, and sobbed herself out in his arms; and he was very tender and gentle with her.

He took her to the Zoo, and though she called the zebra a donkey from Rodier (which delighted him), it was not a success. For Miss Reade was more interested in those before the cages. Had her remarks been naïve, but they were harsh; and once in the ape house were so insistent that he had had to hurry her out. But the restless to-and-fro oppressed her. In the end she walked through every house, past each enclosure, speculating on which caged thing was the most unhappy; and stopping at the golden crested eagle, knew unerringly.

With polar bears cavorting in the background they sipped tea in the sparse sunshine, and Miss Reade developed her theory of how did one wish to convert animals to religion, one would find one's converts only in the Zoological Gardens of the world. But do not open the cages, even after they are convinced and baptised. One could never be too sure with the eagle, for instance.

The following Sunday he took her to Kew Gardens. Willows hung in thin green ropes above the varnished lake. Small yellow ducks threw in their heads and became crocuses. A blackbird put forward his most shining notes. She felt again the beating of the grassy pulse. The beautiful sane green enveloped her.

She ran full tilt over the grass between the trees; then stood waiting for him to come up to her. Another, she could not help feeling, would have run with her, sharing equally the immediate release of gaiety which the sudden sight of trees and grass must always bring the town dweller. But that, she thought, watching him staid and smiling in the distance, was the symbol of their relationship; the waiting was hers. Though knowing the moment too keen and brief to dissipate in words, she tried to be gay and light-hearted to please him. And all at once walking beside him, her hand in his, it occurred to her that this was not herself at all, but was one of Madame Tellier's young females out walking with a kind-hearted habitué. The cruel aptness of the thought shocked her to laughter; and he asked the reason, glad to see her carefree and happy.

Miss Reade replied with a bright immediacy (infallible sign that a woman is lying): I was thinking that what one most admires in D. H. Lawrence is his sturdy independence. He called a table-napkin a serviette to the end.

But he did not seem to relish her wit as he used to. Yet it was keen as ever; so keen that she would not go again to Kew. So, having no garden, she resigned herself to waiting beneath her absurd starry ceiling; staring at the Thames and wishing it were the Seine; discovering that the baubled plane tree is (surely) the invention of a child; and wondering whether her suspicions of the last few days were justified. Not that she cared. In such things her mind was simple and uncomplicated. It was neither a matter for heroics nor repugnance. However, she kept her suspicions to herself for it was too soon to be certain; and even when certain, hesitated. For she clung to the new dark harmony of her life; and at the thought of losing him her resentment left her.

For none knew better that what is desirable in a wife is unpardonable in a mistress. Men were such irrational and frightened creatures. Their sense of honour, or the sense of morality, or sense of responsibility, was always being affronted and made to bear burdens too large for it. The spinster with child was indefinably incorrect. Strange how a man could never feel himself the proud father of his mistress's child! Paternal joy, it seemed, was primarily a legal matter; and in all other cases was a cause either for annoyance, for downright anger, or for a tender pity. It was the tender pity that Miss Reade feared most. It occurred to her that Eve must have borne her punishment cheerily enough and not until she surprised the first look of tender pity on Adam's face did she curse the serpent in her heart. At least M'Hugh had been furious; though later recovering his good humour they went out and celebrated the occasion with unaccustomed ceremony; yet though they were together almost a year after the child was born, she knew exactly in which moment she had lost him.

Although she chose the moment wisely and her words with care, she could not she told herself have foreseen the effect it was to have on him. Afterwards it even occurred to her that had one been suggesting a suicide pact he could not have shrunk from her more palpably. When at last he had left with nothing but that incoherent stammer which she could not catch, she lay down in dismay with her face in the pillows. The next day passed in hope and despondency, and the next and the next. After the third day of sitting by the telephone in a torpor from which she roused herself only at the postman's knock, she rang up the office, to be told that he was away and they did not know when he would return. Then she knew that it was no use sitting and waiting. She was so utterly and incredibly alone that there seemed no place for her to go, so she went to bed; now and then shaken from her thoughts by the undaunted Emily standing with a tray and saying: now, now, Miss, there's nothink like a cupertea I always ses. Have you ever been in love, Emily? asked Miss Reade, aware of Emily's large and placid charm; and Emily holding the tea-cup and bending over her with large maternal impatience, thought: p'raps I seen enough of it with you, me paw dear.

After a fortnight his cheerless impersonal letter arrived with a foreign postmark, assuring her of unfailing financial aid.

—But it would never *occur* to me to worry over money! cried Miss Reade to the letter she was holding, unable to understand the argument that money is the unfailing substitute.

It had not occurred to Harrion that to Miss Reade the essential thing in the letter was his address; possibly because Lavinia Reade as a reality no longer existed for him. Nor ever had. The moment she had told him about her child, bringing their relationship as it were to life, he knew exactly what he had done. He knew what he had always known: that he was a man ridden by the ghost of what could never be.

A moment since and she had called him ill. He was not ill. To be ill is to feel pain, to know sensation, to desire to be well. He was not ill. He was beyond illness. Nor was his mind affected. Only the anæsthetic of indifference had been administered and under it he had died.

Once more bells disturbed the night, maliciously accenting the half-hour as though there must be no sleep for the faithful. It occurred to him suddenly that Christ did not live long enough. After the perfect love would have come the perfect indifference.

The whole earth sang in circles round the sun! Rounded hills, rounded clouds, rounded tree-tops, and wave upon wave of in-coming hill. A concourse of meadow-swifts wrote a Gregorian chant on the telegraph wires. Drawing an empty cart, two pale unhurried oxen with vacant mummer's masks came over the cobbles with the abstracted stare of the sleepwalker. A busy dog was at his nasal observations. A white horse, round and clean as a goose, was being led to the fountain to drink.

Tossing a comb through her hair and tossing her head, Miss Reade was at her window, well-pleased with the view. She put from her mind all night-thoughts of Italy. Besides she had just seen Harrion walk across the little square and vanish down a side turning. Elbows on sill, she had watched him walk away from her. O the completeness of the male who by the mere act of walking away can stress his arrogant isolation! No woman can walk away so completely dead to all things around her. Her hips flutter; her legs look ridiculous and inconclusive; the whole of her is aware of being watched, and irritated by this inescapable awareness of others. Women were scattered in body and scattered in mind; somatic; ever-alert. But the very physical compactness of a man stressed his isolation. So that by chance, looking at a given moment from a window, one surprised this male aura of unapproachableness and indifference. Well, there he went and with him Italy!

Now the incredibly clean horse had finished his drink and was moving off at a merry trot. Two small boys with satchels flying at their backs, chased each other around the fountain. Miss Reade removed her comb and herself to the mirror, reflecting that because the sunlight had played on her face as she watched, a significant thing had seemed almost impersonal; for which, had it happened at night, she would have tossed and re-tossed, accepted and refused, and wearied the hours with whys and nevers. Yet there he was walking away from her in the early sunshine and her thoughts were full of hot coffee. It must be that one dies at night; one dies the small death of sleep and one's vitality is low. The scale of light falls on the mood as on the day. She must remember that.

In the Wynstub Lorwich and Sebastian Doyle were discussing Protection and Mr Ramsay MacDonald. It must have been Mr Ramsay MacDonald for she caught frequent allusions to Little Orphan Annie and Salvation Jane. Lorwich had finished his coffee and was talking across a newspaper. Sebastian sat before his usual breakfast of Traminer and small brezeln. From afar he rose and greeted Miss Reade with elaborate courtesy. Lorwich ignored her. He was saying: So now your London manufacturer brings me my turban or my loin cloth and asks me ten shillings. I see the rest of the world buying that yard of cloth for one shilling. Therefore the British Government is levying on me an extravagant and unbearable tax of every indispensable article I buy; therefore Protection means being ordered to buy the most expensive goods and not necessarily the best: the tea-tax lost America: this would not merely lose India but cause a revolt in every corner of the Empire; who to-day will stand the injustice of being made to pay more for not-always the best goods?; and in many cases having to accept substitutes for the genuine article because England does not happen to produce it? Enforce the exchange of Empire trade and the result will be more swift and disastrous than the enemies of England can wish. (Sebastian nodded and drained his glass.) Besides, in modern goods Britain was behind the times; no-one wanted tin spoons to-day; they wanted Woolworth silvered nickel; novelty and change required elasticity of mind and adaptability: hardly the forte of our British manufacturer, who leaves the nonsense of producing what the world really wants to France, to Germany, to America, to Czecho-Slovakia.

(Käthe, some coffee! Und noch ein viertel, shouted Sebastian.) The British industrialist has proved himself incapable of competing with the rest of the world. Why? Because we British bring our damned caste superciliousness even into trade: anything is good enough for the other fellah. Even in sport we have sought a spurious mental Protection. We have coined the formula that we are gentlemen and the rest of the world professionals, and that we take graciously as diversion what the rest of the world takes as hard work. And there's your whole difference between England and the rest of the earth. A few gentlemen taking things lightly: and highly trained specialists taking them seriously.

Käthe who had been telling Miss Reade that it made one happy to see the sun again after so much rain, flounced away to attend to Lorwich. Käthe always flounced when attending to Lorwich. Her sense of fitness was revolted. Here, indeed, was a good man wasted.

Miss Reade helping herself to the glassy dark-green mountain honey which the bees had gathered in the pine woods, reflected not without malice that no much-married City man could be more aggressive at the breakfast table on certain mornings than could Lorwich. And not even a train to catch. Could it be that he was throwing at politics and the amiable Sebastian the Jovian bolts he had not dared hurl at Corydon?

For Simeon Fenn was not to be seen at so earth-bound a meal as breakfast. Not thus did he reveal himself to mortals. But springing pale and ineffable upon the world (possibly an hour hence) the fair-tressed Apollo, cloud-throned, would appear in the Wynstub doorway and with eyes for none but Lorwich, would utter languidly: I am going for a walk.

Going? It could not be going? Gliding. Or leaping. Or wafting. But going?

Meanwhile Lorwich having turned to the next item on his newspaper was saying that though less benefit to the Bankers than they had hoped, nothing did us so much good as beating Germany. It had got Germany down to work, scientifically advancing the world twenty-five years, while we sit and watch her do it and wonder how it's done. Thanks to the Allies Germany has no military service: consequently Germany has a million picked young brains from whom to choose to do her work. She has no fortifications, no armaments, and therefore more leisure for progressive thought.

So Germany builds; and England stagnates; and France has an army of a million young men to keep in idleness, and nothing to show for Peace but hundreds of little blue soldiers leaning over bridges.

Sebastian nodded and re-filled his glass. Breakfast was not his hour for argument. Also he had been extremely drunk the night before.

From where she sat Miss Reade could see in profile the motion as he talked of Lorwich's rusty beard. And to think that that man had a wife and children perennially suing for maintenance in the English courts while he, on and off, was being politely asked to leave most of the countries he entered.

Squat and gross and powerful, he carried well his deliberate un-washed and unkempt audacity. He had (Miss Reade decided) a subtle and rather pleasing beauty of dirt: that careless beauty of dirt such as one surprises in the true peasant, or in those Italian road workers who grin mischievously up at one as the train passes. Definitely one could admire his robust unkemptness as against such purely negative elegance of well-washed flesh as Simeon Fenn. Which arrogant sense of dirt Lorwich carried also into his work; for (when the Coterie glamour of his personality was discounted, reflected Miss Reade) what were his works but a few salacious post-cards taken haphazard from his literary pocket and distributed in signed copies at so many guineas apiece? But it paid: the glamour, and the dirt, and the Coterie. And particularly the elegant Fenn.

Ach, said Käthe, returning to Miss Reade's corner and leaning from the open window. Ach, it made one happy to see the sun again after so much rain. Ach, could it but last!

A group of holidaying Germans with heavy rucksacks strapped, and large bare knees, marched across the little square singing one of their honest good-natured songs in which the best of friends are for ever parting.

And Lavinia Reade sighed as she sipped her coffee. There he had slunk away, who knew where?, when one should be walking (like this) bare-headed and singing in the morning sunshine. What had she achieved in a week of being here? Twice by waylaying him she had been for a short walk, mostly in silence, for he had nothing to say but that she was provided for and need have no worry. Well and what had she expected? To bring him to her knees again? A line from a poem she had been reading in a literary review came back to her: Iniquitous, knee to knee. No. There seemed no possibility of bringing him to her knees. Then, to her feet? But he never had been at her feet, and he no longer wanted her at his. But he is ill, she reflected, he is ill. But how cold, how dead he was in the sudden unapproachable indifference which he seemed to have spun about him in an aura of decay. And what he was trying to do (O she knew) what he was trying to do was to get away again, to escape her as soon as the best scheme presented itself; and this time leave no address.

—Ach, sighed Käthe drawing-in her head, it made one happy to see the sun again after so much rain.

And there was Lorwich still talking. The room droned with the rumblings from his rusty beard. He seemed to be re-writing in argument the entire newspaper. He had now reached the Come to Britain movement. And of all the damned silly nonsense, when the only salvation for England lay in shutting her doors and keeping to herself, instead of inviting inspection. When only the milords came out of England—the others remaining in a dense fog—the world supposed the rest equal to the sample. But, behold, modern communication and the cinema and the radio had dispersed that fog and revealed the ass under the British lion's skin.

And then poised and languid in the doorway, Simeon Fenn was saying: I am going for a walk; and Lorwich was on his feet, crumpling his newspaper under one arm and stumping across the room in unseemly haste; and Miss Reade was staring rather deliberately toward the window, for though not liking the man she knew his worth, and did not care to see him playing Hercules in petticoats to this lisping inferior; and even Sebastian, who took tactless delight in all things, was studying a brezel as though it were the contortion of a playful grass snake.

But soon he must cross to Miss Reade's table and looking down at her, say: I am going for a walk.

She refused to smile and instead said petulantly: why must you drink wine in the early hours of the morning?

—Possibly to endure more equably the Lover at the Breakfast Table. Why must you drink coffee?

Miss Reade having lost the round, went and got her walking stick, for though Sebastian might be irritating in argument he took the hills with a cloven hoof.

And there, down a side-turning as they all but reached the Andlau Tor, they saw it, small and round and serious, standing on a pile of sand and holding up a little wooden spade and bucket. The infant, surprised by their shouts of recognition, lifted a fat sulky face and stared.

There was no mistake. It was he! And this the first time they had seen him on land. Usually he sat behind the bin in the little manure cart which his brothers, purposeful with their shovels, drew out of the gates each morning on to the main roads. Wherever one saw the little cart, at standstill by the roadside as the children munched their food, or being pulled home at night, there he sat round and solemn and sulky behind the small bin, now full with the day's good gathering. And the very first time they had seen him, such a miniature comedian, such a baby clown, with his high-domed head, his querulous curving brows, the look that he might cry if spoken to, his pugnacious nose and humorous mouth, so serious, so amiable, so delightfully softly incompetent, with everything there but the funny bow and eccentric hat, they had stood still in the street and shouted as one man: *Winston!* And here he was, fat and serious on the top of a sand heap, looking as though about to harangue his bucket.

Startled by their shouts of welcome, and with the suddenness of all well-calculated drama, Winston overbalances and becomes a girl.

—O! cried Lavinia Reade too affronted to help him up. O. O. Now I don't know *what* to call you, for there is nothing in the female line quite so pompous as Winston Churchill. . . .

—Come, come, said Sebastian, astonished. There is — —, and — — —, and ——.

They argued it all the way to Blienschwiller.

But it was not to take the hills with Sebastian that she was here. Nor to assault woods, full with wildboar and gazelle and mosquito, that she had abandoned her bed under its starry ceiling.

And Sebastian was talking; talking in his amiable unhurried voice, that droned among her stubborn thoughts till she took heart and abandoned them. For Sebastian was telling the story of his friend Basil Ollan; and it seemed right that as he told it they should turn from the plain over which the small dark trees were dotted in a pox, and walk on and upward, straight into a sky outstretched like a summer's sea beneath a small thin white sand of fleecy cloud, in which a faint shell of moon still drifted.

Every-one knows the story of Basil Ollan inasmuch as one knows that he committed suicide in a rather grim and delightful manner: choosing the dining-room to do it in, seated ironically at the head of the table, and serving himself up to them for breakfast, as it were, with a slit throat and a bloodstained razor. They said that he did it as an advertisement for his book *Self-Portrait in a Coffee Pot* which had appeared a month earlier. A shallow deduction, since the *Self-Portrait* was the literary success of years and needed no further effort from his part. Or they said that he did it to spite his excellent spouse and deprive her of the only lion she had not been able to appreciate.

For every-one knows the story of Mrs Basil Ollan; that inveterate and courageous hunter of literary lions, to whom the London artistic jungle is one long safari; aided and abetted by one son, an exquisite performer on the clarinet and the virginals, and those twin daughters, who dress alike, who smile alike, and are given to toe-dancing in their mother's drawing-room at day and evening parties with practically nothing on.

The lions laugh; but do not stay away. Living retired, domesticated, and uneventful lives, they realise the importance of such women as Mrs Ollan, who woo and entice them, and show them to advantage against silvered walls, among the lilies and the cocktail bars and the salted almonds and the journalists. The lions laughed a good deal when it was found that the insignificant little man with pale unseeing eyes who would sometimes be noticed sitting in a corner staring in his cocktail glass as though it were poisoned, and whose conversational brilliance began and ended with Quite. Quite. I agree. Could roar of his own accord, and louder and longer than any of them (it is feared) in his *Self-Portrait in a Coffee Pot*. Mrs Ollan laughed also; for the one way to parry ridicule is to gather it up and rejoice in it, and make full and laughing confession.

She staged an immense party for the *Self-Portrait*. The toe-dancing twins learned some of the more ribald contortions of negresses at their intestinal exercises. The Boy sat at his spinet with limpid profile averted. Basil Ollan instead of being somewhere in a corner was standing as though nailed in the very centre of the room. And three days later seated ironically at the head of the dining-room table he sent the under-housemaid into a screaming fit that lasted throughout the morning.

Mrs Ollan's large circle of friends agreed that the poor man had no alternative with such a woman; her enemies on the whole were rather sorry for her. His publishers were naturally delighted, for a dead author is more valuable than a live lion; whilst it was charitably accepted by the Coroner that the nervous strain of a successful book had been too much for the victim. And all the time Basil Ollan had done merely what he had intended doing years ago, but had been too preoccupied, until recently, to set about.

His will held no malice. The Twins and the Boy and their Mother were not humiliated publicly, nor made to feel, beyond the doubts in the minds of their friends, that the dining-room comedy was staged on their behalf. There was, however, a point which long puzzled Mrs Ollan. A cheque for two thousand pounds in her husband's name had been withdrawn from the bank about a week before his suicide, and the money could not be accounted for and certainly had not been spent. But she who had no discretion, was for once discreet. The publicity had been enough.

Meanwhile the money was in Sebastian's pocket. For Sebastian knew of the suicide long before it happened; years before it happened: and also one week before it happened. He even knew of the *Self-Portrait* as it was being written, and had helped with the proof-reading. But at that time Sebastian was not asked to Mrs Ollan's whip-cracking parties; except by proxy when all unknowing she once entertained the highly successful author of the highly successful review, much of whose songs and sketches had been written by the amiable Sebastian.

On the day he withdrew the money from the Bank Ollan had arrived at his friend's rooms in Clifford's Inn with a suitcase packed with papers (with which Sebastian must do as he chose) and the tobacco jar he had used for nearly thirty years, and an array of obviously valuable dress-studs for which he apologised nervously, and putting these down he began to talk of the two thousand pounds which he handed over in an evelope. He was brief, for he was not a talkative man (which silences, incidentally, are among the solaces of the friendships of men). He gave Sebastian an address and vague directions as to how one got there; accepted a brandy and soda; sat smoking awhile, and was gone without even a handshake. And it was not until a few hours later when Sebastian chose to wonder why in the name of God a heap of papers and magnificent dress-studs should be planted on him, as it were, without explanation, that he realised what was going to happen. But he loved the man too much to go to him and remonstrate.

About a week after the news was in the evening papers Sebastian remembered his errand and proceeded to drive himself to Cornwall. Ordinarily it was not a pleasure he would have undertaken willingly. For Sebastian was one of those on whose heart Calais is engraved, and who, when they think of Spring or beauty, turn their heart's eye to other lands. To him the English countryside was but so much unchanging mile of hedgerow, servility, and bad beer. However, Cornwall is the least restrained and gentlemanly of all the slices into which this island is divided against itself. It is stubbled and bleak and thrust out into a cold sea, into an ugly mass of tin shack and towering rock called

Land's End. And arrived there he turned to the right and drove for miles across moors, and through stony hovelled villages lost in what seemed a land of famine, and once again on to a moor, till he came to that wan lurching house set alone in a sea of stone and heather.

So it was here that Ollan had housed his mistress and kept his long secret even from his friend.

It was not a pleasant task that he was about to do, and in this abandoned setting Ollan's death was very near to him. As he stopped the car and got out, his hands were trembling. So he stood awhile to steady himself and stared at the ghostly house, and at the sea of stone and heather, and at the evening sky. A milky sky: one of those evening skies so pale that there is no-thing there. One looks up and there is no-thing there.

Yet the garden, once he had lifted the latch, was full of blue and velvety colour and a warm earthy smell. But there seemed no one about. What a fool's errand! He knocked and knocked; and at last went round to the back of the house and peered through a window. And saw there, in a kitchen and with her back to him, a woman knitting in a rocking-chair. So he knocked on the window, and after a surprisingly long time she turned her head and saw him.

When she came to the door he said: Good evening. Does Mrs Maria Ebbisham live here?

The woman stared at him. A red-faced woman with heavy eyes and big upstanding breasts; her two hands in the pockets of a large blue apron.

He repeated the question and this time she shook her head and pointed to her ear. To try again he shouted the question, and now she smiled and again shook her head and pointed to her mouth, and then to her ear and mouth and back again, so that he should understand that she was deaf and dumb. So he took out the envelope on which her name and address were written and showed it to her. But again she smiled and shook her head. She could not read. She was deaf and she was dumb and she could not read.

And that was altogether too much for Sebastian. He began to laugh and went on laughing. He leaned against the doorpost and laughed and roared and rocked with laughter, till his sides ached and his throat was sore.

But it was she. She led him to Ollan's room, where he was to spend the night. A white-washed room bound and held together by black curving beams; a room so old that it seemed to heave and sway and right itself again; a room that can but close about one and give one up, and on which one leaves no impress. The bed was enormous under a brightly stitched counterpane. Beside a window a table piled with books and papers; a fountain-pen with ink dried on the nib, two much-used pipes, and a tobacco pouch. Small used things which one should take with one in the grave (Sebastian thought) for thus abandoned they are more unreal than the dead.

Now the sky had asserted itself and darkened and brought forth one bold green star; and the silence was so palpable that it was right that all born under it in this waste of heather and sky, should be born speechless and without sound.

Lying in Ollan's bed he was awake a long time thinking of the woman with her deep upstanding breasts and large unhurried movements and her silence, and of the peace she must have brought him. By god, what a solid and fathomless rock on which to build one's church! And here, in this room, he had written the *Self-Portrait*. And what a cook! He would have given much to know whether she now spent her night in tears or in sleep. Not in tears. No, not in tears. She would leave weeping to the official widow. She slept. One knew that she slept her steady untroubled sleep. Besides, to-morrow was Monday. And on Mondays one must be up before six. For Monday (everywhere) is always a washing day.

W e shall be late, said Lavinia Reade, as turning a corner they saw at last the long black crooked steeple struck like an Inquisitor's bonnet above the houses. We shall be late and Madame will be cross again. But we can do it—if we run.

A s a warrior's recreation Madame Jonat was not a success. Although at the moment decked in her silks and finery and spread as invitingly as a nuptial bed, in such capacity she was not at her best. A frigid woman, who took out such energy in hard rages and ugly palpitating fits of temper, violence, and recrimination. Who seemed for ever oppressed by the strain of keeping her head above fat that circled and submerged her: the last waves of which broke against her chin. A heavy white moon of a woman without light or warmth of her own.

Even stretched (as now) in her festal satins Madame's essential self was not more affable. Indeed, was noticeably less so; for the sheen though of silk had the malevolence of armour. But that the intention was festive could be seen in Madame's shrill pomeranian, the rat-eyed Clo-Clo, who wore on his neck his Sunday bow, and was fluffed and arrogant as a pouter pigeon. And by Nicole, Madame's seven year old, that sallow irritable wisp of bone and temper, who seemed more the outcome of her mother's spirit than of her flesh. Nicole who also wore satin, of an uncompromising blue and very short, and among whose black curls flew a bunch of tufted silk.

Seated behind the bar on the raised curved horsehair sofa so oddly like herself, Madame stared at the Wynstub ceiling: that gracious undulating ceiling with richly carved beams, from which the special cast had been taken when, with more good-will than taste, in spacious pre-war days the Germans had restored the Hoch Königsberg and made of it a museum of Alsatian domestic architecture.

Madame was not thinking of the ceiling's undulating grace. She was thinking that cette Mees Ridd and the Monsieur Sebastian were late again; and that not once during the entire week had she known either of them punctual at a meal. A party of strangers was in a far corner of the room; but none of Madame's foreign guests had turned up to luncheon. The Monsieur Leriche and his friend she did not expect. Nor ce pauvre Monsieur (quandmême un drôle de type) who had, as usual, disparu. But cette Mees Ridd and the Monsieur Sebastian: it was too much. Evidently it was not for the English, that cursed and misshapen race, whose palate was dulled with swallowing fog and cokketelle, that one hung one's culinary diplomas about the walls. A race that buys its *soupe* in little cubes and its meat in ice, regards constipation as a national virtue and wine as wicked, and chemist shops as God's greatest gift to man. A barbarous race that should have its food mixed in bowls and served it on the floor!

But to-day no more. After two o'clock nothing for the Mees Ridd. Ab-so-lu-ment no-thing. Karl, cried Madame, après deux heures on ne mange plus rien; deux heures juste, vous entendez. And Karl told Käthe, and winked.

So that it was prophetic and fortunate that Miss Reade had told Sebastian they must run, for when at last they arrived hot and panting in the Wynstub there were a good thirty minutes to spare; and Käthe was delighted. Sweet soul, she hopped about, live as a bird, bringing everything that was wanted before it could be asked.

Miss Reade arching her long independent neck, knew that Madame was displeased again; despite the smile, despite the polite inclination of the head. But why was she all-dressed-up? Miss Reade longed to ask but nothing could have made her: for Madame longed to tell, and would tell just as soon as the moment offered itself. It was not Sunday. Was there a wedding?

Miss Reade smiled gaily at Nicole who, feeling very fine to-day, squirmed in the doorway for all to see. And thought again: what a dreary parody of childhood! And what a largesse of maternal flesh. And how vaguely indecent women were with their fleshy charms hung about them like trophies. Nature has its humours, but it could not be that such an acreage of bosom had been grown to wean this undersized apology of a child? And, decidedly, it was not for the dalliance of her husband: of that one could be certain. Even were its aspects less forbidding, Otto preferred his cellar: and who could blame him?

Indeed, who could blame Otto for anything? mused Lavinia Reade, who adored the masculine virtues. And Otto had them all. Solid, squarely planted, stubborn, cool-tempered, friendly, impersonal. His day's work done he put it from him and gathered his friends for talk and wine, and cards as an excuse for more wine. And the rounder and redder Otto grew and the more full and warm his voice, the more Madame, perched behind the bar, twisted her lips and was affectedly amiable. Madame (did you offer it) graciously drank with you as a particular concession, though more, one suspected, "for the house" than for herself. But Otto drank with any one. Any one, that is, whose eye was humorous and whose face was friendly. Otto could go out on the Marktplatz and bring in any thing from beggars to priests and stuff them with food and drink for the pleasure of hearing them laugh. And made one feel how right it was, drinking and being drunk, and leaving one's friends to sleep it off over (or under) one's table in open acknowledgment of one's hospitality.

Lorwich adored him; and in the evening he could ignore Simeon Fenn (very pink and restrained and looking-on) for hours while he out-drank and out-shouted Otto. And from far Madame watched, looking everywhere but at her husband. Taking in the scene on the very first evening Lavinia Reade (who had a quick eye for the human comedy) had thought how like it was to altar panels of Heaven and Hell, with for centre-piece the wine and Sexual Triad, and on the Right Hand the robust and the joyful and on the Left the soured and the ungainly. And thought how, if Otto was very much a man, Madame was all-woman;

with a woman's addiction to small pleasures and tantrums, and futilities, and no silence.

But what one could not forgive her, thought Lavinia Reade (stirring her coffee and smiling again at some facial pleasantry of Nicole), what one could not forgive was this anæmic sore-eyed child, when Otto should have sons like himself; strong, easy-tempered male creatures, to work as he worked.

The long table near the door had filled, and Madame as she drew the beer, raised her voice. No, she would take the auto-bus. No. It would arrive in Sélestat in plenty of time. It was an inconvenience. But it was just. It was just that she should tell what she had heard. It was an inconvenience. But it was just.

—The girl is mad, said the man with the neat black beard.

Madame pursed her lips: That we do not know.

—The old woman should be guillotined, said a young peasant with a pink square face. And before she knew it, Lavinia Reade had called Hear! Hear! and tossed her head, and thought how right youth always is.

So it was to attend the trial of the Mère Hunon that Madame was in her festal silks and the dog and child wore satin bows.

—But the girl is mad, shrugged the man with the neat black beard. You'll see. The old woman will get off.

Whereupon Nicole rushed to the middle of the room and shrieked in her high falsetto: I'd kill her. I'd kill them all. I'd kill the Judge, too. And then I'd kill everyone here. Everyone. But not you, she said turning nicely to Lavinia Reade. I'd make one of the men kill you first.

—Loathly little beast, thought Miss Reade, joining gaily in the general merriment.

And then one of the men started laughing at the picture of Monsieur le Curé who had come on the mad girl in a ditch with nothing on but a torn rag of chemise. A winter's night a year ago, she had managed to escape at last and lay shivering in a ditch. And the priest had found her there, jabbering away, in her filthy rag of a shirt, a body covered with sores and wounds, and blood still trickling from her head and from her mouth where most of the teeth had been knocked out. And the priest, with gentle words and with infinite patience, had soothed the inhuman creature, and had led her back; had led her back to the mother who had kept her tied in a dark shed for years and starved and tortured her. And the priest had never mentioned the meeting. *Madame Hunon est si dévôte. . . .*

—What on earth are you doing? said Sebastian as the lurching table sent half his papers on the floor.

—O, said Miss Reade who had leapt up suddenly. O, she said, sitting down again, with a white inscrutable face.

Some-one recalled that when the gendarme had come to take the old woman away, she had burst into tears and hung on the neck of her only beast, an eight months' old calf; and had cried in her funny dialect: O bon Diou, et mon p'tit viau . . . qui c'est-t-y qu'en aura soin?

—She'll get off, the bearded man said again. The girl was mad.

The young peasant said suddenly: She wasn't always mad.

—She's mad if the old woman says so. And she will. And she'll stick to it. They all do. And they all get off. Take the Blanche Monnier case, near Tours. Twenty years' starvation and torture, locked in a filthy cupboard. The father answers: but the girl is mad. Acquitted. Take little Andrée Belletier, near Le Mans, chained to a cellar wall for six years and with, among other injuries, an eye knocked out. But the child is mad. Acquitted. Two cases among hundreds. Among hundreds tried, and how many more undiscovered. They all say: mad. And they all get off. And so will the old woman: you'll see.

—That, said Madame pursing her lips. That, we do not know.

—Ach, said Käthe with round eyes. I am glad it was not me! And because Miss Reade looked so white she brought some fresh coffee without being asked; and Sebastian sent for a vieu marc and tipped it in and told her to drink it up, and they laughed at the faces she made; but her cheeks came pink again.

And Sebastian teased her: Lavinia, consider the egg. How elegant an egg. How clean an egg. How immediate, how bloodless, how impersonal a birth!

Which shocked Miss Reade considerably, but she smiled.

Sebastian it seemed was at work on a scene epitomising Walt Whitman's Adamic sons, who, chewing rhythmically and identical in shape and movement, poured from skyscraper doorways, straw hatted, waistcoatless, and spitting. Out they poured identical from identical doorways. A walking Greek chorus (Sebastian explained) conveying an impression of sameness, haste, well-washed teeth, and a cleaner Whitechapel. In the foreground, at the junction where Wall Street meets Lower Broadway, an impressive group, Presidents, Bankers, Congressmen, Kinema Magnates, and world-known American national characters, Big Bill Thompson, Al Capone, Flo Ziegfeld and his Follies, Otto Kahn, Mrs Aimée McPherson, Admiral Byrd, etc., is posed around a flag-draped plinth. It is the unveiling ceremony to the American Unknown Soldier. Or at least (Miss Reade gathered from the half-ear she lent to it) it was intended for the Unknown Soldier. There was a deathless fervour about the sententious patriotic phrases, mouthed nasally to the clockwork kicking of the Ziegfeld Follies Girls, gay as circus ponies; but somehow when it was unveiled it turned out to be the Tomb of the Unknown Dollar that fell so gloriously in the last great Wall Street War.

And now Madame was growing visibly angrier with the bearded man who having given the verdict, was passing-on to the summing up, throwing in here and there imaginary evidence and contradictory statements by the police, and generally by his misplaced animation, robbing her afternoon of dramatic significance.

O wailing Wall Street!

We shall see, we shall see, she thrust in his certainty like a sharp little knife. The echo mad! was like the cry of an ill-omened bird; and at intervals the young peasant with stubborn anger still put in a good word for the girl.

And Miss Reade was thinking that it is not enough. Not enough the little loyalties, the uncertain kindness, the vague sentimental impulse, with which mankind covers up the traces of its dirt; the drop of oil on the ocean of its ugliness.

O Cohens and coins and coins!

Not enough the unshed tear, the sudden charity, the pale-pink glow of good-fellowship, worn penny in the can of the world's misery.

And her heart was cold against Madame preening herself with that bright distinction peculiar to parrots and women of the French middle-classes. It seemed to her (irrationally but not without a grain of truth) that prinked in her satins with her child and dog, she should stand in the dock beside her compatriot. For surely both were accomplices in that they both were French

O profits of our fathers!

and had come from some thin-lipped Northern town, bringing their French-provincial bitterness, their overstrung nerves, and their shrill tempers to these slow-natured, pleasant, indifferent people who used to laugh till France taught them to giggle; who used to talk heartily square till France taught them to talk thinly pointed; and whose once-excellent roads, built by Germans, are left in ruins, while the great forests and passes of the Vosges are trenched and mined for instant destruction.

O Tomb of the Unknown Hero!

Only it was not enough the daily exchange of polite indifference; the rift of faint blue in an immensity of grey. It was not enough to mistrust one's neighbour only a little less than one mistrusted one's self. To bleat one's way into a state of grace before a fabled God and a state of fear before one's fellow man.

O last resting-place of the Unknown Dollar!

There should be the pure curves of stone about human faces (Lavinia Reade was thinking) as on Chinese and Assyrian statues with their benign and serious planes. Or the calm speechless eyes of the Greek thinkers, their brows packed tight and straight about their eyelids. One surprised a measure of it on the faces of these Alsatian peasants. A coolness of soul flowed from them effortlessly; a certain serenity of brow. For they did not deal with men but with the earth, which is less treacherous.

—And you haven't heard a word, said Sebastian, gathering up his papers.

—But surely I am coming to the first night, said Miss Reade with much presence of mind.

And now the motoring party which had been lunching in a far corner of the room was thanking Madame with enthusiasm; and was actually paying the bill without comment, though their speech was distinctly Parisian. And they were praising the painting which hung between the two windows. With some difficulty the date was read: 1744. Three soldiers with a bravura of gesture, drank to and ogled the servant girl, who stood before them in an abandon of rustic wiles. The painting had grace and an enchanting stupidity. It was exquisitely wrong where to have been right would have been to be null.

Miss Reade was glad they praised the painting, which gave her immediate pleasure each time she raised her eyes to it. As though to make reparation for her thoughts in that strange way one has of feeling guiltily that one's mental comments have been overheard, she turned to Madame with a smile, saying impulsively:

—When I am rich, Madame, I shall return and buy that picture from you.

—Then you will have to buy the house, said Madame drily. For it is painted on the wall.

Were I a man, Lavinia Reade was thinking, I would love only men. I would not love women with their vacant chatter and soft ornamental bodies. I would not be charmed by womanly tempers when the coveted hat looked cheap and foolish. Nor treat her as a goddess for bearing me a child or two. To be only a woman is not worth very much; and the man who does not know it is a fool and deserves what he gets.

—Love between man and woman (Lavinia Reade was thinking) is an imperial thing. Leave it to Pericles and Aspasia, and Elizabeth and Robert Browning, and Abelard and Heloise. For the rest, I will feast and talk with my friend, and I will return to Xantippe when I must. For friendship is a thing enduring and safe. The middle course; the emotional Purgatory where one will never see God, nor even Gabriel's impassioned face. Only the lesser saints and an angel or two.

—Purgatory must be very like a small-sized Cathedral town, thought Lavinia Reade, and smiled to see herself elbowing plump Bishops and devout and maiden ladies to attend the weekly lantern lecture. Or coming down the High Street to change her book at the Lending Library and the lean Vicar, with sharp sad little cries, leading the ladies on small clipped wings out of her path to safety.

One clings to the end of things. The end of youth, the end of life, the end of a good dish, a good drink, a good book, a cigarette. Only the fountain endlessly jetting its tireless beads of sound from the mountain's hidden lip. But even that had ended, the legend ran, and once at a saintly prayer had poured wine lavishly as Christ poured his blood. Yet Buddha, said Miss Reade, who argued all things. Buddha needed no crucifixion! And drew-to the shutters.

The trouble was, being so very much alive among the dead. The born dead, the atrophied, the slow-dying. For dying is so slow a process, beginning imperceptibly in the soul and ending perceptibly enough in the stomach; and the walking behind the coffin may be an anti-climax by thirty years.

—Death may be a great adventure, said Lavinia Reade aloud. But life is a great gift! And threw herself on the bed. (If I'm sick, she thought, I shall simply ring for Käthe.)

O life is a great gift! For what right has one to each new day, to each new hour, but the right to accept and enjoy it? Yet so few seemed to know this, urgent though it might be. They seemed so dead, so slowly dying. They seemed disintegrating inwardly, with souls a little sick. The trouble, of course, was being so very much alive among so many dead. People resent it, thought Miss Reade. It is a kind of spiritual Bad Form.

All the unloved faces, the tight mouths, the nervous seeking eyes. It was not to the end of her affair with Harrion that she clung with such tenacity. She knew the signs. A fortnight's tears; a last effort at reconciliation; a few last arguments; and she was free again. Not so blatantly as that, of course. But as soon as the opportunity presented itself, free to love again. For it was essential to her to love the men with whom she slept. Essential to sleep, but essential also to love. For the illusion of love for one's bedfellow is important. It is the difference between pleasure and repeated exercise. Also it saved her from feeling humiliated when men left her. The essential she had had. What shocked her afresh was the ever recurring admission that there is an end. For it is not to the lover that one clings, but to the last of love.

Only one thing shocked and puzzled her. It was so real this revulsion of his, which made of her a laughing-stock and forced on her the arch leer of Madame Jonat and the gentle kindness of the youthful Käthe and the jocose humours of Sebastian. So that she could not turn from a window, nor look up as a door opened, but Madame's vulpine eye intercepted hers. And Sebastian looking up from his writing, murmured: It is not always the Foolish Virgin who sleeps . . . but the Bridegroom.

Miss Reade said coldly: Sebastian, you have all a woman's intuitive cunning. But none of her charm.

And now that to which she clung was nothing more tangible than a serenity of brow such as one surprised on the faces of these people at work in their fields; at rest before their doors. Once again one saw the seasons on the faces of one's fellow-men. One saw the young and serious, and the middle-aged and strong, and the old and humorous. A pleasure made more poignant by a tinge of sadness. For one had no right here. Who had no earth had no right here. Here was the dividing line between the ephemeral and the enduring.

A difference as real as the clerkly fear on the Londoner's face. That clerkly fear which is not a sudden fear, nor a tragic fear: but a small, an hourly fear. A fear of crossing roads, a desperate fear that the omnibus will not stop at one's stopping-place, that the train doors will not slide open at one's station; and that day-long fear of losing his job, which may be called the Londoner's supreme sensation. Under everything, eating at the heart of his restricted life, is the little cancer of the Lost Job. From the day he is accepted in his office and his clerkly life begins, throughout his pale amusements, the daily to-and-fro, marriage and the endless paying-off of house and furniture, the birth of his children; binding all, held together by rheumatism and crowned by premature baldness, is the unspoken fear of losing his job. And there were millions upon millions of them, male and female, moving in and out of shops and banks and city offices, all with the furrowed foreheads, the unloved faces, the tight strained mouths of those to whom life is a happy vale of tears; an inglorious preparation for a better land; the echo of an invitation sent out from a hill-top: You must come and stay with my Father.

—The slave had at least the assurance that his master found him too valuable to lose, thought Lavinia Reade, turning her face to the wall to keep the afternoon sun from beating on her eyes.

Among the tricks which one's tired nerves can play is that it needs but the briefest hour to deny the ambitions of a lifetime. Perched on the wall of one's spirit the cock crows, and its derision has a hollow sound. One does not necessarily go out and weep at this betrayal of one's beliefs; or if one weeps it is only that one must go on living that in which one has ceased to believe.

—Old Willis, said Lavinia Reade with conviction but no enthusiasm, Old Willis will give me back my job.

And needless to say Miss Cullen would be there. One could travel the world round, through fire and shipwreck and famine and plague, and give birth to triplets by way of diversion between the monotony of adventures, and there, on one's return, seated on her swivel chair, in the small office behind the Reporters' Room on the second floor, snipping with large scissors the unalterable pattern of the London social round, ever-alert, ever-believing, ever-faithful, would one find again Miss Cullen, editress of the Woman's Page of the London *Daily World*.

Miss Cullen who believed. Miss Cullen who lived for her beliefs. Miss Cullen whose fervour had, to the onlooker, a pathos of childhood's unfaltering trust in a land of faery. Miss Cullen elongated and white faced, with pale undemonstrative hair, blue eyes misty with looking through rosy glasses at her coroneted world, scissors poised above *The Times* Social Column from which to weave her daily life's reality.

—And lovely Lady Skruschen looking not a day older than her radiant daughter.

—From Antibes I hear that Lady (Diddles) Blim.

—Where in the world could one match such exquisite youth and beauty as were to be seen gathered at the Duchess of Grates' dance for her niece, the enchanting Lady Deidre Dodo.

She wrote to a gay invisible melody. Sweet thrush on a thorny twig, she sang her hymn to the social sun, never doubting but that it would rise eternally and in ever increasing splendour.

And then for a brief space, and because work was short in the Reporters', there was thrust on her Miss Reade the undaunted, world-weary with the wisdom of twenty-two, an illegitimate child, two lovers, and a grievance at having to fill in the Silly Season on "woman's work" as she called it.

It was Miss Cullen who compromised. Finding she could not alter Miss Reade's cold inelegant style, she learnt to withhold comment and re-write it. Though not without a struggle.

—O but surely you ought to say that Lady Missles was looking levely?

—Ought I?

—O but didn't you think she was?

—I hadn't thought about it.

—O but how *could* you say such a thing! You *must* be joking. Ah think she's too-too levely. But then, everyone *does*. When she came out two years ago she was quate the leveliest thing ah've ever seen.

Miss Cullen frowned, re-wrote, sub-edited. Miss Reade returned to *Les Faux-Monnayeurs*.

—O you haven't said what Mrs Tally-Bounce was *wearing*.

—Which is she?

—O Mrs Tally-Bounce is quate too levely. You know her. Of *course* you know her. With very fair hair and very dark eyes and quate petite and O always so exquisitely dressed.

—Probably red.

—But don't you *know*?

—Or green.

—O dear, O dear! Was it *red*? Or was it *green*?

—Put black and be safe. Tell her how too-too anything she looked in black. She'll not contradict you.

Miss Reade had been amazed. She found that social reporting entailed among other things standing in church porches with a crowd of eager gossip-page reporters note-booked and pencilled, taking down the names of those who attended smart weddings. Lacquey among the lacqueys she learnt to stand a little apart, inside the doorway, and to choose and dress the more celebrated names from an Agency report when back at her desk. She early found: call the lady beautiful and she will not protest at a mere colour scheme. So she stood within church doorways, in far thoughts of her own, watching her ardent colleagues name-gathering. And one day a Duchess rushed up to her with light pressure of the hand, crying: My dear, how well you're looking! Where *have* you been? I haven't seen you for ages! and gaily passed on. A not unnatural mistake, for she had an aloof, impudent dignity. And no note-book. Her colleagues who thought her cold and arrogant were momentarily non-plussed and smiled on her.

The sincerity of Miss Cullen touched and appalled her, whose quick mind saw too clearly the ways and means of journalism and its adherents. With a facility for words and a bright-seeing eye it was a game at which a child could play. Except for the crime reporters. For these she was loud and whole-hearted in her praise. Crime reporters and their long struggles with the authorities; often ending in the journalists solving the mystery to everyone's satisfaction and no one's acknowledgment.

So she would watch Miss Cullen living the lives of others by instalment; sipping the heady wine of titled ease by proxy. And she was kind to her. Or rather, she did not tease her more than she could help. Even on the mornings of gloom and resentment (for the affair with M'Hugh was going none too well) she would restrain her natural and now rather acid wit before Miss Cullen's guileless piety.

It was on one such morning that, writing of a party given the night before, on the occasion of some titled game-hunter's return to wife and family, an irresistible impulse made her add: *Or as the eighteenth-century lady's maid wrote home to her mother: M'Lord returned yesterday from the Wars and pleasured M'Lady three times before removing his boots.*

But could not. She looked long and thoughtfully at the back of Miss Cullen's pale undemonstrative hair and at the elongated neck bent rapturously above her devotions. The sight filled her with that faint but quite definite irritation which really gentle and selfless beings at times provoke in one. She sighed, frowned, surrendered. And the words from the succinct pen of the eighteenth-century lady's maid fell piecemeal in a twentieth-century waste-paper basket.

Yet it rankled; and coming back one afternoon from a musical reception held in a room the ornate gilt and satin and cupidon style of which she most particularly resented, she wrote of it as the type of room in which, two centuries since, they seemed for ever living in an amorous atmosphere of unmade beds and overturned chocolate cups.

Miss Cullen was delighted. She gurgled with joy; but it could not be used.

—Ah really think that *one* day you must *trey* and *wraite* a *book*, she breathed.

—Indeed? said Lavinia Reade discomfited.

Miss Cullen shared a flat with a schoolmistress friend who had a sister; which sister was the one crease on the silken texture of her world.

—She is quate mād, said Miss Cullen in a hoarse whisper. So mād that she believes that if she *sat* on an *egg* she could *hatch* it.

—And has she tried? asked Lavinia Reade with interest; to be immediately non-plussed by Miss Cullen's pained surprise. It occurred to her that the one form of madness Miss Cullen would understand would be to sit on an egg and hatch the Holy Ghost. Or another such grave heraldic bird.

Meanwhile Miss Reade was piecing together a paragraph on correct precedence below stairs as still observed in a few great houses.

In referring to Lady Bogg's death, I might have mentioned yesterday that this robs of its chatelaine one of the few great houses the inmates of which still preserve below stairs all the ancient customs, so many of which have passed away since the war.

Thus the maids and valets of week-end visitors take the names of their masters and mistresses and take precedence accordingly in the servants' hall.

The maid of a duchess, for example, will sit upon the butler's right side, and if there be two duchesses in the party the maid of the older family of the two will take precedence.

Usually the butler only comes out of the house-keeper's room to take his pudding in the servants' hall. This is according to a long established custom, but on big occasions all the servants dine together, the butler sitting at the head of the table and acting as host, while the housekeeper acts as hostess.

Etiquette is infinitely more rigid than upstairs and the meals are conducted with a ceremony worthy of the Papal Court.

—I can't! cried Lavinia Reade throwing down her pen in sudden panic, her sense of the ridiculous more than usually outraged. I can't! I *can't* write any more of this wretched tittle-tattle!

—But Miss Reade, said poor Miss Cullen in her high, thin elderly voice. Miss Reade, it isn't just *tittle-tattle*. It is TEA-TABLE GOSSIP.

About this time M'Hugh struck her in the face going down the King's Road; and to his surprise she left him then and there. She gasped, broke in a run, rounded a corner, and that was the last he ever saw of her.

Observers have long been amazed at the discomforts the intolerant Englishwoman will face uncomplainingly abroad. He had fallen on her in a drunken rage one night in Madrid when she was seven months with child. He had struck her several times in Italy, where already he was becoming unreasonable. And once in Paris at Braccard's studio in the Rue Vavin, had decided to try throwing her out of the window. To all of which, this last impulse was as the gentlest expression of sudden rage. But it was also the King's Road, Chelsea. He had miscalculated the geographical significance of a blow. However drunk or irritated one may be, one does not strike an Englishwoman on her own doorstep.

Therefore, amazed, he watched her disappear as she raced home to pack (on a sudden impulse) a suitcase, secure sick-leave by telephone, and rush to catch a train, after agitated but none the less strict instructions to the patient Emily to let no-one in while she was away. (M'Hugh had a habit of living indefinitely on the hospitality of his friends.)

She found Evelyn in the garden of that enviable cottage of hers among the lesser hills of the restrained and gentlemanly Buckinghamshire.

—I never could understand what you saw in him, said Evelyn, later. His books are rubbish.

—A beard, especially a red beard, said Lavinia Reade, can be a powerful aphrodisiac.

—I never liked him.

—I don't like Jeremy, said Miss Reade ungraciously, dabbing at the home-made jam.

—Nor do I, particularly, said Evelyn. But I have such a horror of growing like my Aunt Elizabeth.

Miss Reade finished her tea in silence. She then said: As an erotic stimulant the fear of growing like one's Aunt Elizabeth should rank with the keeping-on of her boots by the German, the keeping-on of her corsets by the Viennese, and the clinging to her stockings and garters by the Parisienne.

Her friend looked up from her book, and smiled.

—And why not? she said pleasantly. We cannot all have naturally wide and hospitable legs.

—Wide and hospitable legs, said Miss Reade, no whit abashed, are the sign of a god-like and of a generous nature. Beware of all who keep their legs in any other way. Legs held together denote fear and servility. It is the symbol of the waiter, the servant, the Ambassador. Whereas legs apart and firmly planted are a proof of strength and independence. By their sign you may recognise the peasant, the Viking, the grande amoureuse.

—Suppose we went for a walk? said Evelyn, jumping up. For though not wishing to become like Aunt Elizabeth, she had an infallible belief in the efficacy of fresh air and exercise as a cure-all for eroticism.

But Miss Reade suddenly remembered that she was unhappy. She protested. She preferred, she said, to stay indoors and read Donne. Donne (she said) was the only poet who had ever made the Muse his mistress and taken her in to bed with him.

However, the house belonged to Evelyn, so they went for a walk.

But in the fresh air Miss Reade grew melancholy. She walked with bent head, and stopping suddenly on the slope of a field, asked: What month is this?

Evelyn told her.

—Then we are a month late. Browning said one should be in England only in April.

Could this be May? in the valley the trees were wintry under their icing of Spring blossom. And this the sun: this chill, uneager disk, as though the least of all the Saints had lost his halo? And this the Spring: this unwilling birth whose tidings the larks bore hysterically aloft, while from distant fields the new lambs threw out their dismal stammer?

Evelyn was saying: This year it's been too perfectly awful! She was apologising, for she knew (though did not share) her friend's climatic distrust of her native land.

But Lavinia Reade made no answer. Indeed, she had not heard. She walked with bent head, in an angry abstract stride, lost in those thoughts which were the despair of her more circumspect and orderly minded friends. At last she said:

—Even Nature, in England, wears a fig-leaf.

A fig-leaf? Plus-fours! Not Ceres. Not the many-breasted Diana. No goat-footed god. But a well-washed, inhibited, and plus-foured Colonel plodding to the nearest golf-course. And the plus-foured Colonel takes no heed of sodden skies and flowerless hedgerows. He says: this, damme Sir, is England. This is not earth. This is land by the half-acre.

One felt it was. One felt, as one stared, that its sense of decency was being affronted. That being entirely sober, it knew its nakedness and was ashamed. It was eager to be clothed; to be cut in little lots and covered in an excrement of brick; to offer itself up in semi-houses for semi-people. The rounded shoulders of the hills were not for burdens of terraced vine, stiffened maize, or heavy corn. They were for villas back to back, a latched gate, a strip of green, a blue lupin or two. Not yet; but soon. In ten years' time when London, that breeding-ground of clerks, had worried its dust-heap of suburb a further thirty miles.

Perhaps I've been too long abroad, she thought; remembering (particularly) a farmhouse, long, two-storied, coloured the familiar etruscan red-ochre, its windows outlined in bands of pinkish lime, lost in the ebb and flow of the hills above Petroio. Tuscan speech is like incense in the mouth. Goat's milk has a heavy acrid taste. One mixes *ricotta* with rum and sugar. Guilletta of the golden face and classic brow brings fruit to the table, sighing: *fa haldo nella hasa.* About the doorways cheerful old women gossip melodiously, and work the long ribbons of leghorn straw to be sent to Florence. There are two streets; one walks up the one which leads to the other. Tuscan peasants with naked feet pass among their vines and fields, for there a man's feet are not white and pitiful but are sunk in the warm earth like stalks with roots.

Yet this, too, was May: this discreet reflection of an ardent act; this onlooker at Nature's festival. The sky was long low-lying cloud. The earth cold and desolate. There was a something inhibited and unwilling about it all. Only the birds, twittering like mice in the heavenly wainscotting. And they seemed foreigners. They were noisy and gay and alive; like the Italians in Soho. And as such were not so much part of the scene as tolerated by the restrained and gentlemanly countryside, the barrier-like hedges, the stony fields. Could it be that in England there must be no display of vitality even on the land and sky? Life's expression must not be extravagant and even Nature's voice may not be raised? All is superior and self-conscious. All things merge. The sun-less tradition of the earth is one with its inhabitants. The people are subdued and the fields are subdued. The people are grey and tweedy, and the fields are grey and tweedy. And over both blows the cold breath of primness and gentility and fear; fear of nakedness, of exuberance, of life.

—Of all the earth England cooled first!

Miss Reade looked back, startled. It rang so clearly in her ears that she stood still. Some-one had spoken. But Evelyn lagged behind and was calling to her dog. Realising that the words were her own, she smiled; her heart fluttered in harmless vanity, for she loved the ruthless summary in a sentence. She looked up and around at the chill and the grey, and repeated slowly and aloud: *Of all the earth England cooled first.*

—Evelyn, she called. O Evelyn! Listen to this. . . .

—He won't COME! Evelyn yelled back. It's no USE. He's after RABBITS!

But by the time Evelyn caught her up, she had ceased distorting a wintry landscape to fit a sudden nostalgia for Spring on a Tuscan hillside. She was leaning on a gate, staring at a cow. The cow (needless to say) was staring back. Her expression was benign. Miss Reade's was hostile. The cow chewed, gently moving her soft and juicy nose. Miss Reade's fine nostrils were distended in surprise and distaste. She seemed never before to have seen a cow, or to have understood its purpose. Such a voluminous, pink, veined, all-too-human appendage appalled her as a source of nourishment. The fat pink fingers were obscene as a fat, soft, money-loving hand. Confronted by her wet-nurse the squeamish citizen revolted. Too near a view of such mammiferous bounty, alarmed her. This then, with its pendulous pink bag, was the source of civilised life. To this swaying breast (for the cow not having to understand sights with her mind, had lost interest in staring, and had returned to her food) to this swollen unappetising fount, the modern mother brought her new-born babe. Here was a field of them, ripping-up with small sharp sound the fresh grass, to be dropped foaming into pails, to be warmed in tens of millions of bottles and held to puling mouths. All this tearing up of grass by these poor patient beasts on whose broad backs the modern woman had shifted her intimate maternal duty.

At last she broke a long silence.

—I am like that, she said thoughtfully.

—I suppose you are, said Evelyn. Only the cow is less emotional. And, of course, never argues.

—Yet I am right, said Miss Reade slowly. And you are wrong. I am old-fashioned. I admit it. I need men. And I need children. I am the human cow. But you are the modern woman. You dislike children. You do not really care for men. Where the fear of Aunt Elizabeth has led you, instinct has led me. Yet one should function correctly, said Lavinia Read with finality. So I am right.

But Evelyn would have none of it. She was coldly derisive. She denied that the act of love was for anything as dull and limited as the mere reproduction of self. She called children the compensation of the unloved. That the act of love should be for anything but pleasure (she said) was both immoral and unthinkable. Women who desire only to be mothers should be mechanically fertilised. Let them be placed apart and tended and graded like cattle. Let them admit their cow-like vocation. Let them be contented by the yearly child. But let them leave the passionate act to the passionate.

Meanwhile the anonymous wet-nurses of the citizens continued grazing peacefully, unperturbed by a distressed onlooker's sudden conversion to beer.

But soon the earth grew warm, serious, productive. The hysteria of Spring was past. The cuckoo's anvil-echoing died down. One lay on one's back in deep clover, in an infinitude of moons which, when picked, told Continental time.

And one thought of M'Hugh who (as Evelyn said) wrote indifferent books; and of how love may become a habit; and of how restless one can be, deprived of it. Not that his books were so very poor. Certainly, they sold.

To pick up a book by M'Hugh was mentally akin to dancing around a maypole. It had charm, a gentle humour, and was instinct with the very breath of English country life. It was also sad, and filled with yeoman farmers who seemed never (until this book began) to have imagined, much less seen, a patch of land other than their own, and off which they were about to be turned. Either they could no longer make it pay, wherein it became a grim battle between the new town and the home of their forefathers; or the sons became slowly mad, through hereditary taint; the cottager's lass was brought to shame by the head of the house; the proud daughter ran away with the commercial traveller. Life for them was monotonously dour and hard. Early M'Hugh seemed to have understood that peasants in literature must suffer, and suffer much. Withal that intoxicating perfume of roses welling in cottage gardens; the thatched roof and straggling street; the light easy touch of dialect; the pewter mugs banged on wooden tables; and the wide wild eyes of love betrayed.

His work was a never-ending source of wonder to one who knew him so well as did Lavinia Reade. The man himself (she had often thought) was so much more arresting in his brutal insensitiveness, that it seemed a pity he should not make use of it in his work. Why, in that little inn in Barcelona, before they had been living together three months, he had insulted her so savagely that even the sailors sitting there had had to ask him to be more gentle to her. What a good story that would have made, though in her case he had not noticed the wide wild eyes. And how often had he not threatened to return home, leaving her without money? Not that he was insensitive to suffering. The sight of a beaten child or a kicked dog could put him to exquisite torment, and to tirades of vengeance.

And how indignant he had been the day of the bullfight when she had laughed and clapped her hands. He had wanted the whole thing stopped. It was revolting. It was barbaric. It was the refinement of torture. He sat withdrawn in anger and disgust. And she had laughed and called it cardboard. Lovely gaudy cardboard. It was Punch and Judy played with bulls and men. They sat high up, on the tightly packed benches among the garlic and the sweat and the orange peel; and all around them the people yelled in their brazen ciccalous voices. She had thought it superb, the lithe mastery of the men; the silken tricked-up insolence of the show. And once when the crowd rose and shouted, she rose and shouted with it, at the blood and the colour and the sun and the cool impertinence of a waving cloak. Straight, swift, sure, and beautiful! Thus should one kill a bull. Thus should one take a woman.

Afterwards he could hardly bring himself to speak to her. Yet he called the child: your brat; and the week it was born he went away. He had gone to buy some cigarettes, and had not returned, leaving her with the few shillings so often threatened. She felt very ill and, unable to ask for a doctor in understandable Spanish, went to bed in that terrifying stone room with the stone floor. And would have gone on lying in bed had not the woman of the house bustled in and throwing up a jet of words like the ceaseless twanging of a guitar, had got her out of bed and sat her between two chairs with a basin beneath; and after a timeless flow of pain it was over, and the woman was laughing and washing the child, and she was back in bed again. And at the end of a week M'Hugh walked in, having bought his cigarettes. He was surprised to see the child. He behaved as though it were an immaculate conception; or as though such things were announced and achieved by incantation, or a form of black magic between witches and women. Later he said that he had gone away because he could not bear to see her suffer.

—That was a mistake, she had told him gently, with that fine candour of hers. One should know every thing that is life. It would have been useful to you.

But mention of his work was the unvarying signal for a display of pained anger on his part. Here was an exposed and acutely sensitive nerve. His work was sacred and above discussion. It must not be tarnished by careless tongues. It was the Pure Woman of the poet's dream. Reality was the harlot.

Besides, was this a time to speak of work? What work? How? When? Weren't they about to be deafened day and night for the next six months?

But if this was an excuse it failed. The infant was so quiet that he both terrified and fascinated Miss Reade, who also had anticipated six sleepless months. He lay peacefully self-communing, self-absorbed, drawing on a store of timeless memories which seemed to amuse him, for he chuckled a great deal. Mother and son were attracted to one another from the start. The admiration was mutual. Possibly because they had the same habit of absorbed staring and laughter came readily to both of them. She would bring a book and would read aloud and charm him with her light, eager voice:

> Busie old foole, unruly Sonne,
> Why dost thou thus,
> Through windowes, and through curtaines call on us?

He liked that. Or:

> Outcrept a sparrow, this soules moving Inne,
> On whose raw armes stiffe feathers now begin.

But all that he knew, the Emperor, and the Post-Horse, and the Mucheron, the spider, the shee wolf, the embryon fish. He slept.

Often she sat bent over the table in the shadow, with her back to him; and sometimes when she was finished would come and read it to him. One day she read: *And here . . . in 1452 . . . the son of God was born. For if God Himself is Omniscience, then none has ever come so near to Him as has Leonardo da Vinci.* This time he not only chuckled, he waved his legs and waved his fists; and his mother was so pleased that she kissed him all over and dropped two large tears on his head in playing.

When M'Hugh came in she told him that Bill would be among the greatest living scientists, and made him watch the child's involuntary response to the word: Vinci.

But Bill was staring sideways at his father.

—And he has the scientist's unwavering eye, said Miss Reade, disappointed.

Why the hell, M'Hugh wanted to know, did she keep on calling the creature Bill. Why not Joe? Or Ed? or Jim? He was working himself up; it was a sore point.

—Bill for Billingsgate, said Miss Reade solemnly, though she had only just thought of it. His father had the manners of a fish porter.

M'Hugh wanted him christened John Andrew Robert after an only (and rich) uncle in Devon; and wanted him christened at once. The rich uncle was not now on speaking terms with his unspeakable nephew, but on hearing of John Andrew Robert and the honour conferred on him, the effect must be magical. He might even offer to adopt the brat and pay its expenses.

But Bill's mother was adamant. She agreed, she said, with the Red Indians. When Bill had shown himself worthy of a name he should receive one and be finally and officially christened. But not till then.

Moreover, the fair name of a future scientist must not be smirched by a cowardly dream of a penitent uncle in distant Devon. From here (for she stood on the balcony looking at the painted boats gliding on a green sea, and at the idling of the dark-skinned men in the toy, white-gleaming harbour) the thought of Devon was as remote as it was fantastic. And she told him why. It was not to the Bills of this world that one gave the names of revered uncles. Strangely enough these had but to appear, to turn avuncular hearts to granite. But somewhere in Devon, midway (socially) between the Hall and the Village, in a simple tennis frock, dewily innocent as though from the pages of one of his own novels (which she kept under her pillow, and wept upon, her underlip between her teeth) She waited. She had heard dark and unmentionable things of her hero's private life; but faith was beautiful; and it must be that one day He and She came face to face.

—And you shall. In time. First the desire will come to you to shave that handsome beard which now makes people turn and wonder who that may be. Which will compel you to tie a neat bow under your chin. Which means shirts of a more-seemly pattern. And even a new suit. And a ticket from Waterloo (for the fight will be over!) to the land of Drake and the Armada. A jocular Uncle. A girl in a tennis frock. At the sight of so much real Innocence your apathy will drop from you: for a simple tennis frock on a Devon lawn is a modern maiden's Belt of Chastity. And later think how uncomfortable you will be in the dead of night when the young mother sleeps, at the thought of another John Andrew Robert who has no right to the proud name of M'Hugh. And you will grow pale and neurasthenic wondering when the blackmailing will begin; just as in your books. And for how much? No, no. Let him leave Uncle John Andrew Robert till true repentance was on him and he decided to settle down. And let him for the moment leave Bill alone. For Bill ever to have a name he must make it.

And it was so true that M'Hugh was angrier than ever. He ground his teeth on his pipe, waved his arms helplessly, vaguely, to take in the child, himself, the sea, the sky, her, the white road to the harbour, and said between his teeth, and practically in tears, that everything, everything was a joke to her. She seemed to have no decent feelings. It was terrifying. Where any real woman would cry, she laughed. She scoffed. She ridiculed. She had no heart. What did he want with his damned uncle but his money, and a decent sort of name for the child, and perhaps someone to look after it.

She had put an arm in his and her head against his shoulder, and said: Dearest, what *is* there to be serious about? We're only poor once! (and even as she had said it, she knew how wasted it was. But how Rollo would have loved that remark!)

The six months past, they boarded a fruit steamer in Malaga which eventually set them down in Naples, and from there walked as fancy took them, vaguely toward Rome and Florence. The infant wore nothing but an enormous red cotton handkerchief knotted round him like a workman's dinner-pail, which made him no trouble at all to carry, and when they came to a village Miss Reade would make straight for the piazzetta and splash him kicking into the fountain, and the women would come tumbling out of doorways with sharp cries and up-lifted hands, wailing: *Il poveretto! Aië, mamma mia, il poveretto!* So shocked they were to see a baby treated like a husband's shirt.

When at last they returned to England, Bill was taken to Cornwall and duly christened with names befitting a future world-scientist, and left at the farmhouse which had been so highly recommended. Already Bill had the thinker's impersonal outlook. He made scarcely any fuss at parting. He was intent on studying a hen and some chickens. Miss Reade wondered would she miss him at all; and in the train it occurred to her how pleasant it must be to be old: old and out of reach.

On the way home she stopped the taxi-cab in the King's Road and bought an armful of tulips, and some mushrooms, and a bundle of asparagus. But M'Hugh was gone to the Ballet with Charles and Edwina. The note added self-righteously that he had put the cat outside.

But it is good to be alone in those moments in which living seems suddenly a thing external, an effort made under pressure; or as though one had been seized against one's will and hurried down turnings one did not wish to take. The glow from the lights on the Embankment outlined the room, the plane trees below, the water's edge, the benches for the homeless and the lovers. All over the world people were drawing their souls out through their mouths. All over the world were farmhouses where children crowed among the hens and chickens. All over the world little blue postmen hurried down streets on their last rounds, dealing joy and pain with an impartial hand.

And she had stared in the faces of the flowers she had bought, and had thought how one does not lose one's innocence with one's virginity, but when first one learns how treacherous people are. It seemed there was a rape of the soul which was of all things the most horrible, because without beauty and without passion. An ugly, solitary, spinsterish act.

I thought you would be ill, Käthe was saying. You looked so white. I thought you would be ill.

She had opened the shutters to let in more air, and hovered anxious and sympathetic.

Miss Reade said nothing. Partly that she found the remark unnecessary; partly that the taste in her mouth was unpleasant. She steadied herself a moment on the edge of the bed, then went to the window and leant on the sill. The warm air played on her face. But it was unreal, too bright, the sudden sight of shouting children tearing over cobbles, the aged houses tilting at each other, the swaying ascent of spires, roofs, hills, to the sun. She went back and sat on the bed, her head on her arms.

Meanwhile Käthe was busy at the wash-hand-stand; but more busy in her mind wondering how to show that she understood these things; that she knew quite well that to be sick like this for no reason one must be wearing a wedding ring.

At last she said: When my mother was sick she always had strong black coffee without sugar, afterwards. And she had eight.

But Miss Reade must have missed the subtlety, for she neither blushed nor frowned. On the contrary, she was extremely grateful and said: Then suppose you go and bring me some, and we'll see whether your mother was right.

So the disappointed Käthe meekly put the finishing touches to the room and hurried away to the kitchen. For how does one resist a smile that is like the mutual sharing of some secret joy?

When next Miss Reade looked up there Käthe stood like an Annunciation angel bringing coffee, but no sugar. And as she drank, Käthe watched with eyes wide, as though hypnotised. And as she drank Miss Reade watched Käthe and thought how Nature is more tittivating than any woman's dress-maker in the matching of earth and man: black hair and eyes with figs and black grapes: straw-coloured hair and blue eyes with white grapes and corn; three steps backward with head on one side, professionally pursed mouth, and a slow satisfied nod.

But it was more than Käthe could bear, the suspense, the being stared through as though she were not there.

—You are not afraid? she whispered.

—Of what? asked Miss Reade startled.

—Of dying, breathed Käthe.

Ach, to look so good and yet to laugh at Sin and Death as though there were no God above! Käthe turned from pink to red. Miss Reade stopped laughing.

She said that it was not nearly as bad as people pretended, and warned her against believing all the silly stories she heard. And suddenly feeling she might have said too much, amended: At least, I can't believe it is!

Not, she felt, that she had anything to conceal, but out of deference to Käthe's sensibilities. It was always as well to remember Sebastian's witty dictum: I never lie. I amplify or I restrict Truth.

She added pleasantly: Besides, look how strong and healthy I am.

And all at once like a dimpled bursting cloud Käthe was pouring her life story, her married sister, her brothers, an old father, a dead mother, the young man they were urging her to marry at once, saying that a year's courting was enough for any girl these hard times. Käthe pouted and tossed her head. For they were marrying her a little (though not altogether) against her will. And she was frightened. She pretended that it was because farm work is long and difficult, and there would be enough to do on her parents-in-law's farm. She spoke resentfully. She seemed to think that she was being pushed into marriage to help with the potatoes, yet all the while was fascinated and half-angry, unwilling and eager for the day when like a piece of furniture and with no more ceremony than the bridal sheets she must spread herself out and render up her possessions, the woman's placing of all her cards on the table, the giving of the only thing she has to give, except help on the farm and the cooking of meals.

Trapped under the confidential cloud-burst Miss Reade sat marvelling that already six years were past. Eighteen! All that part—the

Käthe part—Rollo had had. And how willingly, how thoughtlessly given. My Lord was like a flower upon the brows of lusty May. O, Blake knew! Rollo whose very letters one remembered years afterwards, as though read yesterday, as though still lying half-open on one's lap.

Nice, nice people. I am exhausted. The Countess is more beautiful than I thought. The Countess is more cultured than I thought. She loves Rossetti and particularly the statue of Peter Pan. Art is in the family. Her mother was exhibiting in Liverpool with the British Amateur Water-colour Society. . . .

That, of course, in the days before he was given to painting sleek women as waterfalls of light and colour; acclaimed by the many, mourned by a few early friends who had watched his downfall. That, in the golden days when living could be so plain that it was difficult to think high any more, but by a happy trick one was able to retrieve the shillings one had just dropped in the gas-meter, and spend them on innumerable and unnecessary little jugs of cream, which (did you ask him how he got them) he'd say: . . . ssh. I milked a mouse!

Perhaps Käthe was right. Perhaps one would die. For if death is a sleep, what death was there for a woman but death in childbed? And then, how eager, how more exacting life would become if one could know the day and hour of leaving it. Then only murderers met death bravely with senses alert, facing the inevitable. The newsboys shout, the decent citizen buys a paper, reads with horror, pities the wretch, and, still reading, falls under the first 'bus that thunders by without sounding its horn. That was not death, but an accident. Death should not be made a thing of chance or blackmail, but the body's leaping at the struggle of old and new, with for the vanquished (the woman) the reward of unending sleep. With the first pangs should come a slow gasping for breath; with the first new cry, the death rattle.

Käthe was saying nervously: . . . perhaps . . . now he'll marry you. And blushing yet again.

—Who? said Miss Reade, returning sharply to life.

—. . . the tall one, of course. . . .

But Miss Reade said abruptly, struggling between irritation and a desire not to hurt the girl's feelings, that there was no question of marriage. Adding also that she had no desire or intention of ever marrying.

—Never, she said decisively, as Käthe exclaimed. At least not with the men I seem fated to meet. They are too clever. And clever men are neurotic and unhappy; and about as easy to live with as precocious children. All the men you see downstairs, Käthe, are one-half women. Just as silly, and even more vain.

So Käthe understood that it was all a joke and giggled: Then what is a man!

—Otto, said Lavinia Reade. Otto is a man. And all those you see at night coming home from the fields. Those are men. They work with arms and muscles as a man is meant to do. You will find them carrying their children around in their arms; but not their emotions. The men you see downstairs, Käthe, said Miss Reade, warming to her task, do not need wives and fields and children. They need an audience. Without an audience they are as lost as a pretty woman without a mirror. Or as clowns in an empty tent. No; that is unfair to the clown. He contorts only his face. He can hang his grin on a nail with his tights and spangles. He can go home and rest, drink his soup and smoke his pipe, and grumble at his wife because his toes stick through his socks. But these leap and tumble in their minds, twist and posture in their hearts, and for them there is no rest. They are those enchanting prismatic toys one bought as a child, shaking bright patterns from their tongues and brain; and at each new pattern you must clap your hands and praise it. Then they are happy. For they must never be allowed to think that their pattern is not the best pattern, even though in their hearts they may know it is not the right pattern. Or that the sounds they weave with their tongues are not the strangest sounds; even though they be without soul or substance: but just a little argument. Or they grow melancholy. They wilt. They even die. But even if they throw themselves in the river, my child, it is only that they rush out to embrace their own reflections.

Miss Reade stood up and went to the window.

—Praise them, sl-laugh with them, she said, but never marry them.

Below in the sunlight old men sat still as alligators, absorbing the hours. Children fell in and out of doorways. A beribboned cock strutted. A hen with gracious feathered curves led her fidgeting chicks with sounds like heavy single drops, drip-dripping on a stone.

—Come and look, said Lavinia Reade:

A fat little boy of about four with stuffed pink legs, struggled across the market-place, kicked and pinched another small boy, tore some form of toy from him, and struggled back again. A howl of rage and defeat went up, very like those rancid notes with which sopranos announce that the end is near. Smaller children gathered and stared; slightly older sisters appeared from no-where, surrounded the victim, hugged it tightly in thin arms as though the screams must cease by pressure. Meanwhile the thief was out of sight, though there was much vague pointing and shouting of threats, and at last the screamer, whom only justice would appease, was led away on small unsteady legs and a bodyguard of angry voluble little girls, in the direction the enemy supposedly had taken.

Käthe grinned. She, too, had comforted small fat brothers, unbuttoned them, spoiled them, bullied them, and wiped their noses; all better fun than playing with dolls. She said:

—This year there were two young storks, but the parent-birds have killed one.

—How do you know?

Everyone knew said Käthe. Because they always did. Each time there were two, one was killed. And each year before they flew away they gathered in a field and killed all the weak birds, young and old, whom they thought unfit for the journey. O, yes, they did! They beat them with their beaks, like this. And sometimes one found two or three dead storks in a field, and then one knew that they had gathered there before going away. But there were not so many now. They had been frightened by the guns during the War and had stayed away, and besides they got shot at so much, crossing Italy. Weren't they *funny* things? Standing always on one leg, high above the houses and peering down their long noses; and looking so proud! as though it was too much for them even to touch the earth at all. Just like. . . . And here Käthe blushed once more. But she was a simple soul, with no sense of servility, who thought that having poured out her own story fully entitled her to enter yours. Just like (she said) the tall man who was always running off by himself . . . when here you are . . . and here everything is . . . so happy and so alive . . . but then one looked at him and it was just like the stork standing on one leg, and hating having to stand even on that.

What would be the good of showing annoyance? Besides, the description was so apt. One leg on the earth, and even that was too much for him! She recalled his back, immune, indifferent, hurrying out of sight in the early sunshine.

On, on and on, went Käthe, a torrent of loyalty and partisanship. And all at once Miss Reade found that watching the silly gentle creature babbling away she could not hear a word she said, but only saw her mouth opening and shutting. It was not the first time this had happened to her. Often it was as though sudden intensity of feeling could paralyse her eyes and ear drums, so that she could not see or hear the thing or person who had caused it. And yet she knew she smiled. For there was a queer strain of compassionate indolence in her, so that even in moments of almost hysterical revulsion or boredom Lavinia Reade rarely said the unkind, unnecessary things she might have. A trait which misled many people. But it was only an indolent helplessness. A be good to people. Be kind to them. One sees them but once. Time is so short and its aftermath so long. Say the things they want you to say. And so she thanked Käthe for her help, and said that now she would lie down awhile, and even that she thought she heard some-one calling downstairs and that Käthe had better run; and no sooner was the door shut on the grateful creature than Miss Reade found the tears trickling down her face. For, of course, he had left her. She saw it all clearly, standing at the window while Käthe compared him with a stork. He was gone and would not come back. She saw the train bearing him away, tearing off in an unknown direction with stubborn, foolish secretiveness. So she stood and wept tears that came without effort. All that she knew of them was that they ran down her cheeks. Modern Leda mourned without passion her one-legged stork. She wept, as an hour since she had been sick, meaninglessly. She was not hurt or angry. She was pregnant and so she was sick; she was alone and so she wept. Though it was now too late to weep and quite useless. The real tears had all been shed four weeks ago. And the last. But she felt young and abandoned and empty and at a loss; and what she had feared was not important at all, and really concerned her no more. But it had happened, and so the tears ran down her cheeks as she stared from the window and thought how foolish to waste such an afternoon indoors and that she would go out for a walk.

When, as it happened, he was not gone at all, but at the moment Miss Reade, staring from the window, saw him borne away in foolish and relentless haste, he was somewhere between Muttersholz and Wittisheim, sitting on one of those red-stone benches, half-torii half-druid altar, which line at intervals the Alsatian roads. He was watching a stork, grave enchanted bird, stooping for food in a field. Until a shy straw-haired child who had come down the road with a man and had crept up to stare at him sitting there motionless and unreal, distracted him; but as he turned and looked at her she retreated wildly to the waiting man and held on to his hand and stumbled away, pressed anxiously against familiar legs.

It seemed his life had been but a magnified day. Behind him days stretched by repetition into years and years, by a monotony of hours, habits, and repeated acts, dwindled once more to a day.

Constancy of habit to this tyranny of hours had meant a succession of timed wakings, baths, shaves, breakfasts, work, home-comings, sleep; to wake again to baths, shaves, breakfasts, work, home-comings, sleep. The year-long shuttling between office and home, three hundred and sixty-five breakfasts punctually set, eaten and digested, to each hour of each day its act, in a year three hundred and sixty-five times performed, in ten years three thousand six hundred and fifty times performed; add on; then look back. The answer is a day.

And in these years reduced by routine, by the solemn precision of habit to a few hours, hopes, desires, frustrations, loomed no larger than minutes; or were mere irritants, straws dropped across an insect's mile-long path. For life (he found) is measured by the breakfasts one has eaten rather than by the emotions one has used or avoided; and it was not whether these breakfasts were pleasant or palatable, wanted or unwanted that remained; but the fact of having sat down to them. For in the end detail is eliminated, habits merge in the whole, the whole becomes a lifetime, the lifetime becomes a day.

Possibly they distort some part of one in childhood. They always do. A bleakness of female caution, an excess of male enthusiasm; bleatings, fears, regrets. Regular hours form regular habits. Regular habits ensure long life. A matter of Bleeding Gums and Unsuspected Constipation. But then Harrion never could read advertisements. They reminded him of his mother, whose lips had parted only in things moral and offensive; of himself, a pale thin child, ashamed of his pallor; of his father, even in that mediocre grey-slate town among the most self-effacing, even in his work dependent on the wills of others; and such dull unimaginative wills that could never hope to be queried or disputed: *that* sort (as his wife never tired of pointing out) went to those fortunate beings who kept their own carriage.

If! If if if if. But all the breakfasts had been eaten. Possibly the capacity for emotion is like the capacity for food: gorge and the stomach throws it back. Only a certain measure of affection is given to each: a mother or an aunt, an adopted son, a canary. Beyond that the spent effort cannot be flogged. There comes an end to desire. Life recedes. One is washed up at last on some cold peak of inner solitude. For the bitter parable of Eden is that one first must eat the fruit before finding at its core the dry-rot of indifference.

Harrion looked down. An ant exploring his hand as though it were the road to Lhasa, climbed hills, fell among hairs, and struggled to safety in a valley between fingers; and was no sooner safe than again was up hills, into hairs, panicked, and was safe again. He bent forward, hung his hand over a blade of grass and watched the busy creature lose itself in the meadow's trembling undercurrent.

Unbroken by hedges the vast plain flowed evenly to the very edge of the tree-bordered road, like a grassy sea meeting sand. Fields stretched as far as the eye could follow, stopped only by hills spread in shells across the sky, with here and there a glint of village roof and strip of tilled land. Warm and slumbrous the outer edges dissolved in a mist of heat. A white horse with crimson ear-caps stood with restless tail and stamping hoofs in the shade of an apple tree heavy with its gallant burden.

Who can explain why a child falling under a lorry can make of a lifetime a matter of hours half lived? Perhaps because a child is an innocent untroubled little thing symbol of some lost state of grace. There is no harsh edge to its voice; no memories in its laughter; and to the touch it is as though one put an arm through a branch of apple blossom. Perhaps because a child is oneself re-born, and one will take greater care of this second more precious self; this other chance one dared not hope one had deserved.

From afar and from a church turret graceful as a gazelle came a faint sound of bells, needlessly telling the hour to those who lay beneath it with their lives crossed out. A scented wind gathered up the sounds and odours of the clover. In the nearest meadow a poplar stood above its shadow, stereoscopic against the sky. White butterflies rose on agitated waves bringing tidings to the flowers; and a large dark bee assaults a dandelion that bends under its weight, grips with amorous knees, opens petals, exposes secret places, and releases it, swaying; flies to the next, deflowers them all, a very Mahomet among the virgins.

To-morrow he would leave, would walk away, the last human contact would be broken; he would be free. Since now he could no longer look at his fellow-men, but could look only through and beyond them. It was as though when he looked flesh and blood fell away and he saw a scaffolding of bone, the outline of a skull. In an awful alertness of perception, suspended, apart, he saw the decay in all living matter, the long decomposition above ground which is called life; its fascination, its futility. It pleased him to find that in a walk he could hear the skeleton's dragging of its joints. The child who had crept up to stare at him, had stumbled away as a small heap of bones dancing on strings, crookedly unsure of its legs. Yet people went to extraordinary and pathetic lengths to gain such power as had come to him unsought. They drank, drugged, prayed, in efforts to release, to drown a will and turn consciousness to fluidity. To no purpose. For the drunkard returns to reality only to drink again to escape it; and drink and morphine remain the drugs of the sentimentalist. But indifference is the realist's drug. It does not obscure, it clarifies. It sets life in *relief* and one is borne above and beyond the limits of its bleak mediocrity to chill distances from whence there is no return. Never again will one shrink from that most terrifying of all earthly things: the human eye. One has gone beyond the retina's prying reach. Eyelids are no longer barriers one feared to face, for they close on no-thing; an airpocket; two bony cavities; twin hollows, void and meaningless as the grave.

As though to distract him a stream crossing the field with the small rustle of a silk petticoat quickened its step; and suddenly the air was filled with a busy passing of messages between birds, and as suddenly was so still that one heard that faint whisper in the tops of trees in which peasants at work in fields hear an angel speaking, or the prophecies of saints. Unheeding the meadow shimmered intensely alive and eager in its musical undercurrent of heavy clover, its hoard of new-minted buttercups, blue salvias, ox-eyed daisies, purple campanulas, and the soft pink spire of the field polygonum.

What a weaving, a meadow! How lavish a texture of untroubled hours! What a mirror of that brief moment in which one grows self-absorbed as a field in flower. All the sights and sounds of childhood, when staring in a pond is more than a wizard's staring in space, and the water-spider's giant stride, and the water-beetle's metallic gleam. A meadow is one's first innocence. A meadow is a childhood's memory.

From the incline where she sat looking down on the village (surely the birds had built these houses, so warm, so neatly fitted in the hollows) Lavinia Reade stopped poking the ground with her stick, raised her head and said aloud: I want her to be a gay young thing! I shall call her Bernardine.

For she could not rid herself of the belief that it was good to be alive and happiness enough to be sitting on the earth crying, when one might be sitting under it with no tears to shed, and nothing to be sad about, and no possibility of laughing or wondering what could happen next, or ever again. For let who would call death the great adventure, life (Lavinia Reade decided) life is a great gift.

A decision that had spoilt more than one dramatic moment. As on the day Rollo left her and intent on suicide she had sat down to write a will, only to find that after an hour's tearful staring in the gas fire she had written:

And I leave my spine to the Gas Light and Coke Company,

and had begun to laugh and unable to stop had gone for a walk, and had laughed all down the Embankment till she came to the aged mummified woman in the vast shining car, taking the air under the trees beside the river; the manly chauffeur pacing with the pekingese. And she had paused, shocked back to life at what seemed a bag of putrid flesh, yellow as its gold, pretending (for it could only have been pretending) that it breathed and felt the cool air on the face it turned so sightlessly to the water. One had thought the Bolshevists invented such things for their posters. And not ten steps away sat the man stubbornly staring at the pavement with that cold look the underfed retain even on the mildest days, beside him on the bench his three little girls, with impertinent little Cockney faces, the youngest of whom he was shielding with his battered coat, while she munched a large crust of dry bread.

And Lavinia Reade who not an hour since was on the verge of suicide but for a mis-timed sense of the ridiculous, had walked on thinking of the rich and of how they die and putrify among their possessions; and of how inferior they almost always are to their beasts and servants; riders to their horses, the driven to their chauffeurs. And of the poor, who are invariably superior to their clothes and environment; so much so that one never wishes to harm or attack them, but only to take away and replace their poor mean clothing and their ugly wretched homes.

A poultry farm, she decided. All one had to do to get hundreds of chickens was to give them tea-leaves and potato-peel (or was that pigs?) and they laid eggs and sat on them, which meant more chickens and double as many eggs. Then one added cows, for all *they* needed was a field and they too (and so willingly) gave you double as many cows. Which makes hundreds of gallons of milk and thousands of eggs; lorry-loads of milk and eggs for all the London poor, because it must all be given away, as in a perfect world flowers would be given away (but flowers one would add later); everything should be a gift, for it was unthinkable that people, poor people who shielded their children with battered coats, should be made to pay for food, particularly such food as eggs and milk that was made hourly and with such careless and friendly obedience. Soon lorry-loads of eggs, milk, and butter would descend on London and the poor would come with jugs and baskets, and be sent on their ways rejoicing. Because by then, said Lavinia Reade catching an omnibus on the wing. By then, of course, I shall be rich.

Nevertheless she delayed this matter of wealth and munificence, to sit waiting for the truant Rollo to return and continue their pleasant life, and possibly his unfinished and unintelligible canvases. But Rollo did not return. Rollo was discovering that for an ambitious and penniless artist a mistress in the fifties with money is of more interest than one of twenty with no possessions beyond a seemingly inexhaustible capacity for enjoying all and every hour of the twenty-four. Rollo was in Venice with Mrs Saul Rennet, the enviably notorious Claudia Rennet, wife of the shipping magnate and mother of the lovely Rennet twins; leaving Miss Reade to grind her teeth when she remembered how often she had written: the beautiful Mrs Saul Rennet, the Famous Hostess, that well-known Patroness of the Arts; conscientiously adding those attributes of wealth: wit, fascination, and intellect. How many times had she written of her as looking not a day older than her lovely daughters, when to the unprejudiced unjournalistic eye she was no other than an embalmed and painted old woman with a hunted look of having missed something, life or the latest lion or the morning massage, and could only buy for hard cash what others took by right of youth and love. Still, Rollo was now at the Palazzo Galli, on which its witty and lovely owner (the gossip-writers again) had recently spent more than £100,000, restoring and decorating. Singing for his supper like any of the sycophantic musicians and writers who gather, eager yet deferential vultures, around the carcases and dining-tables of the superlatively rich; except that Rollo sang at any hour; sang at a perpetual Royal Command, beginning possibly before breakfast.

And only a month since he had taken her to Paris on what seemed the last fifty pounds they would ever see. Fortunately she had not known that it was a farewell treat on the last of Rollo's honestly earned pence. And not a week after their return he was celebrating his good fortune (for it was extreme good fortune) with the ageing and exacting Claudia Rennet, adding with happy irony: And she is to give me my holidays on full pay!

Miss Reade could only cry out that he would need them if rumour was true, and that never again would he paint a picture worth painting. But that part of the prophecy could not have been right for Rollo had painted so many pictures that his name came glibly to the lips of lovely women who wished to hang on ancestral and Academy walls, looking as near an expensive fashion plate as they dared and yet with a flourish which gave to the paint a look of expense and permanence. Whereas four years later Miss Reade had got no further than sitting above a village on an afternoon in late July, thinking that nothing would show for another five months at least, and tossing her head on its long independent neck and saying aloud: I want her to be a gay young thing! I shall call her Bernardine.

But a cloud was passing across the sun. The brief spell of good weather, it meant, was about to break. One could see the first faint clouds of white dust whipped by the wind, far down across the plain beyond Schledstadt; where in the far distance the roads breathed a cloud of white dust before the storm. Even where she sat a small sudden wind, insidious agitator, was bending leaves and flowers in discontent.

Miss Reade stood up. She had an irresistible desire to walk to the top of the nearest hill and come suddenly on the sea. Possibly because one always expects to find the sea behind a hill. Behind a hill there can be only the sea. But she had not gone far when the loud and incessant chugging of the saw-mills stopped her. Ugly, inhuman sound. Everywhere the forests were being cut down. Already one could see the mutilated remains on some of the nearer hills, sudden shaved patches like a mange; a sick poodle, all worried. It hurt and dismayed her, the ruthless irreparable damage. Lavinia Reade turned away, as though she knew that she had no courage to face other people's stupidities; but only her own.

She was just in time as she came to the Marktplatz to see the little comedy of the War Memorial; an ugly granite cross enclosed in an iron railing, for which dreary growth the chestnut trees outside the Gemeinehüss had been cut down. Clumps of dahlias grew round it, pushing leaves and heads between the iron spikes. Obviously intent on catching one of the flowers, a little girl of some three or four years was walking slowly around the railing, humming. Miss Reade watched her with amusement; such a good-natured happy little thing, very busy. Suddenly, and as though the impulse was no longer to be resisted, the child reached out and picked a fat yellow dahlia, twice as large as the hand she stretched for it. At once and with a swift possessive fury the woman who was with the child gave her a resounding slap across the face and arm, tore the flower from her hand and threw it back inside the railing. The little thing cried on a long, dazed, hiccoughing note, as though something inside it had been torn. Its fat little legs gave way, and it sat down on the stones to a long bewildered sobbing.

Miss Reade ran across the Marktplatz, gathered the crying child high in her arms, and choosing the largest dahlia she could find, an intricate *rosace* of pink tongues, broke it off and put it between the child's fat tear-stained fingers. It stopped crying quite suddenly, and stared and stared.

—The flowers are for the dead, said the woman slowly and sententiously in German.

—No! said Lavinia Reade in her clear, intelligent voice. For the living! All things, said Lavinia Reade, showing her splendid teeth in a smile, all things are for the living. Only for the living.

She put the child down. In an agony of shyness, its nose buried in petals, it went straight to its mother's skirts and clung there. The woman, with her flat expressionless face turned aside, took the child's hand and they walked slowly away.

—Hello, interference! said an amiable and familiar voice. Now she will be soundly slapped and put to bed without her supper.

They watched the woman and child pass out of sight. Yes, Sebastian was right. The child would now be soundly slapped and put to bed without her supper.

—O women, women! cried Lavinia Reade passionately, as though she spoke of some malignant disease. She ached as though the shame had been hers. To strike a child for picking a flower larger than its own hand! No man could have been guilty of such unimaginative intolerance. Men made foolish mistakes; but not mean ones.

The hour was full of the sounds of home-coming; the grinding wheels of the ox-carts, the tired men trudging beside them, women with large white cloths knotted round their heads, children dangling thin legs and singing, all good-humouredly tired, all rather listless and emptied with fatigue from the day in the fields; all but the oxen with their eyes of onyx and ivory, and their effortless unhurried condescension.

Lorwich and Simeon Fenn coming from a side turning, crossed the Platz and climbed the steps Zum Goldenen Lamm. There was a strength about the squat Lorwich, an indefinable and pleasing reserve of energy; unhurried, ox-like. But the willowy Fenn looked pale and sullen, and as though the day's excursion had cost him a fortnight's energy.

Roused from her thoughts, Lavinia Reade sighed: To think that there are people with so few obstacles that they need climb mountains!

And after a pause she added slowly, and with unaccustomed bitterness: It does seem unfair that with the desires of women . . . they have not also the children.

(. . . the eunuchs of literature . . . the Vestalines of the grammar . . . the White Voices of free verse.

In a room bright as a witchball or the more crude forms of Venetian glass, Gabriel Bethemy receives his friends. Friends on the Bethemy principle that who is not for me is against me. Social and artistic London is or pro-Bethemy or contra-Bethemy. Friends, therefore.

Each is glad to be here. It argues a certain distinction. Gabriel Bethemy does not choose at random. As offering each brings a little story, varying in wit but not in malice. To this, their social exchange and barter, they bring an aëry transient coinage: not even paper, just a little wind. And there is much washing of soiled linen at the literary fountains.

The room, that gaudy prettily self-conscious room, is filled with smoke and people, through which the lilt of tea-cup and glass has a fresh innocent sound of children laughing. The buffet groans under a load of inventive skill noticeably absent from the works of those who so liberally partake of it. Voices rise in mortal combat, rapier on rapier, fist to fist, attack, parry, thrust; to sink to earth, pause, rise again refreshed, uppercuts, body blows, clinchings, knock-out—One—Two—Three—Four—— The clock across the square strikes the hour. It is six o'clock on an evening in late April; an evening of blanched greys and vaporous blue which the trees in the neat Chelsea square turn (it is expected of them) to Whistlerian advantage.

The stage is set and two shall meet, though neither knows it, though as yet but one is in the room, and from the carved and gilded ceiling impatient Cupid, ribbon-girdled, wreathes in soft leaves his stubborn spear. One, wanderer but yesterday returned from foreign shores, hero of many an amorous combat, weary with a weight of reputation grown legendary and irksome, in whose hyacinthine beard Time's greying hand now seeks a resting-place. The other, a woman-virgin boy on whose untroubled brow the rosy light of youth, chaste locks of yellow gold in ardent disarray; one who, standing on the strand when the winds have soothed the seas (the mirrored semblance cannot lie!) surveys himself, and fears not Daphnis.

Lorwich lowering himself on to a chair groans: God! An antique! and poor

Miss Fiffers at whom he stares in horror without seeing her, is never again quite sure, and to the end of life dares not finger the secret doubts of that thoughtless moment.

But Lorwich is referring to the chair whose tapered legs sway and creak at the burden so tactlessly imposed on them. He would get up, but dare not. He remembers that Gabriel Bethemy is very much the gentleman and therefore puts much of his soul and most of his pride in his furniture legs; and wishes that a gentleman's taste would occasionally run to something as decently solid as a tap-room bench. Lorwich, therefore, remains seated, hoping for the best. He is subdued and completely bored, and wonders how long it will be before some grinning and hospitable female will place a tea-cup in his hand, binding him more securely than Prometheus to his rock. It is eight years since Lorwich was last in England. He arrived from Paris but yesterday, and is already wondering where he will go to-morrow.

Meanwhile Gabriel Bethemy with grave, sleepy, impertinent face relaxed in welcome, picks, chooses, favours: like the sun, like a golden bee. He is speaking with that invisible but very audible silver spoon in his mouth. For some reason he avoids Lorwich, perched there helplessly on those legs more ridiculous than his own, and gazing fixedly at the wall where a blue Chirico stallion rears beside a pink-foaming sea. One can never be sure what Lorwich is thinking. He may be bored, and say so. He may use his sense of his fine theatrical presence to insist on his right as King of the assembled beasts.

As it happens Lorwich is thinking how splendidly Gabriel Bethemy and his brother Tressilian, maintain the English tradition of the gentleman. Gentlemen farmers, gentlemen trainers, gentlemen jockeys, gentlemen poets. And of how, by some inestimable dispensation of Providence, these two may sit astride life's fence; gentlemen among the artists: artists among the gentlemen. Rarely is a book of theirs published without it being remembered that an ancestor, one de Broy de Cuiy, came over with or after or before the Conqueror; and often they buy for sums not exceeding five guineas the works of struggling French and English painters, becoming with the minimum of effort and expense connoisseurs and patrons.

It gives Lorwich a definite malicious pleasure to observe how even Time has stayed his hour-glass for Gabriel, who, the room being warm, is calling to his brother Tressilian: dear heart, would you open a window? Time stands still for Gabriel (Lorwich decides with feline insight) at an eternal thirty-three. What price had he paid, what bribe had he offered, to be allowed thus in the advance-guard of young moderns; though writing well before the War? And how rightly disdainful he looks; like some exquisite sheep perfumed for what slaughter? to be torn by what ridicule in the literary fangs of his enemies? to be . . . but a high

playful voice is saying: Well, well, well, well! and what are you doing here!
*And behold, high above Lorwich's chair now hangs the leaning tower of Alicia
Prothero, whose novels are all they should be, and sell accordingly.*

*Very gaunt and skittish and pencil-thin is Miss Prothero, holding aloft a
champagne glass as a torch to light her wit and guide her footsteps in the ways of
toothy charm. She is laughing now at Lorwich's plight, trapped on those spidery
legs of undoubted worth but impoverished health; and Lorwich is laughing also
(thank God, he has now an excuse not to move for the remainder of the evening)
and dimly understanding why fundamentally he has never been able to appreciate
women. An ungenerous thought, for this specimen (intellectually, at least) is
above sample.*

—*What what, what what are you writing now? Miss Prothero asks. A
repetition of words due to a studious technique of charm; girlish, light-hearted,
irrepressible, irresistible. But Lorwich does not know this and thinks she has been
drinking. He decides that he is writing a sequel to* Lady Chatterley's Lover.
*He makes a sign. From afar Miss Prothero bends. He whispers the title in her
ear. It is more than a little shocking; it is even disgusting. Miss Prothero shoots up
again. Her cheeks are flushed. Her mouth is open. Her eyes are wide. She
grimaces with excitement. So much so that Lorwich has almost the impression
that she has this instant been raped, and has liked it. He leans back and watches
this gaunt hollow campanile of a woman from the top of whom the thin sounds
rock and jangle. From her height Miss Prothero is rapidly passing in review the
various groups, choosing which shall be first recipient of her news; hesitates,
falters, rallies, aghast and elated at such a word in her mouth, who till now has
always sinned by proxy; and floats away heavy with the mystic burden of her
secret.*

*Fragments of conversation detach themselves, are borne aloft, drift unclaimed,
dying in wreaths of smoke, unmourned.*

*Some-one has just told Odo Quimpel (nervous as lightning and with the
angular lines of a congolese mask) that Adrian Tims is not here as his wife is
having a baby, and Odo is drawling: Now how did Adrian do that, d'you
suppose? Breathe down her nostrils? A voice says quickly: O no. Adrian is a
sadist. He probably poured hot tea down her back.*

*A large lady who has been dipped in flour and left unfried, is saying that all his
virility (my dear) seems to have gone to his nose. And adds that, of course, he is
fat. But that one expects of tenors; they spend so much of their time swallowing
their words.*

*The thin little Jewess with the black ancestral curls on her shoulders is saying
plaintively: But you forget, surely you forget?, there is a life below the stomach.*

Once again Pirrie Ounce is complaining that his wife steals all his mistresses.

At the mention of wives Lorwich scowls mentally. His thoughts of Sidonie de Lagresin are hardly gracious; and certainly unfair. A wife has every right to enter the Casino and ask if her husband is still there, and on being told that Monsieur le Comte will be back but has left an hour ago, may add: alone?, and on hearing that a friend left with him, may decide to wait; may even wait one hour, two hours, three hours, motionless in shadow against a pillar, her mouth hard, her chin deep in the folds of her velvet cloak. There is a touch of frost in the air; one by one the lights go out; soon the street-cleaners will appear with their clatter of brooms and backchat; but such things do not trouble her static vigil and her eyes are fixed on the distance. At last a large yellow car turns in the drive and stops at the portico. It takes a certain time for the occupants to descend, but with much laughter and confusion they eventually do so. Le Comte Etienne de Lagresin comes first. Let alone walk he appears to find it difficult to stand, but with much good-humour and a little assistance he succeeds at last in staggering up the Casino steps. In his arms he carries a boy in the tightly buttoned scarlet of a page's uniform. The cherub's golden head lies sleepily against his shoulder, and as they pass through the lighted doors, the woman hidden in shadow hears a tired child-voice, half-sob: Mais non. Mais laisse-moi. Laisse-moi donc, cheri. A stout bearded man follows with another page tucked, like a bright little pig, under an arm. The child is very pale and has been sick all over the man's evening trousers. The chauffeur after handing out empty bottles to one of the Club servants, slams the car door, and drives off. The woman has not moved. Transfixed, frozen, she has let them pass. For nothing now avails Madame de Lagresin; nor her jewels, nor smoothly classic brow and tapering arms, nor the full-length pictures in those illustrated monthlies which set their worldly seal upon her beauty. On all these she may call; there is no answer. There is, however, influence; and three days later Lorwich leaves Paris. O all very politely, all very much as though it were a charming joke between man and man; but quite definitely leaves Paris. Who? How? fumes Lorwich, perched on four expensive legs and horribly bored. Jealousy? Inadequate tips? Didi, le groom du Magentá? The de Lagresin chauffeur, under threat of dismissal?

And then a voice that cuts like a sun through heavy cloud, dispelling with its rays his boredom and his anger. It is a languid voice, elongated, throaty, slurred, provocative. The voice is saying: Rome? But what is Rome but a beautiful and commodious water-closet surrounded by magnificent buildings?

The sentence does not by right of invention belong to Simeon Fenn, however well he uses it. He has overheard it not a month since, near the fountains of the Piazza di Spagna or coming down the steps of Santa Maria dei Monti, when the busy group of American tourists coming to a standstill, he was to hear the elderly bird-like little thing (from Polygon, O.) say shrilly: Waal, if you aarsk me, it's

one laang worrer-claset surrounded by just-too-luvverly buildings! But his
listeners cannot know this. Besides he has accented it almost beyond recognition,
and also has had the good sense to see its possibilities. It goes well. The laughter is
immediate.

Lorwich has turned. His gaze travels from the length and elegance of the
speaker's leg to that fair starry face surveying the room as from its cloud. And all at
once Lorwich is aware that he is carrying about with him an enormous stomach
which floats when he walks, jellies when he laughs, sags when he sits. So
humbling is love that he is on an instant and for the first time aware of his colossal
and stunted frame: gross, uncouth, unworthy. But he has turned and gazes across
his shoulder, his full eyes fixed and steady; and slowly, and as though willed,
Simeon Fenn has turned and is looking at him. Sees, though his eyes do not move
from the face, that heavy neck, that subtle perturbing varnish of dirt and brute
force. As at a command Cytherea's rosy babe awakes, yawns, apprehends: takes
aim. A moment and their wanton eyes (love's twin pools, the soul's fond mirror)
are troubled. A blush is on youth's pale cheek. He lowers his eyes and is the first to
turn away.)

B oum! Bou-bou-boum-boum. *Boum!* Heady martial sounds shattered the Sunday calm. A few mournful recruits sprang to attention, pranced about the cobbles, making solemn and spiritless clatter to
an audience of delighted children and two barking dogs.

But Madame eyed the clock and snorted. Now the procession would
be ruined. Bah! Les anti-clericaux!

Some-one reassured her. This, at its worst, could last but another
twenty minutes, and the procession did not pass until four.

The military music crashed on: tuneless, discordant, insidious.
Impossible to resist, impossible to think. At the door and out of the
house before a man has realised what he is doing.

Sebastian was saying: To become a saint, my dear Lavinia, you need
but transfer your erotic centre to your knees. Karl, noch ein viertel.

—As easy, said Miss Reade wearily, as easy as pinning one's colours
to one's nose. No, thank you. No; no more for me.

No more wine (thought Lavinia Reade) and no more words. There
was enough noise at the moment on the Marktplatz. Words and military
music had much in common; both insidious and equally disturbing: the
one to the ear, the one to the mind.

But Sebastian would talk. He was calling the American woman cold, angry, and ungrateful. He said she was her own punishment. He said the American woman was woman before she had been brought to her senses. Civilised woman, on the other hand, was woman made pleasant and palatable. The American woman was true woman: woman before she had been beaten into shape.

—But beautiful, said Lavinia Reade, half-heartedly.

Beauty? What on earth had beauty to do with it? Excrement was beauty to a fly! And Sebastian would have started once again on his theory that woman was made not for love but for pleasure, had not Miss Reade stood up and without ceremony walked to the window and stood staring.

After a while she said:

—Otto, your dog has no sex appeal. The other dogs avoid him.

—That is because he loves only me, grinned Otto.

—What a house! cried Miss Reade in mock alarm. What a house!

Meanwhile as an alternative to leaning over bridges by the hour and spitting at the water, the little blue soldiers leapt apart and back again, swung left and started off, swung right and were once more whence they started. Their discipline, French and individual, was disarmingly imperfect. It impressed the children. But the dogs seemed critical.

No more words (thought Lavinia Reade), no more words. At least not just now. Not on a Sunday afternoon. (How many times had Aunt Deborah used those cheerless words?) Could one not resuscitate or invent some god or hero to whom Sunday afternoon could be sacred in silence? And there fell a great calm upon the heart and ear of man, and the spirit of peace rested upon his habitation.

Standing there, staring from the window at the blue prancing soldiers, she felt a sudden, sharp, quivering movement. Once again, and it ceased. And she found it strange, and perhaps symbolic, that as she looked on at this clatter and mimicry of destruction, the new life she was to bear shuddered in the depths of her body.

Yet Sebastian had said that though biologically woman created, psychologically she could but destroy. Then men, one must assume, destroyed physically and created mentally, and the balance adjusts itself. Cold comfort this masquerade of war. Now even Sebastian's absurd prophecy had a disquieting threat of truth about it. For Sebastian held that men were becoming unnecessary, and must disappear. Indeed, the entire morning and that long road back from Engwiller now seemed to have been but a platform for Sebastian's theories and speculations.

They had been to the Ossuary. Fourteen thousand bodies had once packed it tightly to the ceiling (from some peasant war which the people spoke of as though it were yesterday); but the bones had crumbled until there was left only a heap of fragmentary dust, with here and there a skull and thigh and arm bone intact; big bones and large round skulls that still triumphantly proclaimed themselves the bones of strong men. (Looking at the skulls with their firm grinning teeth beautifully in place, she had thought: If I die now I shall look like this, and they will say: that one was young, look at those teeth! And it gave her a mournful pleasure to think of her teeth for ever whole and strongly clenched in death, as though the last word had been hers.) Above the Ossuary door was written:

WAS IHR SEID, SIND WIR GEWESEN.

WAS WIR SIND, WERDET IHR SEIN.

An official touch, misplaced, misunderstood, for the young dead are not sententious or vindictive. On the walls hung military buttons, caps, belts, and other oddments; left, the man in charge had told them, by the young men who went away to fight in the last war. Before they went they had come here to pray and light a candle, and those who returned had come again to hang these offerings on the walls. And that had troubled her more than the pile of young bones, the thought of the young coming to pray to the young, who also, some three hundred years since, had marched away from these villages.

But Sebastian was indifferent. He said that the last war was probably the end of man in more ways than one. The modern woman with her militant sterility could quite easily run the world on her own. He said the female was now active and in the ascendant, while to-day the function of the male was limited. For the mere continuance of the race man could be reduced to the male sexual organ. The world was changing too radically and the male virtues were no longer needed. War was not a need; it would become obsolete and the soldier would disappear. Man-power was not a need, soon all would be calculated by mechanical horse-power. Courage, enterprise, foresight, endurance were useless in a modernly organised community. Therefore all the qualities which made man supreme fell away. The men grew effeminate. Their services were not required. Only the women (said Sebastian) remained women. Their new activity and independence (a lack of servility) was mistaken for masculinity, but was merely adaptation. Already the more civilised (industrialised) a community, the more easily were the men dispensed with. A natural process. Where not so long ago it needed a man to guide a horse, to-day you had a woman guiding from 40 to 4000 horse-power. The more mechanical a community, the more feminine: as America, Russia, England. Only in natural (peasant) communities, such as Italy, Spain, the Balkans, France, the man still retained his power. To fight Nature it still required a man. To fight with machines, woman sufficed.

Sebastian said that the fact that a man always puts up a better performance than a woman did not matter at all. It did not make him indispensable. Small degrees of efficiency did not count. Man was no longer necessary when his job could be done almost as well by a woman and a machine. And as soon as he was no longer indispensable he ceased to exist. Only the indispensable is needed and created. That is Nature's demand and supply. In time all that would be required of man was the male semen.

As a living example of how well this worked there were the Ceratoids, most grotesque and efficient of all living creatures, the oceanic angler-fishes, who are all female, the male being dwarfed and parasitic on the females. One might say that here at last the female has found the perpetual male. And he told her how these female fish, solitary, sluggish, floating about in the darkness of the middle depths of the ocean, had at first found it difficult to find a mate, until this difficulty was overcome by the males themselves, who, as soon as they were hatched, and when they were relatively numerous, sought the females and if they found one held on to her and remained attached for life. They first held on by the mouth, but in time the lips and tongue fused with the skin of the female and the two became completely united. This mouth is toothless and closed in front and he is unable to feed himself, so he is fed by the blood of the female, for the blood streams are now continuous. And she now has an infinitesimal male permanently attached to the top of her head between the eyes, or under the body below the jaws. The Ceratoids were unique among back-boned animals in having dwarfed males of this kind, and unlike all other animals in having males fed in such a manner by the females. But that was only a matter of time, said Sebastian. The idea was too sound for Nature's humour and requirements to overlook. The trouble saved would be incalculable. And how much more pleasant a world, with women no longer dissatisfied and masters of the situation, and the harassed male no longer compelled to work for them.

All of which had been less real than the sight of a field of cabbages so exultantly blue that it had seemed to reflect the sky.

—Not merely blue blood, had said Lavinia Reade ironically, but the authentic purple.

Yet the rash prophecy of the perpetual and parasitic male which had not concerned her at all this morning, had now become less amusing. For no words, however plausible, could weigh against that tender and despairing grip that had clutched her a moment since, while the mimic soldiers pranced and Sebastian's cynical words made ugly echo among these simple unalterable things. Such as the old woman at the window opposite jumping a child above the flower-pots so that it might see what all that noise meant in the square. The old woman was taking the child most seriously and pointing out dogs, and the stork nest, and possibly several small members of the family gaping in the square; explaining how brave and significant it all was, quite as though the whole world was but a background for this latest arrival on it. (But in a village a baby *is* the very latest news, thought Lavinia Reade.)

Simple things, she thought. Simple, unalterable things. There was the woman with the tiny child in the scarlet boots, who came each evening to the inn corner to meet her husband home from work. When he appeared far down the street she would hold the child high for them to catch a first sight of each other, and then start running. Such a swift, lovely, unalterable impulse, the woman's holding-up of the child to its father home from work. And when she had remarked on the profusion of walnuts on the trees lining the roads, she had been told: Ah, a good year for nuts means that many women are pregnant! That, too, was a lovely eternal thing, linking their women so warmly, so unquestioningly, with the earth, sharing the effortless burden of trees and fields.

How pleasant, here among these people. Why could one not live here always? This village was big enough. This was a world. A woman's world: world without end. Why go back? To what? To words? To the hermaphroditism of modern woman in a modern world? To that bright protective-colouring of good fellowship that is life in a great city? From a long dissembled frustration to the dissatisfactions of old age? Must she, too, capitulate? Of all ugly decaying things, a woman dissatisfied. How wearying it was, that modern indecency: the frustrated woman. And how futile, seeing that nothing could be done about it. A woman's dissatisfaction led nowhere. Women should be pleasant peaceful creatures, generous in youth and wise in age. What more could one ask of them? What more could they ask? Men might be restless, because men could achieve. But women achieve mostly a half-achievement, and at best nothing that a man cannot better. Except the holding-up of a child with scarlet boots to see its father in the distance; or explaining with extreme seriousness to a doll-face peering over the geranium pots, as though nothing was so important in all the world as the proper understanding between grandmother and her very latest grandchild. Perhaps if Aunt Deborah had not been so strict, so coldly hostile, and she had not run away and had never written that absurd napoleonic letter: when I am famous I shall return! (Whenever she saw black earth she thought of Norfolk and of how in winter the powdery frost sits on it like sugar on plum-pudding and the windmills are like old men or witches with faggots on their backs, and sometimes on Sunday afternoons when one has been more than usually severely punished like a Cross being lifted once again.) Here in this changeless setting, in some angular house, a husband with few words, whom one would help in his fields, a table-full of children, one's own wine in the cellars, one's food stored for the winter, and washing-days and baking bread, and never again to say a bright or witty thing, and to become old without noticing it, having no regrets. Here where it was a matter of man and beast: food and shelter. For they were shelters, not houses, either for their animals or themselves, or for the storing of food. And all the sounds were animal sounds. Hens and children. Swallow calling swallow. And man preparing for winter as for a siege.

A voice cried excitedly: Here they come!

For the soldiers were gone, faces were at the windows, people were looking over her shoulders, and beside her Otto in his black Sunday clothes was leaning on the sill.

First the children in white and pale blue innocence, supplying with short steps and high astringent voices the pace and rhythm to which the procession moved; and then the priest whose lean face wasted its subtlety on the village air (a disappointed man, thought Lavinia Reade); and then several handsome young novices from the seminary, a few sisters of mercy, pale gulls with spread wings, planeing behind them. Several saints, male and female, swayed howdah-wise above the procession, but which exactly on this particular day had risen and gone to Heaven was a difficult choice. The men were painted plaster, but the women were gracious in gaudy skirts stiff with tinsel, the large lumps of glass jewellery on their crowns and breasts glinting prettily in the light and distracting from the enormous bunches of grapes with which they were hung. For grapes were everywhere: the real reason and the best one. Hung over Saint Sebastian's arrows and round the women's hands and throats, threaded through Saint Joseph's halo and over Saint

Anthony's outstretched arms; everywhere wreaths of white and purple grapes in a profusion of leaf and tendril. Re-enthroned Bacchus moved in sober measure to the Agnus Dei. Now came the girls who left the village each morning for the Schledstadt factories, very self-conscious and very condescending in their silk stockings, their high-heeled shoes, their rouged lips. (Another generation and we'll have millions more tin cans and no children, said a voice.) And lastly the old women, clutching long candles in tenacious yellowed claws. Miss Reade who had seen them at work in the vineyards was surprised. Why are they the last? she wanted to know. Without them there would be no grapes!

Some-one pointed proudly to Karl's grandmother, an astonishingly robust and monumental old lady carrying a heavy banner as readily as though it were an umbrella.

—Your grandmother certainly is a remarkable woman, Sebastian said to Karl.

—She is silent, said the youth indifferently. An excellent thing in grandmothers.

Miss Reade looked on without pleasure. The town-crier and his little drum was a more amusing sight, yet it brought scarcely one head to a window. Besides it was such a joyless slow-moving thing, out of harmony with its true purpose and reduced to the measure of a few subdued children chanting in questionable Latin. And Sunday, as usual, seemed to have fallen on them like a blight, leaving them ill at ease and incredibly mediocre. How drearily people misunderstood their purpose and the harmony of a setting! These should be flushed with love and wine and rosy-cheeked children. How willingly people denied themselves; and what a constant betrayal they were, friends or strangers, however little one asked of them; by their stupidity or by their meanness, or an unawareness, or an indifference. They failed. They fell short. They cheated. In the kingdom of the blind the one-eyed may be king, thought Lavinia Reade. The two-eyed is outcast.

Otto seeing the look on her face, misconstrued it. Some-one must have told her the man was gone. Or had she guessed? Women had an instinct for such things. And she was sad and unusually pale. Otto had a romantic eye; he would have been surprised to learn, among other things, that Miss Reade was no longer nineteen. He admired her. She gave him an impression of good-humour and courage. And there was no French mincing nonsense about her; no airs; no paint and powder; no pin-point heels. A companion for any man, thought Otto. And of how many women could a man say that? And Otto felt a sudden anger against the fool who, for a moment and as he left, had seemed to clutch at his hand like a drowning man. Enjoying himself now, thought Otto. Ingrate. Deserter. And where could he find such another? Not where he was looking now, thought Otto. He'd soon find his mistake. And serve him right if it was too late.

Thoughts which would have surprised Harrion who, tired of watching the liquefaction of the Strasbourg houses in the oily surface of the canal, had at last found a bench in a park, and was sitting there lost in the contemplation of an ornamental flower-bed.

He must have been hungry, for he could think of nothing but hors-d'œuvre.

O men were gay and filled with a bright nonsense! They saw things as children saw them: for the first time; where women saw them with the old old eyes of women, nothing escaping them. It was as though men were born with new eyes, and women with women's eyes.

Particularly at this hour the Wynstub was loud with masculine good-humour, drink, argument, and laughter. Not what was said, nor how wise, nor how foolish, but a zest that gave to the hour its charm and emphasis. Here and thus men had argued, laughed, drunk the centuries away; and would again. Inevitably at this evening hour it would be alive with such sounds; the same arguments would break, the same complaints be made, the same conclusions reached; as serious, as ribald, and as ephemeral.

It had the mellowness (she thought) of the Dutch still-life hung, ever-crooked, above the door. An advertisement, a cheap German oleograph used by a local poultry merchant; but no oleograph however cheap could make vulgar the Dutch school. Perhaps because their values were true; fruit, game, people grouped about their tables, above their music. They had their conventions. No Fra Angelico saint was more frail than the transparent asparagus bundles of these incomparable food and flower painters. A glass half-filled or overturned; a few nuts broken in the foreground; a fly; a lady-bird; a lemon trailing a luminous curl. For drama: the fish's eye.

Caught in the swirl of sound, Miss Reade was marvelling at how good men were, how unself-conscious; how gay and how nonsensical. (A fly falls in some beer and one of them drinks it, or to every one's dismay sees it in time!, and all the business of cards and argument is held-up for the laughter to stop, and stop only to break again louder and merrier than before.) Women: why could they not laugh? Why was the divine male gift of nonsense denied them? Why had men alone this gift of effortless gaiety? Did Eve bite it off with the apple, that vague female resentment as though life must be always pleasant, made of an elegant, fadeless, rosy texture; and that sense of brooding responsibility, that censorious outlook, that small intolerance? Man laughed (Lavinia Reade was thinking) without effort or after-thought; yet man worked, worked and saved and cared for and fed wife and children, fought, invented, rolled the earth along somehow on his back, and was always ready to laugh at nothing; particularly at a fly dropped in a mug of beer and all but swallowed.

—And after that what do we do when we want to honour a man? We put a chain round his neck and call him a watchdog of the city! (A dig this at some local councillor who drank only at l'Agneau Noir.)

To which the owner of the superb red mushroom of a nose, prime cellar-grown under the barrel, said: And where's the difference between them, anyway, except that one lifts an elbow at every corner and the other a leg?

At intervals the group of young Germans on a walking tour broke into song, in that lush German voice of a man who has eaten and drunk well, and sings to thank for it. They were noticeably German with their rounded buttocks, handsome blond faces, and pink moist lips.

Now Lorwich was talking on wine countries and their supremacy in Art, and proving that the picturesque is a remnant of barbarism.

A voice (Otto, she thought half-turning) boomed: . . . a case of do not touch my goods. But stealing itself is not immoral. It is only that it affects the man who had the money and now has it no longer!

An uproar, a thunderclap of protest and agreement. A glance risked at Madame. But Madame was laughing; perched on the black horse-hair sofa so curiously like herself, her soul's sister. Madame is in extreme good-humour; for the verdict is not till next week; the trial is again postponed, and her importance is no longer momentary but cumulative.

The large man with the béret pulled down so tightly that it seemed to have hit him on the head, was saying that you can give them the freshest eggs and still they will make the heaviest omelettes. A matter of climate. No wonder they left their own country and were to be found the world over! What other people had ever been so eager to leave their own part of the earth? When the English boasted themselves world colonisers and victors, they should remember their climate and be more humble. A cold selfish people. The climate again. No endearment except for the dog. No sugar except for the horse. And a people utterly without religion. Had they ever seen an English clergyman? The bony sort with large teeth and long noses and reedy necks wriggling in a large collar? But it was unbelievable! It was something made for Christmas to amuse the children.

Sebastian was beating on the table as though thumping himself on the back. He was insisting that genteel people work more than the honest worker, only they produce nothing. Hence genteel discontent and the worker's hearty disposition. Whilst the simple person (the worker, the peasant) is positive, he finds joy only in positive things: a good feed, a good drink, a good laugh. The genteel person finds joy only in genteel pleasures: a little snicker, a little bitter word, a little criticism of appearances: in fact, in purely negative non-existent things. A hearty man understands a solid hefty female: he gets, so to speak, a good meal out of her. The genteel male will find his pleasure in parading some feathers and paint and does not ask for a woman to be there at all.

—The fascination of glass is the fascination of the eye. . . . Take this dark green-black bottle. A pool of water has an hypnotic effect. In an open space, a light in the distance is eerie, haunting. And the moon, the sycophantic moon staring a man in the face. . . . Instinct then has always been a finer instrument than science. Much that science has dismissed she has had to re-admit. If telepathy exists it means there is a human receiving and broadcasting set. One (that of science) was invented yesterday. One is eternal. We may dismiss such things as phantasy. But our mechanical receiving and broadcasting set is primitive and unfinished compared with telepathy. In other words, Science is coarse and full of errors where Nature is subtle and infallible. To come to the ridiculous: you say to a peasant (an illiterate): there is a machine and you put a pig in at one end and it comes out a sausage at the other. He laughs. He laughs at mechanical science: you are affronted and amazed at his stupidity. But when he says to you: I was in a field and I felt that something was wrong and I had to stop work and ran home to find that the horse had kicked my little son and killed or injured him, you (the scientist) laugh. That is the coarse and imperfect (mechanical) laughing at the infallible and subtle. Saying peasant means, of course, a man nearer to Nature than the scientist. If we knew more, we should probably know why Nature gives us this instinct of fear for the unknown.

Possibly to preserve us. To prevent us falling into a trap or facing a danger. For all we know, whatever is mystery may be Nature's self-preservation for man. . . .

One of the young Germans, angry at the new red-brick fire-station stark in its utilitarian rawness in the street behind the Gemeinehüss, was saying: They keep history so sacred in a book and obliterate it in life. They give away the original and keep a description of it.

Madame said impatiently: But, of course, your history books will put out our fires.

Everyone laughed; no doubt excessively to propitiate Bellona, who acknowledged the tribute by polishing the rim of a glass with contentious vigour. For a fraction of a second her glance intercepted that of the English Mees. He is gone! said Madame's bright malicious eye. He is gone!

Let him go! cried Lavinia Reade's quickened pulse. Let him go! And good-bye to all regrets and yesterday's mistakes. For now she knew that she would always be as foolish as she was now, even when she was quite an old woman. For always she would be in the midst of life and feeling. She was not one of life's spectators, but its ardent participant. How then regret mistakes, when one could but repeat and repeat them? She who lived too intensely to see herself as the centre of the situation until it was too late, or long past. But never again would she be ashamed when she laughed or cried or found things more than she could bear, only to forget them a month hence. She knew that this must always be, for hers was the secret of the artist: intensity. Where there was no intensity there was no enthusiasm, and where there was no enthusiasm there was deadness and decay. And to be without emotion was to be old. For the old are without emotion. It hardens like their arteries, and is politely called being wise. But intensity was youth. And not merely youth but eternal youth. It might be frowned on. It might not be fashionable. It might not be correct: but it was right. For intensity was life. And life she had abundantly. She was not fortunate in her love affairs. She gave before being asked, and again when they had ceased asking. She was the type of woman who runs calling through the street: Gilbert! Gilbert! And to the very end, if there was any giving to be done, she would be the one who gave. But never mind. Some women had security; security of affection, security of possessions. But security was not for her. Only when she was tired, disappointed, sick or fearful of old age, did she long for this security and unimaginativeness of other women. But were it offered she would not accept it. For she took life as men take it: as it came. And all that it had taught her could be summed-up in: now. Now. Not yesterday nor to-morrow: but now. This hour. This moment. This was all. This the answer to every question: *now*. Later one was swept aside like a floor that is tidied, new sand is sprinkled like earth on one's grave and others sit and drink and argue. But there is Now. And that was the sum-total of all happiness. That was the secret of intensity, of life, of eternal youth. And she thought of the many people she knew, interesting enough people, drifting in far-away London as in the middle depths of an ocean, and all of them neither happy nor unhappy, but only distracted. And she thought that whatever else she lost in life, never must she lose this sense of living for the moment, and of denying that moment nothing: for what was each hour but a gift that brought one nearer death?

Miss Reade shook back her head, an unconsciously arrogant movement, as though to hold it high, high above all other heads; and Sebastian happening to look up just then was reminded of Maurice Barrès: J'aime la femme un peu folle: l'inspirée.

But he did not mention it, being occupied with an exquisitely sensitive drunken song:

> Ah, ciel! quelle ivresse!
> Quatre seins et quatre fesses. . . .

—No, no, no. A matter of climate. Catholicism and wine. Protestantism and beer. And if you wanted a practical working religion then Catholicism was the more amenable of the two, for it had the only pagan rites left. Its devotees might lose anything from their virginity to a buttonhook and there was always some-one to complain to about it.

—And did God model or carve when he was making the English? And did he blow into them a soul or just a little wind? And why did this most carnivorous of nations have its teeth set like rabbits?

—But in a village the burden is shared equally, each man and woman contributing. In the city father is a little clerk and all the family lives on his back.

—Destroy a human being in five seconds and it is a crime. Destroy him in thirty years and it is right and natural. What do you see when you go for a walk? Church—fort—castle, castle—fort—church, surrounding each village. Wherever human beings are gathered there you found the castle and fort to milk them. Christ said Feed them. The Church misunderstood and sheared them.

But Lorwich seemed to think it was being taken altogether too seriously. Probably it was all an advertisement for the Jewish genius for being born in a manger and ending in the bank manager's chair.

Whereupon Sebastian (doubtless wishing he had thought of it himself) raised a heavy head and called out: Maestro Rafaello, non te n'incaricar!

—Perspiration for the many, my dear friend. Perspiration for the many and inspiration for the few.

—What a waste it was! What a waste! And it will come again. Not in my day, but you, young woman, you will see it. . . . (The old man nods and nods as though this makes his prophecy unassailable. He is telling Miss Reade about the War, in which he lost two sons. He is very old and brittle, and as though held together secretly by wire and string, as old people so often seem. The marionette made man.) All the vines were ruined. What could one expect with only women and children in the fields and vineyards, and the artillery commanding the mountains. No, his sons were not killed in France. In Poland. POLAND. Ya, Poland. Poland was an awful place, it seemed. Poor, hungry, filthy. The people live like pigs. All in rags and on a crust of bread. It was a shock to the Alsatian troops, used to a good table and warm beds and plenty in the cellars. They hated Poland and the stupid superstitious Poles. Only the churches were rich and filled with gold, and jewels sewn all over the statues of their saints. But my sons said our pigs lived warmer! Then why were they sent to Poland? Herrje, because you had to send them as far away as you could or they'd come home again: and rightly, too, with the corn and wine all spoiling and nothing but women and children scurrying about like frightened hens, and the soldiers trampling everything and always drunk and threatening civilians. That's why they were in Poland. They sent the Paris troops to Africa, the southern troops to the north, the northerns south or overseas, and our boys to Poland. Because you can shoot deserters by the handful but not by the battalion. That was one of the gravest problems of the War, especially for France and Belgium. It takes a great deal more than patriotism for a boy who has been brought up on the land to see the corn trampled. They don't mind fighting in the towns, that's all right, that's all towns are for because towns don't count. But it hurts them most in the fields. . . .

I should have been called Pandora! she thought; full of hope again. Not that she knew that it was hope. She knew only that she was alive and at peace with herself once more. Even this old man with his prophecy of War could not frighten her now. Not even a prophetic glimpse of the folly of men in a world without vision, world in which she must live, the old had made it, the young must accept it, and all who came after must accept what they found here. It didn't matter! One was alive. Only the moment mattered, now and always. Once again she felt that exhilaration of the blood when one is so aware of being alive that one could die and not know it until long afterwards. And that, of course, meant the return of hope. For hope attacks, where possession can only defend. (Which may be why few rich people are really happy, thought Lavinia Reade.) So that hope creates energy and energy creates life. Against evidence, against experience, still hope does not give up. Because, of course, everything had disappointed (did one sit down to think of it), beginning with the nightingale. How angry, how cheated she had felt, waiting, waiting, sitting on the windowsill, her knees drawn up to her chin, her toes tucked in her long flannel nightdress, waiting for the first fluted notes of *La donna è mobile* to come trilling above the woods. What, was that all? But a blackbird was prettier! Was it for this that one had pinched oneself awake until the whole house slept? With their: sings like a nightingale! What *could* one expect from a nightingale but to sing like an operatic tenor? And not even a ballad. And everything was a little like that. But in the end one emerged. One discarded Make Believe at last for the happiness of being alive. Reality transcended the illusory, and this was life's reward, the having of one's finger-tips tingling with a certain drunkenness in merely being alive, and being enclosed, as now, in a drowsy warmth of friendly voices.

This exhilaration of life was her gift, though she had never understood it before, to those she met or had loved. But only Rollo had known. Rollo loving both God and Mammon, and deciding that though God might be necessary Mammon was indispensable. M'Hugh was not among those who mattered either to God or Mammon. Harrion had known it, and because of something secret and confused, had for a time extinguished it. But not for long.

—I should have been called Pandora! thought Lavinia Reade, and would have liked to lean her head out of the window and get it soaked in rain. For outside the rain was bearing down on the stones as though to crush them. It had begun an hour ago, the first drops ringing on the ground like large pennies, and then a summer storm had set in, whipping up the air, gathering up the winds, washing everything clean, washing everything away, making things fresh and new again. Rain was an eager thing.

(But Harrion, who loathed it, lay on the bed in a fitful doze. The miauling of a child came to him through an open window. The roof drip-dripped. On, on and on, the sounds of water flowing. It was as though the ceaseless battering was a deluge threatening to bear him down; he put out a hand and clutched the edge of the bed. The rain poured on. Through it all the crying child hiccoughed meaningless things.)

. . . and so you think he has the right to appeal to the rest of the world to interfere in the Russian religious persecutions? And it is not political, no? No! Very well. But when in 1922 the Turks were massacring the Armenians and a deputy of Armenian refugees begged the Pope to help them . . . I know, dear children. I suffer. I am praying for you. And they were gently pushed on to Cardinal Gasparri. We know, dear children. We suffer. We are praying for you. Yes, says the deputation, but can you not make some public gesture? Cannot our cause be put before the world? Cannot prayers be said in every Catholic Church throughout the world for the souls of our poor martyrs? Ah that . . . *that,* no! For that we have no power, dear children. . . .

—What's that? said Sebastian, suddenly alert.

It was repeated, vehemently. The Pope interfering in Russia's affairs and appealing to the world. But when the Turks were massacring the Armenians . . .

—When the *what?*

The narrator was losing patience. When the Turks were massacring the Armenians . . .

Sebastian groaned. Good God! Haven't they caught Michael Arlen *yet?*

Some-one suggested that the Book of Revelation was the work of a man in the last stages of D.T.'s. Didn't he first see two candelabra, and the next time he looked they were six, and then they were nine. . . . If the Bible survived it would be thanks to sailors!

Lapped by the warmth and friendly flow of voices, Miss Reade smiled upon the room. The young German student, who throughout the evening had been trying unsuccessfully to attract her attention, responded eagerly. But her smile was unseeing, impartial. It rested awhile on Simeon Fenn, languidly suffering this plebeian hour for love's sake; and she wondered again (as she never ceased to wonder) wherein his vaunted attraction lay, and decided finally that the fact that Lorwich had need of him temporarily justified his existence. And thought how each and every vice was acceptable, except meanness: for meanness alone of them all could not bc explained by an excess of emotion or pleasure. It was the one vice that was not a misdirection of energy or generosity.

. . . till we come to *l'obolo di San Pietro*. Only the Pope could have found the way to exploit both worlds so neatly by making earth and heaven work for him. What a super rag-and-bone shop they had started in Rome! Pieces of rag and bits of bone hawked down the ages by super-ragmen. . . .

Whereupon Lorwich urging that one God was ample for the shop-keeper though inadequate to the creative artist, and (as an impartial observer) stressing the dour provincialism of the Protestant sects, struck the final and victorious blow for Catholicism by leaning across the table and saying quietly: Tell me. Which would you rather: dine with the Borgias or take tea with Dean Inge?

S trasbourg is a diversion of the Comic Muse; a work of the Foolish Virgins. Unserious, cross-stitched houses appear to have been playing leap-frog and to have been caught in the act. One looks up, they steady themselves. Their smile is Voltairian. The swaying argus-eyed roofs stare, wink, hiccough. At no hour are they quite sober.

Yet the effect is deliberate; nothing has been left to chance. All is composed as a flower-piece; the whole linnet-coloured with care and tenderness. The river moves thickly, the crude oil surface unhurried, and at its edge the houses in full sail anchor a moment. After the night's storm the air is fresh and pleasing, and the activity everywhere is Monday's rebuke to Sunday's idleness. In the wash-houses the women kneel in their boxes of straw, scrubbing with large brushes, thrusting out their arms from time to time to swish the linen in the oily waters. Clothes baskets litter everything, and cats, and children. Above towers the Cathedral's single spire, that mighty amphora raised to heaven. The bells begin a deep, slow, reverberation; now a warning, now a command. In such a voice God spoke to Adam, to Michelangelo.

Harrion stood up. The young woman with the child in her arms, who had shared the bench, watched him from sight, wondering why she should be filled with pity for him. She was pale and sickly looking, as though the child had been wrenched from her leaving her bloodless and transparent.

Unmistakably the produce of a picturesque old town, he was think-ing. In small dark rooms, pale, ill children, ugliness and ill-health on all their faces; bad teeth, unhealthy skins. (An epidemic of infantile paralysis was spreading alarmingly just then in the Bas Rhin, but one did not need to wait on the newspapers for the information.) The more narrow and picturesque the street, the sicklier seemed the children. The people themselves were white-faced, unindividual, hard-working, *abbruti;* with ill-fitting clothes of mediocre colour. Faces matched houses, stubbornly out of square. But in their physical disability lay their architectural advantage, as by their faces one saw how it came that they could no more have built symmetrically than the Italians could have built asymmetrically.

Little blue soldiers bobbed about, their humorous alert French faces in immediate contrast. But blue was the wrong colour. Blue became an eyesore. Everywhere the French had put up their hard, Parisian-blue plaques and taken away the German script, so that the houses were no longer written across, their names clinging like tendrils to a vine, and spread to the grateful eye as a page from Gutenberg's own Bible. Everywhere the beautiful wrought-ironwork had been taken down, lost or shut away in museums, and replaced by bits of white and blue enamelled tin.

Suddenly between the streets the Cathedral hangs like some precious tapestry that has caught fire in a thousand places. High above the world in an ecstasy of their own the bells plunge and crash, as though hammering at the door of heaven itself. But the Cathedral square was thronged with people. He hesitated. But something of immediate importance seemed about to happen, and before he could retreat the crowd had grown larger. He was shut in by a troupe of boy-scouts whose willing knees seemed (as usual) frail for such an exaggeration of cooking array and rucksack; and by eager voluble Americans with their strange insensitive children.

Standing directly beneath it, the Cathedral had the glow of rusty ironwork. The treatment of the stone is the treatment of wrought-iron, as involved, as wayward. Here has been done with stone what the Chinese did with ivory; air has been let in, a third dimension added. At intervals blue doves rose and scattered, exchanging scrolls for apostolic beards, cherub heads for saintly wrists.

But the crowd was moving, and the effect was hypnotic. Many brave men have done many brave deeds, but among them has not as yet been the moving backward through a mass of advancing crowd. So that it was only when he was inside, wedged at the back against a wall, that he found he was in the side chapel, given-up to the worship of its famed astronomical Clock. But going out now was too great an effort, even had it been possible. The attendants were fussy and irritable enough, with their brusque little rudenesses and their Silence là-bas! Silence!

There was too much light, though the doors were now closed. It came in broad shafts from windows behind the altar, through stiff staring apostles, bright blue, bright red, bright green; new as a pack of unshuffled cards. How misunderstood, these modern efforts at stained glass. The colours are crude, the pieces of glass are large, where the colours should not only be sober in the extreme, but the pieces of glass minute and held together by lead-work in such a way that there is more lead than either glass or colour. The modern effect becomes that of a bar-parlour by daylight, when it should be that of a forest at sunset. He turned gratefully to a small rose-window glowing like jewelled earth, and remembered that traveller's tale of the old craftsmen using the blood of traitors for the sombreness of their reds. But the blood of innocent men would scarcely have been too high a price for such perfection. And he thought how the impermanence of to-day was not the result of war or the decline in religious belief, though that counted, but was due to the impermanence of the goods of life; the manufactured goods, the plethora of religious beliefs; and the impermanence of these goods is responsible for the sense of impermanence in spiritual matters. When men built this they knew that it was for ever. They built their homes for ever, their beliefs for ever, and, in some unfathomable way, their literature and their arts for ever. We build for to-day, we live for to-day, we think for to-day, we die to-day.

But the *Silence!* and the sh-shings were growing louder. It needed but a minute to the hour for the little figures in the mechanical clock to do their turn, bob out, be blessed, all except Judas, when the Cock must crow and flap his wings; and then everyone would breathe a sigh of awed relief (as though wireless, cinema, refrigerators, telephones, wrist-watches, and other hourly instances of ingenious mechanism were unknown) and push back again into the street.

Yet to have seen one thing is to have seen all things. A grain of sand and all shores, an incoming tide and the farthest ocean. A certain number of words, and nothing is left to say. If this was all and afterwards there was nothing: then this was not enough. And if there were other worlds, then this was but a waste of time. Christ's remark about gaining the world and losing one's soul was so good as to be unnecessary. For who has lost his soul has lost his world. Once attained the solitudes are too bleak. The urges, good or ill, of one's fellow-men are no longer impressive. Life's most urgent function remains that of defecation, and man's most pressing need washes down to the rivers

(however weary or not these may be). The rest is a lid to cover putre-
faction; a warding-off of the inevitable nothing. The earth contracts to
a few square feet, seeing that it is bounded individually by man, and
man is sewer-bound. (Which may partly explain why the naïveté of a
Jean-Jacques Rousseau can undermine the godhead of a Voltaire. And
not only can, but invariably does.)

It was then, just as the first stroke summoned the first apostle, that
Harrion looked up. But it was not at the Clock, with the others, that he
looked. He was seeing for the first time that column rising like smoke,
umbilical cord binding earth and heaven, revealing itself slowly
without visible beginning and end; and understanding how it came that
he rose at the sound of the bells as though summoned.

If the window was blood then this was bone, for whatever is austere
and sepulchral in the Gothic was here in this fluted column carved from
the very bones of acolytes, from the emaciated ribs of saints. And there
suspended, leaning a little forward, her lips to the swirl of trumpet
along whose length her Gothic fingers rested, her wings in shadow,
brave, outward-looking, poised for stony flight, she looked down at
him. Up, up, up the fluted column in ascension perpetual: calm, other,
sexless. It is looking up that makes one giddy, and leaves one dazed,
cutting off reason in the pushing back of the head. Such the messenger,
such the message. And it is for him, for he alone had looked up and
answered it. All sick things must be thrust aside. All that is tired and
sick, he thought, is human garbage. It seemed to him then that she
smiled. It was not impartial. It was the bringing of a message and to
those who understood it, she smiled. Now it was a matter of days or
hours, yet when the moment came to him (he felt) she would know.

Yet it was an ugly thing, seen face to face. Not death itself, but that
which came after; those about one, all the unpleasantness of disposing
of a dead thing, the putting of it in a box and the wheeling of it away,
and the digging of the fewest possible inches of earth in which to hide
it. For now he saw, accepting as he did the decision, that the horror
of death lay in what they did to one afterwards, when there was no
redress, no restraint, no privacy. And he shrank from the sudden
realisation that soon he, who recoiled from contact with his fellow-
men, who all his life had feared the crowd, he, who with difficulty had
taken another's hand in his own, would lie packed among the crowd in
death, shoulder to shoulder, depth to depth, powerless, indiscriminate,
uncaring. Then not in the loneliness of the grave lay its horror, but in its
promiscuity. Then not even in death was one alone. Yet she smiled.

Suspended in an ecstasy of stone in ascension perpetual, lifted above man and his tumult, one looked down and one smiled. Granted that, one would smile. At last one could smile if one might lean thus in endless half-light from a piece of tessellated stone; or swing in the light of day from a dizzy height looking downward with sightless eyes; or standing on a shaft of filigree point a hand to lure a pigeon, and rest seven hundred years.

The rainbow struck the earth in a shaft of light: the javelin Saul threw in anger. A bowl of light has been shaken and cracked and the pieces float, pause, drift, and sink, leaving on the sky the justification of the soul's folly, the damnation of common sense, all the miracles of the Middle Ages, all mysticism, all mystification. Cities of the plain, ascensions, annunciations, fiery chariot trails, rays whose swords pierce infidel and martyr, blue holes ripped in the grey through which chant the heavenly hosts, and in the distance the hills where God walked with his prophets.

—It was worth the bites, said Miss Reade at last, slapping her bare arms.

But Ittswiller was still a mile away. And at the thought of turning away from it all, from the great length of plain spread at her feet (for that pencil *was* the Cathedral holding a Paternal finger above the plain, and that at the other end should be Colmar, and that range the Black Forest, and everywhere the apple-red roofs of villages, the white bony spires of their churches accenting the plain) she mused on all that it had meant, and of how the symbolism of what unconsciously one had dismissed as another of the sacred fairy tales of one's childhood, was so simple and obvious that how in the world had it escaped her till now. For she saw it all, standing on a high hill, looking down, and about to turn away. And I will give you all the cities of the earth! So He had stood there, like this, looking down at the distances and turning it over in his mind, knowing that they were afraid and would offer any bribe, and dallying with power and wealth and all its implications. For He was sorely tempted. Only of course they had made it unreal by bringing in the Devil, so that with childhood one outgrew it as one outgrew other childish tales, and years later when one never opened a Bible for months on end (except to prove that it was not Shakespeare) one suddenly saw its undimmed significance. And actually that was all one needed to know about Christ: that and the casting of the first stone. For to the East miracles were nothing new, and prove little except that the masses were the fools then that they are now; and the trial was not more interesting than the trial of Joan of Arc, or the recantation of Galileo, or the excommunication of Spinoza; but the struggle between power and integrity, or gain and conviction, between the retaining and losing of one's essential self, struggle which in greater or lesser degree each carried within himself, *that* they managed somehow to distort for children so that it lay useless and half-remembered as something very noble, very remote, very Guido Reni.

—I'm glad that I'm not rich, said Miss Reade suddenly; forgetting that let alone all the cities of the earth, no one was going to offer her the nearest village unless she got-going and walked to it.

—For I should so loathe to be cluttered-up with possessions, said Miss Reade emphatically. And turned her back on the sunset.

But Sebastian reproved her. One should be more tolerant. One should remember that of all mankind the rich alone enjoyed the privilege of never growing-up. They alone were allowed, without ill consequence to themselves, to remain children all their lives; and might therefore without effort to themselves be dressed and fed and amused. The French must dress and feed them; the Italian provide them with a playground; the Jew with theatres and entertainments. For unlike children in only one particular, they could not provide their own amusement. Therefore the Italian had to let them in his garden, sing to them, and serve their food. The French had to dress and perfume them, and prepare that food. The Jew had to bring them furs, jewels, entertainments, and luxury. To this add the shooting of any bird or beast that was at all swift or graceful, as an excuse for a little lust and exercise.

And just as children who wish to play undisturbed avoid grown-ups who are sure to ask them pertinent questions, so to them the rest of the world was untouchable. Abroad they communicated only with ruins. They shook hands with Museum pieces and patronised the dead Cæsars. (Though not if the effort could be avoided.) For what were trains-deluxe and Splendide-Splendides but guarantees of isolation? They will travel thousands of miles, only if they are sure of finding their neighbours at their journey's end. They will go only where their neighbours go: possibly to demonstrate to each other that they each have done the same thing. For one must remember they are children. They merely extend the game of hide-and-seek from the nursery to the outside world.

Miss Reade considered this. She said: And do you really make as much money as they say you do, Sebastian?

He reassured her. He also said that if he didn't, he wouldn't work. He said there were only two kinds of writers: those who made money, and those who tried but couldn't. It so happened that he could and did. And had he not been able to do so, he would have given it up long ago and tried his hand at something more lucrative.

At which Miss Reade, who was of a romantic disposition, laughed; convinced that he was teasing her.

Ittswiller (unable to compete with ardent sunsets and proffered cities) proved a dull little anticlimax of a village. But it was all prinked out with flags and bunting, and the children had their heads in curling rags. For to-morrow was a day of days. The new bells were to be consecrated by an imposing, though minor, Bishop.

They found the bells propped on a heavy scaffolding inside the church; very bright and factory-new, and the engraving on their rather pompous stomachs told how in War they had been melted into guns for their country's defence, and how when peace was come again a grateful country gave them back once more to the service of God. This day: this month: this year.

For a while they had stood staring in silence, until Sebastian had said very quietly:

—Having ceased the destruction of the body, they will now resume the destruction of the mind. . . .

Whereupon, in sheer delight, Miss Reade had looked up at him in rueful admiration. But as she could not know the look that lit her face at that moment, she never realised quite how it happened; though once again she was to discover that although the spine may serve some useful purpose, the lips have a disconcerting way of containing most of the essential nerves.

—But this, gasped Miss Reade (whose thoughts but half-an-hour since had been so exalted). But this is a church. . . .

—But there is a carpet on the floor, urged Sebastian, who was very much in earnest.

But there were also footsteps outside. So they wandered again into the courtyard. Sebastian flushed and extremely annoyed, Miss Reade calm and with confidence in the future. Yet she leaned against the first tree she came to as though her knees were unwilling to support her further; and suddenly looking-up and seeing that it was an apple tree, impulsively picked the first at hand, bit in it, and held it out to him.

For now at last we know, she said, in which season Eve tempted Adam.

H e seemed to have been walking a long time and to be always in the same place. Or not so much walking as prowling round an hour that drew no nearer.

In the August heat Paris was its familiar untidy self; very much the French: why should I use a suitcase when string and paper will do as well? Here one might pause mile after mile and never know that anything new existed in the world; old angles, old architecture, old writing of signs, old furniture shops; a gigantic bric-à-brac; Napoleon's writing-table. One walked on through a confusion of Bébé Cadum and Nicholas and scarlet cheeks and cheap (female) scents and shoddy clothes, and grey and white houses against their grey and white clouds, and all the good standing about in the street in the friendly haphazard of a long *marché aux puces* through which one picks a way. For air, that sweetish blend of incense, garlic, drains, and river.

But he had left the river long ago. Hours ago, it seemed, when the thought that three o'clock might come on him unaware and find him far from his objective, miles out of his way, had for a moment made him physically weak with fear so that his hand had trembled as he put back the book he was fingering sightlessly, and had begun walking in the direction he had avoided all the morning. Curious these scruples he had developed, and the sudden protective self-loathing, as certain men develop a physical horror of their wives and feel themselves contaminated each time that resistance is no longer possible. No one seeing his quick step could have guessed the reluctance with which he climbed the steep street, much less have understood his morbid pretence at being in quite a different part of the city. Yet bandage his eyes and he could have passed correctly the butchers' shops with their gilt horses' heads, the rolls of linoleum and strips of cheap carpet, the quincallerie, the narrow sordid shops spilling their cheap goods on the pavement, the untidy *bistros* with the fly-blown paper on the tables, the sickly beggars. For this was the slope of Menilmontant leading to Père Lachaise, and the first impression had been indelible in that detailed stereoscopic way in which the mind recalls at will the few backgrounds by which it has set store.

And here already was the long stone wall and the side gate he used, for he disdained the imposing main avenue with its steps and ascending cypresses, bronze busts and poetic willow, and trumpery frieze of naked huddled men and women dragging children and the aged after them through an open doorway, and all the other theatrical accessories that tricked it out in a semblance of hope and decency. For was he not an intimate? No sitting in the auditorium for him, who might loiter at will in the wings and lift the curtain on the make-believe.

But now that the wall rose in front of him, Harrion relaxed his step; and as though to drag out still more subtly the pleasures of anticipation, lingered before the last of that dreary array of pokey shops, littered with all the sordid traffic that goes on around the dead; counting again the pots of dusty leaves, the weary bunches of dark leafless flowers (for not a flower that was gay or vital), the beaded wire wreaths of neutral colouring, the trite farewells in enamelled tin of drab design, the whole reminiscent of old serge, of cheerless' rooms: a last unlovely echo of their spent lives.

But already the air had a different taste to it; a taste one never forgot, that burnt for hours in mouth and nostrils, so that no smoke is ever afterwards quite the same, even if it is only the burning of leaves in a garden.

An icy moment of panic seized him, till he looked at his wrist and was reassured. It needed twenty minutes to the hour. He turned away from the window and let himself in at the gate with an almost proprietary air of absorbed excitement, passed familiarly between the graves without giving them a glance, and turned down a narrow pathway to the left.

But one of the attendants who saw him coming got up from a bench and came to meet him.

—Le gros-Michel n'est pas là, he whispered. Il est allé casser la croute.

Harrion stopped; frowned. Would he be back? He would be back; the attendant adding that the ceremony could hardly begin without him, and smiling wanly at his own joke. His was a thin sad face, with rather bleak grey eyes; he pocketed the tip Harrion had pressed in his hand with a curt nod and scarcely a pretence at gratitude (yet he had a wife and three children and could hope for no further promotion for two years at least); watching his benefactor make his quick way in the direction of the Crematorium with something not unlike contempt on his face, and perhaps reflecting that even the gros-Michel, surely the lowest of God's creatures, spat when he spoke of this man.

And Harrion knew perfectly well that he despised him, and that when the attendants saw him they winked at each other, and even that they were a little repelled by the notes he thrust in their expectant palms. But that, if anything, only heightened the exultation that was his the moment he closed the gate behind him and was admitted, however contemptuously, to their midst; for with the shutting of the gate and the attainment, as it were, of his object, all his polite reluctance and self-loathing dropped from him, as though they had been there only to heighten the enjoyment of the moment when it came (at last) after the dreary struggle to put it from him. For here he was a different being. Here once more desire returned to him. Once again life held an interest; an interest that now could never fail and which he shared alone. For here and at last one could love without fear or rebuff. Indeed, could be so filled with a love for all mankind as to burn in a glowing heat of ecstasy that made one's footsteps light and suspect as one picked a way between the graves and made oneself not a little ridiculous to the attendants. But that he did not mind. He would not have had it otherwise. He welcomed it. One bore ridicule with humility when one loved humanity as he did. For at last one could love humanity when it suffered as it suffered here. Here, shorn of all its pretence and at its most pitiful; here where all its bitterest tears were shed and its darkest fears went uncomforted. Here where the very air reeked with the stench of man, so that as one took in a breath one drank the flesh and blood of one's fellows in an awful communion of fear and ecstasy. For no sooner was the body on its asbestos mat placed on the altar and the iron doors swung-to, than out of the turret-chimney it rushed, the heavy wave of black and swirling smoke, pouring voluptuously heavenward or forced down to earth like an unwanted sacrifice, and slowly from its dense and angry mass came the aroma of pine-wood as the coffin burnt itself out, then the black smoke thinned and turned to grey and with the change came the subtle retching smell of burning flesh and grease, which in turn changed to a foul penetrating odour of excrement consuming itself, until at last, when one was exhausted and one scarcely could bear more, the grey changed to a thin steady spiral of white, with its acrid taste of burning bone.

But not yet. He looked again at his wrist. It needed still fifteen minutes to the hour. Then the funeral party would arrive, and someone would help the widow or the old people up the steps leading to the Crematorium chapel, and they would disappear, and then his friend the gros-Michel and his men would shoulder the coffin and follow with no more ceremony than if this had been the bringing in of the piano, and still in their blue cotton workmen's blouses, which never failed to call comment from the sad-faced attendant (On dirait des tonneliers! he would murmur indignantly. But then he had a sad face, and scruples, and even after years the sight of weeping widows could still move him to look away), and once the mourners were seated inside the chapel the coffin would be placed on the high curtained altar, and, like a conjurer's best trick, soft music from the organ would be the signal for the draw-ing-to of the curtains, and from a small trapdoor at the back (but *they* think it all happens here, the gros-Michel had winked at him one day) the coffin would be removed to the furnace-room, and be returned to them later, when the curtains would again be solemnly drawn, as the casket which must be fitted neatly in the walls of the Columbarium outside, with its small marble stones and wall-fitments for a few flowers.

Strange how surprised they always were to see the little box, after the heavy coffin which they had brought there. And what scenes they made, sometimes. As the woman who had come screaming down the steps: My child! My child! Is this all that is left of my child! and crying reproaches at the man with her, who had persuaded her to do this thing.

—But after all, my dear, it is so much cleaner, was all he could find to say in his defence.

O yes one needed a strong stomach for the job, as the pale-faced attendant would emphasize, nodding in the direction of the colossal indifferent Michel and his sturdy assistants. The sad attendant never could hide his disgust of the great hulking jovial red-faced workman who controlled the Crematorium as he the cemetery grounds. For sometimes, the attendant said, the bodies burst their coffins, when they had travelled a long way, for instance, or were the corpses of very fat people in an advanced state of decomposition. Only last month there was that hindou (qu'il était affreux! qu'il était horrible!) whose head had swollen to an enormous size, and the mouth had widened inches outwards across the face and bubbled with a hissing of blood and putres-cence. (Bien sûr qu'il faut avoir l'estomac bien placé!) And all the work they got from the hospitals, the abortions, the refuse from the dissect-ing tables, all arriving pell-mell, human joints, heads, arms, thighs, and to see those great hulking brutes jamming them in the coffins like bits of meat and banging them down with their fists when the lids wouldn't shut. But they were less than men, they were human butchers, they were barbarians. And they've got rubber gloves, too; but do you think they'll use them? And do you think they'll change their filthy clothes after being hours soaked in the smell of decomposition? Try and make them! They go straight out, just as they are, to get a drink. But they won't serve them any more. The barmen say: Get out. It's horrible! Your clothes stink! Still, some-one has got to do it. People do die.

But Harrion was growing restless sitting there on the stone bench in front of the Columbarium and with nothing to do but change his place from one end of it to the other. Whenever he looked up his eye caught the glitter of gold writing on the squares in the nearest walls: *Un bon souvenir de Madeleine. Une bonne pensée. Regrêts. Au-revoir, Joseph.* And the gaps where many a niche had been torn open, as were some of the graves outside. Their payments, then, had lapsed. That was what it meant. For five years they could have the few inches, the few feet, then out of consideration (for the survivors were not all neglectful, but might be ill or in momentary financial difficulties) the grave or urn was left another year. But after that, no more. The bones were tipped in the *fosse communal* and there the matter ended. There was no appeal, no redress. Pick them out, if you can. For again the wealthy were in their palaces and the poor were in their tenements. And again the poor could not pay the rent and suffered the Ultimate Eviction. My dear Sir, my dear Madam, the rent is due. We regret, but. Out you go. For he must pay rent all his life and his bones must pay rent, or they, too, shall not rest in peace. Not even rest in his length of earth, nor stop a seven-inch hole in a wall. Even that is not conceded man in his last abject attempt at privacy. But there is humanity in the deed. They will not throw his bones out in the street as when he was alive. Nor will they scatter them, as he might have hoped, to the impartial winds. For human bones must be respected and may not be thrown heedlessly away. They may be thrown only in the public ossuary. So get out. We are sorry. But we need this room. Get out. Shuffle your bones with the least of your fellows, with the unknown, and the unloved, and the forgotten.

But how little all that mattered, Harrion was thinking (at last one could love humanity when it suffered like this, at its most pitiful, at its most desolate!) for the last flame goes up from the brain. From the brain, not from the heart. Though he hadn't believed it, until they had proved it to him. But when at last the grey column of smoke ascending the air grew barely perceptible, and the tang of burning bone began to die away, and all flesh consumed, the framework of bone lay in cinders on its asbestos mat, then the heart and the brain ran their last macabre race, ironically staging their last fight over a victim long past caring.

And when the doors were opened and the mat drawn out with its bright calcinous trail, only the brain burned on in its burst shell of skull. For at the end, it seemed, man's inconstant heart must bow down before his spirit, the last white flame to leave the body.

Less than five minutes now. Should he stay where he was when the funeral drove up, or go indoors in the furnace-room? But he had been too often behind the scenes, lately. Michel was growing annoyed, and even an extra large tip had not stopped him grumbling yesterday, when, as he said, there had been nothing to see, rien que des foetus et des nouveau-né sent from the maternity hospitals, and for that he'd probably lose his job, if all this got about. Even though (thought Harrion) he couldn't be seen, standing there behind the furnace with his eyes glued to the mica opening for as long as the heat was bearable. How unreal it was the way the whole thing swayed and split, sizzling like fat that has caught fire in a frying-pan, and the maddened gathering of the roaring cataract of flame as the light pine covering burst away and then like two fiery swords cutting it up, the flames fastened on the flesh. Sometimes Michel would prod the body like an enormous sausage, turning it over with a curse, if it were that of a very fat person that wouldn't burn quickly enough. (So the pale attendant said, with disgust. He hadn't seen that yet.) But once he had been allowed to scoop the bones into the urn with the long wire brush, and watch them grow cold after all the fury and recede from fiery red to an indifferent grey.

But this must be the funeral. A carriage was drawing up. And there was Michel and his men coming down the steps. (Then he had been there all the time, and hadn't let him know!) And now he was pretending not to see him. It was quite obvious that he was pretending not to see him, as he sat there on the bench trying to ask by signs whether he might come or not. Still, he must use tact. He mustn't anger him.

The mourners in the first coach, Harrion noticed, were anything but sorrowful. Particularly the men, who seemed to have drunk rather more than was wise and were grinning together and cracking jokes. Their women, sitting at the back, pursed their lips resentfully at their fun, and seemed not to be enjoying this part of the afternoon at all. They didn't care, he reflected. They wouldn't mind. They might even say: yes, come along! Still, he must be patient. Another day would do as well. Now the coffin was being lifted from the hearse. Now it was being carried up the steps. And still no one looked round at him. The door shut with a bang.

And with the shutting of the door, he had (he always had) a spasm of self-loathing, a longing to get away. And again resistance made him sick and excited, till he felt his stomach dragged down as though falling out of his body. But to-day he would stay where he was. Nothing should move him. No; he'd shut his eyes. No; that was not enough. He must go away. He must go now, before it began. To-day he would be strong. He would leave before it could overpower him.

With the suddenness of an explosion the column of black smoke rushed up from the furnace chimney, mounted, wavered, and swept down to the ground, away from him, on the opposite side of the Columbarium.

Then the wind was in the north to-day. He should have thought of that. He hadn't realised. He leapt up and, breathing hard, reached the other side, only just in time, it seemed to him. He leaned against a pillar to steady himself, with nostrils distended like an animal flaring the scent of another; and it came surprisingly quickly after the black burning of the wood, the thin grey column in ascension perpetual with its stench of grease and putrescence. He smiled, and held up his face.

From a height the sun chose, drowsy fastidious bee, now this village, now that.

—There is a future for these people, Sebastian was saying.

And Lavinia Reade, shading her eyes from the bright look of the day, and gazing down at the bacchic frieze of grapes, the tumbling children and burdened fields, and oxen remote in their unhurried condescension, said: No! There is an eternity.

THE APPLE
IS BITTEN AGAIN
(Self Portrait)

Se tu sarai solo sarai tutto tuo.

LEONARDO DA VINCI.

Further Reflections on the Death of a Porcupine was published by The Blue Moon Press in 1933, in a limited edition of 99 copies, signed, numbered, and exhausted before publication.

I re-publish it among this selection from my notebooks for no reason but that I am sick and tired of being quoted and plagiarised without acknowledgement.

Having sampled the literary manners of the Few (for whom presumably such luxuries as Limited Editions are issued) I wish to protect myself by offering it to the Many, who, rightly suspicious of wit, will feel no urge to claim it as their own.

O. M.

CONTENTS

NOTEBOOK NUMBER ONE, TWO, THREE, FOUR, FIVE, SIX, SEVEN, EIGHT, NINE, TEN, AND ELEVEN   339
Observation, Comment, Thought.

NOTEBOOK NUMBER TWELVE   381
London, Eng.

NOTEBOOK NUMBER THIRTEEN   386
Woman as Uncreative Artist.

NOTEBOOK NUMBER FOURTEEN   394
Further Reflections on the Death of a Porcupine.
Final Word on D. H. Lawrence.

NOTEBOOK NUMBER FIFTEEN   403
The Apple is Bitten Again. Personal and Empiric theory of Local Brain; denial of instinct and nature; all Life a happy combination; Soul as Fifth Element; and exploration without balloons into a psychosphere and ultra-psychosphere.

NOTEBOOK NUMBER SIXTEEN   413
Eternal Death: Credo for Adults Only.

C ivilisation is the distance man has placed between himself and his excrement.

Selective Spirit. The same soil produces potatoes, sun-flowers, grapes. The potato root knows only how to find nourishment for being a potato. It is the selective spirit of the root which makes the artist.

Origin of Kingship. Wherever there are three, one is chaired.

An egg. It all depends on what you do with an egg. The Italian hatches a zabaglione, food for the pregnant Madonna. Or a poached egg, salt-less, on wet toast. Restorative for the typist.

Negation. People are not to be despised for not doing their own think-ing. One does not ask of them to be able to think. But one does ask of them to be able to function correctly.

One asks of them to be able to sleep, eat, digest, without the aid of ten million pills, patent drugs, and irritability. One despises them not for not having a life of the mind (which is, and should be, rigorously denied them) but in not having a life of the body. They have made their choice. They could at least delight in that choice; exaggerate their senses; take to their beds with anticipation; their tables with zest.

Yet they take to their beds with fear, their food with indifference, put their glasses to their eyes instead of to their mouths, and assault their bowels instead of their women.

It is because of this that a child, fresh, new, inquiring, can be such an unreal and bitter sight. Much like witnessing a crime one is not able to prevent.

On Pain. People who suffer in their minds should be exempt from physical pain. They suffer enough.

Physical pain is unproductive emotion. It teaches nothing, but possibly the incompetence of the medical professions. (*Patience?* But patience *is* the virtue of the infirm.)

From fear, shock, loss, miscalculation, one learns and remembers. But not from toothache.

German war-film. Beyond the horror of warfare (one is, by now, used to film evocation of bombardment, trench-life, dying agonies, wounded) the bitter ineffectuality of women in times of war. A matter of food-queues and being unfaithful.

Yet is there more a woman can be, but unfaithful? Is not unfaithfulness her ultimate achievement? By the act of unfaithfulness and all its emotional-nervous excitements woman is crowned queen of her restricted kingdom. Her dominion the eruptive, useless, emotions: jealousy, uncertainty, despair.

The lasting irony: the physical insignificance of this thing called being unfaithful. At most, the outcome of a kind word or well-chosen dinner. Yet even when deliberate, how mean a life achievement. And once past, the power to sway by being faithless or no, there is an end. No more triumph. No more make-believe.

In this lies all the powerlessness of woman, and her limited horizon.

Promethean theft. The secret of the gods is scepticism. This, in its audacity, their power. This, in its simplicity, the fire they took such care no mortal might share or intercept.

Man has only faith.

On Giving. Only the creative artist has any thing to give. Others give externally; paying in kind or coin. But the artist gives of himself; gift inevitable, unpremeditated, unceasing.

One must not be afraid of giving. Or ashamed. It is better to give than to receive, if only that one can receive only that which one gives.

Else surround oneself like China by a Great Wall and stagnate inside it, till even a monkey people like the Japanese can come and knock one to pieces.

Lines for a Play. Thought (unvoiced) at a Reception. I wonder how many times Lady Dash's face has been lifted?
—And her legs?

Religious Art. When religion was simple, pure, Art was simple, pure. When it became mendacious and corrupt, Art became tortuous and corrupt. The thing itself was not enough. It had to have curtains and poles and curves and tassels and stones made of lace and wood fashioned by the pastry cook and all the arrogant profusions of baroque.

To make plausible a lie you need much detail.

Credo. Believe in anger. Not the anger at some-one stepping on your toe. But the anger at some-one stepping on some-one else's toe.

Lost Sense. Destroy man and there will remain in Shakespeare's works the encyclopedia of his complete psychology.

There seems, once, to have been a common collective psychology. Not a collective newspaper thought (man could not then afford his life lived for him) but an acute common-sense, lost to us.

That is why a Shakespearean fool in five lines can tell you more about psychology than a present-day professor in five tomes. Then, its use was impulsive and universal. Now, it is specialised. Man having to do his own summing-up developed a universal defensive observation; as the flair, the smell-sense of danger or approach, in the beast.

Where we deal in the Collective life, a life of corporations, groups, masses; they dealt in human life: a human life less complicated by unnecessary detail.

Still to-day we say: the shrewd peasant, the canny countryman. He alone of men has been the least touched by the second-hand knowledge of reading and writing.

Once man looked on man and knew him. Read in a gesture, sound, aspect, that which not all the printed word and compulsory education of to-day can teach him. Within himself lay his defence and his guide.

He had the wisdom of illiteracy.

Watching a bee, instead of working. The season for work is not Spring. The time, not youth.

Man must not be shamed by the industry of insects. He must remember when he sees a bee at work that a bee is born old. Likewise the ant. These are instinctively antipathetic to man, for, like God, they have had no growth, no doubts, no youth.

Defence of Brevity. Time eliminates all detail. Time is no respecter of detail. A timeless thing has no detail. Therefore measure a thing's brief-ness by its verbosity; its hour by its opulent overloading.

Take a lesson from Time in judging Art.

Notebook Number Two

D*enial.* I refuse to believe that after the company he had kept the Prodigal Son found the proximity of the pigs uncongenial.

On Wine. Wine soothes the palate, perfumes the veins, multiplies the heart-beats. Wine puts Olympian fire in man's fist, with none of the uncertainties of stealing it.

Bacchus has as many thunders as Jove. And none of his pomposities.

On a friend, reluctantly crossing a field. Cows, dosing in the shade, meditate simple, immediate, physical needs: sleep, cold, heat, food. Principally food.

Suppose, timeless in their passive staring, sculptural in their mossy planes, they lay meditating the frenzied (human) appositions: Truth and Beauty, Heaven and Hell, Good and Evil, Love and Morality, Peace and War.

That would be the time to run!

The New Kruschen. Sagas, epics, tri-volume-inous memoirs, and all novels over 360 pages. Each morning, before sitting down to work, they take as much as can be held on a threepenny piece. But instead of going to the bowels it goes to the brain.

In both cases, afterwards, there is a copious use of paper.

Strength. A human being is down-and-out not because of a weakness but because of a strength. A drunkard's capacity for drink is the strongest thing about him. The weakness of the swindler, gambler, waster, criminal, the virtue he does not possess.

Man is the outcome of his strength. If this applies to greatness, why deny it to littleness and mediocrity?

On Death. Not altogether fear of the void, the inevitable nothing. But that one's curiosity resists. One is too curious to be tolerant of dying. One resents being unable to live for ever; watch, comment, weep, exult.

Prophecy is man's ultimate victory over curiosity. Prophecy is man's last means of cheating death.

You cannot wait, so you guess.

Distinction. The most formidable of Big Business Men is at the level of the humblest street-stall vendor.

The humblest of artists, in direct line of succession to Giotto and Michelangelo.

Survival of the Fittest. Domesticity (at which some still scoff) is the survival of man. Savage he can no more survive than a fabled Cyclops or a dinosaur. Therefore the bowler hat, the villa row, the perambulator in the hall, are the symbols of his victory.

Then what is defeat?

Newsreel. Suddenly the world fills with savages, children, lunatics.

And the period of sanity seems all too short.

Car-racing, steeple-chasing, all-in-wrestling; and a crowd yelling in the hopeful fear that a neck shall be broken. These, the savages.

Football, cricket, boat-racing; and another crowd yells. These, the children.

A few politicians are speaking: Joey the Clown in a larger ring. You realise that each has had a period of sanity. You realise, also, that true *gagaisme* seems to be the malady of elderly politicians.

Remain a few lunatics. Either balanced on a head on the outer rim of the Eiffel Tower playing a piano with a toe, or suspended from a beam writing home to mother with pencil in its teeth.

But these are few, as genius is few.

On Woman. Woman is the vacuum which Nature abhors and must see filled. Consequently woman is always slightly ridiculous unless stretched on a bed or with a child in her arms.

All the rest is marking time.

He Died for You. He took on the Sins of the World. He gave His life. But of course he did.

Every man who thinks for mankind, who does the thinking of the unthinking mass, takes on man's sins. Takes on his shoulders the follies of his fellow-men, assumes the responsibility for their thoughtless sinning, their ignorance, their limitation, their stupidity. And dies because of it.

He is in the paradoxical position of being at once the Oracle and the Sacrifice.

Formation of Self. More than to parent, background, family, education, we owe the chance remark, the chance sentence in the chance book, the chance turning in a street, the chance opening of a door.

Grammar versus Poetry. The Greeks compiled the grammar and dictionary of nature and the human form. But the Greeks were not the artists. They were the technicians, grammarians, erudites.

The poets and the visionaries were never the Greeks. They were the Egyptians, Chinese, Assyrians, Indians. Those who have learned and forgotten grammar; not those who never attained grammar.

For perfection is not Art. Art and perfection are enemies which no declension shall ever reconcile.

Virtue. Leave the brave virtues, the enduring virtues, to the few. The impulsive virtues to the many.

The impulsive virtues: charity, kindness, pity, courage.

The brave virtues: purposefulness, gentleness, steadfastness, fidelity.

On hearing of a young man who, to listen to Duke Ellington and his Band, put on his best bracelet. For there is more joy in the artist over the one best bracelet than over the hundred who have put down their money.

Always wear your best bracelet when you approach the artist. Clean your hands before writing our name. Your mouth, before destroying us in words.

Approach us always on your mental knees. We are the last of the aristocrats.

Notebook Number Three

L ittle Brother. Sentimentality goes preaching to the birds. Wisdom lets the birds do the preaching.

Disposing of the body. Squatting semi-circles of loin-clothed Indians, a Salvation Army Band with trumpets of pure gold, or a whirling in space without instruments to measure the distance or the monotony, is more one's idea of novelty than of eternal rest.

Because of the pleasure its sight has been to me, I shall lie (unboxed) in the clean active earth, companied by clean active androgynous worms who lift on their narrow Atlas shoulders the dark crust of the world.

Standing in Covent Garden remembering the South. A square mile around, bread, wine, honey, figs, flowers. In the morning on the tree or in the earth; at mid-day set before you, warmly bearing sun-distilled their taste and perfume. Because of which, a dish of zucchini cooked over a charcoal fire to a high cicalous Neapolitan commentary shames Eschoffier's elaborate sauce-covered art.

Tightly packed in boxes, the four corners of the Empire rot in the cellars of Covent Garden. Picked unripe in worthless natural condition; packed before reaching maturity to travel unbruised; coloured and warmed by artificial means in damp underground vaults. Passing from a state of prematureness to a state of decomposition. As do men in towns.

Cannibalism. A young man is more virile than a young sheep. Consequently the finest restorative, the most easily assimilated meat, should be human flesh.

Moreover cannibals do not eat their friends. They eat their enemies and occasionally an inquisitive stranger. To enhance their self-respect and restore their strength they use prime unfrozen meat. To which excellence of flesh they add the spiritual exultation of conquest, the sacramental sense of destiny, and the acquiring of renewed vigour by eating the heart of a brave and formidable rival killed in single combat.

The Romans found us drinking from our enemies' skulls. Civilisation permits the Communion service and the blooding of a child at its first kill. Or what is blood transfusion but a genteel later-version of cannibalism?

All of which prove our arguments against the eating of human flesh to be sentimental and based on a code of behaviour which none ever bothers to think about because it is called morality.

Certainly man's argument cannot be hygiene. Man eats the slimiest and least aesthetic of things from bacilli, gland pills made from (refined) human excreta, frogs, winkles, snails, oysters, spiders, eels, snakes, old horses (France and Belgium), dogs (China and Japan, where cannibalistic practices, incidentally, are neither unknown nor infrequent). Indeed, do we take the whole human race there is not one thing it does not accept as food, though portions of it (in the name of refinement) bar the human flesh.

It cannot be that it is distasteful. Whenever man has eaten of it he has enjoyed it. The pies of Sweeney Todd, Demon-Barber of Fleet Street, were famous, though made of quite haphazard meat. Of anyone, indeed, who called-in for a shave.

In Venice, children thought to have fallen in the canal were disappearing in a stewpot. All Venice and surroundings knew of those luscious stews. Till a doctor found a small-finger bone in his soup. Now a red light burns above the entrance and the Venetians cross themselves as they pass without loitering.

Having neither honour nor self-respect (except a collective honour and a collective self-respect called Patriotism and Morality) man does not kill for food or vengeance as do animals or savages. He kills to kill. Which is a pity, for cannibalism carried to its logical conclusion is the only means left to civilised man to stop all wars for all time. Even the most formal sense of honour and the strongest desire to die for a freedom in which cloth caps and cheap cameras shall be sold in unwilling markets, would not lure a man to seize a bayonet if it meant eating the men he had to kill.

Morally, to starve a man is more ruthless than to eat him. Few people have much feeling for what may happen to their bodies once they are dead. Such refinements in living merely make for refinements in cruelty. They enable us to weep with the mother cat mewing for her lost kittens and give the human cat five shillings a week for the upkeep of hers.

Finally, to a black and savage people a white man cannot seem a man, but must seem rather some skinned form of comic animal. So that actually to a Cannibal Chief a missionary is not a man.

—And who shall say that he is wrong?

More Cannibalism. Artistic-emotional. They hand round the work of others like a dish of cakes: Have you seen? Have you read? Have you heard?

Likewise the emotions. She adores, he hates, they loathe, dread, love, ignore, avoid, despise one another.

Wildly their hearts beat to the energy of others. Sleight-of-mind one would have thought too difficult to be worth while. And too dull.

Girl Guides in Passing hold-up a Tram. No wonder men rape children! They seem the only female things that have softness, gentleness, curiosity, sex-appeal, and no moral consciousness. From fourteen onward they harden to granite. Frigid, and with strident hygienic voices.

Definition of a Fool. One who does not learn from experience. From *first* experience.

Under-water feature Reel. The poetry and brio of the native diver among the coral, shell fern, and anemone. They pick flowers on the floor of the sea and play at loitering with an arrogant childlike simplicity. Their movement is beautiful as joy, and an aim in itself. The willingness of their action is sparkling. At the surface, they shake the drops from their heads and smile like sudden light. But you have smiled first.

Then the European divers, scavenging for gold; dragging their distorted shapes with weighted boots through the horror of dead ships in fog-thick seas. They perform as an end to an aim. Creeping, courageous, strained, painful, vicious, hired movements. Their gropings to reach the bars of gold are almost too painful to watch. The end, harrowing and symbolic, a duel between man and octopus.

One sees why natives need no kinema or football after the day's work, as befits office clerk, factory worker, and shop assistant.

In the European, for driving power, there is discipline. In the negro, there is desire.

Illustrating Joy. If you want a thing humorous and light-hearted, you cannot achieve it with the white man.

You must eliminate us where there is need of the care-free and the impulsive. Caricaturists, comic-strip artists, find it difficult to make a humorous thing with white men. They can make only that at which we laugh; not that which does the laughing. Negroes are the sole living beings with whom such liberties can be taken. Else substitute pigs, cows, hens, birds, mice. We may yet have the last laugh, that cold chattering of the teeth. But they have still the first laugh, that bright look of the morning.

O lost simplicity of the laughing soul!

You cannot ask more of a human animal than to see him complete and free from care. You cannot bring to man treasures greater than a care-free and a joyous life.

Yet we reduce him to a state that when his watch is in pawn he has lost his soul. While a gentleman has lost his soul merely at the thought of parting with his cuff links.

Strange the balance, the compensation, which gives to the white man a black soul, and a white soul to a black man.

To pedants and sentimentalists who bemoan the Vulgarisation of the world through the Kinematograph in particular and Machinery in general. But mankind has always had its cheap stories, only they magnified them into Literature and Art. They had the same tale scratched out again and again, as *Manon,* as *La Bohème,* as *La Dame aux Camelias,* as *Samson et Delilah.*

Now at least their same tale has found the forty-two positions and samples the fifty-seven varieties.

The Grin. Children and old women, having no protection, grin.

How many professions have to be grinned for! Every job in which there is a grin has in it an element of prostitution. One of the reasons one should never meet people. The grin to please becomes the anxious grin. A few for a brief moment have a grin of triumph.

Final Judgment. Not by the master but by the pupil. Judge Karl Marx by Lenin. Lord Beaverbrook by the third-class compartment of a City-bound train.

Notebook Number Four

B*itterness.* To be saying now truths which one day they must come to. To know that it is a matter of days multiplied through intolerant years. To know that what they blame you for now they will not thank you for then.

That is despair.

Compromise. Man does in a lifetime, embryo, growth, decay, that which the earth does in aeons and humanity in centuries.

What makes man the more interesting is that he goes through his small growth and decay blunderingly. The rest are movements and temperatures. But man knows all about it, protests, and gives a little cry.

The cry is religion. The protest is Art.

Love. (The perfect definition is found.) There is always some-one to whom we are not ridiculous.

La Grande Logique et La Petite Logique. I would call phantasy and imagination La Grande Logique. It belongs to the creative artist, to children, to the exalted. La Petite Logique belongs to metaphysicians and professors. Example: La Grande Logique: Turner *vecchio,* Pieter Breughel, Bach, le Douanier Rousseau. La Petite Logique: Kreisler, Paolo Uccello, Aldous Huxley.

Man. A person, how like a cloud. It shapes itself as the wind blows. Like a cloud it is a dragon and becomes a lamb.

Sipping wine at a Sicilian Inn. Wine at last as Bacchus drank it; before it had been served to the Cardinals.

Walking through Hyde Park toward the British Museum Reading Room. The Gentleman, the rebellious Greeks, Seagulls, Brigands. The man stands at the edge of the Serpentine, watching the seagulls. He gilt-edged, null, incorruptible. They scavengers, raucous, thieving, angry, bold, free.

He watches them expressionless and long, lost in the rhythm of their swift purposeful weaving against the sky. Something in their freedom, wildness, vitality, touches him, so untouchable, walking before luncheon from his admirable home to his admirable Club; a man of set purpose, set habit, set belief. But he cannot understand them. He sees that they are free, angry, vital, and something in him responds, is made to pause before their wildness and their grace. But he cannot *understand* that wildness and that grace, for these are emotions he can never know and must instinctively shrink from, lest he is to deny his days and their purpose.

And watching both, one thinks: the gentleman and the seagulls, how like the Gentleman and the rebellious Greeks. They may stare and scream at one another, but they can never be introduced!

Prophecy on seeing an iceberg in a newsreel. The Ice Age sweeping aside the hot vegetable life will come again. And not only will come again but its advent can be calculated; its date, within limits, predicted. When the Poles become too heavy with snow they will swing the world round. Africa to the ice. The ice to the Equator. Such the earth's safety valve; its protection against being cracked and roasted like a chestnut.

(And when it happens I hope they will not ascribe it to a revengeful Second Deluge, but will remember that I warned them, after an iceberg had pushed clumsily across a screen and told me so.)

Origin of the Gargoyle. Cats on roofs. Hungry cats peering down over the edges of drain pipes. Hungry artists in their garrets peering back at them. The closest human thing to the starving cat. One step more and they are on the roofs themselves!

Why we cannot Think lying in Bed, and Why, lying awake, become Inconsolably Depressed. The horizontal position. Position of defeat, death, surrender. Flat on one's back and finished.

Art. Classes, professions, trades, all are limited. You know their end at their beginning. Their depths and heights are calculable and mechanical. There are setbacks or advances. But there are no *surprises.*

Having no limitations, creative art is the one freedom. The creative artist the one free being, in that he can impose his own limits (within limits!). But at least such limits are his own and not imposed by class, community, or profession.

Pan adapted to the English-speaking peoples. From Arcadian groves to the perambulating nurse-maid alley.

The King confers on him the key to Kensington Gardens, so that he may go there after hours; so that at night in pride and solitude he may look on his creation, his capture.

None ever knows what takes place between the two. Or hears the curses, recriminations, fury. Or the soothing mother-noises of the little old man. Sometimes from the park at dusk comes a long nostalgic painful cry. They say it is the geese.

And the sculptor was knighted, too.

War. The Bombing of Non-Combatants. By all means let us bomb cities and civilians. Let us rid ourselves of cant in this matter of just how politely bombs and shrapnel may behave.

In war there is no innocent victim. Each one of us participates. The innocent victim, the self-righteous civilian, patriotic wife, elderly man, thoughtless child, send armies to their death as ruthlessly as the politicians who begin the slaughter and the armament firms who profit by it.

Nor can we find conclusive argument against the bombing of women. Women are guilty as the rest, and more hysterical. Men have been known to argue that they do not want to fight and will not. But women are the morality-economic fiends. The eggers-on, without responsibility or honour, given to the sentimental cruelty of personal tears.

Therefore that city and those inhabitants, having made no protest, are not neutrals but accomplices. Bad education, bad emotional up-bringing, bad ideals, must take its medicine. We all are instigators and collaborators in the next war. Let us, at least, accept with dignity our chance of being wiped out with the rest.

As to the bombing of children (on which cringing pleas against civilian bombing are ever hung in the Popular Press) it is both logic and precaution to exterminate them. They are the future weapon; the avengers of to-morrow. You kill malarial mosquito-larvae in the swamps. You do not say: he did not bite me but his father did, or possibly it was his uncle. You spray paraffin on the malarial dump, taking no chances. Spray your gasses on the human larvae doomed to the mock heroics, shoddy newspaper patriotism, and sham morality of the Great City.

It is not War we need end at these farcical heart-searing Conferences. It is frontiers. Conferences to abolish frontiers would automatically abolish wars. (See Switzerland, North America, Russia.)

But reflect rather on the noble time-serving of politicians, the pompositics of vested interest, the howl from befogged masses and their ardent befogged leaders. And turn aside.

Reflect also that man has fallen so far from grace that though one half of him goes out to die and be maimed, the other half is concerned with how safely it can sleep in its bed and pursue uninterrupted its daily life. Reflect that when the next war comes, they still want to live. Their hearts are to be strong to bear the heroic reports of death and sacrifice, but not strong enough to break at the folly and desolation.

Then let it be the end. Let them bomb and be finished. Let our little brick worlds fall about our ears. And let the few who are left crawl out and start again the long painful coma relieved by moments of lucidity, which man calls growth and history.

Notebook Number Five

F*reedom.* How long the fight! Generations fight for one hour more freedom a day.

Freedom—a policeman to guard your car while you are at the office.

Freedom—free speech. Yet free people want no speech. They have little to say. They live.

Freedom—getting it, what do you do? Nothing. The perfect state of happiness is repose.

Freedom—all humanity's struggle for freedom is the struggle to get one half-hour off. A few more minutes of the day for his own. Which shows how man loves work! All is reduced to a ceaseless fight to escape it. Harness river, thunder, camel, oxen, engine; all but himself. For man is only trapped into it. He's corralled.

The moment a man has caught the ass and put the sack on its back, he has done it. He has dodged work.

The peasant has a hard life. Did he think he could sow to-morrow or turn his field next week, he would be sitting peacefully sucking his pipe. But the skies continually threaten: I'll bring down snow. I'll manage a good long frost. Yet where skies are generous, people delightedly take their ease and Time loses its tyranny and significance.

Only the creative artist can love his work. In it he takes his freedom.

For Phalliculturists. Final Word. Thought alone makes life. All else is decay.

Compared with the thinking person the strongest athlete has an aura of decomposition. One senses the body's invisible disintegration. Only in thinkers does one avoid this immediate sense of flesh decay. They have another dimension; a respite.

The wreck of a mind may be a generation's loss: the collapse of a boxer or cricketer (at most) a season's setback.

Let us remember this when tempted sentimentally to exalt man's few copulative years above the centuries his mind can fertilise.

(*Explanation.* Where the word thinking occurs in these pages is meant creative, original, germinative thinking. Only. Not Pedants (male) and Higher Governesses (Female) whose path is always safe, imitative, explanatory; however efficient.)

Education. Avoid knowing all there is (assumed) to be known about a thing. This is death to curiosity, which is the source of all knowledge.

One should ask one or two relevant technical questions on a subject in which one is interested. The rest one should find out by puzzling over.

Any thing that is not worth thinking about is not worth knowing (*bis*).

Anger. Anger is of the first importance to the creative artist. It is the difference between the permanent and the fashionable.

(Example: Mr Maugham and Mr Coward are rarely angry but invariably cynical. The great Strindberg was a burning bush of creative wrath; Ibsen, merely academic.)

Anger is the creative principle of the mind. Its physical action identical to that of love. The violent pulsing of the blood, the quick angry breath.

Only take care to choose your anger as carefully as you choose your love.

Pre-Sentimental Age. What one definitely can admire in the old biblical prophets is that they said: My punishment is more than I can bear. They never said: My punishment is more than I deserve.

That is left to us. We with our overstrained and dewy mercy. Yet an eye for an eye is correct emotional perspective. It is integrity. It is mathematically exact. It admits of no uncertain (human) element. Mercy more often than not asks two eyes for one, if not the whole head.

It means: I will stand by what I do. I take my neighbour's eye, he takes mine. I take his hand, he takes mine. Thus each man answers for himself and to himself. No tears. No second tries. No excuses. No sophistry.

Nationalisation of the emotions. Kindness, gentleness, tolerance, charity, can be imposed by law. And far more satisfactorily. These virtues shall become commonplace and universal only when raised to the dignity of an Act of Parliament; not by being left to the hazard of free-will-less-ness, and the emotional-chance of organised religion.

Peaceless Man. A man on his land has for horizon the hedge of his neighbour's field. His needs are adequate to his demands.

Most manual workers are happy, or it is extremely easy to make them so by adequate recreation and payment. Their brain is not a hampering factor. The fight, the dissatisfaction, comes where there is more brain than power.

Whilst all other species live unaltered, uninterrupted, intelligent lives, man is in ceaseless mental convulsions. Then is the thinker the curse of humanity as are its warriors its scourge.

The negro now far too intelligent and civilised to be care-free, already has started asking questions which he was not asked to answer.

China, most intelligent of nations long before these others even began acquiring intelligence, has all the curses of humanity and civilisation: famines, tortures, tyranny, slavery, war.

The moment man went beyond the ancestral ape, he lost peace. When the ape bettered its social position by becoming a man it paid an unfair price.

Immeasurably beyond that which even the gentleman has paid in ceasing to be a human being.

One does not see that when they were painted blue they were more ignorant than now that they need a lifetime in which to buy a bowler hat and a white tie. What did the Romans do for them? Took oysters back to Cæsar; left a few pebbled floors to be undusted to-morrow; and a Wall for elderly archaeologists to break their heads on and bury their days beneath.

Fallacy that Science will eliminate Superstition. Science will never eliminate superstition. It can eliminate only a belief in miracles or in less popular creeds. No sooner does a certain pedestal of a certain god become unsafe through Science, than humanity immediately transports its god to another pedestal.

So far Science has definitely established that the Almighty does not wear a beard. But having shaved him they have turned him into a nebula.

If physicists, mathematicians, scientists, are still wrapped in such stupidities, what can one expect of the *popolino*?

Sleight-of-hand. You have but to look at a field of stars, at a sky cold and salty with stars, to know that man is nothing beyond a further pulsing of earth dust. A further leafless, furless, featherless pulsing of earth dust.

Man alone matters, mattering not at all. His arrogance and insignificance are such that he can look on the stars, unnumbered, undistanced, and believe that his alone is inhabited, intelligent, sentient.

This arrogance and insignificance give him the fear through which he hoists on pedestals conjurors and magicians of his own invention. Only thus can he reduce the Galaxy to mere sleight-of-hand and comfort himself in amazed admiration at the cosmic-bunting issuing from beards and vestments. Obsequious, he yet occasionally has been known to question, and even to call the Magician to account for his methods. But never for his authority.

Piteously afraid lest the Magician himself disappear and the pigeons, flags, bunting, become only pigeons and flags and bunting.

Man and his Friend. When a dog shows intelligence, men cheer. When a man shows intelligence, they hiss. As though intelligence were not an attribute of dogs.

Genius is the attribute of man.

Genius. Genius can almost always be known at sight. For it is almost always a little ridiculous; almost always a little out of focus. In the street, in the room, in the house, in the work. Some-one at whom the crowd looks askance, instinctively, defensively.

It is the dancing bear in the world's dark forest.

Art. According to Spengler, Art dies and finishes and cannot carry into or influence another culture or decade.

Not so. Art is a mineral deposit, stream of coal, strata of radium, dug up century on century for the warming and well-being of man.

But a few of us (only) are allowed to know its source.

Notebook Number Six

M an. Man is the vulgarian among animals. Studying him it is impossible not to despise him. Impossible also not to realise that he alone matters.

Change and Regret. Once you did your best (Bach, Mozart, El Greco, Orcagna) and you offered it to God or the ruling Prince.

Now you do your best and it is offered (roughly) to seventy-four book reviewers, three-quarters of whom glance first at the name of the publisher to see if it may be mentioned; next at that of the author to see if it be a friend. To a Great General Public whose bread-and-circuses is the adult fairy-tale called Popular Novel; and whose verdict must be accepted, though it were never asked.

Wise Diogenes with a lantern is outshone by the meanest fool with a hundred power flash-light.

Genius. (Final Word.) Man must cease condoning his creative limitation by coupling genius with insanity. Savage and childlike confusion! Genius is the supreme sanity.

If insanity be the attribute of genius, then is every asylum the elysium of great minds and creative energies. Talent in its varying degree may be akin to insanity: which is uncertainty, lack of control, and misdirection. But the peculiar quality of genius is that the nearer it approaches madness the less it remains genius.

Genius is common-sense. Genius is only common-sense. Genius is common-sense uncommonly used.

Hatred. Be careful with hatred. Handle hatred with respect. Hatred is too noble an emotion to be frittered away in little personal animosities.

Whereas love is of itself a reward and an object worth striving for, personal hatred has no triumphs that are not trivial, secondary, and human. Therefore love as foolishly as you may. But hate only after long and ardent deliberation.

Hatred is a passion requiring one hundred times the energy of love. Keep it for a cause, not an individual. Keep it for intolerance, injustice, stupidity. For hatred is the strength of the sensitive. Its power and its greatness depend on the selflessness of its use.

Truth. Metaphysics is the psychology of the mob in various stages of advance or retrogression. No more. Morality, collective self-defense.

Truth has nothing to do with ethics and the two must not be confused. Ethics is common (protective) experience. Truth is personal experience.

Leonardo da Vinci's dictum *Experience is the only certainty* is final and absolute.

Then there can be no (emotional) truth. For your certainty is not my certainty.

The sneer. The sneer is the blow in cold blood. The inferior's defence. The weapon of the mediocre.

Why the world loves its Musicians. It feels so safe. Nothing is so safe as an imitative artist.

It has its little fence around it. It cannot run amok. Once off its little rails it would be lost.

That is why the composer dies in poverty and the fashionable performer of the moment gets his thousand guineas for performing at the fashionable reception.

Whether in art or mechanics originality and inventiveness are automatically ridiculed and mistrusted. The more unusual, the more ridicule. The inventor has to wait for the generation that takes him with the others: with the adapters and modifiers of his original idea. To this public ignorance is to be ascribed the prosperity and vogue of all imitators in all lines, from a —— to a —— ——.

Whatever Dante may have found writ above Hell, we find this writ above the world: " 'Ware the dangers of being creative! Safety lies in numbers and imitation."

Neapolitan Street Scene. To sing full-throated in the street. Your only excuse that being in the street gives you a desire to sing.

Much seems to have become tarnished through being brought indoors and boxed between walls, whether called opera house or art gallery. There are things which must walk the streets, where they began. We must take the Arts off the payroll if we want them to find shelter again in the heart of man.

Limitation. What most one distrusts in the human creature is his limitation: his smug acceptance of that limitation. To which is due the increasing and unreasoning (modern) distrust of versatility.

Yet versatility is an off-shoot of vitality, one of the primary sources of genius. The common house-fly can boast several thousand facets to an eye. Why then should man boast but one to the eye of his mind?

An age was when the artist designed not only the cathedral for the town and the palace for its duke, but the brothel, sewage system, citadel, defences and weapons of war, monuments to whoever won that war, statues and frescoes commemorating the saints who helped win that war, busts and portraits of the lords who led the fighting and (occasionally) the paying for that war, sonnets enshrining deed and dead, music by which such sonnets became song, the ducal festas at which they first were sung.

The test of the creative mind is that, in whatever its form, a laugh follows a sigh; joy merges in melancholy; the tear ends in the guffaw. Versatility is the aesthetic impatience without which no effort is higher in the creative scale than the efficient sameness of a ledger clerk balancing his weekly accounts.

—Hence the distrust.

The Human Social-Barometer. Art is a truer indication of the social and political trend than is the stock-market or the speeches of politicians. One more of the lessons humanity has failed to learn: Art as infallible barometer of social change.

When prosperity grows increasingly fat, heavy, smug, Art becomes increasingly fat, heavy, smug. Exactly then study most carefully the walls of contemporary art exhibitions, the flow from the printing presses, the first notes of a Poulenc or an Ellington.

Example: The Ingres–Lord Leighton period of fatty well-being is at an end. Yet outwardly there is no sign. In industry, in the home, in the street, sleeps stability seemingly without end. Suddenly there is a commotion and a great deal of laughter. Edouard Manet has painted his *Femmes au Balcon* and all Paris flocks to give unrestrained vent to its anger and ridicule.

Finished the fat years of abundance! A blot of colour heralds the dissolution, the change, the war, the Soviet, the long lean years of industrial depression.

The world could have known, could have foreseen its doom, could have saved itself by the canvases of the Impressionists. These the prophecies and warning which none could read and had they been able to read would not have heeded.

Unfortunately the lean unstable years are best for a nation's art. No sooner does life become settled than it sags from a Michelangelo (already bad enough) to a Carlo Dolci, a Canova, a Sargent. Then when the despair and gangrene are about to take effect a Goya, a Manet, a Picasso, a Voltaire, a Stendhal, a James Joyce appear, their works bold as the flag of anarchy or the cold gleam of the scalpel.

The creative artist is the forerunner of a civilisation's beginnings and end. Priestless oracle; Cassandra whose message is read too late, if at all; world barometer; sensitive desert fern that shrinks and dies before an earthquake is due; a certain brave wintry flower that foretells an earlier approach of spring, a richer garnering of autumn.

Devil Worshipper. Steal fire from Olympus, apples from Eden, answer why with why not, and bring fiery reason to man. And man will curse, revile, deny, and thank with ridicule, hatred, and abuse.

Fortunately man can only torture a Galileo, vilify a Macchiavelli, chain a Bakounine to a prison wall. Can hinder, cannot destroy.

—(But tell me, O my devout hearts, was man worth it?)

Notebook Number Seven

The Poet Consoles his Loneliness. Not parents, friends, wine, have been near to me as a sudden turn of stone head, the flight of wings in sound, a colour framed, a thought that is of itself perpetual motion.

To these alone blood-deep the self has answered, pulsing in recognition and approval. On such a table I too have drained and brought down my glass.

So would I plant a word. Sow a sentence and reap a life. A life unknown, that not wife, child, friend, or love, shall ever wholly reclaim.

Across the timeless space-flow which in our arrogance we call the centuries, I salute my human sacrifice!

Thought. Never deliberately bruise another's soul. Souls must be vindicated. Souls must wave bravely as flags.

A human soul should perplex by its range. It should be a labyrinth in which none has yet wandered without losing himself.

Reason for resisting the blandishments of saints. Because they acquiesce. They accept. They withdraw.

Yet rebellion and curiosity are the only virtues which raise man above the commonplace. These two alone have relieved the tedium of the maudlin and the vulgar; *i.e.,* his virtues indistinguishable from vices, his vices indistinguishable from virtues.

Meet People Once Only. There is an eagerness, a shy intimacy, a charm of the unfamiliar, each is out to please, the hours pass prettily. But not again.

Afterwards there are rumours, acquaintances in common, personalities, irritations. And all that was impersonal, spontaneous, vivid, becomes the suspicion, gossip, and familiarity which is friendship.

Uses for laurels. (To a friend who sends a spray from Italy.) Cæsarian brows, suburban front lawns, and soups. And the best and most lasting is soups.

Ducks all leaving a pond together because a horse comes to drink. How middle-class ducks! How like people, domestic animals. Horses, hens, pigs; dogs with their wistful endearing faces; cats subtle as children and elderly actresses. Harmless stupid animals always remind one of people. But rarely wild animals or strange animals. Only tame ones. Possibly because people wish only to be like tame animals, those they have tamed and understood.

Of all men only the savage dare wish to look bold and angry, imitating the belly-crouch of the leopard, the majestic buffoonery of the lion.

On Reading a Book of Noble and Coroneted Ghosts. The reason Family Ghosts are found only in Castles, Ruins, and the Very Best Families, seems to be that people who have been used to being ordered about all their lives find a Ghostly Butler indispensable.

Dinner is served, M'Lady. The car is at the door, M'Lord. Death called while you were out, Your Grace. A headless gentleman to see you, Sir, he says you know him.

Else, presumably, they would never die.

Slogans. Most lasting and most important was the first: Thou shalt eat thy bread by the sweat of thy brow.

Brow. Not Back. But as nothing is more disheartening, uncongenial, and unrewarded than the sweat of the brow, man understood early that the best sweat was the sweat of the backs of his fellow-men. Moreover, only by transferring his sweat to another's back has man ever earned bread sufficiently varied to be worth the eating.

Counterblast to this slogan (capable of such personal and remunerative interpretation) was: Man does not live by bread alone.

But by this time, baker, industrialist, and middle-man had sweated their brows to such effect that those of their fellow-men were no longer able to function, the sweat-glands having been permanently transferred to the shoulder blades.

Which goes to prove that you must read a slogan very, very carefully if you intend to profit by it.

Pre-Sentimental Age. We must return to man as destined, as gage. We must return to a lost sense of destiny if man is to be saved.

So far only in art forms and in war has civilised man shown any sense of purpose and unity of aim. But such sense of purpose cannot be left merely to the mystic sentimentalities of priests, soldiers, visionaries, while the rest of mankind jog along indifferent and complaining. Unless each individual life becomes fore-ordained, man cannot be saved. The creative principle, the sense of attack and defence, must be brought again to daily life if it is to remain worth living. If it be destiny to put word before word, colour upon colour, thought on thought, it is destiny to plough and reap, assemble machinery, heap-up bricks, answer door-bells, stamp out buttons. Man must accept his limitation.

They now find that one atom has two molecules. For all one knows the distance between molecules and atom, air-space, may be by comparison great as the distance between sun, moon, and earth. We might be just minusculous cells of some colossal being. Or globules streaming through the veins of some monstrous atom.

The smallest cell seems to have consciousness of attack and defence. Swallows or is swallowed. Man alone meanders aimless, accepting economic depressions and monetary upheavals thrust on his world as though they were movements as real as earthquake and cyclone.

Man must be simplified. Must reconcile his limitation and his desire. Happiness and emotional development are personal matters, whether for kings or card-sharpers. They are the trappings of a life, made bright or dulled by individual temperament and outlook. They further or they obstruct an aim, but they cannot deflect it.

No thing is higher than its aim. No aim higher than the training for one's destiny. The conscious discipline, selfishness, purposefulness of the creative artist or inventor, must be brought to each individual life, trade, profession. The running sore of civilisation is exactly this aimlessness of daily life, its lacking of all dignity and purpose.

To-day instead of life we have the human millions without purpose. Instead of Reason we have faith. Instead of joy, sentimentality. Instead of a controlled perfection, an impulsive excellence. A return to a personal sense of destiny is the only anchor by which man can escape the horror of his present-day drifting. But let us not confuse a sense of destiny with a sense of fatalism. We have but to take its secret from the Few and reveal it to the many. Man must accept his limitation. Must learn to shoulder such limitation as the earth shoulders its seasons; calmly, logically, inevitably.

—Might not as well the sun tire?

Thought (unspoken) at a banquet in honour of Two Famous Flyers. Courageous, undoubtedly. But suppose some-one were to stand up now and accuse them loudly, publicly, of not being nicely, safely, and legally married. ... (Proving that courage is moral courage. All else is impulse, patience, lack of imagination, or vanity.)

To an unknown correspondent who (falsely) accuses Fugue *of indecency and licentiousness.* Dung? Maybe. But from the Augean stables!

Second sight; clairvoyance; starers in crystal and sand. One more lost human sense among the many acute senses which man has mislaid in the evolutionary teething period. Possibly a survival from the pre-reading, pre-writing ages.

A few still have this sense, and they take a crystal, card, bowl of sand or water, as point of departure, focus of concentration. Not as proof of trickery or magic as large policemen, angry clients, and aged magistrates suppose.

Clairvoyance is the most romantic of all the senses man has lost; it being the one sense lost through stupidity and not necessity. Day came when man had grown too wise to condescend to these prophetic utterances, these future warnings, these auguries of events and conduct.

Protesting to the last, the weary Cassandras laid aside their gift, helpless before man's incredulousness and vindictive stupidity.

Copyright. Greece has no boots. Or rather Plato dies and his sons have no boots. Thomas H., and shorthand-typist collect the money. Yet smack a king's face or tweak an ambassadorial nose and England pays that family tax and homage six hundred years. We find this justice, where we would find it unreasonable to pay a yearly royalty for a formula of behaviour or an architectural principle.

The Parthenon might be built of pure gold had all the Western peoples who went there and filched the pattern paid royalties on its copyright. If there were but the smallest, most inadequate, tax on the rights of her architects, sculptors, philosophers, poets, dramatists, scientists, Greece would be the most flourishing garden in the world.

But we Westerners have been clever. We have decided that the flattery we confer in our thank-you-very-much-you-are-altogether-too-wonderful is enough. One of the higher examples of politeness paying.

Those Believers in Other Lives. Strange, the people who tell one (apologetically) that they are the re-incarnation of Cleopatra, remember intimately being Queen of Sheba, recall the thousand and second night of Scherazade. Always Joan of Arc, Aspasia, Napoleon. Never a policeman, dress-maker, cook-general.

Even pre-natal memory, it seems, has its social code.

African newsreel. (Witch-doctor.) But *are* the African savages so superstitious? How readily they humour the camera-fiends and play-up with their sacred paraphernalia and local witch-doctor.

I have yet to see a native cameraman persuade *us* to lend the Bishop of London to be hunted by firemen and comic police and run madly about Piccadilly in all his war paint!

Notebook Number Eight

Joys of the Humanitarian. Both Christ and Don Quixote repented at the last.

Pre-Sentimental Age. Joan of Arc's favourite oath: Dusse-je ne pas boire de vin jusqu'a Pâques! Elizabeth's: But I have the stomach of a king!

Great women swear on and by their stomachs. Or rather, when their stomachs were repositories of wine and kingship women were great.

On Friendship. To have friends one must see people as they see themselves. If this is impossible and one can see people only as they are, one must be resigned to not having friends.

But one must not be surprised.

Man and Animal. Man is the only animal whose brain has been led astray by morality and overlaid all impulse.

A young cat howls and knows why it is howling. A young girl reads poetry or takes up the dream or novel where she left it yesterday. The cat gets its bellyful and stops howling. Which is just when the girl decides it is time to start. The cat now becomes restful, proud, fulfilled, conscious of virtue. The girl becomes angry, afraid, restless, and ashamed. Everything is denied, forgotten, but the recriminations and the family and the antagonism of the suburb, street, village, of whichever acre and latitude she inhabits.

Thus it would seem civilised man's sexual impulse is just sufficient to teach him to abuse himself and betray the body for the rest of its days.

Yet take the most commonplace of creatures: a mole, frog, sparrow, beetle. They manage to live self-sufficient lives, breed till useless, resourceful, unerring, active, all by their own effort. Their condition, ideal and useful. They cannot better such condition.

Compared with these man is stupid and limited. He cannot defend himself without studying, buying, acquiring, arming; cannot live without inheriting, depending, being protected. Any thing that comes to question or alter these artificial rules and regulations so necessary to his spiritual well-being he declares a menace to civilisation, a return to the dark ages, the greatest ill that could befall humanity.

As though humanity were not its own greatest ill. Or could know a menace greater than its own limitation.

Collar and Tie. The collar and tie is the halter of humanity. The more civilised the more it fits the neck, so that proudly they may assert that they labour under the yoke of civilisation.

Consolation on being plagiarised without Acknowledgement. No civilisation would have grown or survived were copying not an essential part of human nature!

Darwin was too sensitive. He seems to have kept to himself that later evolutionary change where the ape got crossed with the parrot.

Advice on how to write a popular novel. Les puces de l'amour l'obsedait. L'insecte de la vie voltigeait autour d'elle sans la toucher. . . .

—And already we are willing to give a life to know what happens to such a girl!

Old People and why they love Children. Because children are the only beings they still have authority over. The only beings they still can be of use to. The only beings who possibly can need them. The last impression left to them to make.

City-bound Train. Popular Newspaper. The caterwauling of a great city. The fig-leaf placed against the Unmentionable Triangle. Amnesia's small daily dose.

Collective. To-day everything is collectivised, heightened, improved. Collective business: trusts. Collective humour: the Four Marx Brothers. Charlie Chaplin with his sneaking tear-in-my-laugh humour is no longer enough to carry humanity's cross.

Only the thinker goes on alone in a collectivised trust world.

Best for Both. The artist can be hungry. But the connoisseur must be always well-fed.

They say! Denying the few senses left to him, man sees with his ears.

Lesbos. Seventy per cent. of lesbianism is woman's attempt to assert herself; a borrowing of attributes; a manifestation that a woman in her strength and power borrows man's attributes, as a man in his decadence and weakness takes on woman's attributes. The mediocre woman remains a woman. The strong woman becomes a light-weight man.

From personal and unbiased observation, all lesbians one has met have been hyper-feminine, more especially the masculine ones. The artistic or literary have been (at their best) efficient and imitative. At their worst, abysmally woman.

Again from personal and unbiased observation, the only impressively strong-willed women one has met or who exist have been married women with children, who joyfully have done the thinking, earning, acting, and scheming of a half-dozen men.

The drawback of lesbianism is its extreme femininity.

Greeks and the Sea. It is on the third day out that one understands why the Greeks loathed the sea. To a reasoning people, so much useless expanse of water. Above all, an uncertainty which neither logic, theory, nor rhetoric could explain away or control.

The Writer ponders the Humiliations of weekly Wage-earning and voices the Bitterness of being the daily butt of refrained Illiteracy and scoffing Suburbia. O seven swords in the heart are as nothing, Madonna mia!, to the daily pinpricks against which, try as one will, one cannot defend oneself.

Pinprick No. 1. But why must your brains be any better than other peoples'? (It is not that they are better. It is that they are different.)

Pinprick No. 2. And why must you call yourself a poet? (Because I write only prose.)

Pinprick No. 3. And now, I suppose, you are writing another of your queer books? (Yes. I must have something to read.)

Pinprick No. 4. Must you always be laughing? Nothing but the noise of your laughter about the place. . . . (So that in time you may boast that you heard it!)

Comment on the above. Eaten by worms before my time.

Art. A horse has more justice done it than a man. Or take the boxer. When he is down he is down. Useless saying the other man is superior even though knocked out at the beginning of the round. There is no argument. There is but the supreme justice of fact. Justice for ever denied the creative artist. For him there is only opinion.

Pain. Remember if you are hurt that it is always deliberate. There is no such thing as undeliberate pain inflicted by another.

In each of us there is a snake, and when we have struck either we are shamed or we are vindicated. Even the least subtle among us carries his own poison.

All hurt is deliberate. And it is only because it is deliberate that it can be borne. If such pain were impartial, its blow would be mortal.

Notebook Number Nine

Pleasurable *Reflection.* Like my pen I drank from a bottle. One debt less I owe my fellow-men!

On Death. While there is a room to pace, a wine to drink, a laugh to share, I shall know that I am alive.

Good Clean Fun. "*When a man recognises another man's sister as of equal value to his own sister, then the sort of thing the bishop complains of will not take place. That is what we aim at.*" Mr George Lansbury, M.P., replying to the Bishop of London.

Admittedly incest has everything in its favour, but for that aspect so desolating to physical love: the too-familiar. It worked efficiently enough among the Aztecs and would have continued working efficiently enough among the Egyptians had not Cleopatra preferred Cæsar to brother Ptolemy.

And that exactly is where incest is not practicable in the mass, and why the bringing of all relations between man and woman to the plane of brother and sister has not proved as easy as reformers have hoped.

It is not that suburban and provincial young ladies are less hedonistic than a Lucrezia Borgia. It is that few brothers are as desirable or exquisite as a Cesare Borgia. As even fewer fathers are as amorous or as cynical as a Pope Alexander.

Or truly it would need no Mr Lansbury to say: Go to, go to!

Sudden glimpse of Heaven's Front Parlour on coming on the Salvation Army calling loudly in a side street. Disheartening that the Almighty has still so little aesthetic sense. . . .

Why the best murders happen always in the dullest streets and quietest suburbs. A potato left to go to seed will produce berries as deadly as nightshade.

To understand man, make a study of the vegetable.

To those who are afraid of Love. But it is not love that hurts! It is when one has ceased to love.

Opera. It takes three seconds to cross from one end of a stage to the other. To music it takes three hours.

City Bred. Sees a petrified forest and believes it. Sees a dead civilisation and cannot believe his own will one day be like it. The top may be off the Colosseum or the Bagni de Caracalla. But not, *not* the Splendide-Splendide and the Super-Magnifico Kinema.

Unmentionable Triangle. O the North, the North! Mr Lawrence, Mr Huxley, Mr James Douglas, fingering mentally, ashamedly, that which it has never occurred to the South to question. It is time we learned to blame religion, conduct, impulse, on climate and latitude rather than on the non-conformist gods and ourselves!

City-bound crowd. To sacrifice yearly a few thousand handsome fresh-picked virgins, is paganism, savagery, and cannibalism.

To sacrifice daily a million smug, undecorative, self-patterned people, is civilisation, christianity, and progress.

How to Judge. Judge always by the lowest. The highest is so rare as to be practically an unnatural growth; an exotic poisonous bloom on the human dunghill. By taking the lowest you get man's measure and the happy mean. As a nation's test it is infallible.

Thick and thin and round and square. (On seeing a newsreel of imposing excavators amid the latest excavations.) Scientists and distinguished archaeologists dig about in the sands and lose themselves in the discovery of a ring of the Shepherd Kings.

But who is to tell us why, since Egypt, it has all been much like children playing at bricks with bucket and spade? Who is to tell us why the Great Pyramid built over five thousand years is so planned and constructed that the variations of the compass may be determined by the position of its sides? Who shall explain the impulse behind the thought and fact of the Great Wall of China, ruin of Ankhor Vhat, the Aztec temples over which the jungle has closed?

The Greek, the Roman, is too near to us. It is our every-day. It is too human. We have passed through and beyond. Yet Egypt was dying as Greece was being born. As China dies to-day. And still since these two, all effort has been childlike and unfinished.

It is not facts we need. A stone on a stone is a fact but it does not unbuild the pyramids. Here it is no longer what we know, but what we apprehend.

Take the noblest piece of stone or brick the Greeks have left us. The appeal is to eye and memory. We honour, we understand, we imitate. In the modern, we better. (Beside the sweep of a le Corbusier design how tawdry the realistic frieze, the enlarged public-mantelpiece temple ornamentation. To be acceptable the antique must be a fragment or a ruin, with connoisseur Time eliminating all detail and knocking off arms, legs, and noses.) Rome merely piled the bricks four times higher and one hundred times more vulgarly.

Brick, stone, marble, cement, which the best or worst of human limitation has strung together. None of these fills us with awe, even with terror, but principally with the sense that if these were men then are we not even pigmies.

Not a question of scale but of conception. Climate cannot explain it as it can explain all other mental phenomena from the loin-clothed squatting Indian staring life away in suspended animation under a broiling sun under which it would require herculean energy to bother about to-morrow, to the little soured sects of chapel-going protestantism under lowering skies beneath which it would require equally herculean effort to persuade oneself that there is not going to be a to-morrow. Ever and always man's buildings fit his mind. What then must have been the lost mind of Egypt if such stones remain?

Strayed in the wastes of Africa, with which it has nothing in common. Africans are mere dancing baboons; gramophones and flannel shirts will not make them less so. Here then is a check to sentimentality. Nations and individuals are to be judged by their works. By their works only. Deeds are impulsive.

From the Mediterranean-European shores civilisation has penetrated even to the barbaric furthermost northern islands (England, Ireland, Greenland) of the continent. In the Mediterranean the communication from shore to shore, from age to age, has been vital and intense. From the African shores of the Mediterranean it has not moved. Therefore is there no assimilating power in that land. No absorption of culture. No growth, no expansion. Then niggers remain niggers.

The Egyptian was a fine, thin-nosed, thin-lipped people. The negro has large thick lips and flattened nostrils. Far more by the mouth than by the grubbing about in sand after buried trifles, may we yet come to an understanding, an apprehension of a race and its achievement. Thick lips seem to belong to a people whose food is succulent large fruits and is stuffed in the mouth with fists. Thin-lipped people have evolved to the spoon for millenniums and fed on small grains (China) and wheat (the white races).

The Africans work in mud. They still can carve only a wooden spoon. The primitive (African) is round. The civilised (Egyptian) is square. Again the Chinese are proof of this. These two are the artists who have experimented the longest.

O that round pot, unearthed everywhere!

The Round—the kraal, Stonehenge, the popular ring dance, the magic circle.

Oppose to that Greek, Chinese, Babylonian, Egyptian, Assyrian, Byzantine, Cubisme.

No high civilisation has passed without coming to the square. Whilst the round requires only feeling, the square requires brain. The square is the triumph of thought over emotion.

There are no round crystals. You analyse from a prism. Analysis is prismatic. Therefore that which analyses (thought) is always pointed, angular, sharp, square-edged.

If in six thousand years the negro has produced nothing, he is not likely to produce it now. Let us then not sentimentalise him merely because Harlem can find a voice worthy of the concert platform or a sufficient electric vitality to caper with a string of bananas round its thighs.

And let us stop disturbing the hot sand for that round pot and primitive ring, however pleasant an excuse it may be for escaping an English winter!

Freud and the rest. Where wrong. Because of a patching-up which takes people seriously. But people are not to be taken seriously in their little psychic belly aches, induced by wrong emotional feeding.

Individual psychic ailments are to be taken seriously only when man's education, mental standard, emotional control, have been brought to sanity and in touch with modern needs.

Petted and given a toy each time it cries, the individual is a nuisance and romantic millstone round the neck of sane thinking and constructive action.

What have you achieved if in a fool's world you cure a fool? In a sane world only can you diagnose the insane and unbalanced and thus be useful to the community at large.

Therefore Freud and his fellow-workers are but a psycho-sexual Salvation Army, repairing, soothing, tidying, covering-up the evil after the event. But not removing the cause.

We have gone too far for the individual to matter. The individual can have his ills cured and prevented by gland treatment. But civilisation is now too far out of control and proportion for a revivalist band to explain it away at the corners of streets or in the private confessionals of expensive consulting-rooms.

Such luxuries are of the past. Events are too serious.

The one-ness, the blood brotherhood, the unbreakable link by which Sir James Barrie, O.M., and the late D. H. Lawrence are made one. Men who know women only in the guise of mothers; their own mothers. Therefore, themselves.

The petulant, the sentimental, the weak, the ungrown. Emotional lack of inches is as much a freak as the physical midget. And the literary tumblings and posturings which follow spread evil and panic, where the gay little midget spreads only a thoughtless and kindly laughter.

Men whose love of woman is mother love, who know women from having clung to their skirts. To whom woman is a comfort but never a discontent. To whom the mistress recalls the copy book.

All of which makes reading Mr Lawrence very much like attending a revivalist meeting; Sir James, a kindergarten. Mix the kindergarten and the revivalist meeting and you have the Great General Public.

—And who cares to batter a head against *that* wall.

Notebook Number Ten

First *Poem. Statement.*

> However absurd
> Any bird
> Can get itself heard.
>
> But no man
> Worth a damn
> Can.

And Last Poem. E pur' si muove. . . .

> The peasant drives an ox
> The millionaire a Rolls
> The jew a bargain
> The gentleman a ball.

Sanctus Spiritus. Of the three the Holy Ghost alone is free. His throne, the Universe. God and Son are seated on an earthly throne. He hovers.

Consider the egg. How bloodless, how clean, how impersonal a birth.

Pre-Sentimental Age. Of the Queen Bee's fifty thousand children one hundred only are sons. The rest daughters, young, old, sterile. All work in and out of the hive is now theirs.

But then this state of work and virginity should be accepted as permanent and inevitable. They should be left alone, apart, sterilised by industry.

They should not be tormented by daily newspapers and popular magazines with stories of love, of freedom, of happiness, of plenty.

The Old. Never trust the old. The old can only take. That would not matter but that they think it their right. As though unproductive people have any rights! The old have no life; but they have the position and the pedestal.

Big City. Everything in a town is calculated to stimulate envy, greed, desire. Life is not to be grasped. Everything is out of reach. Everything is behind plate glass.

And we still teach children the legend of a Tantalus!

Suicide. How many would commit suicide were there nothing to hide. A man will be ten years on the verge of bankruptcy, to the last twelve hours when the news is a certainty. Till that moment he does not take his revolver from the drawer. On the contrary he argues: If I shoot myself they will know. Likewise the young girl who commits suicide only when her condition becomes noticeable.

Such secrets keep a man alive. Meaning you can humiliate and deny the body and it can withstand it. You cannot humiliate the spirit.

To propitiate this spirit man will go to fantastic lengths, outside himself. He will crystalise his spirit in the arts. On his dying day he does not wish his neighbours to insult that spirit and leaves his hoarded old masters to the local picture gallery. Herein is the great desire of people to leave something to posterity. Only for that name, that spirit, do the Rockefellers of the world leave their hundred millions to the incurables of Little Rock, Ark.

Scapegoat. After each Big Business crash when a leading stockbroker finds himself in the dock, the General Public alternates between horror at the business man's astuteness and gratitude at a justice alike for rich and poor.

But it never tells itself that had there been no crash, that particular stockbroker could have continued uninterrupted that same astuteness. Nor that the State in treating him as a common thief is both libelling the thief and condemning itself.

A thief only takes money. So far it has not occurred to him to promise to return it with interest.

Likewise the State turns a blind eye when mass-swindling goes well. Its moral indignation, therefore, when things go wrong is a sanctimonious hypocrisy of the meanest kind. You cannot deny the result and uphold the principle.

(But that would be asking the General Public to think. . . .)

The Writer consoles Herself on not getting a Thought. Even a hen does not lay an egg a day. And if she can manage to lay three hundred in a year (helped by patent foods and artificial daylight) she wins a prize.

We with three thousand thoughts in a year are never likely to win a prize, both because thought is not considered prizeworthy, and because in our case the hens are busy judging the literary laying.

So let us take the day off and play!

Whenever in despair one has thought of hens as a possible means of being able to live in the country and of achieving solitude and monetary independence, one has had to abandon the idea. The smell of hencoops and their restrained activity remind one only too forcefully of the estimable middle classes, their mental sobriety, their thoughtless security, their uncompromisingly utilitarian outlook.

On Death. All fear springs from the fear of death; unconscious force behind all thought and action.

Loss, finality, oblivion. It is the shortness, the uncertainty, the comparative uselessness of our life that corrodes the heart and dulls the finer edges of the spirit.

He who can see himself going down to the earth and accept the grave as final, living again only in that no matter can be destroyed or energy lost, has intensified despair—but has conquered fear.

This is hard. Except in calm moments of vision when the unity of all life is understood and acknowledged, this is practically impossible. Especially when one loves, and the length of youth and life seems still more pitiful.

A whale cleaves the water five hundred years. A tortoise retreats into its shell for anything up to a thousand years. Either they are more important than man or Time has no significance beyond individual brevity and desire.

Credo. One belief alone can stand the test of any hour, age, emotion, mood. One belief alone which can be neither denied nor betrayed. A belief in happiness. A belief that if pain is an evil, then is sorrow an evil.

The gift one would give man would be laughter. Laughter in all its forms from the finality of irony to the guffaw of the drunkard.

But laughter!

Memory. As a child, standing near the great windows on late winter afternoons waiting for the convent to light. For only then could the earth shine and throb more brightly than all other stars, once our great building had come alight, its windows blazing their challenge.

They said we were a star. They said that each star shining at night was but a world like our own. From where then could it come, that light, but from the houses, their windows gleaming boldly through the darkness? And so one waited, impatient, believing, for the convent windows to put all other stars to shame.

Curiously right, this childish delusion. For the light must come from within oneself. In all things, light comes from within, from the core of the spirit or of the sun. Fortunately one was not then to know that life was to be lived among people whose light is the wan reflection of others' sun, who themselves are reflections of reflections, till they are so many millions of miles away that some of them cannot even be seen.

Pre-Sentimental Age. Gothic offends the reason. Stone is not to be treated as lace or ivory. Milan is the ultimate of vulgar tripotage. Strasbourg a masterpiece of materialised vision, for the local stone used is a dull red and the result not white lace, lard, or sugar, but rusted and entangled iron.

Gothic needed men of taste. Norman needed men of character. Stone is strength, might, majesty. It is a material symbol of male power. We must go back; back to the first vision before men put frills on their buildings and their minds.

As a child one believed that people built their houses first and put the windows in only afterwards. Else (one argued) how could one know where one wanted windows to be? Curiously right, this childish assumption. For form is all and detail mere accessory. In all matter is form the foundation and conception: detail the impulsive addition. One must come straight to the point in stone and in words. A sentence, like an arch, must be hewn in a line, bearing the full weight of its thought.

The Poet consoles his Loneliness. At intervals here and there; ardent, unknown, invisible. Friends whose hand one shall never take; whose finding shall not be marred by familiarity; whom one shall never speak to or know but by knowing and speaking to oneself.

Pis-en-lit. Let us leave daisies and buttercups to True Poets. We cannot all be cows.

Six months in New York. The *rapide* tears with its boat-load of passengers toward Paris. But this is not a moment to be for ever lost by hurrying to the first train that is to hand. In the pale grey of an early spring morning Havre is preparing itself for the quiet busyness of its day.

Again the sense of cobbles to the foot and ear. So man still builds his own house with his own hands! They are about us everywhere, made with the care and precision of a bird's nest; each straw, each fluff, each twig, placed to advantage with care and love. Hand-made with the beautiful crookedness of hand-made things: that perfect balance of irregularity.

The ascending houses hang, time-faded, hand-embroidered. A stitchery of brick, spring leaf, and peeled bark.

A *Gobelin* tapestry at early day; a bead embroidery in the noonday sun. The composition that of a bunch of flowers, picked with a laugh and arranged still smiling.

And everywhere deep breaths of incense, manure, coffee, drains, and wood shavings.

The Cuckoo. (In Homage.) The cuckoo is the patron saint of the upstart artist. Alone of birds it does not twitter. It states. There is no answer to its call. Into the stern reproving silence that greets its challenge it sends again that clear triumphant echoing. It is the true contemptuous solitary.

And what a labour and what a cunning that placing of its eggs and the slow pushing aside of all obstacles in the calm knowledge of its superior and unlawful destiny!

No singing bird can make so arrogant a sound. Woods and hedgerows are live with a busy flow of twittering and taking tea and charm and rivalry and gossip. And then, ringing in all parts of the air at once, bold, unheralded, unseen, there falls in warm drops through the sudden silence the oil of doubt on love's complacent shoulder.

Notebook Number Eleven

Self-Portrait. All my life I have seemed slightly ridiculous to people. And people have always seemed damnably ridiculous to me.

Advice to the Living. Measure your life by the depth of your mind, the state of your bowels, the range of your laughter, and the subtlety of your palate.

Distinction. Christ turned water to wine. Process known to all good wine sellers.
Turn blood to wine. Process known only to good poets.

On reading Saint Teresa of Avila. Done with the hand it becomes certifiable and ends in a lunatic asylum. Done with the mind it becomes canonised and ends in a message to mankind.

Martyrdom. On watching an expanse of singer from above. So much disfigurement and for such poor song! With the final acute child-birth note such bosom should recede, shrink, unswell, deflate, in preparation for the next mechanical lark eager to nest in its heaving acreage.

Bucolic. On watching the futile efforts of a field of sheep to interest a ram and the equally futile efforts of the ram to interest the sheep. No wonder the shepherd does it himself!

Copied from a notebook kept at the age of sixteen. Beware the handicap of polite thinking!

Our Two (literary) Schools. The rage of impotence or the ignorance of impotence? To be angry or to be unaware? And both these old wives' tales re-told on the high thin falsetto of old women's voices.

Martyr-exile. Spring in Sicily. Summer on hilltops near Florence. Winters on the Italian lakes. Months in Mexico. More months about Southern France and Naples. And year upon year spent thus, as an alternative to sipping tea and competing in parochial drawing-room mischief among the little London cliques of literary tea-cup fishers.
Exile the staunchest patriot might envy!

Man, woman, child. The male child is cruel, warm-hearted, ruthless. The female child gentle, vicious, motherly. Man grows into a reasoning and dutiful being, obsessed by many forms of honour. Woman emancipates herself and becomes naturally tyrannical and possessive.
A young woman dreams of a home and a family. An old woman of

reform clubs and Rescue Societies. Both must (benevolently) interfere.

On Woman. Woman's creative gift is self-sacrifice. This, their deepest impulse, militates against any creative genius they could have. For the creative artist is the supreme selfish being: Art that which you alone can do and to which you will sacrifice all things—but yourself, who must be alone, secure and impregnable, to create it.

Only to dwell on the sacrifice women as mothers make, in towns, cottages, war, poverty. Even though they have made motherhood so vulgar a sentimentality, one would like to follow these sacrifices, these humiliations for their children (tired women, not lovable) when term fees are due; study the wiles a full-grown woman will contrive (who for herself would not endure a moment more the insolence, drunkenness, indifference, stupidity of some-one whom she secretly despises) to send a boy back with his shoes in decent repair, his school trunk correctly filled.

Because of a child, unformed, unimaginative, waiting the day when it shall be freed from the restraint of the too-familiar four walls of home, sacrifice like a disease is imposed by these thoughtless beings on their vulnerable parents. Sacrifice passing unnoted; dark heroisms for which a General would be so weighted with honours as to look like a prize booth at the local fair.

Deliver the child from the tyranny of the parent: the parent from the tyranny of the child. Self-sacrifice is an impulse artificially induced and sustained. This family business does not work. Family means that there has got to be a victim. And fortunate indeed that in which there is but one!

Civilisation. The family is the enemy of progress; the main cause of civilisation's backwardness. (This is proved by the religious outcry each time a voice is raised against it.)

Too long has mankind had the hearth for horizon. Too long has he judged all things by mother, Aunt Euphemia, Uncle George, and the twins. And looked no further.

Thus the same narrow mental standard persists through the centuries, the only noticeable difference being that the women cook less willingly and wireless adorns the side table. And man is where he was centuries since, when he should be as different from that early self as is the gramophone from the clavichord, the Marx Brothers from Grimaldi.

The family is the decay of man. The questioner, the rebel, humanity's black sheep, the unruly son turned from the door and deleted from the will. For the family has nothing to learn. It is slovenly, smug, and limited.

The individual develops only when he has left the family. So shall the human race.

Mob. Awe and reverence: distinction between wild and tame animal.

Where the individual is weak and unreliable, herds of people are gathered together for their protection. Consequently the one grave sin against the herd is independence. The herd can forgive only its own weakness. It cannot forgive another's strength.

Dog, child, man, family, parents, friends. The need of us, of you, of it, of all. We need you. You must need us. Do not question the common need. At the first hint of independence (of thought, word, action), they hate as inevitably as the rich the poor, the crowd the solitary, the safe the rebel.

Numbers smell stupidity. Civilisation will have been reached only when man is separate, inviolate, alone. Not a common weakness but an individual strength.

Brotherhood of Man. Put him in uniform and study the brotherhood. A coloured rag on his back, a coloured rag in his hand, a coloured rag of skin, creed, shift.

Are we then bulls to be frightened and made violent by a sudden patch of arbitrary colour?

Foremost sample of mass thinking: Poems are made by fools like me, but only God can make a tree. Then God deals in second-rate goods. Trees are everywhere; there still is not a handful of good poems.

An acorn can make a tree. Try and make a poem.

As Poets might well question their Mirrors. Why after tiresome hours lost in pursuit of a vision or a word, should we look no different? There is no visible difference between ourselves and other men, jostled in buses, elbowed in streets, but that they look neater and more composed.

Why is there none to see the nimbus about our heads, wings at our back and feet, dove above our brows? Only a stride and an abstract stare to proclaim to others that we are objects of derision.

Grateful Acknowledgement. There are meetings in print exciting as one's own thought; that find one trembling again as at the first words of love one listened to and believed.

For me that encounter was Stendhal. Nor was it a gentle meeting. It was a shock which for days left one between anger and enthusiasm. An idle unsought meeting with mirror-like sentences in which one stared, defensively refusing to believe that more than a hundred years ago their content had been taken from one's mouth.

—Il me faut trois ou quatre pieds cubes d'idées par jour, comme il faut du charbon a un bateau a vapeur.

—J'ai un tort qui nuira a mon avancement dans le monde, c'est l'amour de la solitude.

—Quand serai-je assez riche pour n'avoir plus de rapports forcés avec aucun homme?

—Une reverie tendre en 1821 et, plus tard, philosophique et melancholique, est devenue un si grand plaisir pour moi que, quand un ami m'aborde, je donnerais un boulet pour qu'il ne m'adressât pas la parole. La vue seule de quelqu'un que je connais me contrarie. Quand je vois un tel être de loin, et qu'il faut que je pense à le saluer, cela me contrarie cinquante pas à l'avance.

—De là, mon bonheur à me promener fièrement dans une ville étrangère, ou je suis arrivé depuis une heure et où je suis sûr de n'être connu de personne.

This is the first time a written word spoke and in a voice which I recognised. One knew then that literature had always seemed sentimentally a great many words, stories, poems, plays. And that one had no use for literature. And that a passion for facts, change, solitude, and thought, could never again seem the eccentricity it was held to be.

Only twice before had a voice spoken in a sentence, as though written for one's ear. Each time in adolescence. One in a book, ponderous, erudite, on the human mind of which one understood nothing, till one came on this: *There can be no production without reproduction.* So *that* the art-philtre's essence! And one had thought such mysteries heaven-sent, haphazard by divine-right, in which a chosen few indulged in a form of superior magic while the rest of humanity respectfully kept off the artistic grass!

The other, was to change a nervous and petrified mental approach to the people with whom (it seemed) one must share this world: *And who's afraid of you? said Alice, why you're nothing but a pack of cards!*

These few words and certain of the sayings of Leonardo da Vinci have been the written moments of illumination real to me as my daily

life; dearer than many of its happiest experiences. All the reading-rest
has been words and situations more or less ably or vividly or breath-
takingly or incompetently or unforgettably strung together. Not more.

To these alone could I apply that supreme test of book-writing laid
down by Metastasio: Chi fa un libro fa meno che niente se il libro fatto
non rifá la gente.

Strange to me and saddening that there can be no way of repaying
such a debt. . . .

O*n approaching a London terminus.* Twenty-four thousand eight hundred and thirty-nine chimneys. And one tree.

London, Eng. London is not for passionate people. The unraised voice, the deadened tread, the restricted smile. The neat uncompromisingly utilitarian aspect of its changeless mile of shop-bordered street, about which Londoners (most parochial of the world's crowds) creep and murmur through their daily life with an old-age cautiousness. They do not laugh: they titter. But they are good-natured and cowed and non-aggressive.

Talk to them of dissatisfaction; talk to them of having missed something; talk to them of a here-after. Talk to them of anything, in fact, but life.

But hang it all, I mean to say. Unvaryingly one's first impression on returning home from the Continent is once again the restrained street-life of the Londoner. Their singleness of desire seeming to be to efface themselves from the presence of their fellow-men, for whom they have at sight a genteel, ignorant, and unreasoning contempt.

In despite of Eros in Piccadilly (that enlarged Sèvres on the public mantelpiece) there would seem to be no love that a lady cannot forget in a little shopping. No passion a gentleman cannot dissipate in a round of golf.

Untouchable. Neat London, efficient, dull, parochial. It may well be that (apart from our climate and lack of clear air, sun, wine, and argument) the level drabness of our English town-life is due to our ideals of Untouchable.

India has but three million Untouchables. We have over sixty million. The entire British population at home and abroad.

After a few Dukes and the few thousands of the Upper Middle region, come the compartmented classes, all gentlemen in varying degree, till they cannot squeeze another ounce out of the wretched creature and it becomes a manual worker.

And all are Untouchable one to the other with their set eating-places, quarters, habits, entrances. The workman who wants a drink cannot come and sit at the next café table to our own (there are no café tables at which to sit), as before the surrounding gentry can protest a waiter appears, frowning. Worse, it could never occur to the workman to sit there and have that drink, for the Untouchableness (our peculiar anti-human British brand) is inborn, imbibed early, never lost.

The sniff, the whisper, the genteel snicker at the manners and appearance of our fellow Untouchables is characteristic and peculiar to London. Everything is dehumanised. And it works.

Laugh in a London train, street, restaurant, and all within earshot stare coldly; at once hostile and defensive. In every corner of the world they would grin, ignore, or join in. But in London a laugh is felt subtly as a personal affront; resented as both unnatural and ill-bred. One is left always with the shamefaced impression of having burst out laughing in church. Which makes for good manners and an exceptional dullness.

The pleasant friendliness of the street-life of Paris, New York, Rome, is the singularly shocking sense that the town and everything in it belongs to the people. Londoners look guiltily as though they were being tolerated on some-one else's street. As a drive in the English countryside is being politely allowed through some-one else's park or garden.

That pleasing Continental impression of variety and exuberance comes from the unconfined life of the streets. Ours, the mistrustful insular confinement of life chopped-up in rooms. Safe in our water-tight compartments from which all other Untouchables are excluded by prejudice, upbringing, and a plus-four cut of unused intellect.

O land without wine, with restricted movement, without song!

The Club: the Café. The difference between the Club and the Café is the protection which the Club affords. Protection from one's fellow-men.

The gloom of England comes from the correct. It may not be the highest expression of life, but it is the highest expression of our life. Consequently the gentleman is the only man who questions the usefulness of women. He can do without women but he cannot do without men. He is not right, but he is correct.

Thus the telephone is his only passionate connection. Very angry if interrupted on the telephone, he yet remains philosophic if interrupted in love.

Joylessness. There can be no life when in place of hope you put fear.

Take a census of their ambitions and each and all would vote for the continuance *ad perpetuum* of their jobs.

A few daring ambitious souls would ask for a rise of £2.

Thought on approaching Oxford. How many pinnacles in the seat of learning!

Public School. Young England. Where he was to learn the pleasures of a bad table and a solitary bed.

He then sits on a bench for three years and acquires an Oxford polish.

And now for the rest of his life, perpetual adolescent among the world's men, may put his school tie around his neck and strangle himself.

Motoring through pretty villages. On the sunnier side, the drier side, the healthier side, and the Cornish Riviera. Not a fountain! Not a well-head! Not a cackling of women or crowing of child.

Do you remember that first sight of Viterbo, swirl of stone basin over which the water bounds in flowing light?

Do you remember, centre-piece to each Alsatian village, the steady drip of the fluted mouth as the serene octagonal fountains pipe their reedy tune?

Do you remember the massive baroque stone contortions of Forio Ponte and the high cicalous clamour of the women, to which the children join their thin pointed voices of young and amorous cats? And for less than a penny you drink a glass of local wine, ice-cold from a bronze wine bin you had admired yesterday in Pompei?

—Not do you remember, but can you forget!

Lost on a winter's day in Wandsworth, S.E. Miles of tram and two-storied soot-soaked brick house. And no protest.

Yet the depression of London, the sick ache of its dullness to the sensitive colour-starved eye, nerve, spirit, is not that three-quarters of its fifteen-mile radius is slum. But that it is hopeless slum.

Out of every slum of the world, out of the poorest quarters of the great cities, from the tenements of New York, Berlin, Paris, Moscow, Spain, Dublin, Clydeside, an Italian village, a lesser industrial town, from the dreariest homes and most dilapidated of hovels, it is possible to believe, to accept, to know, that a great talent, an anger, a genius, may emerge. A sense of striving, a sense of activity beyond mere struggle. But the London slum, stretching its mile on mile, alternating the very poor and the lesser genteel, leaves a consciousness only of minor clerk, shop-assistant, and tram conductor.

A dull unquestioning in which they neither strive nor starve. And from which not artist nor genius can be produced, they having in themselves, surroundings, or blood-stream, neither music, colour, beauty, nor eloquence. The highest that is open to them is to better their social position through enterprise and application and be received into the wholly middle class.

There is an emigration from the Bowery to Park Avenue; from the East-End to Upper Brook Street and Park Lane; but there is no stir from the depths of Balham, Tooting, Wandsworth, and the Old Kent Road. The local kinema acts as sedative; never as stimulant.

Why these spawned million? Their opinions? Their emotions? Brought into being for Black Cat, lower grade ale, and the margarine magnates.

For it is not the slums that make the people. It is the people who finally make the slums. If Wandsworth did not want to live in its slum it would be emigrating to Canada, or conquering Paris, or clamouring for munitions to take the South of France by storm!

Instead of being moribund, it would be empty.

Fog. They should use the London streets for smoking bacon, hams, and sausages, as they use the sun in Italy. But we keep our smoke for our lungs.

A post-mortem examination on a Londoner reveals his lungs to be not only atrophied but black. And a third generation of Londoner is considered as uninsurable.

On reading Lady Chatterley *in French.* In English three-parts of it read as the sniffling of an adolescent vulgarian. But to read it in the language of Montaigne, Stendhal, Balzac, is to understand to its full horror the police-court censoriousness, the immovable death-in-life millstone around the neck of *la tristesse puritaine et methodiste.*

Its glorification of the amorous artlessness of the working-man becomes more than suspect when one remembers that in Paris a person wishing to make clear that another knows few of the subtleties of amatory combat, will qualify the remark by saying that it is done: *à la maçon.* And no doubt will add with a raising of eyebrow and shoulder: *le français, lui, il fait ça à la confiture.*

And Uller, laughing, was saying: The character of Art is exuberant. That of the Englishman, sober.

Personifying Art you will find it to be a warm, exuberant, generous, giving, frank sort of person, utterly unself-conscious, possibly gesticulating, talkative, unconventional.

Melt all the English in one and you will get a form of person well-bred, well-behaved, moderate of language, modest of demeanour, showing little his emotions (unless his dog die suddenly), not expressing very strong opinions if opinions at all, gesticulating never, rather trying to take than to give, always insisting on his money's value, intelligent, and slowly observant.

The education such a person receives directly and indirectly, at school, the home, the street, makes him a gentleman: gentleman of rule and order and safety first. And he must be sure he has his chin well shaved before he can consider looking at a woman passing in the street.

So modest is he that he does not ask for fruit or flowers or blue skies. The country produces only green and rain, and do you wish to make him happy send him out in the rain on the green.

These two people are so differently born and bred that there can be no understanding or sympathy between them. One, silent and unmoved, on a misty, chilly, raining island; one on the shores of the Mediterranean, loud, generous, vital, conscious.

The meagre sunshine and sparse crops make the Englishman wise, secretive, saving, cautious. He does not belong to the other, cannot walk in step, or sympathise. How then should he transplant the flower of Art from abroad?

The English can grow and will grow Art, but it must not be an imported mongrel Art, as it always has been till now. It must be an art as national as the art of daily journalism, of betting, and plus-fours.

W*oman as Uncreative Artist.* Art is a masculine prerogative. Its prizes go to man with his sewn-up body and thicker blood-stream. Art is the fertilisation of life. Man, the fertiliser.

Woman's Sphere. Art is to the spirit what thought is to the mind, desire to the body, words to the mouth. It is exactly this sense of the essentiality of the task that is lacking in women's work. Diligence is no substitute.

For the creation of Art is needed universality, curiosity, impersonality. For fiction you need only emotion.

Women are excellent at fiction.

Woman as Uncreative Artist. Women are not born with creative souls. They are born with virtues and emotions. So that they may disturb only for a little while.

Five hundred a year and a Room of one's Own. If creative achievement were a matter of a room of one's own, then since the first dawn in which the first woman was pushed to safety in the first cave, she should have been the world's creative artist.

At no time in the world's history has woman been without a room of her own. But it has always been the kitchen. Then write on the kitchen table! Paint on the kitchen walls! Draw on the kitchen floor! Carve into shape the pastry and the butter! And so she would have had it been essential to her nature.

The bitter story of the Arts urges one to ask what man has ever had a room of his own that he did not have to earn with cadging, pandering, humiliation, fill with wives and children and bailiffs, and still produce by the spirit-alchemy of sweat and desire the works he is remembered by?

As though England were not honeycombed with passive aesthetically sterile women of all ages, in rooms of their own ranging from five hundred to five thousand a year! Possibly it produces a local (village) industry. That is as much as five hundred a year will produce anywhere.

To the creative artist £500 is not enough. It must be five millions. Or five pence.

Woman as Uncreative Artist. Women confuse sincerity with art, achievement with purpose. Which is the cause of the shoddy literary goods and sentimental thinking of the day. The female public is one with its sister supply.

For women bring the charitable virtues to the Arts. The lame, the halt, the blind are succoured. They drop pennies only in the bottomless cans of sincerity and good-will.

On a gift of the Diaries and Letters of Katherine Mansfield. ("I knew you'd like these, being a writer yourself." "O you come from London? Then you must know a man called Brown. . . .") Twittering, twittering, female twittering. Bird baths, quick linnet wings, canary seed, a lump of sugar, and suddenly a raised throat, a pause (a self-conscious literary pause), and a sudden jet of delicate twittering, melancholy snow-clad female twittering. The whole neatly photographed with the ever-watching feline literary eye.

Self-consciously to dedicate a lifetime. And then to twitter!

Lament. Oppose the twin (female) gifts of Good Clean Fun and Diligence to the twin (male) gifts of Nonsense and Curiosity. And you will know why on reaching Parnassus woman sips tea quietly in the drawing-room while man sups royally with the gods.

Distinction. Woman takes on the colouring of her surroundings. Man makes his surroundings and colours them.

Two Points of View. The sun has smiled on man and woman alike; the earth flowed onward; the seas swung their rhythmic course; the skies opened and revealed their depths; trees budded and let fall their fruits; grandeur and decay and rebirth have been revealed to each impartially. And only man has marvelled.

Tea-Shoppe. They seem to take to the Arts rather as a marriage recommended as a cure-all for a delicate woman.

Woman as Uncreative Artist. Women have many drawing-room beliefs. The hearth, the vicar, the cup of tea. And the toast.

To the Temple of Art they bring their small corner of baroque gilding. Charmingly the ladies take down their harps and produce a little grey-haired music in F Superior and G Squat.

Among those invited we find Thought with its tea-cup in its hand.

And Venus with her sterile pubic gesture which may be modesty and may very well be something less than modest.

Curiosity. Curiosity, most male of male gifts, thanks to which man cracked the earth in his fist like a walnut. And then invented Art to help himself digest it!

Sappho. Who still is used as proof of woman's aesthetic equality to man. Not on her fragments (which are mostly pedestrian and genteel notations of an able and conscientious woman versifier) does one condemn Sappho, but on the testimony of her day.

To be bludgeoned into accepting her poetic superiority as final, sacred, and unquestioned, because her work was praised by one or two important men of her times, is carrying a woman's privilege of the doubt to extremes. On what evidence is Plato, conscientious politician and mystic muddle-head, an authority on the lyric arts?

Mr H. G. Wells is unstinted in his praise of the novels of Mr J. B. Priestley. Mr Stanley Baldwin an ardent advocate of the works of the late Mary Webb. Mr Bernard Shaw sits for his portrait to the Honourable John Collier.

Therefore a few fragments of the works of Mary Webb, a few thousand pages of Mr J. B. Priestley, and we are to assume down the ages that these were the sweetest songsters of the early twentieth century.

The judgements of its Public Men on Art are surely too well known by now to be taken as testimony for greatness or enduring worth. This is one of posterity's verdicts which should always go by contraries.

Tea-Shoppe. Sappho bitterly rebukes her brother for his marriage to a woman of the streets. *This from a poet!* This from a woman with a private brothel of her own which she called an Academy.

Here in the outlook (and is there a woman to say she was wrong?) of their foremost example of aesthetic excellence, one comes near to uncovering the source of the failure of women as creative artists. We come near to explaining that mincing elegance, that devoted lifetime of pedantic sterility, that warm menstrous flow of womanly prose, which give to their works all the negative virtues of the male soprano.

A comfortable income; a room of one's own; respectability for others. In short, woman's trump card: security.

. . . secondary woman. On watching two Indian dancers. The man meditates. The woman disturbs him.

Female Elephants have no Tusks. Both the desire and the capacity for creative art are organic. If therefore the necessary structural impulsion were latent in woman it would have made itself manifest before this weary date in the world's antiquity.

It is typical of woman that she should put forward that justificatory plea of centuries of slavery and repression, for she is essentially imitative and purposeful and feels (rightly) that had she been told about the fine arts earlier she might have competed.

Unfortunately the creation of art is in no sense an acquired characteristic. Were it so, women would have more than a fair chance of competing with men; though not of excelling.

Art must not be confused with freedom or education. A natural manifestation in woman is self-adornment. Centuries of irate fathers, despotic husbands, or lack of facilities have not prevented woman from giving expression to this urge and need of her nature. How then not Art, had it been as womb-rooted as her impulse to physical procreation and personal adornment?

Woman is an outward appearance. Her realm the minor emotional realm of Dance, Stage, and Fiction.

Distinction. Men are cunning in their works. Women in their lives.

Further distinction. Man opens his arms: woman her thighs.

Good Clean Fun. Woman has (supposedly) so many temptations to resist. It is a pity she does not realise that Art is the most insatiable of all the vices, and resist its assault on her dishonour.

Example of how a verdict is obtained in the English Literary Courts. Mrs Woolf in a literary weekly reviews the books of newcomers, and finds neither interest nor distinction. ". . . Down they come from the two Universities. . . ."
Down and DOWN.
Left to the Two Universities England would be illiterate.

Mark Twain quotes a School-Boy essay: On Girls. "Girls are very stuck up and dignified in their manner and behav Your. They think more of dress than anything and like to play with dolls and rags. They cry if they see a cow in a far distance and are afraid of guns. They stay at home all the time and go to church on Sunday. They are al-ways sick. They are al-ways funy and making fun of boy's hands and they say How dirty. They can't play marbels. I pity them poor things. They make fun of boys and then turn round and love them. I don't believe they ever killed a cat or anything. They look out every nite and say O ant the moon lovely. Ther is one thing I have not told and that is they al-ways know their lessons bettern boys."

Carefully read this is a most complete and sympathetic exposition of the problem of woman as uncreative artist.

Until woman can kill a cat and play marbels and do her lessons as badly as boys, she must give up all hope of attaining to man's creative level.

Ignore the moon, she cannot.

Impotence. Impotence should be relegated once more to the Law Courts. A conclusive plea for divorce, it has strayed too long into Poetry and the Arts.

Lesbos. One would have thought that lesbianism, most provocative and interesting of the feminine vices, would have found its gentle or tempestuous voice at intervals down the artistic centuries.

But not a groan, not a sigh, not an articulate murmur. Where women have sung their pain they have sung of men (Héloïse and Elizabeth Barrett Browning) or of God (Christina Rossetti).

The Well of Loneliness, rambling, apologetic, and emotional outpouring, is proof of the subject's misuse; and of how dull, how sober, how domestic, such a theme becomes in woman's literary hands. Yet de Maupassant in a few pen-strokes of a minor short-story ("La Femme de Paul") transmits an undercurrent of fascination, excitement, and passion with an artistic finality which neither education nor freedom can wholly account for or explain.

Whatever the complete outpourings of Sappho we still may doubt, and rightly doubt, that she ever came within poetic half-distance of that yearning tormented cry which Donne wrote in her name to Philaenis.

Art. Art is desire, control, finality. It is a spiritual-organic urge comparable to the rising sap in tree and man. Its seed, the intensity of its vision. Its womb, the mind.

Creative Reality. One agrees with Stendhal that it does not matter what mistakes are made so long as they are the outcome of exuberance and brio.

Unfortunately this is a mistake we are never called on to forgive in woman. To expect exuberance and brio in women's spiritual make-up is rather like expecting them to give an uncontrolled and sudden guffaw instead of an appraising and well-mannered smile. Woman's limitation is that she is only physically adventurous and a-moral. Mentally she is circumscribed, passive, and censorious; estimable qualities for the home and State: inadequate to the higher creative efforts of mankind.

This does not mean that women in their work have not charm, sensitiveness, psychological observation, serious intent, and considerable achievement. But it means that all these qualities are not enough.

For creation is needed audacity, controlled architectonic power of mood and sentence, a brooding deliberation, a superabundance of purely physical energy, and an integrity of thought and purpose that is of itself so exhausting as to explain why it is so rare. In Art there are no second tries. No next time; no audience; no praise; no blame. There is only Oneself.

Good Clean Fun. I have read and enjoyed many clever books by many talented women. But I have never yet finished a book written by a woman without, for all its charm and excellence, a sense of limitation. An accurate and deadly knowledge that the writer would rather be taken for a lady than mistaken for an artist. A lack of virility; a lack of rebellion; the sad certainty that their literary mock marriages are never consummated.

(*Amendment.* To this last paragraph there is an exception. *Maurice Guest,* by Henry Handel Richardson, can take its place among the best novels by men, masters of their craft.)

Woman as Uncreative Artist. A quotation which one regrets, but which proves one's point. Miklucho-Macleay, speaking of Papuan art in North-east Guinea, remarks: "I have been struck by the absolute absence of ornament on the pottery, the clay easily lending itself to all sorts of ornamentation; this lack of ornament is due to the fact that the manufacture of pottery is exclusively confined to women, who are not usually very artistic by nature. I have found confirmation of this ancient and just observation even among Papuan women. I am able to state that I have not seen the slightest ornament invented or executed by a woman. During a visit to the island of Bibi-Bibi, where pottery is manufactured for all the neighbouring villages, when observing a dozen women and young girls fashioning pottery, I saw several women doing nothing. As they had in front of them a mass of pots without the slightest ornament, I asked why they did not ornament them. 'What is the good? It is not necessary!' were the replies they gave. But this did not prevent two young boys from finding pleasure in imprinting with their nails and a pointed stick a sort of ornamental border on some of the pots."

O merda, ó berrétta rossa! To be judged on the texture of one's thought and the disposition of one's sentences.

Vision, enthusiasm, and inner counsel.

Tea-Shoppe. "But . . . what is this? This blazing jewel that I have at the bottom of my pocket, this crystalline concentration of glory, this deep and serene and intense emotion that I feel before the greatest works of art" (Miss Rebecca West: This Strange Necessity). "You know what Roger Fry means when he says somewhere: 'That is just how I felt when I first saw Michael Angelo's frescoes in the Sistine Chapel.' I get it myself most powerfully from 'King Lear.' It overflows the confines of the mind and becomes an important physical event. The blood leaves the hands, the feet, the limbs, and flows back to the heart, which for the time being seems to have become an immensely high temple whose pillars are several sorts of illumination, returning to the numb flesh diluted with some substance swifter and lighter and more electric than itself. Unlike that other pleasure one feels at less climatic contacts with art it does not call for any action other than complete experience of it. Rather one rests in its lap. Now, what in the world is this emotion? What is the bearing of supremely great works of Art on my life which makes me feel so glad?"

This quotation justified one's contention that women should be allowed nowhere near the Arts, if only for physical reasons. The blood immediately leaves heart and extremities, and by the time it has returned they find themselves resting in some-one else's lap.

One had often wondered what women really felt on looking at "supremely great works of Art." Particularly Sistine-Chapel-King-Lear works of Art. Now we know that in that long look of ecstasy they are digesting temples. And not merely digesting temples, but immensely high temples with flood-lighting on the columns. In fact, Jonah swallowing the whale.

And all this on merely beholding it. Imagine what would happen did they produce it. One lady after another dying of undigested columns and coloured electric bulbs "which have overflowed the confines of the mind and become an important physical event."

In other words, Art as laxative.

On n'est pas né seulement pour boucher des trous.
POPULAR FRENCH SAYING.

F urther reflections on the Death of a Porcupine. (Final Word on D. H. Lawrence.) Deeply as the English may approve Marcel Proust they could not possibly have produced him. No literate Englishman could so offend as to suck a madeleine that has been dipped in a cup of milk.

In soil so disinclined to exotic growth such things are not left to chance or individual device. There are laws, restraints, limitations. Endeavour (as in dress) must be distinguished but not distinguishable. Form (however intense the vision) must be Good Form. The first need (however strong the creative urge) must be the need of clerk and floor-walker: five hundred pounds a year and a room of one's own.

Thus armed, steadfast in security, one now is free to creep and whisper through well-pruned literary glades where stride those tweedy nymphs so solicitous of the passions of their dogs, so heedless of their own; here to tease the drowsy argument; sport on a playful wind of words; indite a sunrise, slightly inflamed; a sunset, slightly passionate; relax in comfortable after-dinner glow induced by thoughts of the extreme worthiness, the Galsworthyness, of current literature, whose profit and loss account is the measure of its worth; strict as any trade.

Small wonder then that when, amid such even-tempered excellence, a voice is heard too loud and too emphatic to be quite the voice of the Gentleman it becomes, by virtue of its singularity, the voice of the Prophet.

How otherwise explain a deification more exciting for the zest of its disciples than for the message of its Messiah? Here was that uncomfortable phenomenon spared to English letters for so long: a self-willed man. A parallel must be found.

Another such, bold and passionate and controversial. They hesitate. William Blake? (Unfair to Blake, who could say in a sentence what it took D. H. Lawrence several novels, innumerable poems, and a sheaf of essays to insist on.[1]) But the hesitation is brief; the temptation sore;

---

[1] *He whose face does not show a light, will never be a star.*

the fall inevitable.

A mining village, how near a Stable. Apostles gathered, from the windy shores of literary tea-cups. To each his rôle, of Beloved, Doubter, Chronicler, Betrayer. Sermons from the Etruscan Mount. An Agony in the American Garden. A Last Supper at the Café Royal.

Only a definite racial squeamishness concerning the social stigma of illegitimacy has so far saved us from proof of Virgin Birth.

To concern oneself with any slur cast upon Christ would be irrelevant. There can be few aesthetic surprises left from a nation that made Pan acceptable to its sixty million people by turning him into Peter.

The argument by which partisans effectively silence the sceptic is the unvarying: *he was so sincere!*

Yet sincerity (in Art) is not enough. Possibly Lord Leighton was sincere. Michelangelo, one feels, had something to be sincere about.

It is significant that in all that has been written on D. H. Lawrence since his death, only one writer has approached him solely and seriously as creative artist.[2] To none other has this fact seemed relevant.

One mourns him as the pleasant companion, talkative, eager, doubly important since even Mr Aldous Huxley, so beyond the humdrum of London literati, dare not ignore him.[3] Another, on the weakness of having been called a genius by the late Mr Arnold Bennett, giggles (not ungracefully) at his clothes and mannerisms.[4] Yet another exalts the wanderer, "solitary, scorned, betrayed, bloody-headed but unbowed."[5] And one subtly mixing eroticism, mother-love, impotence, homosexuality, and Jesus Christ, cries with authoritative sweetness: Behold the Man![6]

So it goes, the fight above the literary remains. The angry social activity about the dead. Pleadings, justifications, counter-attacks, intimacies revealed, implications denied, until the creative artist is submerged in a Message; the life-work is reduced to the man.

It is to this bickering of the Apostles that we owe the belittling of their Lord. While John kicks Matthew and Luke floors Mark, each accusing each of having slept while told to watch, the impression left by

[2] Richard Aldington.
[3] Rebecca West: *D. H. Lawrence.*
[4] William Gerhardi, *Memoirs of a Polyglot.*
[5] Catherine Carswell, *The Savage Pilgrimage.*
[6] Middleton Murry, *Son of Woman.*

the varying Gospels is of a shrill petulant little man harassed by a lady of spacious germanic form, given to breaking earthenware dishes on his head and scoffing at his marital supremacy.

For Message we are led to a bedroom keyhole and asked to share in the intricacies of a mystic, palpable, real otherness of ultra-phallic worship; a dark knowledge subtly mindless; source of pure and magic control; and depending (principally) on touch.

Bounded in infinite space and lord of a nutshell!

Continents new and old come in double-bedded size. Oceans are pools in which to outstare a troubled reflection. Flowering Nature with her manifold insistence on two painfully similar shapes, must have made a walk a disquieting experience and given to flowers an erotic significance that had escaped the bee. Everywhere in unself-conscious profusion the mindless hen is being trod by an imperious cock. Busy dogs are at their nasal observations. Goats sardonically amorous are at the bottom of the garden. Small irritable male tortoises disconsolately harry large indifferent female tortoises.

Yet there is more to a tortoise than a middle-class bedroom comedy. And a tomcat is not howling because of a problem, but because of a need.

In what corner, then, of this unsatisfactory earth would a colony of London literary people (however amenable to Leadership, homespun, and the lighting of fires in the rain) have been other than a colony of London literary people amenable to Leadership, homespun, and the lighting of fires in the rain?

Love and Sun! What then do people want? Fog and Hate? Give a Salvation Army Lass a glass of wine and she'll babble of Love; though never having been beyond Worthing Pier or the Brixton High Street, she'll not add Sun.

It is a testimony to the essential blood-brotherhood of man that what the vulgar will accept standing in a pious ring at the corners of streets, the Few will accept standing in pious rings at the corners of drawing-rooms. (Only the Salvation of the Few must be administered in the form of Forbidden Fruit.)

Yet a lifetime spent in an exalted mental pursuit of the proper relationship between man and woman is of doubtful social value seeing that neither by augury, indictment, nor divination, can the answer be other than that the woman should be agreeably passive and the male agreeably active.

It is right (it is inevitable) that those sated with the over-refinements of intellectualised passion should envy the lordly navvy who holds his woman down without the fuss of asking her permission, and instead of arguing about it afterwards turns over and sleeps.

But any farmyard problem is in the (intellectualised) eye of the beholder. The hen and cock would be surprised.

What a wearisome waste of time, this soul-probing of a problem that does not exist! The *proper* relationship between man and woman is the making of children. This apart, any sexual relationship between them becomes immediately so improper, that it can only justify itself by becoming also as pleasurable as it is possible to make it.

But had it been a matter of pleasure (*comedite, amici, et bibite, et inebriamini, carissimi!*) Apostles would not have left their perilous saucers.

All is nobly done in the name of Right. For God and Salvation! The day has yet to dawn when England's rebel sons will say what they have to say without the protection of the Salvationist's bonnet and drum.

A chastening thought is that D. H. Lawrence preferred this spectacular rôle of popular prophet to the more forbidding rôle of artist. And if the zeal of his Apostles has made him temporarily ridiculous, he asked for it in asking for them. He lived aloud. The personal taint of an inspired gossip-writer is everywhere. And now that his Apostles obstinately insist on proving more exactly which scene took place where, and whom, and why, the Spirit has become Matter. And matters so much less.

The gibe that he lacked humour is unfounded. His was an amusing, penetrating, and malicious humour, which the Introduction to the Maurice Magnus memoirs shows at its best. What he had not, was light-heartedness. It was principally this lack of lightheartedness that evolved the phoenix idyll with the coals leaping from beneath. They should have been in a brazier on the head. For who touches Lawrence touches the English middle-class conscience; outcome of our prurience, witness against our climate. Whether upward or outward, his mental finger was ever rigidly accusing. How often he was ashamed, this sun-worshipper in a seamless shirt. How grimly for our sakes he shouldered the dread burden woman—that Cross on which he so unwillingly lay down.

One sees in D. H. Lawrence the ill effects of our tight-lipped puritanism. One sees also proof of England's easy-breathing freedom.

Make what they will of the war experiences and the flight abroad, the Mockery and the Exile, Apostle and Messiah can produce no deeper impression on the unbiased than the truth that though England may not be (socially) free, by God, she is safe!

Much is unpleasant in Lawrence's baiting of the unfortunate Maurice Magnus (particularly unfortunate in having borrowed a few pence from him), a man of great sensitiveness and generosity, who showed the highest courage and endurance both in serving and in escaping from the French Foreign Legion, when one contrasts the shrill scream he himself set up on being made to go through the usual army medical examination, when, over-conscious of his nakedness, they handled his private parts and looked into them.

But you must read the chapter "The Nightmare" in *Kangaroo* (they say). Then you will see what he suffered in the War. And one reads the chapter "The Nightmare" in *Kangaroo,* and one says: and what did he suffer in the War?

More than his private parts would have been mishandled in France, in Germany, in America, had he lived there with an enemy-alien wife who "was not only German but loudly provocative and indiscreet."[7]

Yet all that seems to have happened, after much loud singing of German songs at the piano and more loud and more provocative intellectual argument concerning the excellence of the enemy and the futility of war, is that the simple suspicious Cornish villagers at last became openly hostile; and finally and with a great many Yes, Sirs, and Thank you, Sirs, and Sorry you've been troubled, Sirs, an army officer and two men descended on the cottage, searched and took away a few meaningless papers, and respectfully told them to leave Cornwall in three days.

England, my England! The heart responds with amused gratitude to this unsolicited testimonial to your smug, polite, and kindly security!

Yet this same England suppressed *The Rainbow;* and later seized poems and drawings; and still disclaims *Lady Chatterley's Lover,* as though any other country in the world could have produced it.

Of these the poems are the most interesting and important. The paintings, apart from a sense of rhythmic design and an unusual feeling for colour, are cheap literary clap-trap. And *Lady Chatterley's Lover* is possibly the best example in English letters of emotion remembered in tranquillity.

Sexually it is an improbable study, though a most useful lesson in elementary botany. What it most definitely is not, is pornography.

The odourless excellence of our puritan make-believe which is our

---

[7] Catherine Carswell, *The Savage Pilgrimage.*

daily life, has reached a stage of mechanised inhibition at which anyone painting the undepilated bodies and heaped thighs of large ladies in attitudes of surrender, is labelled (and suppressed) as pornographic. Yet pornography is an Art needing much subtlety, both of evocation and response. And at its best, it is clothed.

It is not enough for a naked man and woman to twine hedge-flowers in each other's navels. Such wilful barefaced innocence may hint at depravity: it cannot approach pornography.

Moralists forget that though there may be forty-two positions, there is but one sensation. It is said that Pietro Aretino died from falling from his chair and cracking his skull in a fit of laughter on hearing a bawdy story told about his sister. Such the essential difference in the spirit of pornography and the spirit of depravity! The one is solemn, the one is gay. The one is masked virtue, the one is open-countenanced ribaldry. The one is of the prig. The one is of the jester.

Just as caricature deals in outward peculiarities, emphasising the ludicrous and exciting to immediate laughter, so pornography delights and heightens the sexual excitements of healthy nerves. (A degenerate can grow spasmodic on his mistress's shoe-string.) It is therefore an indictment of the weak and atrophied state of our English nerves that a pleasing, unsubtle, Arcadian attempt at nude interplay should aggravate such extremes of horror and partisanship.

Dare one hint that the nose of Punch (that pleasure-giving organ of the British middle-classes) is infinitely more erotically suggestive than amateurish paintings of abandoned nudes? But subtlety in sex is not the Englishman's forte; hence his confusing the minor depravity of an adolescent with the adult wit of an Aretino.

From the very circumstance of his upbringing, sexual moralising ill-suited Lawrence. Try as he will, the impression left by his fulminations on sex is of those very nice, those very young young-men in American advertisements, so hyper-sensitively aware of the fore- and under-arm of their dancing partners.[8]

Subtlety was ever the handmaid of Art. It is a taste which the middle-classes do not acquire; the lower-classes do not need; but which finer minds dare not be without.

If you would be more than human do not feed from a human source. Drink (like a pen) from a bottle.

[8] *And she thought she had been so careful. . . .*

Here is dignity, indifference, variety. It is the sole mouthpiece for the artist.

Chief among the handicaps of the Breast-Fed School is that however violent the ensuing struggle, it will be confined always within the arms of a woman. Yet the Madonnina is a woman's saint. Men should be made of sterner stuff.

To be believed in by one's mother seems altogether too easy a victory to be worth striving for. What may be the delight of childhood, is not necessarily the crown of maturity. They may receive us back upon our shield: they are not asked to carry it.

Too long has Nero been blamed for much that was praiseworthy in his outlook. His way with his womenfolk may have been the refinement of exasperated cruelty, but he never thought of embalming them in excrement or in treacle. He needed their goods and their silence; it never occurred to him to need their good opinion.

There is an end to a bottle. It asks no return for the drink it gives. The first and last word is with the drinker.

If we are to believe his followers, most of D. H. Lawrence's defects, literary and personal, were due to the influence of his mother, whose tragic death when he was twenty-six was the deepest emotional tragedy of his life.

Be that as it may, the only convincing scenes of passion in his books are the love scenes between men. He was a man obsessed as a maid by thoughts of his own virginity. Eager and voluble as a woman in his work and observation, in daily life he seems to have had all the house-wifely virtues, the love of cooking, scrubbing, sewing, and the making of clothes. And a woman's passion for power and dominance. His was also that peculiarly feminine trait: petulance. There was the ultra-phallic relationship of touch with which to supplant the distasteful normal act of love that to him was like the rape of himself. There was the final exultation of the Dark Gods who must come from below; almost the auto-erotic visions of an ageing spinster.

It is to the Breast-Fed School that is due the ecstatic discovery that hens and cocks are free from the mental ills of civilisation because they do not know their children's names nor read the latest book reviews. (This is true also of other barnyard fowl, and of all feathered denizens of the forest.)

But the Breast-Fed School is strong. It is perplexed and it is spiritual. Its appeal is to the frustrate and the uncertain.

"*Un sein, c'est rond, c'est chaud! Si Dieu n'avait crée la gorge de la femme, je ne sais si j'aurais été peintre!"*[9]

But that is not an expression of faith that could win Apostles. It is too sure of itself. It is complete, real, uncompromising. It is an adult remark, straight from the mouth of the bottle.

Possibly it is only in England that the artist is a problem rather than a need.

On the Continent where the Rimbauds, Baudelaires, Van Goghs, Douanier Rousseaus, Modiglianis, are almost daily occurrences, such apostolic manifestations of astonishment, of blame, of adulation, are not encouraged.

A work of art is sufficient unto itself; it need not be also a prayer meeting. The wilfulness of its creator needs no excuse or explanation. The correct answer to Why? is Why not?

D. H. Lawrence is principally explained (and endeared) by his restlessness. He had to an unusual degree that passion for freedom which artists, criminals, and tramps share of all living men.

The source of his relentless creative urge was a passionate revolt. Indifference was impossible to him. And it is exactly such undercurrent of anger and pain that matters and makes memorable a man's work. However useless the struggle and expended on however trivial an issue, even at the risk of its becoming a bonfire rather than a torch, if that struggle has been laocoönean enough, the gesture is sufficient.

Without it, not all the monied erudition of Mr Such-and-Such's prose, nor the passionless charm of Mr So-and-So's verse, can be other than dishes having all the necessary ingredients—but served cold.

When he has ceased to be a demi-god in a few drawings-rooms, D. H. Lawrence will take his place as one of the finest imaginative prose writers in English letters. Nor is there a poet of his generation to approach him in language and intensity.

Only then will domineering wives and infantile-mother-fixations and friends and enemies and unsympathetic publishers and poverty and anger and ill-health be as unreal as the cults and indignations they once aroused.

But the dead can wait; so long, that they have invariably the last word.

D. H. Lawrence's mistrust of England was not simply caprice or illness or inferiority-complex or persecution-mania. (He had these in other countries.)

[9]Renoir.

But the artist is almost always a practical person. He leaves romance to lesser beings; their desire is not strong enough.

To belong to the world is one thing: to belong to a corner of it, quite another. And England is too secure to satisfy or to understand the needs of the restless. Also, it is too watery.

Fire is a moment, a flash, a spark. It gives light, however briefly. Water is dull, but it persists. The earth is three-parts water; man likewise. Water cannot be other than water. There is no light in it. Raise it to the sun, it can return again but as water. It is the one element that can quench fire; and how effectively! There are no water-worshippers. In water live fish, frogs, molluscs; cold-blooded, mistrustful each of the other. And with mist, fog, mud, rain, and drizzle there comes a damping down of gesture, of voice, of movement. An unawareness; a moving in shoals; apart; indifference upon indifference.

Here all that is angry, or aware, or warm-blooded, or questioning, is a betrayal of the mass instinct of a people ever-ready to accept anything that will distinguish them from others; not individually but in a class. Not an individual excellence, but the mass distinction of Club, Class, School. A herd distinction; a desire to be distinguished, but in small bands. A land of amateur undefended titles, where the highest expression of Art in literature and painting is and has ever been the art of Portraiture. But portraitists are lacqueys. One despises them. They hold to the wall.

Where the mimic is exalted, the visionary is outcast.

The creative artist is not an individual. He is not to be judged by the virtues which make the clerk or unmake the banker. Impotence neither hampers nor stimulates. Amorousness neither explains nor justifies. All that matters is that he takes up his brush, or his pen, or his chisel, and that that which he has done has been worth the doing.

The cistern contains: the fountain overflows.[10] And the little stagnant cistern can contain only that which the generous fountain has poured into it. And that (for what it is worth) is the artist's compensation.

[10]Blake, again.

T*he Apple is Bitten Again.* We are a ligament. A small adhesive matter. A running of two colours. An ebb and flow of light.

Drowsing in an orchard the writer cuts her finger on a blade of grass, watches apples growing, and discovers that a Brain as fine, as reasoning, has been given to the smallest sentient thing. Man loves to give to trees and natural phenomena in general an Outside Directing Intelligence: god, providence, nature.

So proud, so limited, that we call man the reasoning being. For him a vegetable, flower, tree, has neither brain nor feeling. (As though purpose were not the highest form of brain and emotion!) Yet this tree, fruit, plant, has in common with us that it is born, it feeds, it breathes, wakes, sleeps, reproduces, dies, is born again. We with our huge brains cannot perform such acts efficiently, yet a tree with only some inexplicable mystic Outside Direction, some nice fatherly olde gentleman God or the scientist's All-Comprehending Nature, surpasses us in normal functioning.

This little blade which bores its sharpness through the soil sees a stone and goes round it, directed by its own brain-power. Then in the small root of this plant must live a directive spirit. It need not be a full brain (he may decide not to work but to climb up the leaf and enjoy the air and sunshine), but there is a brain cell, an infinitesimal part of a brain, that knows only one task: to find a way round pebbles, obstacles, earth. Then are there brains clumsy and large as those of man and subtle and small as those of the mosquito and subtler and smaller as those of a bacille. It could not Move otherwise. It could not Be.

A look, not a glance. One look at a bird, a root, a leaf, and there can be but one conclusion: that no such thing as an Outside Direction exists. And that not only is an Outside Direction neither possible nor needed, but that it could not work.

That anyone cares for us but ourselves is a sentimental exaggeration on a level with Immortality and the linking of the Firmament to the forceps at our birth.

Not a thing could exist for a moment did it not have all the Brain it needed for that existence. Who yet has lived on advice given it by others?

Arum maculatum, Utricularia vulgaris, Dionœa, Darlingtonia. . . . There are plants semi-animal, catching and feeding on insects.

If we cannot be imaginative enough to grant a Brain to a blade of grass, we surely must admit that a plant, semi-animal, which angles for and digests insects, is already a high degree of brain-power with a complex life system.

Only when we shall be capable of detecting these brain cells in plants and roots, shall we be capable of detecting similar and finer cells in every part of our and the animal body.

A hedge-sparrow chirrups. Each manifestation of life is provided with as much brain as it needs. Man alone has a concentration of brain far in excess of his needs and therefrom derives his troubles.

A sparrow has kept his breed over thousands of years, is still as gay, as impertinent, nor shows signs of degeneration, thanks to the fact that his brain is adequate to his self-protection, which sober allotment of intelligence will keep him going in comfort and ease long after our learned self-extinction.

Reason and mechanics. Why must man fight thus against Brain in all its manifestations, including that of his own species? Why must he always inherit, like a lazy and elder son? Why must all efforts be lifted from his sluggish shoulders to those of an ancient and sleepless watchman with a passion for interfering in the business of an entire growth of an entire world? Why does he think the sweet strong grasses will wave as vigorously above the earth when he long since has disappeared from its surface, if not that grass has singleness of self-directed purpose while man has but an outer-directed morality.

The apple falls. There are movements, Unconscious, Unintelligent movements, which are caused by the gravity of the earth, or the different consistencies, rarity, condensations, temperatures, dictated by physical laws.

All other movements can be only Conscious-Intelligent movements. Whether directed by our brain or various nerve centres, they are self-intelligent. When therefore we notice an intelligent movement as the healing of a wound on a hand or tree or the forming of an apple, that healing and that forming are simply and incontestably an action of what

I shall call Local Brain.

In the apple it is the accumulation of food around the seed for the preservation and first feeding of future generations. A savings bank, a granary. And in it then and there they carry their sacks on their backs, have a transport system, a traffic regulation, a packers' department in which is made the skin; their painters colour it; their polishers and waxers make it waterproof; millions of lives depend on it and go to its making, and all that brain-power is provided locally on that spot, in that world.

Let us bite that apple with no remorse. Generations have lived, died, and been buried on it. It is but an expected cataclysm; a Final Judgement. In the two minutes in which we shall pick, carry away, and chew, the minusculous builders and inhabitants will live three centuries and see many generations pass. And from the picking of the apple to the sending of it down our throat, will be an unrecorded history that loses itself in remotest antiquity.

How wonderful is Nature, providing us with all things, making all things harmonious and interdependent! One should write with a lisp when repeating such inanities.

Each piece of man and vegetation is independent. A tree, it seems to me, has several different and separate lives. So we. There is neither harmony in Nature nor in ourselves.

Man's very body which he is wont to praise as proof, miracle, and embodiment of all harmony (when it works) is at perpetual war with itself. In no sense is it a charitable organisation. When the bones want calcium they take all the calcium they can find, raiding parts beyond themselves, no matter how they rot the teeth or disturb the rest of the organism. The sexual organs want satisfaction at the cost of whatever excess, no matter how this may enhance or detract from the health-flow of the whole.

So much are we independent that our hearts will beat, removed, cared for, artificially supplied with blood and oxygen. A lump of flesh or skin will grow in cultures. Teeth form either in the mouth or stomach. The stomach does not care from which end it gets its food; the veins from whence the blood that fills them; the heart will have no sentimental regrets that it is not feeding our particular brain or nerves. Each is dependent on the need, but not on the source of supply. The source is unimportant, provided the need is satisfied.

Nature provides nothing but the simple elements, atmosphere, heat, light, cold, moisture. All the rest is sweat and Local Brain.

Exploration without Balloons. A brain is given in charge a few organs to direct, and if an intelligent manifestation has been performed in any natural phenomena from the forming of an apple, corn, or fungus, millions of organs directed by millions of brains must be responsible.

Yet we not wanting, not daring, to admit that the world about us teems with Great Thinkers who bring reforms and improvements in all their manifestations, dismiss the problems elegantly by inventing Nature and the sleight-of-hand Creator.

Were we courageous enough to admit the existence of these millions of brains we should have to admit that man, though the most interesting, is not necessarily the highest form of life on our planet. Should have to admit brains not only as good as ours but superior. So far we have admitted only gods' brains to be superior. But unfortunately we have to dismiss the Olde Man and the brains remain. As they have performed bigger constructions and reforms in medicine, defence, inventions, than we have, so must their brains be superior to our own.

Therefore watching our own activity, invention, organisation, we find them but a copy of such inventions in the vegetal world. From which we may deduct that all plants and all the microscopic world and the ultra-microscopic world, as the telescopic and ultra-telescopic world, is ruled by the same means and laws. All experience leading to same conclusions; all life a repetition on various scales of the same principles.

Intelligence is localised, not universal. Up to now, whether mystically, religiously, philosophically, scientifically, the verdict has always been: There is One who Knows all. Or, Nature provides.

Rubbish. "Nature" provides all the mechanical-movements, rain, winds, atmosphere, heat from sun and earth, cold. And there "Nature" stops. In this provision we (all living beings from corals to man to eagles) fight for æons to hold our ground and assert ourselves. All this is personal matter; a personal responsibility. All this is Local Brain.

(By Local Brain is not meant an actual miniature copy of that under the skull. But that Brain which inhabits vegetables and is as yet undetected to science or microscope, and which might be a few atoms concerned in the direction of one single activity.)

Nature neither provides nor cares, hence the extinct and the living. For Mother-Goose-Nature they starve and they die and they cease to be. Let us bury the Olde Dame, ceaselessly watching. For the result of all life is the personal initiative of all the component parts.

A Happy Combination of a most Unholy Family. Much borrowing and copying from all sides and much coming to the same conclusions through identical needs and conditions (all tropic fruits being liquid and hot-coloured; northern trees being pines as leaves cannot resist winds; Londoners alike in semi-desire, semi-play, semi-senses) submitted and adapted to the requirements of their surroundings, produces the various species and families, similar and dissimilar, fraternal and divergent.

Thus a man, a tree, a bird, is but a happy combination. The variety of species due to the fact that one happy combination has borrowed or given of its components to yet another happy combination.

Further exploration without Balloons. Soul and Vitality. Where there is a living brain there is a soul. From a cut finger it would seem that part of the brain is localised in the skull and the rest of the brain (so called because it performs intelligent functions) lies posted at various strategic points in the body or plant; there being a great possibility of ambulant particles of brain which are called-in in emergency cases. (You send soldiers with an officer; workmen with a foreman.)

With the soul as the life-giving spirit in the human-animal-plant body, divided in as many parts as it need be, each particle giving life to one part of the body, we possess possibly a thousand souls, the sum-total of which makes up the so-called human soul. Moreover, we shall detect the main seat of the Soul centuries before we detect the little scattered centres. Whether seen or unseen, weighed or not weighed, from this logical deduction of Local Brain, we know it to be there.

If each time the body deteriorates the soul diminishes, the soul must be measured mechanically by the state of the body.

It is absurd to give a great soul to a sickly old man and the proof is given daily in our hospitals. The weak, the old, the drunken, the dissipated, drop their souls at the first shaking.

SOUL AND VITALITY GO HAND IN HAND. Then has a healthy horse ten times the soul of a normal man.

Immortality is off. Sans fleus, ni pleurs, ni couronnes. Then are there millions upon millions of molecular-atomic little souls and different beings and growths are allotted as many as they need.

But soul is no blanket. Each body and each component part of a body while living captures for itself a certain number of soul-molecules which impregnate every part of the body, animating our brains, our brains animating our organs, our organs animating our actions. When the body expands and acquires a greater number of matter-molecules, automatically it attracts the corresponding number of soul-molecules.

These can come but from the air, so that logically we take it from the ether, use it at our convenience, breathing it in and spitting it out. And not only is the soul not immortal—but renewable.

Soul as Fifth Element. A psychosphere and an ultra-psychosphere. We must dismiss our soul and body fable. No longer speak of one soul and another soul. But of soul. There is no human soul and animal soul, as there is no human air and animal air. There is air. There is soul. Which, like water, like air, should be considered an element. *I would call soul the Fifth Element.*

Then like air, like water, soul must be penetrating and surrounding the earth. This surrounding layer I would call *the psychosphere.* A layer rich in soul element. The present theory that after the stratosphere there is only ether spread over the universe, is too simple. The stratosphere is not the last wrapping of a planet and in time we shall prove it.

This layer, this psychosphere being finer than rarefied air should extend many times further; but even this layer must rarefy its soul element and give place to a new and finer envelope which I shall call *the ultra-psychosphere.* This expansion must be so vast as to intersect similar ultra-psychospheres belonging to other planets and so form an interplanetary contact.

Soul then is a combination of magnet and electricity; of the family of electro-magnetic fluids. What I have ignorantly called soul-molecules and soul-atoms might more accurately be called soul-waves and wavelets, or soul-vibrations and second-vibrations: the ether waves, the light vibrations. When a man dies he does not give up his soul. He gives up the last insignificant remains of a polluted viciated element that would not keep a rat alive.

A guess at a question that has never yet been answered: what is blood? THE IRON IN THE BLOOD MIGHT—SHOULD—MUST—CON-DUCT AND ATTRACT SOUL.

The cold sweat of a fright. The popular saying: frightened to death, comes near to discovering this truth. The cold sweat of a dying man may yet prove that soul and water are closely linked in all living things.

(*Sudden Aside, showing impatience and considerable irritation.* I have no seventy years in which to grow dusty and old, dedicated to this subject. Its implications are both too vast and too obvious. I know nothing of what I am talking, but that I know it to be true.

These few lines scribbled in a notebook under an apple-tree, drowsy with light and heat, are a moment, a glimpse, a guess, an apprehension. And I would be a fool to waste more time on them. I never could do sums and no sudden reverie is going to start me adding up the obvious to make a universe I'll back to my grim interpretative last! Particularly as I choose to think it, in this melancholy world, a greater tragedy for one artist to be lost than for one pseudo-scientist-philosopher more to be added to the hundred million so busily engaged in wordy and test-tube retort!)

The Artist as Fore-Runner. Man having bungled the centuries and crawled stupidly through the time allotted him, is discerning three or four shades of the universe. But it is not given to him yet to see the ultra-violet of the rainbow, nor to fathom the infinitesimal range of both sides.

The mediaeval artist of pre-microscopic days evolved labyrinthine ornamentations, inspiring motives, beautiful and fantastic convolutions, for which inventiveness we have honoured him. Only to find to-day that the microscopic-photographic proves them to exist; and to have existed for millions of years in plants, in minerals, existing as a common state of being which the creator-artist not only ignored but had no possible means of suspecting.

Soul, the Universal Glue. There is no thing in all the world at which man need gasp, except for breath.

What to-day we carelessly call spiritual are but those invisible magnetic and electric powers which impregnate all animate and inanimate things and which project themselves from one to the other, migrate from place to place according to physical laws, circulate, create currents, storms, disturbances, always under normal physical conditions, and which project themselves from inanimate to inanimate things, from animate to inanimate, from inanimate to animate, from semi-inanimate to animate, and all other combinations.

If the cap fits. With soul as electric fluid let us call the eyes to account. Eyes that hypnotise; eyes through which you project your will.

Eyes through which a man, in the act of giving up his life, stares. And in that stare imbibes, hooks with his eyes, on a window, ceiling, cupboard; nails his will with his last breath; nails his will like an old overcoat to that wall or window, and his energy is impressed and stays there. And now take a man who enters, comes to sleep in that room after a day or century. In the night when a part of us departs, vitality is weak, we are in a semi-live state, and that old coat comes and fits us because there is room in the body for it. Or photographically it reprojects itself, the imprint on the wall. And the crime is re-enacted.

In the morning you wake and retake possession of yourself. Or being a weak person your own fluid returns to take possession of your body and the other refuses to leave. And we get ghosts in cellars and obsessions and lunacy and possession by devils, or whatever the popular definition of the times may be.

Or love. Love which is always a desire to give oneself, or possess, or belong to, another. You willingly disembody your spirit. The self in detaching itself creates an emptiness or semi-emptiness, struggling to give or to possess.

The Poet is saddened to find that he is not so lonely as he had hoped or thought. Only an exchange and ceaseless metamorphosis. Sickly and humbling the thought that we have no new materials; that the distribution varies but not the quality; that we must put back in circulation the same quantity of matter, same quantity of energy, reshaped in myriad forms; the same familiar amount of energy and matter kept eternally in circulation.

—Who shall say whose Eternal Grit we rub so irritably from the corner of an eye!

Instinct, that mythical beast of burden. We are so lazy and so vain that we accept that all things are done for us and gods and providence protect our simplicity (we, their especial favourites) by sending us out of nowhere: Instinct.

Man learns all things and learns them from the Brain. Warm in the womb the foetus learns its first lesson. A small steady beating of an embryo heart, pum-pum, pum, pum, pum, learning to beat from the womb's blood-pulse; egged on to the movement of its first lesson which it learns so well that the movement becomes unconscious.

Second lesson. The foetus starts turning and learns movement, getting its impulse to movement from the mother body. A bird sits on its eggs, shakes them, turns them about. Already the parent bird is giving a lesson, awakening the embryo to movement. So all womb-carried things.

Third lesson. The embryo assimilates food through the umbilical cord. Moving, breathing, it now is learning to use the food pumped into it.

Fourth lesson. Comes the moment to break into the air. It has lungs, but has not learned to use them, knowing feeding, breathing, only from within. On its passage to the world, in the dual struggle of child and woman, it is being squeezed at high pressure. Its lungs, squeezed tight as a sponge, open out at the first contact with the air. Automatically you get the first cry.

Now the infant starts by itself a small artificial respiration, agitating its arms, its little breast squirming. And I contend that its brain is sweating with hard thinking and it is even in a panic, so hard its brain works to do that simple act of soaking and expelling air from its new-opened lungs.

Much later comes the desire to feed. Later still the desire for sight; having at first no need of such distraction the small unused brain must concentrate on the urgent matter of keeping itself in breath. Only after having learned the two lessons of breathing and feeding, can it afford time to look about it and observe slow incredible nebulæ.

Then the lesson of walking; birds teach to fly; all other beings learn from example. And all this time at each lesson the brain of the individual is working at high pressure.

And after your long, difficult, new-learned lesson, Man, what is left of your vaunted instinct?

(*Poetic digression. Poor man invents money.* Once only in all his days has man free board and lodging and that is for the first nine months of his life. After which he buys his daily, hourly, life on the instalment plan.

His first boarding-house, his mother's womb. After which he becomes a cumbersome thing, paying for the body's shelter even when tired and wanting rest. The space he occupies belongs now to someone else. Standing he pays; sitting he pays; lying he pays three times more. So many head of cattle, so many head of man. Children half price.

Ah, but how free one could live without this body's daily fee! To be able to break through and walk this earth without money, what an escape, what peace, what a mirage!

Every space becomes valuable by the fact that man sits on it, stands on it, or lies down, leaving his few pence as immediate security. And all this payment because the gravity of the earth keeps man to its crust and man is persecuted by his fellow beings and made to pay for taking space on a crust which is thrown at him only when, his last payment made, he lies as precariously beneath it as he once lay above.)

Slow, forgotten, oft-repeated lesson. They please to say that instinct is every thing the Brain does not know, making a small concession for the beats of the heart and the gangliar system. But as there is no thing the Brain does not know, ninety-nine per cent. of what is miscalled Instinct must be attributed to Local Brain.

Instinct either protects you or does some good to your species. It is a lesson, wise and sane, which man learns through long experience. But which each must learn afresh.

Life is a lesson learned from its beginning by all animate things. Man starts learning in the womb. Learning is imitation. (That is why a very learned man is nothing; a great copyist.)

Thought is construction.

Reason is godhead.

It seems not for nothing that the apple comes always to the rescue of humanity.

One woman, meaning well, bit an apple. Circumstances were against her (she was ahead of her times) and it turned to superstition.

Another woman bites an apple. Circumstances are against her and she still may be ahead of her times, and gives back Reason through the medium of Common Sense.

L*ight and Water. (Only.)* This thing called Soul is so sacred that it can be revived by a cylinder of oxygen or a glass of cognac. Mechanics, gentlemen, mechanics.

Happy Ending. The Last Trump will not disturb me. I shall be the Last Cabbage!

After the mind of Leonardo da Vinci: a field of cabbages. Approach both in the same spirit of awe and humility.

Supreme Purpose. Man no longer needs a Paradise. He needs an earth. Let him fight for the social status of the Turnip. The franchise of the Carrot. The rights of the Potato.

For the greatness of the turnip is its Purpose. Man has only morality.

Danger from Falling Debris. Man's moral skies are overworked, over-crowded, and nearing their end. But the Earth shall outlast him.

Only the skies and man show signs of moral wear and tear. Skies filled with singing zealots whose eternal bliss and chorus he shall share if his days be sufficiently mournful and unprotesting here below. Skies across which prophetic meteors have blazed, sybilline planets rushed to extinction, fiery moons dripped blood, suns suspended their motionless motion, all to bring him arbitrary and occasional proof of paternal interest and yet another creed.

Cold Storage Comfort. Is this what they have done to you, Humanity, the dark æons through which you have crept, with their denials and their messages, their martyrdoms and their doubts, the dreary clash of arms which precedes the clash of bells, peaceless on earth, good-will in death, for which men have hanged and burned and crucified and laid down lives, all to bring you the comfort of an eternal life?

Eternal life? But you cannot escape eternal life! You have no choice. That you are alive implies eternity of being. Strike a mindless match and you have cast its breath down the ages to the last flicker of infinitude.

Too many, too long, too often, these passionate misinterpretations of a primary mechanical law, with their tears and negative joys, little soured sects, anger, pain, mistrust, despair, and chill futility. Eternal life has had its cheerless day.

I would offer you Eternal Death.

But for Death. But for death man would be as stupid as the gods.

It is the inevitability of death that sharpens our wits; the uncertainty of death that gives us curiosity; the finality of death that gives us rebellion. From these, and from this Uncertain Certainty, spring our (brief) greatness, our (momentary) heroic stature: the Arts, our protest; Science, our questioning; Thought, our arrogance; Reason, our godhead. All these man owes to death. To death alone.

Argument. I am against all gods. Benevolent because they are paternal. Heroic because they are brief. Angry because they are foolish.

Man has yet to invent a god who can approach him in profundity, folly, audacity. A god willing to stand against a wall and be shot for holding an opinion contrary to the day's safe belief. A god who could murmur through his pain . . . *and yet it moves!*

Anger. Too late! Man has thrown his chance away; does not deserve another; could not take it were it given him.

But for the gods it might have been worth while. Who knows to what perfection man might have attained had he not limited himself in his bearded dogmas born of fear and credulity.

(Interruption. But you forget that man must have his gods to worship! And sacred monkeys, sacred cows, sacred cats.)

As worn. Fashions in gods may change but not man's urge to raise his hat.

Humanity's ceaseless religious conflict has been but to decide on which or on how many puppets. Tell them that the gods do not exist and they not only will not believe, they will not listen.

Tell them that it is not this god but that god, and they are eager to consider, refute, accept. For there are fashions in gods, but the same puppets wear them.

Idolatry. So God made man in his own image. A compliment man has never yet returned. For no god that man has made has come near to the godhead of man.

So that man in making gods has made an inferior copy of himself for consumption among the weakest part of humanity. And as the best brains had no hand in the creating of gods, it has been left to second-rate brains (priests, saints, martyrs) to create a second-rate image (Luthers, Calvins, reactionaries, have merely undressed the existing gods) to be believed in by third-rate inhabitants and tenth-rate brains. When the second-rate want to convert they have to find still smaller brains in the swamps of Africa, the slums of London, the depths of the Americas.

And the cry is: Faith. Magical, unreasoning faith; vulgarian among the questionable virtues.

By lack of faith alone shall man be saved.

By the certainty of Eternal Death and Reason: twin realities he has spent the lost centuries in evasion and denial.

Reason. A dog can dream. Pursuing ghostly rabbits; burying celestial bones; hallooing across elysian hunting fields.

The mystic is the mental drunkard. And the liquor he has distilled has sent humanity reeling down the unlit ways of credulity and fear.

Hit a man on the head and he will see stars. Give him opium and he will see visions. Give him chloroform and he will see nothing.

Give him Reason and he will see all things clear, whole, and true. Only through Reason shall life break from the confines of dreams and the mystic's drunken embrace.

Occultism, voodoo, thought transference. These must not be confused with the mental erotics of the mystics. These are facts. These are physical-mechanical laws appealing directly to Reason. If I can turn a button and get music from Rome or New Zealand, I can turn an invisible button and get other currents, wave-lengths, psychic distances. It is a more-lost sense than clairvoyance; comparable to the migration of birds. It is principally desire, space, necessity. It is still unsolved. Look only to the source.

The incredible is always real. And usually commonplace. The incredible can always be brought to the light of Reason and examined. For the incredible is always a fact. Mysticism is always an emotion.

Defence of Reason. For the But-You-Forget-Emotionists. Emotion is the mainspring of human life, minute on minute. Without it not an eyelid could be raised or nostril dilated. It is because of emotion that man surpasses the vegetable, and shall not survive it.

Paradoxically only a boundless capacity for emotion can lead one to the worship of Reason. Were Reason sentimentally no higher than fantasy we should all be barking in our sleep.

For dreams and fantasy are natural to all, as Reason is foreign to all. Emotion is the daily bread of life, but as man (erroneously) cannot live by bread alone, Reason is the wine by which life becomes poetry. For (contrary to all literary belief) poetry is not asking the moon what it is doing there. It is telling the moon what and why.

Emotion that by which we live: Reason that by which we control life. Emotion is all life. Alone Reason is beyond mere life, as Art is beyond mere moment.

Final Test. Pick at random among the Reasoning Beings: Aristotle, Galileo, Leonardo da Vinci, Einstein, Marconi.

Proving that man can be great for all things. But that rarely can he be Great Enough for Reason.

Meanwhile man is afraid. Yet why should one give man hope, when one can have no hope of man?

O my devout hearts! The one thought with which the Few have consoled and sustained themselves down the ages has been that if they might eventually reach the masses they would be able to drag the rest of mankind after them to sanity. A sorry fiction.

I dare to take this consolation from them.

Neither time nor education shall ever make the mass less stupid. For the mass must first unmass itself, becoming singly aristocratic and self-sufficient; and all civilised education and thought are against this principle. (Should it ever attain to it, it will be too late, too old, too decayed. This is not a thing which should be done last, but first.)

Thanks to the mystical restrictions of religion and its extra-terrestrial rights, mankind has used but a fraction of its power, its brain, its creative impulse. It shall continue doing so.

For you may move mountains by faith. But you shall not move the human mass by Reason.

Summing Up. Were I your judge, Humanity, I could think of no conclusive plea by which you might justify the continuance of your existence.

—Wine and laughter?

But you have diluted wine. And you have almost ceased to laugh.

Futility. Cowed, limited, thoughtless. What can it matter if man perish or save himself? Better to cease to be than drag in semi-lucid state across more time, repeating the same mistakes with the same shouts, the same pomposity, the same bloodshed, the same self-satisfaction.

FOR THE TRAGEDY OF MAN'S LONG MARTYRDOM IS NOT MAN, BUT THE FUTILITY OF THE CAUSES FOR WHICH HE HAS BEEN MARTYRED. Stigma of the unmarried woman bearing the unauthorised child; rage of priests and mob at change and reason; pillage and starvations and mass-murderings; morbidities of sex and marriage; persecutions of the scientist; despair of the thinker; havoc of missionaries; ruthlessness of commerce; passions, mutilations, vandalisms. Burnings, heroics, and sacrifice for faiths and laws which do not stand the test of time and reason.

Vision and Truth. No man has ever been ahead of his Time. His Time has always been behind its great men. His Time has always, like Savonarola's Army of Innocents, gathered in his inventions of the devil and printed heresies and lewd pictures, and burned them on the little bonfire which they assumed was Oblivion.

Only two people have ever profited from the lessons of the past: the artist and the scientist.

The one understands beauty. The other, truth.

Eternal Death. Impossible to study man and not despise him.

Impossible also to see a child crying in the street and not pause to comfort it, though one knows it to be lying and its tears to be brief.

This comfort is reality. The reality of death: Eternal Death.

Credo. Whatever Time may be to the mathematician or Eternity to the zealot, to man it can be but: NOW. This moment, this hour, this day.

For Death is the intensification of life; the answer to all doubt. Because of Death we put forward our finest urge; our silkiest plumage; our most luminous song.

He who intends to challenge Death must have in his life an object or a love. The one achieved, the one ended, he now can die without protest or regret.

For Adults Only. All life is brief and uncertain. All death is long and without end.

These things are, and there is no comfort. No extra-terrestrial concession. No mystical-emotional bargaining. Each must accept these facts according to temperament: despairing, stoical, indifferent; bearing the knowledge as best he can.

Life gives us many gifts to counterbalance our brief being, our implacable end. Passion, sudden and intense happiness, vitality, wine, hazard, laughter, the satisfaction of work, Memory which is the subtlety of sensation, and Thought, greatest of all adventures a man may know.

There is none who can shoulder these our joys. How then can they take on themselves our despair?

Man wears his own thorns. Equally he may crown himself with sedge and dance to his own measure.

Before the beginning and after the end man is alone. Each thing struggles separately. Each blade of grass, each man.

All he can be certain of at the last is that he has made the most of the days which have been given him.

Finale. I know the cold of all cold, wound of all injustice, despair of all loss, abyss of all remorse, depths of all solitude, the suicide's last grimace, the closed eyes of love.

I have seen winter's black entanglement of bough and I have seen Spring come bounding over the hills like a child's ball.

All these pass. Man cannot hold a moment or a breath. In this alone the hurt of life. Not its pain, but its transitoriness.

I love life. I would not barter with the most illustrious dead the privilege of being alive; my feet above ground, my eyes in their sockets.

APPENDIX

FUGUE

BY

OLIVE MOORE

JARROLDS *Publishers* LONDON
Limited, 34 Paternoster Row, E.C.4

Title page for *Fugue,* reproduced full size to show Moore's minuscule handwriting

Although Olive Moore's four published books constitute a remarkable achievement, placing her among the best British novelists of the twentieth century, she is virtually unknown to literary historians. She isn't listed in any of the encyclopedias of women writers that have appeared recently, nor is she mentioned in any of the many books on modern British literature we've consulted. The only reference book that does take note of her is *Authors Today and Yesterday* (an early version of the now-standard *Twentieth Century Authors*), for which Moore furnished this autobiographical sketch in 1933:

I was born in Hereford, on the border of Wales, which in my childhood used to upset me greatly as I felt London, or Rome, or Ancient Greece, or something really grandiose was the only place to be born in. I was sent abroad to a Convent at the age of five; I suppose I learned to read and write; a great war broke out, which meant less than nothing to me, except that now I realise how fortunate I was to escape mob educational methods by which the brains and digestive organs of millions of small children are still being ruined daily. Since growing up, and of my own free will, I have studied art in Italy, and subjects which interested me, such as literature and language, at the Sorbonne.

My life is so completely dull and uneventful, that there is absolutely nothing to tell you about it. O yes. I was in New York November 1929–May 1930. Memorable to me—indeed unforgettable—because it was there that the MS of my book *Spleen* (Harper's published it as *Repentance at Leisure*) was burnt out in a hotel fire. Together with every garment I possessed, except an aged mackintosh in which I had been walking round Central Park in the rain. But *Spleen.* I would like to be stoical and exalted about it; but I cannot; it was an unhappy and deadly experience. I sat down and re-wrote it. Fortunately my prose is such that I have to write very slowly. I spend days reducing 500 words to 50. I loathe the easy and the slip-shod. So in a sense I memorise as I go along. I know some passages in my books word for word, because of this passion for simplifying. I remembered a great deal of *Spleen,* the rhythm, the construction. At least I can see that *now.* But *then,* it was torture. I don't know why I re-wrote it. I used to say that if I'd had a few pounds a week of my own, I'd never have touched a pen again. But I didn't have; so perhaps it was just as well.

But that wasn't my first book, which was *Celestial Seraglio: A Tale of Convent Life.* Appeared 1929, October. England only. *Spleen* in November 1930.

Fugue, March 1932. A limited edition, signed and numbered, of an essay on D. H. Lawrence (published by C. Lahr, the Blue Moon Press, London) *Further Reflections on the Death of a Porcupine,* came out November 1932. I shall be re-publishing it in a book of essays this autumn or early next year.

There is little to tell you, or that matters, about me. I am by nature solitary and contemplative, very happy, very morose. I loathe books and never read them. Except informative books, giving me facts, any facts and all facts. I love travel best of all, and yet get very impatient with it. I like walking. I like talking. I love meeting people once. I love best knowing absolutely no one; but watching every one. I dislike having to live in London, a parochial little village. But I have to. I dislike it so much, that it does me (creatively) an awful lot of good. It's the pearl in my oyster. I dislike things very thoroughly indeed. I like disliking them. Otherwise (I live in London, Eng.) one gets genteel, tea shoppe, bored, refined, amateurish. All things which make it so difficult for the creative artist to live in England, which is secure, pleasant, imitative, watery. But fortunately I never meet people, and so am saved from contamination.

I have no sense of hero-worship. I respect all men who are master of their jobs; I say men, meaning men. I don't believe in women. They seem able to do everything but think. Yet they get away with it.

I believe only in the conscious artist. I would wish my work to be judged on the texture of my thought and the disposition of my sentences.

This provocative sketch was reprinted (slightly abridged) in the 1942 edition of *Twentieth Century Authors,* where a few more facts are given by the editor:

Her *Amazon and Hero: The Drama of the Greek War for Independence,* on which she has been at work since 1931, has not yet been published. There is no recent word of her, in an England which she can no longer describe as "secure, pleasant, imitative, watery." She is unmarried, and though she does not give her birthdate, it was probably about 1905.

No further documentary evidence is available; there is no indication that *Amazon and Hero* was ever published, nor has any obituary been found.

A request for further information in the *Times Literary Supplement* elicited a reply from David Goodway of the University of Leeds, who informed us that "Olive Moore" was actually a pseudonym for Constance Vaughan and that she "is almost certainly dead (and died before 1970 or thereabouts)." Prof. Goodway also noted that "Connie" Vaughan was part of Charles Lahr's Red Lion Street circle, a literary group that gravitated towards a bookstore specializing in radical literature located at 68 Red Lion Street, Holborn. The proprietor, Charles Lahr, published literary pamphlets as well, including stories by such writers as D. H. Lawrence, T. F. Powys, Rhys Davies, and, as she notes in her sketch, Moore's essay on Lawrence. (See David Goodway, "Charles Lahr: Anarchist, Bookseller, Publisher," *London Magazine,* June/July 1977, 46-55.) Lahr also published occasional Christmas cards consisting of short verses by some of his writers. Moore contributed one for Christmas 1932, one of a set of six signed copies of poems by various authors; hers is entitled "Statement" and was reprinted in *The Apple Is Bitten Again,* as was her Lawrence essay (pp. 371 and 394-402, respectively, in this edition).

Alec Bristow, one of the few surviving members of the Red Lion Street circle, wrote us an informative letter that is worth quoting at length; regretting that he didn't know when she died (or even that she was dead), he explained:

We had completely lost touch many years ago, though in the early thirties we spent a good deal of time together. I have no letters from her either; we both lived in Bloomsbury (she in Doughty Street and I in Mecklenburgh Street), only a couple of minutes' walk from each other, so we had no need to correspond by letter when it was so easy to visit.

We first met at Charles Lahr's bookshop in Red Lion Street, which was a focal point in Bloomsbury for writers to meet each other. I had reviewed O.M.'s novel *Fugue* very favourably in a literary-cum-political publication of the day called the *Twentieth Century,* and she had expressed to Charles a wish to meet me, which he arranged. We soon became friends, sharing as we did similar likes and (particularly) dislikes.

She gave me copies of her other two novels, which I still have. The first, *Celestial Seraglio,* was of course largely autobiographical, and she confessed to me that the character Mavis was very much a self-portrait. The second, *Spleen,* was much more a novel of ideas; the title, she told me, was inspired by the poem sequence "Spleen et Idéal" in *Les Fleurs du Mal* by Charles Baudelaire, whose work she greatly admired. Indeed, she gave me her copies, which I have still, of both *Les Fleurs du Mal* and *La Vie Douloureuse de Charles Baudelaire,* on the title page of which she had written in her tiny writing "Olive Moore, Bruxelles 1929"—so she must by then have given herself the pseudonym under which her books were published during the next few years.

Her real name, as you know, was Constance Vaughan. She was known as Connie by her colleagues at the *Daily Sketch,* a (long defunct) newspaper where she worked as a journalist. I never called her anything but Olive, since she made it clear that she much preferred that name. She once told me that the reason why she had chosen her pseudonym was that Olive represented an acquired taste, dry and sophisticated, and Moore suggested that once the taste had been acquired her readers would want more.

Our conversations were almost entirely about books and writing. She hardly ever referred to her background and upbringing, which she clearly wanted to forget. I did, however, have the impression that her parents had separated, like those of Mavis in *Celestial Seraglio,* and that she had preferred her father to her mother—who, she told me in passing, had once called her a monster. I do not know what other personal ties, if any, she had at the time we knew each other, though I believe she had had an affair with Sava Botzaris, whose fierce-looking sculpture of her appears as the frontispiece to *The Apple Is Bitten Again,* the last of her books to be published, as far as I am aware.

We had used the same portrait in *Further Reflections on the Death of a Porcupine,* which first appeared in 1933 in a limited edition of 99 copies, published by the Blue Moon Press, of which I was then chairman, in partnership with Charles Lahr. The way it happened is that O.M. told me that she had written an essay on D. H. Lawrence but thought it unsuitable for Jarrolds, who had published her novels but were not in the field of *belles lettres.* I said I would finance a limited edition, and I wrote the prospectus for it (signed A.B. because Olive did not want people to think she had written her own blurb). To the best of my recollection all the copies were sold and I nearly recouped the money I had paid. We hit on the title not only because Lawrence had published an essay entitled *Reflections on the Death of a Porcupine* but because he had been rather a prickly character himself.

It was in acknowledgment of my role in getting the book published that my copy is inscribed "To Alec Bristow, who is responsible for this—Olive Moore." Later, of course, *Further Reflections* was included in full in her collection of *pensées* entitled *The Apple Is Bitten Again,* published by Wishart & Co— who, like Jarrolds and the Blue Moon Press, ceased to exist many years ago.

The highly stylised portrait sculpture by Sava Botzaris does not give me a satisfactory impression of the O.M. that I knew—except perhaps for the somewhat intimidating air which she could convey to people who bored her. Though of medium height and unremarkable features and build, she certainly made her presence felt in any company. Dining with her in a restaurant was quite an experience; her carrying voice and penetrating laugh would make the glasses ring and other diners look round. . . .

You are, I am sure, quite correct in assuming that her projected book *Amazon and Hero* was never published. I very much doubt whether she ever finished it; she had started making notes for it when I knew her, but I think she was finding the prospect of doing the necessary research rather daunting, quite apart from the labour of the actual writing. Her style may be easy to read, but being a perfectionist she found it agony to write.

Aside from the fact that she was acquainted with the Scottish poet Hugh MacDiarmid, nothing further is known of Olive Moore at this time. Anyone knowing more is encouraged to write to the Publisher.

A Note on the Texts

The whereabouts of her manuscripts unknown, the texts for this edition have been taken from the published versions of Moore's books, as noted below. One uniform departure has been made from all of them, however: it was Moore's habit to begin each new paragraph flush left with a one-line space separating it from the previous one. Section breaks within chapters (in *Celestial Seraglio* and *The Apple Is Bitten Again*) used four or five line spaces, resulting in some pages where the amount of space dwarfs the amount of type. We find this wasteful and often aesthetically displeasing (especially in exchanges of dialogue and one-sentence paragraphs) and consequently decided to indicate paragraphs in the standard manner: indented and closed up. Otherwise, we follow Moore's texts faithfully, retaining her old-fashioned orthography, British spelling, and occasional eccentricities. (In *Spleen,* for example, nationalities like English and Italian are not capitalized.) Typos and various inconsistencies in the treatment of words have been silently corrected.

Celestial Seraglio was published in 1929 by Jarrolds Publishers of London, who were to publish all three of Moore's novels. The subtitle *A Tale of Convent Life* doesn't appear on the title page of the book but is used on the "by the same author" page of her later books and by Moore herself in her autobiographical statement for *Authors Today and Yesterday. Celestial Seraglio* is unique among her novels in using quotation marks to indicate dialogue (rather than the European dash) and in being divided into chapters. These may reflect the publisher's wishes rather than Moore's; in our edition, the quotation marks have been retained but new chapters don't begin on new pages; instead they are separated by a three-line space to make the format consistent with the later books. (In the original, the four extended quotations from the *Méditations de Sœur Marie Saint-Anselm* that begin the four parts of the novel are placed on separate pages; in our edition they appear at the top of the page of each new part.) Sometimes Moore uses italics for dialogue in a foreign language, sometimes not; following standard practice, we have left dialogue in roman type and used italics only for single words or short phrases in a foreign language throughout this omnibus.

Spleen was published in 1930 by Jarrolds and by Harper & Brothers of New York in October of the same year, who gave it the singularly inappropriate title *Repentance at Leisure.* There is every indication, however, that the American edition is closer to Moore's original manuscript than the British edition, and for that reason we have used it as our text. Some of these indications are spaces between paragraphs (where the British edition closes them up, causing some confusion when the last line of a paragraph ends flush right); the absence of periods after such abbreviations as Mrs and Dr; at least one instance where a word is missing from the British edition, which suggests that the American edition was set from a manuscript rather than from the British edition; and numerous indications in the British edition of the hand of a conventionally minded copy-editor: inserting many correct but unnecessary commas, capitalizing nationalities that Moore apparently preferred in lower-case, and correcting a few errors. Only these corrections and the title *Spleen* have been used from the British edition, since this seems to be the title Moore preferred.

Fugue was published by Jarrolds in 1932 and by Dial Press (under the Lincoln MacVeagh imprint) of New York in August of the same year. The two editions are nearly identical, both running to 283 pages and differing only in typeface and display type. The American edition has a few superior readings over the British edition ("reumuthig" for "renmuthig" in the German inscription on p. 238) and has a few other indications that it may be closer to Moore's original (though not nearly as many as in *Spleen*), so here too this edition has been used as our text.

The Apple Is Bitten Again was published by Wishart in London in 1934 and by E. P. Dutton of New York the following year. The latter was offset from the former, so the two texts are identical. Certain inconsistencies in the use of italics have been eliminated (in the chapter on D. H. Lawrence, for example, she italicizes *Lady Chatterley's Lover* but not *Kangaroo*); otherwise, our text follows hers, even to retaining some odd spellings (Bakounine for Bakunin, for example). Both editions used as a frontispiece Sava Botzaris's striking sculpture of Olive Moore, which we too have used as a frontispiece as well as on the dustjacket.

STEVEN MOORE